White Rose

A Mystery from a Dark Past

David W. Roberts

SILVERBIRD
PUBLISHING

About the Author

David Roberts migrated as a qualified teacher from the United Kingdom. After seventeen years working as a teacher, deputy principal and principal in country New South Wales, he became a university academic. University appointments and consultancies enabled David to travel widely and broaden his horizons. Now retired, he lives with his wife in Adelaide.

This is his eighth novel.

Books by David Roberts

One Thing Leads to Another

Easytimes

Graham's Story

Eve

Murder on the Heysen Trail

Scrubber McDade

PART ONE

1.   Saturday, 24th August, 1962

Upper Bybridge hummed and buzzed with bees and other noisy insects this steamy afternoon in August. The sleepy village nestled between hills on the Sussex South Downs was content to sit quietly and mind its own business. Nothing much happened in Upper Bybridge although its villagers insisted it was a much livelier community than its neighbour, Lower Bybridge, languishing two miles away on the gently winding River Bye. A tumble of pretty cottages lined the main street jostling for space as if randomly cast there by some careless giant dropping bread crumbs. The village proudly boasted a clutch of thatched cottages dating back as far as the sixteenth century and, up on the hill, the attractive Anglican church of Saint David was of similar age.

This being an overly warm Saturday, most Upper Bybridge villagers had retired to their television sets to watch sport. There, scoffing sugary snacks and drinks, they tried to convince any visitors that the game was played better in *their* day and that today's players were no longer as accomplished. The only establishment in Upper Bybridge where a boisterous crowd was assembled was the pub which rejoiced under the rather peculiar name "The Squirrel and Porcupine". Squirrels there were in abundance in and around Upper Bybridge, but everyone was at a loss to explain how a porcupine managed to get in on the act since porcupines certainly didn't live in Sussex and never had.

BBC television had been broadcasting regular Saturday afternoon sports programs since the mid-fifties but television was yet to be accepted as a permanent fixture in British pubs. The customers imbibing this particular afternoon at "The Squirrel and Porcupine" had other matters to discuss and argue about. As usual in this deeply class-conscious country the pub's clientele had naturally divided into three distinct drinking groups. At one end of the bar, lolling about in the easy chairs, were the local landed gentry together with a handful of professional men: the bank manager, a retired major, a lawyer and the local doctor. At the opposite end of the bar, as far away as possible from the "snobs," was a raucous group of working-class blokes smoking and knocking back beers as if the pub was about to run dry at any moment. These were the unemployed and lowly-paid farm labourers working in the district. Sandwiched between these two groups, perched uncomfortably on bar stools, were the tradespeople: the butcher, the owner of the general store, a couple of sales staff, a carpenter, an electrician, a builder and the village baker. Scarcely a woman was to be seen or heard in "The Squirrel and Porcupine" at this time of day.

Behind the bar and pleasingly busy this particular Saturday afternoon were Jack Duncan, the proprietor, his wife Betty and their sixteen-year-old daughter, Jenny. Jack was a roly-poly fellow somewhat overweight and well-liked by one and all. Nothing seemed to worry Jack and he always had a broad smile and an encouraging greeting for whoever entered his pub. When things were extra busy his face would redden and today his face was verging on beetroot. Being in his mid-forties, Jack's doctor was starting to worry about his elevated blood pressure but Jack was a simple uncomplicated sort of a fellow who, as they said in these parts, "called a spade a spade."

The brain of the establishment was Jack's wife, Betty. She had sole charge of the finances, handled the ordering of stock, completed the tax returns and reams of tedious forms constantly requested by an army of faceless government bureaucrats. Betty Duncan was also the Vicar's Church Warden at the afore mentioned Anglican Church of Saint David which sat like a brooding mother-hen over-looking the collection of cottages and shops that was Upper Bybridge. There were some in the upstanding congregation of St David's who questioned how Betty could be a good Christian as well as the wife of a publican dealing with all those "nasty drunks." Betty, however, never considered these two roles incompatible. In her own quiet way, she felt she did much to keep the peace at "The Squirrel and Porcupine" by listening to distressed souls whenever they needed to unburden and by maintaining a level of decorum when things got rough.

And it was a matter of decorum that was worrying Betty this particular Saturday afternoon. When their daughter Jenny turned sixteen recently, her parents agreed to let her work behind the bar at weekends. Jenny loved the bar work because she was earning money at last, but more so because it gave her the opportunity to flirt with the gorgeous young men who drank there. She took considerable care to dress in such a way that showed off her figure to full advantage. Teenage Jenny was experimenting with perfumes, lipsticks, eye shadow and even hair styles. Today she sported a jaunty pony-tail and was wearing her most daring dress revealing considerably more of her cleavage than her mother liked. When there was a short break in the demand for bar service, Betty Duncan collared her husband.

'Jack dear, Jenny's wearing that dress again.'

'What dress, love?'

'Have a look…the one that's cut far too low and everything's just about falling out!'

'Oh yea…'

'We must do something about it. Some of the young fellows can't keep their eyes off.'

'Well, as long as it's only their eyes dear, we shouldn't need to worry.'

'It lowers the tone.'

Jack wiped clean the last glass he'd been rinsing and looked at his wife, 'To be perfectly honest dear, having our attractive daughter serving behind the bar is excellent for business.'

As soon as he'd said it Jack realised how inflammatory his comment must have sounded and Betty bristled. At forty-two she was still a handsome woman and if the truth be known, she enjoyed subtle, refined extra attention from some of the middle-aged men when they thought Jack wasn't watching. Allowing Jenny to work in the pub also meant that Betty was no longer the most attractive female in the place so there was more than a tinge of envy which Betty did her Christian best to suppress. Betty decided, however, to say nothing more about the matter for the time being and instead turned her attention to her daughter to see what she was doing.

Jenny had left the bar area and was picking up the empties and wiping down tables. Several pairs of hungry male eyes followed her progress. There was no doubt about it, Jenny had developed the same stunning figure Betty had once enjoyed: slim, long legged and full breasted. As she watched, Jenny moved to the darkest corner of the establishment where someone was sitting alone largely hidden behind a newspaper. An empty glass sat on the table. For a brief moment the paper was lowered and Jenny exchanged a few words with the person there. A few minutes later, Jenny delivered another half-pint of frothy beer to the customer. Betty wondered who the shy lone drinker might be. Certainly not a local she concluded.

❦

At the other end of Upper Bybridge, near the village green, stood Hollyhock Cottage home of Rolf and Doreen Summers. The house sat on a bend in the road and was much admired by tourists since it was built of traditional Sussex flint stones and boasted a recently re-thatched roof. "Quaint", "cute", "gorgeous" were descriptors typically on the lips of visitors who passed by. Those who had the time to linger noticed Hollyhock Cottage had tiny cosy windows, a front door painted bright green that tall folk had to duck under and a splendid front garden full of roses. Sometime in the past, the elderly locals recalled, the garden had been full of bright red, white and pink hollyhocks which was why it had been originally named "Hollyhock Cottage." Rolf and Doreen Summers shared the gardening chores although for them it was really a labour of love. For some reason when the Summers couple moved in, Rolf had insisted the hollyhocks must go and be replaced with roses.

Being such a hot afternoon, Mr and Mrs Summers had retreated indoors where the thick flint stone walls guaranteed coolness even during rare heatwaves. Doreen was in the kitchen making a pot of tea and wondering whether to break apart the four chocolate fingers that make up a packet of KitKat. Two fingers each wouldn't be too fattening surely? Rolf was already comfortably ensconced in his favourite armchair thumbing through the latest book he had borrowed from the Petworth library. Inside Hollyhock Cottage it was a scene of domestic bliss.

Last week Rolf had celebrated his sixty-second birthday. Since a sixty-second birthday is hardly remarkable, the couple had stayed home and simply invited their next-door neighbours in for dinner. It had been a pleasant enough evening and Rolf had been in good form. Doreen was pleased to see her husband so happy as he was inclined to be a moody man. One day he would be on a high, cheerful and motivated, the next day down in the dumps, sour and grumpy. Their doctor had advised some years ago that Rolf suffered a mild form of bi-polar and had prescribed some appropriate medication. Over the years Doreen had gently tried to cajole Rolf into talking about his past in an attempt to better understand the cause of his mental illness. Once, the doctor had suggested a psychoanalyst might help get to the heart of the problem but Rolf had angrily rejected the idea.

Doreen was still rather ashamed about what she did one night to try to get Rolf to talk about his past. She planned her special evening meticulously. Rolf seldom went to the pub but he did enjoy the occasional drink at home with Doreen so she set things up so he had more to drink than usual. Extra alcohol, she knew, made him amorous and she would be ready wearing her sexiest lingerie to encourage him so that he was frantic for her. However, before she would consent, she would insist on him talking about what it was in his past that was troubling him. It was the oldest trick in the book. Doreen reasoned her strategy was defensible on the grounds that Rolf would feel some relief having shared his past history and she would be better able to understand his moods in the future. It didn't work but they enjoyed the best sex they'd had for years.

A cabinet maker by trade Rolf had worked the last twelve years with E.J. Thomas and Sons who had an expanding business in the nearby town of Petworth. Rolf was good at his work and had become a valued member of staff. Doreen knew he reserved his bad moods for home and she alone had to be his amateur therapist. The staff at E. J. Thomas and Sons were totally unaware of Rolf's mental issues. She looked lovingly at her husband now as she waited for the kettle to boil. Rolf was overweight despite being on his feet working all day. He had set his sights on retirement at sixty-five. He needed glasses nowadays and she was sure his hearing was deteriorating, not surprising when he worked with noisy machinery all week. She wondered, rather gloomily, what it would be like when they were both retired.

Doreen was two years younger than Rolf and this was her second marriage. The great love of her life first husband, James, had willingly volunteered for military service and like so many others paid the supreme sacrifice dying from his wounds late in 1941. Doreen was left shattered at the age of 39 to bring up their only child, Douglas, on her own. Douglas, at the time of his father's death, was a vulnerable fourteen-year-old and he reacted badly to the news becoming unruly and rebellious. The teenager rightly directed his pent-up anger at Hitler and the Nazis and was determined to join up to fight. When he turned seventeen, he was accepted into the army but it was already late 1944 so he saw little action. Army discipline was exactly what he needed, however, and after two years in the armed forces he emerged a better grounded more balanced young man. Now he was a happily married man and living in London.

Throughout these troubling times Doreen had carried on with

her teaching career. She taught infants and credited working with "her little ones" as being her saviour. There was something hugely satisfying about pouring her energies into helping and loving "her little ones" which helped compensate for the needless cruelty, death and destruction of war. At sixty Doreen was still teaching and had become somewhat of an institution at the small state school in Upper Bybridge where she had worked since marrying Rolf and purchasing Hollyhock Cottage in 1947.

After tragically losing husband James, Doreen initially had no interest in re-marrying. They had had almost sixteen years together and it had been a happy, rewarding union. She liked reminiscing about the places they had visited together and the fun they had in bringing up Douglas. After years of looking back, Doreen gradually came to realise she should instead be looking to the future. Life in Britain was slowly recovering after the horrors of war; she had a reasonable salary and was fit and healthy. What was the point of wallowing in a life past when so many new opportunities were popping up everywhere?

One day a friend suggested she join the local golf club where she could play ladies golf every Sunday. It was at the golf club during one of their social nights when she first met Rolf Summers and ended up marrying him. Initially she was intrigued by his accent and relaxed conversational style. She felt at ease with him and was hugely flattered that in her mid-forties he wanted to have a romantic relationship. After a few months of serious courting, Rolf popped the question and she accepted. A long life alone no longer appealed; sharing it with this excellent and loving handyman seemed almost too good to be true. They were married on July 7th 1947 in a quiet ceremony at the Reading Registry office.

Rolf Summers never talked about his background. Doreen had several family members present at their wedding. Rolf had nobody, except a work mate and a friend from the golf club. Surely, Doreen reasoned, he must have family somewhere but where were they?

Gently she prodded and cajoled but Rolf remained stubbornly silent and secretive. After years of married life, she had established a few meagre details. He was brought up in Austria, his parents were long dead and he never spoke of any other family members. Rolf had arrived in the United Kingdom a few years prior to the outbreak of the second world war and was subsequently interned as a category A "enemy alien" for the duration of the war. Rolf claimed he had spent most of his internment on the Isle of Man. Once Doreen had suggested they take a holiday on the Isle of Man so he could show her where he had lived for four or five years but Rolf reacted surprisingly angrily to the idea.

Now, as Doreen brought in the tray with the teapot, two rattling cups, teaspoons, milk and sugar and all four sticks of KitKat, she wondered whether the man sitting in front of her could possibly have had a criminal past. Was there something really sinister in Rolf's background that he was still hiding? Perhaps he had robbed a bank or raped a woman? Could he have been a deserter? God forbid, was she married to a murderer? Alternatively, perhaps Rolf had been sent by the Gestapo to Britain as a spy? If only she could unlock Rolf's intriguing past.

'KitKat dear?'

'Oh, yes please.'

'Are you still trying to cut back on sugar?'

'Yes, two lumps only please.'

She poured the tea, plonked the sugar lumps in and placed the cup and saucer on his side table. Rolf looked contented and relaxed. Doreen berated herself for ever thinking her quiet, attentive husband of fifteen years could ever have been some kind of nasty criminal or Nazi spy. She dismissed these negative thoughts and picked up her sewing. She had two pairs of Rolf's winter socks that needed darning.

A few minutes later there was a furious knocking on the front door.

'Could you go please, dear? I'm in the middle of darning this sock of yours.'

Grumpily, Rolf climbed out of his armchair and walked slowly the short distance to the front door which he opened to the sound of squeaky hinges.

'Rolf Summers?'

'Yes.'

There were three noises then a gasp, a grunt followed by another. Something heavy landed on the floor. The front door slammed shut. Alarmed, Doreen jumped to her feet and hurried to the door. Rolf was lying on his back groaning, his eyes wide with terror, clutching his stomach. Three blood-red stains were spreading rapidly across his torso.

2.   Later the Same Day...

'Brian...forty-four across, it's five letters. The clue is luke warm?'

'That's easy mate...tepid.'

'Yup...'

Sergeant Frank Smithton pencilled in the word "tepid" and moved to the next clue. This long serving member of the West Sussex Constabulary chewed pensively on the end of his pencil. As he approached retirement Sergeant Frank Smithton had increasingly become a man of habit and doing the crossword puzzle in the local paper was something he always did on Saturday afternoons. The police station at Lower Bybridge was seldom called into service at such times unless there was a car accident somewhere in the vicinity. With young Constable Brian Brooks' help, Frank usually managed to complete the Saturday crossword. He officially knocked off at six o'clock when he took his completed crossword home to show his wife, who would cluck-cluck admiringly and praise Frank for yet another of his amazing intellectual achievements. The two of them would then sit down to enjoy a sherry together, dry for him sweet for her before his kindly wife served up their hot evening meal.

The smooth flow of events on this particular Saturday afternoon was rudely interrupted, however, by a phone call that the two policemen noted in the day's log book as coming in at 4.46 pm. Constable Brian took the call.

'Okay...okay...calm down please, madam... madam please...I can't help you if you keep yelling at me...that's better. Now... kindly start again and speak slowly...a stabbing you say...your husband? Yes, we will come round immediately. Is he breathing? ...Is he conscious? ...What's your name please madam? ... Where are you? I see...Hock

Cottage? …Aah, Hollyhock Cottage. In Upper Bybridge?… Yes, yes… we're on our way. We'll order an ambulance too. Now, Mrs Summers stay where you are and don't touch anything. Yes, yes I understand… five minutes.'

Sergeant Smithton was already on his feet car keys in hand. 'I know the house and I know the Summers. Nice enough folk. Mind the station for me Brian. Oh, and get the ambulance to go to Upper Bybridge.' And with that the sergeant hurriedly disappeared into the small parking lot at the rear of the station.

A minute later Sergeant Smithton was winding his way as fast as he dared up the pretty country lane that connected the two Bybridge villages. He swerved to avoid a tractor emerging from a farm gate and narrowly missed a pheasant ambling regally along the road. This sounded horribly like a murder. He racked his brains to recall the date of the last murder he had had to deal with in these parts. Must have been the Symons's case back in the winter of fifty-five…seven years ago.

The police radio crackled into action as he reached the first houses of Upper Bybridge. It was Constable Brian Brooks confirming the ambulance was on its way from Petworth, expected time of arrival half past five. There were no signs of life as he pulled into the short driveway at Hollyhock Cottage. For a moment he wondered if this had been some kind of a malicious hoax. The bright green front door was shut as he reached for the brass door knocker shaped like the head of a fox.

'Who is it?' a frightened voice called out.

'Sergeant Smithton, West Sussex police.'

'Thank heavens you're here. Come in, come in sergeant…'

Sergeant Smithton pushed the heavy green door open gently to discover a man lying there. Blood completely covered his chest and stomach and was oozing onto the carpet. Moving adroitly for a man of his age, the sergeant checked the man's pulse and breathing. Nothing! He checked again. Still nothing. He carefully closed the dead man's eye-lids, confirming at the same time that this body certainly looked like Mr Rolf Summers.

Mrs Summers remained seated on the couch sobbing helplessly into a delicate handkerchief, understandably in a state of shock. Smithton was far too experienced to make premature assumptions. Nevertheless, he knew it was a well-known fact that with murders in a home, the most likely perpetrator was the spouse. For all he knew Mrs Summers could be an accomplished actress. Like it or not, she immediately became his number one suspect.

The sergeant pulled out his trusty note-pad and started gently quizzing Mrs Summers. He jotted down the few facts she was able to provide then suggested she make them both a nice cup of tea while he looked around outside for a few moments. Sergeant Smithton found no obvious signs to indicate who might have perpetrated such a vicious attack, no footprints on the ground, no murder weapon, nothing he could see that might assist.

As he was securing the front garden as an official crime scene the next-door neighbours came wandering over wanting to know what had brought the local police to the Summers' place. The neighbours appeared genuinely shocked when told what had happened. They claimed not to have seen or heard anything untoward. The sergeant instructed them to return home and not to visit Mrs Summers until he gave them permission. Frank Smithton then returned to his car to radio head office to report a major crime and request the urgent assistance of the murder squad. Next, the sergeant went back indoors to have that cup of tea with the distraught Mrs Summers.

The ambulance was on the scene soon after. The paramedics were advised to bide their time until the murder squad had carried out its preliminary investigations and given them permission to remove the body. With the arrival of the ambulance and a second police car bearing two plain clothes police, a small crowd of inquisitive villagers started assembling on the other side of the street. Soon the rumour mill was working overtime. Old Fred Granger who hailed from further down the road was of the opinion, 'It were Mrs Summers wot had been done in,' Fred told anyone prepared to listen, 'that Rolf bloke was too quiet for me liking. You never can tell with 'em foreigners. Probably one of 'em bloody Nazis.'

'I reckon it's been a robbery,' counter-claimed Mrs Bradberry, 'a nice cottage like that, I expect they've some lovely stuff well worth nicking.'

There was general support for this suggestion from most of the onlookers. The idea that there had been a murder in Upper Bybridge was simply too awful to contemplate.

'Could've been be a rape,' piped up a young man up the back of the crowd.

'Bullshit. You're just talking through your balls!' Tom Fisher, a local farmer responded angrily.

'At least I've got some,' the youngster fired back cheekily.

'Gentlemen, gentlemen can we *please* have a little decorum?' It was Mrs Bates, President of the Combined Bybridge Canasta Club who interjected and for a short time no more wild ideas were publicly aired.

☾

Recently Belinda Purcell had been promoted to be a detective in the Criminal Investigation Department (CID). For the last seven years she had served as a "copper on the beat" working in the Brighton and Hove district and later Hastings where, eighteen months back, she had achieved notoriety for the way she had single-handedly brought down a violent young criminal and effected his arrest. Her courage had earnt her a coveted police medal for bravery and considerable exposure in the local newspapers. Shortly after this dramatic event she sat her examination for promotion to sergeant and passed with distinction. A couple of months back, when top brass at the CID were looking for new staff, Belinda Purcell's file had impressed them.

A number of highly positive remarks appeared therein. She was described as being loyal, highly intelligent, a lateral thinker, resilient, conscientious and an excellent team member. Belinda Purcell was called for an interview with the CID Appointments Board and had presented as a cheerful, enthusiastic person with strong analytical skills. It didn't matter that she was barely twenty-five years old.

Belinda was posted to Petworth as the third and most junior member of a small team of detectives working in that area. She found accommodation with a kindly Scottish widow who was thrilled to have a member of the police force living in the one-bedroom flat at the back of her house. The flat boasted a neat kitchen, a bathroom with a decent sized bath and a small bedroom with a single bed. Belinda was responsible for her own meals but had shared use of the attractive garden and laundry. The flat was most conveniently located being less than a mile from the police station in one direction and the shops in the opposite direction. The newly appointed detective sergeant believed the flat would suit her needs well and happily paid a week's rent in advance.

The senior member of the Petworth CID threesome was Nigel Sandham, a tall bean-pole of a man who smoked like a chimney and coughed incessantly. Belinda immediately presumed cancer, but was too polite to ask. Nigel was grey and gaunt and openly admitted he was hanging out for retirement in a couple of years' time. Chief Inspector Sandham was perfectly content to remain in his Petworth office doing the paper work because he quickly became breathless if required to move about. Despite his unhealthy disposition Nigel had his finger on the local pulse having served the district for nigh on twenty years. He claimed to personally know most of the criminals "on his patch" and whenever a crime was committed would immediately produce a short list of likely suspects worth following up.

The third member of the Petworth CID team was twenty-nine-year-old Hank Zagalski who had already been working with Nigel

Sandham for just over two years. Belinda didn't know what to make of Hank. He was a man of few words, the strong silent type. With Nigel determined to remain glued to his office, like it or not, she was stuck with Hank and the pair of them were obliged to go out on calls together. Zagalski was strikingly handsome with a shock of wavy blonde hair, blue eyes, a firm jaw and a beautifully proportioned physique as a result of the intensive training he underwent for the sport he lived for, rugby union or "rugger" as it was still referred to in some quarters.

After two weeks working alongside Hank Zagalski, Belinda still felt awkward around him. He was highly efficient and did everything by the book as you might expect from any true professional. She didn't know whether his aloofness was because he was shy, a poor communicator or he didn't even like her. Belinda knew her attractiveness sometimes scared men and they'd get embarrassed and end up behaving like nervous wrecks. But that was certainly not how Hank was behaving. She wondered if he was gay? He was such a fine figure of a man, a talented rugby player and a fitness fanatic so she felt this was unlikely but you could never be sure. Possibly he was seriously dating someone and felt it wise to keep his distance. Whatever the reason for his remoteness she still found Detective Inspector Hank Zagalski intriguing and longed to know him better.

Shortly after five o'clock Belinda was sunbaking in the privacy of the small back garden behind her flat. It was still beautifully warm and she was lying back on an old faded deckchair dressed only in a revealing two-piece swimming costume and straw hat. Polaroid sunglasses reduced the sun's glare as she flicked over the next page of the romantic novel she was enjoying. As a member of the police force there had been many occasions when she had had to be authoritative, in command, giving orders and asserting herself but at heart she was a gentle romantic soul. Belinda's mother had never quite understood why her daughter had decided to join the police force.

Belinda was just beginning to feel sleepy when her Scottish

landlady popped out of the back-door to tell her she was wanted on the phone. 'It's your boss,' she said, 'Chief Inspector Nigel Sandham.' Fifteen minutes later Belinda was standing outside her apartment as Hank Zagalski pulled up in a police car. She'd done a lightening change, spruced herself up and was surprised to find Hank covered in mud. He had been playing in a pre-season rugby match and claimed he'd not had time to get showered and changed. Belinda couldn't help surreptitiously admiring his fine muscular physique now on full display. Chief Inspector Sandham had been frustratingly short on details Hank told her. Apparently, they were to investigate a stabbing murder in the small village of Upper Bybridge. Hank then reverted to his usual uncommunicative self. All Belinda was able to wheedle out of him was that his rugby team had won 15-14 in a tight game and he'd scored a try under the posts.

Hank was a fast, safe driver who switched on the emergency siren only when absolutely necessary. Belinda felt comfortable with him at the wheel. She used the car radio to contact their boss again to see if he could furnish further details. All Sandham could tell her was that a call for help had come from a Mrs Summers, wife of the alleged murder victim. She had been almost hysterical. The local Bybridge police were attending. Normally, whenever a major crime was committed, Nigel Sandham would quickly shortlist the most likely candidates but this crime had him baffled. Knife attacks were thankfully rare in the district. The last one the chief inspector could recall was in 1952 when a terrified woman had successfully used a kitchen carving knife to fight off a potential rapist. In that case, the knife had been used as a weapon of self-defence.

When the detectives entered Upper Bybridge it was easy to find the location, a score of cars were already parked around the cottage creating a serious hazard for through traffic. In addition, perhaps fifty locals were milling about chatting, laughing and wandering to and fro across the road.

'Get the plod to clear the area,' barked Hank, 'before we have more deaths in Upper bloody Bybridge.' Sensible, thought Belinda, just a shame he had to speak to her so authoritatively.

There was nowhere near the cottage for them to park but Hank soon fixed that too. He lowered his window, lent well out and ordered every car parked on his side of the road to be moved immediately. His message circulated amongst the crowd fast and within ten minutes the car owners had all been found and the offending vehicles re-located. Hank parked close to Hollyhock Cottage. There was no doubt who was in charge. Since this was Belinda's first murder case, she was more than grateful to have Hank's expertise and experience.

Sergeant Frank Smithton appeared. He introduced himself then briefed them quietly, well out of earshot of Mrs Summers. Nobody, as far as he knew, had been near the crime scene although he couldn't definitely vouch for Mrs Summers who claimed to have witnessed the murder.

'Mrs Summers says she never touched her husband's body. He died almost instantly right before her eyes. He was trying to speak to her as he faded away.'

'What did he say?'

'She's not a hundred percent certain. She's sure she heard the sound," ose" but couldn't quite catch what sound came before it. She thinks it might have been "rose."'

'How's she coping?'

'She's in a bad way. Mainly shock, I think. She was hysterical when she rang us. I've given her a cup of tea and a blanket because she's been shivering even though it's hot.'

'Thank you, sergeant. Stay outside and keep all those nosey-parkers well away. Belinda, go and comfort Mrs Summers please and see what you make of her. Remember, currently she's our number one suspect. I'm going to search the area outside the cottage and get the fingerprint boys on the job.'

❦

Mrs Summers was still seated on the sofa; head down and seemingly lost in a world of her own. Belinda approached quietly and asked gently if she might sit down next to her. Mrs Summers looked up briefly and gave a slight nod. Belinda had previously dealt with people suffering from shock when working on the beat and knew to take things slowly and calmly. If she was to ascertain anything of value the kindly, empathetic approach was the most productive. For a few minutes Belinda said nothing allowing Mrs Summers to get used to her close physical presence. Then, as Belinda had hoped, Mrs Summers was moved to speak.

'Who would do such a terrible thing? Rolf never hurt anybody… He was well accepted in the village. He never had any enemies. It's all just too awful… I can't believe this has happened…' The unfortunate lady broke down again and buried her face in the sodden handkerchief. Belinda waited patiently.

'You will catch him, won't you?' Doreen Summers blurted out.

'We'll do our very best. That's a promise. Mrs Summers…may I ask you a few questions, please?'

Doreen Summers blew her nose, 'Yes, I suppose you must…'

'Mrs Summers, did you hear anyone speak when this happened?'

'Oh yes it was a man, definitely a man, a man with an accent.'

'What did the man say?'

'He said…he said…' Mrs Summers broke down again.

'Take your time, there's no hurry.'

'He asked "Rolf Summers?" My husband said "yes" and then it happened. It happened in a matter of seconds. Next thing I heard Rolf fall heavily to the ground and the door slammed shut.'

'Did you see anyone?'

Mrs Summers shook her head, 'I only heard the voice. I couldn't see the front door from where I was sitting.'

'You say the man had an accent?'

'Yes.'

'How would you describe the accent?'

'Like Rolf's, German or Austrian.'

'Where exactly were you when you heard the commotion?'

'Over there on that chair. I was busy darning Rolf's sock,' the distressed woman broke down again, 'he won't need his sock now, will he?'

Belinda felt genuinely sad for Doreen Summers and found it hard to believe this woman could possibly be a murderer. If she was, then she was giving an Oscar winning performance. Now that Belinda had successfully engaged Mrs Summers in conversation she pressed on with her low-key questioning.

'So, Rolf was German or Austrian, was he?'

Mrs Summers nodded, 'He was German, but he didn't fight us during the war. He was interned for years in a camp somewhere on the Isle of Man.'

'Did he ever talk about his time there?'

'No, hardly ever. It was not a happy time he said and he wanted to forget about it.'

'Was Mr Summers in England at the start of the war?'

'I think so.'

'Do you know what he was doing then and where he lived?'

'He never told me where he was living. He's…he was…a cabinet maker. For the whole time we've been married he's been with E.J Thomas & Sons the local cabinet makers.'

'I see. Mrs Summers, can you think of anyone who disliked your husband?'

She shook her head vigorously, 'He was well liked.'

'How old was Mr Summers?'

'Sixty-two.'

'Coming up to retirement?'

The crying started again. Belinda sat quietly by, waiting for Mrs Summers to recover some composure.

'We were going to go on a world trip when he retired. He had a few aches and pains, arthritis the doctor said, but he hoped to keep going until he turned sixty-five.'

'Mrs Summers, did you ever hear your husband speaking to anyone in German? On the phone, perhaps? Or maybe a German friend visited you?'

'No, never.'

'Do you have someone who can come and stay with you for a few nights or someone nearby you can go and stay with? We are going to need to talk to you again, of course, so you must stay in the district.'

'I'm sure my friends next door will put me up. To be perfectly honest, I don't want to stay in this house tonight.'

'I can quite understand that. Now what are your friends' names, please?'

'Mike and Sandra Leighton.'

At this point Hank appeared at the front door and stepping over the body of Rolf Summers, came over and stood before the two women sitting together on the sofa.

'I think I'm done out there for now.' He gave Mrs Summers a curt nod followed by a flick of the head to Belinda that clearly indicated he wanted to leave. 'The ambulance boys are about to come in to remove the body.'

Belinda wished Hank could be a little more tactful. It was Mrs Summers' husband lying there at the door!

☾

A few villagers were still hanging about as the two detectives exited Hollyhock Cottage. Hank had given strict instructions for the cottage to remain a crime scene until further notice and had ordered the local police to maintain a visible presence there day and night.

'Feel like a drink?'

'But we're on duty, even though you don't look the part still dressed in your rugby gear!'

'Just joking,' he grinned, 'there's only one pub in the village "The

Squirrel and Porcupine." Always the best place to pick up on any local gossip. Somebody there may have seen or heard something unusual. Tell me what did you glean from Mrs Summers?'

In the five minutes it took to drive to the other end of Upper Bybridge Belinda filled Hank in with the few details she had managed to elicit from a very distressed Mrs Summers. Hank listened intently but made no comment. They drove to a vacant parking spot at the rear of the pub beneath a large holly tree for shade. Here they sat for a few minutes while Hank briefed Belinda on what he had found.

'No sign of a weapon. Obviously from the stab wounds, it was a reasonably large knife or some other sharp weapon, in what appears to have been a frenzied attack. We'll get the local coppers to do a more thorough search tomorrow morning in case the weapon was tossed away somewhere nearby. It's possible the attacker had blood spattered on him too. At the same time the local police can doorknock everyone living nearby who might have seen or heard something. A ferocious attack like this suggests it's a pre-meditated crime of hate. What do you think?'

Belinda wasn't expecting to be suddenly asked for her opinion. She was both pleased and surprised and ended up giving a rather wishy-washy response, 'Yes, that makes sense.'

'Oh… I did find something of note,' continued Hank, 'no footprints unfortunately since it's been bone dry, but I did find this…' he fumbled in his jacket pocket before extracting a small clear packet like the ones used by stamp collectors. 'It's a half-used cigarette butt. Interestingly it has what looks like part of the cigarette's make or brand name on it. See…' He showed it to Belinda who lent over to inspect it better. Peering carefully at the object she could just decipher three small upper-case letters "MER". The rest of the word was missing having been smoked.

'MER? I don't know any English cigarettes with "MER" in the name. Do you?'

Hank shook his head, 'Could be a rare kind of coffin nail we haven't heard of before. Or perhaps it's foreign? I'll check it out when I get back to the office.'

Belinda looked puzzled.

'Come on,' he said, back to his typically authoritative tone, 'let's see what the pub comes up with.'

Belinda straightened up her hair and followed the striding Hank into the bar. She had not been to this particular pub before.

Pubs vary enormously. There are the sleezy ones where you immediately hang tightly onto your wallet or handbag and stick out the cautionary antennae before speaking to anyone. These are the "one drink only" places and you feel a sense of relief if you escape outside unscathed. Belinda wouldn't stay for a minute in such places, unless obliged to in the course of her police work. At the other end of the spectrum are the classy snobby joints, where you pay far more for your drinks than you should because you are paying for the ambience and the high-class exclusive clientele who choose to drink there. Between these two extremes are the friendly, family-oriented places where you can feel safe and relaxed in the knowledge you have mostly pleasant, unassuming folk surrounding you. "The Squirrel and Porcupine" was definitely one of these. Instinctively, on entering you knew you would receive value for money.

"The Squirrel and Porcupine" oozed atmosphere. Exposed black timber beams, heavy oak tables and twenty or more jolly souls sitting or standing about enjoying each other's company. It was surprisingly cool considering it had been such a warm day. Three or four young studs were winging darts at a much-punctured dart-board and nearby a serious game of dominoes was in progress. There was an air of good-natured jollity. Belinda noted there were very few females present. Hank strode directly to the bar where a middle-aged man was pulling a couple of golden coloured pints.

A tall strongly built stranger wearing muddy rugby clothes heading confidently up to the bar through a bunch of locals does not go unnoticed and there was an instant quietening of voices.

Belinda followed a couple of paces behind Hank and soon diverted the attention of most of the men. With a couple of beers under their belts some of the blokes were in the right mood to appreciate a stunning young woman suddenly turning up in their midst. A couple of wolf-whistles rang out.

'Inspector Zagalski and this is Detective Sergeant Purcell,' announced Hank flashing his ID card.

'Welcome to "The Squirrel and Porcupine,"' responded Jack with the broad smile he extended to everyone who entered his establishment, even police. He retained his smile long enough to include Belinda. 'My name's Jack Duncan, I'm the proprietor. How can I help you officers?'

The chatter in the pub had been running hot for the last hour or so with regard to the nasty business that had happened up at Hollyhock Cottage. All kinds of crazy ideas had been bandied about and the more the grog went down the more outlandish these stories became. Old Charlie, a regular, had been telling anyone who cared to listen he had predicted this murder was going to happen years ago.

'I knew the village were in trouble when me cabbages went black overnight. It were an omen. Black cabbages me old grandma always said, meant black death. Aye, she'd seen it 'appen and all. One mornin' she found her cabbages had gone black overnight and afore the day were done two villagers lay dead. I don't know how its 'appened, but I reckon Mr and Mrs Summers are both goners. You mark my words!'

Charlie's ramblings hadn't garnered much support because Alf, the village undertaker, who happened to live right next door to Charlie and could see over Charlie's fence, was adamant Charlie didn't have any cabbages in the ground this year. 'How can you have black cabbages Charlie? You ain't got no bloody cabbages in yer vegie patch!'

Charlie's sinister black cabbage predictions were put on hold because the pub's clientele had turned its collective attention towards the two strangers who had just marched in as if they owned the joint.

'Jack, I'd very much appreciate your help please,' requested Hank,

'I want to speak to everyone in here and ask for their assistance.' Although Hank had used the word 'please' this was clearly a police directive.

'By all means,' replied Jack, affably.

Seeing an empty glass sitting on the counter Hank tapped it with a spoon making sufficient noise for the pub's clientele to stop talking and listen.

'Ladies and gentlemen, my name is Inspector Zagalski and this is Detective Sergeant Purcell. We are from the CID. I apologise for briefly interrupting your evening; however, an urgent matter has arisen in Upper Bybridge today. No doubt you have already heard some rumours. I want to tell you what has *actually* happened and ask for your assistance.'

'You're welcome officer,' came a cheeky voice from someone at the back of the pub.

'Shut-up Jim,' came a second voice.

Ignoring the interjections, Hank continued. 'This afternoon around a quarter to five, there was a savage stabbing murder at Hollyhock Cottage. Mr Summers was the victim. Mrs Summers thankfully was unharmed. The immediate area has been cordoned off and will remain a crime scene until further notice. Mrs Summers is staying with friends.'

There was a chorus of concerned voices as this "official" news was received.

Hank tapped his glass again and waited for quiet. 'Crimes of this nature are, I'm glad to say, extremely rare in rural Sussex. Naturally we are most anxious to apprehend the man responsible as quickly as possible. In cases like this the quicker we can follow up any leads, the easier our job is. We've come in here to ask you to think hard whether you've seen anything unusual today. Have you noticed any strangers in the village? Was anyone in the village behaving oddly or suspiciously? Any strange vehicles about? Don't be afraid to come forward with *anything*, even if it's only slightly unusual.'

'How do you know it was a man?' someone called out.

'Because the murderer called out "Rolf Summers" when he came to the door. Mrs Summers heard it clearly and she's positive it was a man's voice. She thinks the person spoke with the same accent as her husband, German or Austrian probably.'

'Oh God! I think I served him!' All eyes turned to Jenny Duncan the attractive sixteen-year-old daughter of the proprietor. The distressed lass covered her mouth with both hands in shock.

Once more there was a hub-hub of raised voices and Hank had to call for quiet again.

'This could be really valuable information. Did anyone else see a stranger in here today?'

'I reckon I might have seen the bloke,' called out Barney Hobbs, a local chicken farmer, 'he was sat over there in the corner. On his own he was. Only a half pint, a newspaper and a cigarette for company.'

'Have you been cavorting with murderers again Barney?' called out someone, good naturedly, a comment followed by a raucous round of laughter.

'I thought you only murdered them chickens of yours,' yelled another. More laughter.

'Where exactly was this man sitting?' asked Hank, raising his voice above the noise.

'Right there,' replied Barney, pointing to a small table in a dark corner with only two seats.

'Okay that area is now a crime scene too. Nobody is to touch anything there. We might be able to pick up some fingerprints.'

Hank quickly established that nobody else had seen this mysterious stranger and thanked the drinkers for their help. Meanwhile, Belinda disappeared behind the bar with Jenny Duncan to ask some probing questions. Hank hastily placed police tape around the table and chairs in the dark corner and then remained standing at the bar with a glass of lemonade and a bowl of crisps in case anybody wanted to speak with him.

3.   Pub Interviews

Hank called for Barney Hobbs, the chicken farmer and led him outside for further questioning. Meanwhile Belinda asked Jack if there was a room out the back she could use to talk privately to Jenny. Hearing this request, Jenny's mother asked to be present during her daughter's questioning and this was agreed to. Betty led them to a small untidy office with only one chair. The desk was strewn with forms, letters and bills and the waste-paper basket was over-flowing. She apologised for the mess and then brightening up suggested it might be more comfortable if the three of them went out the back door and sat around the old table there.

Belinda looked at her watch noting it was a few minutes past seven yet still pleasantly warm. There was a couple of hours of sunshine still to enjoy. Running a pub was a full-time job and the neglected back garden reflected the long hours required indoors keeping the thirsty local drinkers happy. Several overgrown fruit trees had dropped most of this summer's fruit on the ground where bees, wasps and other insects were relishing a feast of the over-ripe, sweet remains. A couple of grey squirrels cavorted about at the end of the uncut lawn undeterred by the appearance of the three humans. Blackbirds and thrushes stopped their tuneful singing when the threesome first appeared, but soon resumed their cheerful choruses once they felt safe.

Belinda examined the young lass more closely. She was very pretty, sported an attractive pony-tail and was wearing a loose top that might be just a little too daring for the likes of some of the blokes that frequented pubs. Her parents should have a quiet word with her about wearing more appropriate clothing. Jenny's good looks could not, however, hide her obvious nervousness in having to be questioned by a policewoman. She sat with her long legs crossed chewing on her finger nails. Feeling empathetic, Belinda once again opted for the gentle, easy-going approach.

'Thank you, Jenny for coming into the back garden with me for a bit of a chat. There's nothing for you to worry about, you're not in trouble but you may be able to help us find this person of interest.' As she spoke, Belinda pulled out a notebook and pencil and flicked over to a clean page.

'Do you think he's the murderer?' Jenny asked nervously as she switched her attention to a new fingernail to chew.

'It's much too early to say, Jenny. We have to follow up every possibility. It maybe that the stranger who was in your pub today is totally innocent, but we need to make sure. Now can you tell me when you first saw this man, please?'

Jenny looked across to her mother for assurance before she answered fearing what she was about to say might not be well received.

'I was chatting to one of the boys at the bar.'

'Who dear?' inquired her mother.

'Frank Stubbs.'

Belinda sensed from her body language that Mrs Duncan did not approve of her daughter's choice of young man.

'And what happened?'

'I suppose I wasn't looking to see if there was anyone waiting to be served,' confessed Jenny, blushing. 'Then I heard this cough. When I turned this man was standing there. I don't know how long he'd been there. Sorry mum.' Jenny flicked another anxious glance at her mother who remained tight lipped.

'Go on…'

'I think I apologised to the man for keeping him waiting and then asked him what he would like.'

'Can you describe what he looked like, Jenny?'

'Average height…'

'As tall as you, Jenny?'

'A bit taller.'

'And do you know your height?'

'I'm five foot seven and a half. I know that because I applied to get into a modelling course and girls had to be five-seven or more to apply.'

'Okay, so this man would be about five foot eight or perhaps five foot nine?'

'Yes,' said Jenny moving onto a fresh fingernail, this time on the other hand.

'How old do you think he was?'

'In his thirties, perhaps thirty-five.'

'Was he handsome, attractive…?'

'I guess so but too old for me.'

'Hair colour?'

'Dark.'

'Was it styled? Like a teddy boy? Duck's arse, for example?'

'No, just ordinary. I think he had a parting in his hair.'

'Left, or right?'

'I can't remember.'

'That's all right, you're doing very well. Can you describe his physique?'

'What do you mean?'

'Was he thin, well built, over weight?'

'No, just ordinary.'

'What about his face?'

'He had a moustache, I remember that.'

'Describe it for me please.'

'It was very neat like those military moustaches you see in films.'

'Excellent. Now what about his clothing?'

'It looked a bit different. I don't know why, it just didn't look English.'

'Okay, that's interesting. Now what did this gentleman say to you?'

'I remember it clearly. He said, "Please beer." It sounded funny because he said "please" first.'

'And what did you say?'

'What kind of beer, sir? We have beer on tap and several kinds of bottled beers.'

'And what did he reply?'

'He just shrugged his shoulders as if he didn't mind. So, I asked if a Guinness would be okay and he nodded.'

'Did he say anything more?'

'No… Oh yes, he did. When I handed the beer to him, he said "danker" or something like that.'

'So, do you think he was a foreigner?'

'Definitely. I reckon he was a German.'

'This has all been a terrific help, Jenny. I'm getting an excellent picture of him. This man went over to the dark corner. What then?'

'I forgot all about him and served some other people.'

'Did you see him again?'

'Yes, perhaps half an hour later. I was going around collecting the empties and wiping the tables down. I do that when things are not too busy.'

'Go on…'

'Well, he was still there in the corner sitting by himself almost hidden behind a newspaper. I picked up his empty glass and asked him if he wanted another one. He shook his head and got up to leave.'

'Now, this is very important. What time was it when he left?'

'Oh, I don't know. It must have been before five o'clock because mum only wanted me to work until five.'

'Was there anything else you noticed that might help us to identify this man?' Did he have any distinguishing features? Was he wearing any rings, for example? Or a watch perhaps?'

'I didn't see anything else.'

'The other man in the pub who noticed the stranger, Barney I think his name was, said he thought our friend in the corner was sitting there with a cigarette. Do you remember the stranger smoking?'

'Oh yes, he was. I forgot about that, so many people smoke. After he left, I took his ash-tray away.'

'What did you do with the cigarette butts?'

'What we always do. I threw them in the dustbin then washed the ashtray ready to put out again.'

'I want to get hold of those cigarette butts, please.'

'Whatever for?'

'It always helps to know what kind of a cigarette a person smokes.'

Belinda turned to Jenny's mother. 'Do you mind, Mrs Duncan, if I look in your dustbin for the butts?'

'Not at all. It won't be very pleasant though. You're lucky the bin was emptied yesterday afternoon so there will only be a few butts in there from today. Did you empty any other ash-trays, dear?'

'Only a couple of others. I remember now there were three cigarette butts in his ashtray and they all looked the same.'

'Jenny, you have been brilliant. Thank you both for your time. Mrs Duncan, may I rummage through your dustbin now please?'

Ten minutes later Belinda washed her hands thoroughly in the small bathroom basin reserved for staff. She was pleased with the result of her dustbin search. In a plastic bag she had placed three cigarette butts, each one displaying the start of what appeared to be the same brand name as the cigarette butt Hank had found outside Hollyhock Cottage. One butt had the letters "ME…", another only the letter "M…" but the third butt, which must have been discarded in a hurry, had "MERCE…".

❦

Hank interviewed the man known as Barney, the local farmer who had also claimed to have seen the stranger in the pub during the afternoon. Next, he collared Frank Stubbs, the young man who had been chatting with Jenny at the counter when the stranger ordered his first beer. Neither of his interviewees gave him anything particularly useful. Barney had had a couple of beers too many and any further details about the mystery man in the corner had eluded him. Young stud Frank confessed his attention was focused on the gorgeous Jenny who he claimed was openly flirting with him. As Frank unashamedly remarked to Hank, 'Who cares about some bloody foreigner when Jenny's giving me "the come and get me" treatment.'

Having thanked and dismissed both men, Hank idled away his time sitting out in front of "The Squirrel and Porcupine" sans beer, sans any kind of alcoholic drink and feeling stupid sitting there on his own with the patrons coming and going. Finally, after half an hour, an elated Belinda appeared. Hank thought she looked even more attractive than usual when in such a happy radiant mood. She couldn't wait to sit down and read out what she had written in her notebook. For a brief moment Hank allowed himself to wonder what it would be like to have this stunning woman out with him on a date. With some difficulty he pulled his mind back into gear and concentrated on what Belinda was so enthusiastically reporting. When she'd finished, he congratulated her, a rare occurrence since Hank seldom complimented anyone.

It was getting late and there was nothing more they could do. The two detectives returned to their car and headed back to Petworth. Along the way Hank told Belinda to put the following dot points in her notebook. He was a great believer in putting his ideas down in writing for fear of losing them.

- The mystery man in the pub now becomes our number one suspect
- Mrs Summers is a close second
- We have sufficient details of the foreigner's appearance to have an artist draw up a facial likeness
- The man is most likely German or possibly Austrian
- Identical brands of cigarettes have been found at the site of the murder and in the corner where the man was sitting in the pub providing a powerful link

- As soon as possible we must track down the full name and origin of the cigarette brand
- The fact the man was careless about his cigarette butts suggests he's an amateur not a trained professional killer
- The finger-print experts must examine the cigarette butts and the table in the corner of the pub asap for further evidence
- The man is probably a visitor to the country. If he is the murderer he will be anxious to leave the country asap. Immediate steps must be taken to stop his departure from the UK.

Hank stopped giving Belinda any more dot points and parked the car. He used his car radio to ask Chief Inspector Nigel Sandham to contact his superiors to request urgent police and security checks be established at the country's major air and sea embarkation points. He then provided a full description of the stranger's appearance. This done, he asked Belinda to resume her listing of dot points.

- Interview Mrs Summers again to understand more about Mr Summers' past. She may have valuable information that could provide clues as to why someone would wish to murder him
- Find out how this man travelled to Upper Bybridge. This might help us track him down. There are no public buses or trains servicing Upper Bybridge so he must have come by car or motor bike Did he hitch-hike, steal a car, hire a car or get someone to drive him to the village?
- Redouble our efforts at door-knocking the people who live in Upper Bybridge. Locals are very perceptive of anything out of the ordinary
- Where is the murder weapon? We must find it!
- This intensive investigative work requires additional personnel to be appointed asap.

It was well after eight-thirty when they drove onto Chief Inspector Nigel Sandham's gravel-crunchy driveway. The sun was dipping behind his garden trees and the temperature was a little more pleasant. They hadn't eaten all day and were delighted when their boss inquired whether they would like something to eat. The Sandhams were empty nesters, all three of their children having found work elsewhere with two already married. Joan Sandham, Nigel's wife, was only too pleased to prepare them a quick meal.

The Chief Inspector led them to a room that doubled as his study and library. An impressive array of books filled the shelves, neatly arranged indexed and in good condition. A heavy carved wooden desk sat facing the bay window together with a matching chair. The Chief Inspector lowered himself gingerly onto his chair and waved to his subordinates to take the two remaining seats.

'Okay action! I've already been in touch with Head Office and they've ordered customs and immigration at all major ports and airports in the country to be on high alert for your man as soon as they receive final confirmation from you. Here's the phone number for you to ring, Hank. I suggest you do this straightaway while you're waiting for Joan to bring you your meal.'

Hank picked up the phone and dialled the number. With Belinda's help he confirmed the descriptive details they had received from young Jenny in the pub. It would have been better had they had a photograph. Nevertheless, the description was good enough for a police artist to create an "artist's impression" for circulation.

Hank borrowed Belinda's list of dot points and ran through these with Sandham. The boss agreed to have the police researchers work on the source of the cigarettes first thing in the morning and to call in an additional sergeant and six constables to begin the painstaking work of hunting for the murder weapon. Two other police would be assigned the task of door knocking every house in Upper Bybridge. Hank, with Belinda's assistance would oversee the entire operation. Sandham agreed Belinda and Hank should return to re-interview Mrs Summers and ascertain how the mystery man travelled to Upper Bybridge and fled afterwards.

As soon as they had agreed on their strategies for the ensuing day, there was a tentative knock on the door. Joan Sandham was standing there and invited Belinda and Hank to come to the dining table. In quick time she had laid the table and put out their heated plates loaded with pork sausages, carrots, greens and bubble and squeak. This, she informed them, would be followed by fruit salad and ice-cream. Nigel Sandham poured them a beer and stayed to discuss further details.

4.   Saturday Evening

Later that Saturday evening, after Joan Sandham's excellent meal, Hank drove Belinda back to her small flat near the park en route to his own place which he shared with two of his rugby mates. After spending so much time with his young female assistant Hank was finding her more and more attractive. They were both behaving entirely professionally, of course, and he made no attempt to reveal his increasingly strong feelings for her. During the day, when he thought it safe to do so, Hank had glanced at Belinda and marvelled at her good looks. She was always so composed, like a model, yet strong and athletic enough to have survived the robust police training. He wondered whether she was also attracted to him.

As soon as Hank arrived home, he changed and went for a training run. The rugby season would be getting underway soon with the first competition matches starting mid-September. He hit the road running at least three times a week and made sure he covered no less than ten miles each time. It was getting dark so he planned to run along the better lit streets. One of his flat mates was the sports master at the local high school and he usually invited the three of them to come to the well-equipped school gym at weekends. Here they worked out using medicine balls, ropes and weights. Combined with the running, the gym work was enough exercise to maintain a base level of fitness during the off season so that Hank continued to feel good about his overall health.

As Hank started up the long hill that led out of town his mind reverted back to Belinda. He felt pangs of guilt about this though because he was still dating Suzette, an attractive blonde school teacher he had been seeing on and off for several months. Suzette was great fun and he always enjoyed going out with her but he never felt she was "the one." Recently, Suzette was becoming far too serious about their relationship. After an outing to the cinema last week followed by drinks at her place, she had made it abundantly clear she was "available" and wasn't just talking about cuddles and kisses on the couch anymore. So far, he had resisted her charms but his refusal to go any further appeared to have fired Suzette up to being even more passionately inclined. Now she was ringing him almost daily and begging him to come round in the evenings.

Hank was twenty-nine and rising steadily up through the police ranks. He knew he was good at his job and had impressed the senior ranks. He had attended every opportunity extended to him for further training and could boast a faultless police record. According to his annual reports he was regarded as a tough, principled young man, highly intelligent, uncompromising but perceptive. Sometimes he came over as rather too cold or insensitive, but if anything, this was considered a fault on the right side for the kind of detective work in which he was engaged. Hank was objective, able to think laterally and avoided showing his emotions.

Every couple of months Hank tried to get away to visit his parents living in Bristol. His old man was a public servant who had returned from the war with a smashed leg and now found a desk job suited him. Mum had learnt typing and shorthand and had been a secretary before taking fifteen years off from paid work to look after Hank and his sister during their younger years. Hank supposed his parents were considered "ordinary" folk. Nevertheless, he loved them dearly. The one thing he had learnt from them was the importance of providing a stable, loving family environment and this he yearned to establish in his own life. Could the lovely Belinda be the person to join him?

❧

For a time after the horrific murder of her husband, Doreen Summers was unable to process what was going on around her.

She moved in a ghastly fog of confusion, interrupted at times by sudden panic attacks when she imagined her life was also in imminent danger. She had a vague memory of some policewoman speaking to her but had no idea what responses she had given to her questions. At some stage her next-door neighbours, Mike and Sandra Leighton, had taken her into their bungalow where she sat now on the settee next to Sandra nursing a hot cup of Ovaltine. It was approaching eleven o'clock at night, some six hours after her life had been violently shattered in a few horrifying seconds. She felt numb, trapped in some weird game of make-believe. Had she really been present at the murder of her loving husband or was she going insane? Was this just some ghastly nightmare? If so, why couldn't she wake up?

'Doreen dear, the doctor has suggested you take a couple of these sleeping pills to help you through the night.'

'I never take sleeping pills thank you Sandra. I always sleep very well.'

'But you have had an awful shock dear. Mike rang Doctor Thornberry to ask his advice and he strongly recommended you take these tablets. They are often prescribed in situations like this. Mike went to the chemist specially for you. They have a calming effect too.'

'If I can't sleep Rolf snuggles into me and then I go out like a light.'

'Well, suit yourself dear. How about I leave two tablets by your bed with a glass of water?'

'If you like.'

'It's past Mike's and my bedtime so I think we'll go upstairs. If you need anything during the night, just knock on our door.'

'Thank you, Sandra. You and Mike are the most marvellous neighbours. If you don't mind, I think I'll stay down here a bit longer. I'm not quite ready for bed.'

'Of course, dear. We'll see you in the morning then. Just get up when you feel like it. Help yourself to whatever you want for breakfast if we're not around.'

Mike and Sandra headed up to bed, leaving the forlorn figure of Doreen huddled alone on the settee. They skipped their evening baths and climbed into bed but sleep was a long way off.

'The poor girl. How's she ever going to get over this Mike?'

'Only with a lot of love and support from everyone in the village.'

'It's just too awful! Do you think it was some madman on drugs or something? It must have been a crazy random killing, don't you think?'

'No.'

'Oh…Why do you say that?'

'Whoever came to their door asked if he was speaking to Rolf Summers. So, this definitely wasn't a random killing. Rolf was singled out. The killer checked first that he had the right person.'

'Yes, I guess you're right. Whoever did this must have really hated poor old Rolf. But why? Rolf has lived here for fifteen years and seemed to get on well with everyone. I've never heard anyone complain about Rolf. He never got into any of the village's petty issues as far as I know.'

'Perhaps he dared disagree with the judge's final decision on who won this year's sponge cake competition at the Upper Bybridge Show,' suggested Mike.

'Oh, don't be so silly, Mike.' All the same, Sandra gave her husband a loving dig in the ribs.

'Did you ever hear any nasty whispers about Rolf when you were down at the pub?'

'Nah, although when the Summers first came to live in the village, fifteen years ago, there was the usual speculation and scuttlebutt that flies about whenever strangers come to live in Upper Bybridge. Rolf being German didn't help, either.'

'We've got to do all we can to support dear Doreen. She doesn't deserve this, poor girl. I think I'll…'

Mike was already asleep.

5.   Sunday, 25th August

Belinda was up with the dawn on Sunday clad in her pink track suit and plimsolls ready to do a few laps around the football oval behind her flat. This was her favourite time of day, the air fresh, the birds in full song to greet the new day and a light dew glistening on the grass. Few people were abroad at this early hour and the hum of traffic on the nearby main road was yet to become a constant. Although it was a Sunday, she happily accepted the expectation that detectives don't take days off when there's been a murder. The niggle she had felt in her thigh yesterday after her run had disappeared overnight and she decided on five laps at a comfortable steady pace.

Ninety minutes later showered and breakfasted, she was ready for Hank to sound the horn when he pulled up outside in the police car. She needn't have hurried as he was ten minutes late. Normally Belinda walked the mile to work and back, however, last night for the first time, she had allowed Hank to drive her home. Now he knew where she lived, she wondered whether this had been such a good idea. Would Hank driving her to work in the mornings and back home in the evenings become a regular event? Did she really want such close attention? Belinda had always highly valued her independence and didn't want Hank to start regulating what time she had to be ready every morning and when she would be coming home. And yet, this morning she sensed a bit of a thrill that Hank was out there waiting for her. Belinda had to admit a day in Hank's company was something she looked forward to.

Half an hour later the detectives drove back into Upper Bybridge and headed straight for "The Gables," the cottage where Doreen

Summers had spent Saturday night with her neighbours, Mike and Sandra Leighton. It was a few minutes before nine o'clock, not too early to speak with Mrs Summers again. They were pleased to see the uniformed police were already busy at work searching for the murder weapon and anything else that might be helpful. So far nothing more of interest had turned up.

"The Gables" was another sixteenth century cottage with a newly thatched roof and a small garden surrounded by a low brick wall. Obviously, the Leightons were not keen gardeners since much of their garden was overgrown with dandelions, thistles and stinging nettles. There was even a wild blackberry bush straggling over the sidewall. Belinda noted the decent sized berries were starting to change from a deep red to black. The detectives walked up the short curving path and knocked loudly on the front door. Mike Leighton appeared and obligingly ushered them through to the sitting room where Mrs Summers was reclining on the settee with her feet up. The detectives politely declined the offer of a cup of tea and pulled over two chairs so as to be closer to Mrs Summers. The purpose of this second interview was to probe deeper into Rolf Summers' background. The detectives hoped that something in Rolf's past might shed light on the reason for his sudden and violent demise. Belinda opened the proceedings.

'Good morning, Mrs Summers. I expect you remember me speaking to you yesterday afternoon?'

Doreen stared blankly at Belinda for a moment. Then, realising it was the policewoman she had seen before gave a faint nod and swung her legs down so she was sitting upright.

'I hope you managed to get some sleep last night?'

'Not much.'

Mrs Summers had only made a half-hearted effort to do her hair, wore no make-up and looked at them through red blood-shot eyes. Belinda's heart went out to the poor woman and she resolved to once again take things slowly and gently.

'Mrs Summers, my colleague here is Detective Inspector Hank Zagalski.'

Hank was also accorded a slight nod.

'We are anxious to find out some more about Mr Summers' background because it might help us with our inquiries. Do you feel able to talk to us?'

Doreen sniffed and pulled out a handkerchief from under her sleeve, 'I suppose so.'

'When did you first meet Rolf?'

'Just after the war, November 1945.'

'Where did you meet?'

'At a jazz club in Reading.'

'Why were you living in Reading?'

'I was working in an arms factory there.'

'And what was Rolf doing in Reading?'

'He said he'd just been released from internment at a camp on the Isle of Man.'

'That's interesting. Do you know the name of the camp?'

Doreen shook her head.

'Did he tell you why he was interned?'

'Because he was German and happened to be working in England when the war broke out in thirty-nine.'

'What kind of work was he doing?'

'Fitting and turning. He was a qualified tradesman.'

'Do you know when he first came to England?'

'No.'

'Did you have any reason to doubt his story?'

'No, not at all. It was very difficult courting because people still hated the Nazis and they thought I was going out with a Nazi. Many of my friends spurned me. Rolf didn't tell me much about his life in the internment camp because it was very unpleasant there and he wanted to try to forget what the British had done to him.'

At this point Hank asked a question. Belinda was pleased to see him being respectfully polite. 'Mrs Summers, did your husband mention anyone at the internment camp that he didn't get along with?' Did he have any enemies there?'

'No, I don't think so.'

'How old was Rolf when you first met him back in forty-five?'

'He was forty-five and I was forty-three.'

'Had he been married before?'

'No.'

'Are you sure?'

'Yes. I think he would have told me before we got married if he had been married before.'

'Let's talk now about Rolf's life in Germany. Did he serve in the German army in the first world war?'

'Yes, but only for the last year or two, after he turned seventeen.'

'So, he was in the German Army in 1918?'

'I think so.'

'Do you know his regiment?'

Mrs Summers shook her head, 'He never talked much about his life in Germany.'

'Doesn't that strike you as strange, Mrs Summers? He never spoke much about his family, his school, what he did in Germany between the wars?'

Doreen Summers shook her head again and wiped her nose with a handkerchief, 'He always said he came to England before the second world war because he wanted to start a new life. He didn't like what was happening in Germany with the Hitler Youth and the Nazis and that awful man, Hitler.'

'Do you think Rolf came to England to get away from someone? Perhaps he had enemies there or had fallen out with somebody?'

Once again Mrs Summers shook her head. The interrogation wasn't going anywhere and Doreen Summers looked as though she had had enough questioning for the time being. The detectives left shortly afterwards promising to return to interview Mrs Summers again soon.

Belinda checked her watch as she and Hank left Mrs Summers in the kindly care of her next-door neighbours. It was a quarter to ten. Thoughtfully, Belinda had brought along a thermos of hot coffee and two mugs and suggested they return to their police car for a drink and a quick debrief. The detectives were about to discover they had rather different takes on the interrogation they had just conducted with Doreen Summers. As Belinda passed a cup of steaming coffee over to her colleague she opened up the discussion.

'Do you think Mrs Summers is telling the truth?'

Hank looked surprised, 'Certainly, why would you have any doubts?'

'I think she knows far more about Rolf's time in Germany, before he came to the UK, than she's letting on.'

'Really? Whatever makes you think that?'

'I can't believe two people married for fifteen years didn't know more about each other's background. Surely, Mrs Summers would have wanted to know *something* about the man she was marrying back in 1947? They'd been going out for nearly two years when they tied the knot. So, they were actually together for seventeen years in total.'

'I think she was telling us the truth,' replied Hank, 'being a German and living in the UK after the war must have been tough going. Rolf would have been keen to forget everything about his disgraced Nazi country. He certainly wouldn't be telling everyone he was German or enthusing about his family or schooling back there.'

Belinda sipped her coffee a couple of times before speaking again. 'Well, you can call it a woman's intuition if you wish, but I wouldn't go out with someone for a couple of years and end up marrying them if I didn't know something about their family and their background. I think Doreen Summers does know more about Rolf's time in Nazi Germany but she isn't divulging. Perhaps he was a German spy? Who knows... I still think she's definitely hiding something.'

'I guess you're entitled to think that way, Belinda. I'm a bit more trusting I suppose. That's nice coffee by the way. Do you have a bit more?'

Belinda topped up Hank's mug, 'Remember, Doreen was forty-five when she married Rolf in 1947.'

'What's that got to do with it?'

'She was getting a bit long in the tooth. It was probably a case of get married now or forget it. I reckon she was so desperate to get married she was prepared to ignore Rolf's past. Rolf would have been thrilled to find someone who would accept him too. After all, he was a forty-seven-year-old German without much money behind him. Not many women would jump at the chance to marry a bloke like that.'

Hank smiled and shrugged his shoulders. Belinda was pleased there was no apparent animosity, they had simply agreed to disagree in a mature sensible way. She screwed the lid back on the thermos flask and waited for Hank to finish his coffee.

A few minutes later feeling refreshed, they left the car to speak with the sergeant in charge of the uniformed police still combing the garden around Hollyhock Cottage looking for the murder weapon. Finding nothing in the immediate vicinity the squad had spread out farther. Apart from a few drops of blood on the ground outside the Summers' front door they had uncovered nothing of interest. The sergeant wanted to know how much longer the squad should keep looking. Hank advised the sergeant that if nothing came to light by the end of the evening, he could call the search off.

Next, the two detectives caught up with the senior officer supervising the door-to-door inquiries. The uniformed police had contacted the owners of most of the houses nestled around Hollyhock Cottage. Nobody had seen anything unusual. Several nearby house owners, however, had reported hearing what they thought was a gunshot at about the time of the murder Another villager, a returned serviceman currently working as a car mechanic, swore he knew the difference between a gun-shot and a car back-firing. He was one hundred percent certain it was only a car back-firing. Hank accepted the ex-serviceman's explanation as being the correct one. The bang was an interesting observation, although it was difficult to see how it might in anyway be connected to the demise of Mr Summers.

Belinda and Hank spent the rest of the day carrying out what turned out to be fruitless activities. They revisited "The Squirrel and Porcupine" in the hope someone there would come forward with new evidence and they re-interviewed Jenny Duncan. They helped the uniformed police with their door-to-door questioning and even joined the team searching for the murder weapon for an hour or two. It was one of those frustrating days when virtually no progress was made. At four o'clock they called it a day and drove back to Petworth. Hank would have dearly liked to have taken Belinda out for dinner that evening, but he still hadn't broken off with Suzette.

℃

Sunday afternoon in "The Squirrel and Porcupine" was far more lively than usual. Rare dramatic events in the quiet village of Upper Bybridge were guaranteed to bring out the locals in droves to have a good old chin-wag and gossip session down at the village's only watering hole. There was always something comforting there for the imbibers who would journey home at the end of the day knowing they had shared their concerns, picked up the latest news, renewed acquaintances and had a good belly laugh. Usually there was some wag at the pub who could see the funny side of everything even if it was a murder.

The Duncans had anticipated this busy Sunday and brought in extra snacks, chairs, ash-trays and glasses. Jenny had been signed up for a whole eight-hour shift, a first for her. They had even persuaded Charlie Cruickshank, who filled in if Jack or Betty were away, to help out for the day. Right on the dot they opened their doors to find a dozen customers already waiting outside deep in discussion about the murder of Rolf Summers. As the day wore on, it became clear there was general agreement about *how* the murder had occurred, however, *who* the villain was had become a topic of endless speculation. Just about every male who resided in the village came up for consideration as a possible suspect at some stage. Try as they may, nobody in the village emerged as the number one suspect and the villagers eventually went home shaking their heads and tut-tutting. What was most extraordinary was that nobody had observed anything out of the ordinary on Saturday except for the mysterious stranger who had been seen briefly drinking in the pub during the afternoon. By a process of elimination, the villagers decided it must have been the stranger who murdered the unfortunate Rolf.

Sixteen-year-old Jenny Duncan was in her element. The pub was full of men and they all seemed to appreciate her good looks and friendly way of interacting. Much to her mother's annoyance she was wearing a particularly short mini-skirt and a top that gaped open invitingly whenever she bent over the tables to pick up glasses. Jenny enjoyed seeing the men trying to have a peek and got a thrill from the extra attention. Of course, she had her favourites and made a point of checking on their tables more often. There was much good-hearted banter, heaps of jokes and even a couple of suggestive comments made when she was still within earshot. Jenny lapped it all up.

This being a Sunday, the pub was required to close its doors at seven o'clock. As was his custom, twenty minutes before closing Jack Duncan called out in his best ex-Sergeant Major's voice, 'Last drinks ladies and gentlemen, please.' There was the expected sudden flurry of activity as the late stayers came dashing up to the counter to order a final round of drinks. Jack and Betty, already aware they had had their best sales day ever, pulled hard and fast on the beers to satisfy demand.

6.   Doreen Summers

By Sunday afternoon Mike and Sandra Leighton were becoming increasingly anxious. Doreen Summers had been depressed all day, eating little and wandering around in a stupor. When Sandra tried to settle her down for some afternoon tea and a chat, she did little more than sit on the settee whimpering. Engaging in any meaningful conversation seemed beyond her. The doctor had warned them this kind of behaviour was a typical reaction to the traumatic loss of a dear one and she would gradually come out of it over the next few days. It was, the doctor assured them, a form of delayed shock and the beginning of the grieving process. Doreen ignored her cup of tea and went off to her bedroom for a lie down.

An hour later Doreen suddenly re-appeared in the lounge room dressed in her Sunday clothes as if going to church. It was five o'clock.

'Where are you going Doreen, dear? inquired Sandra.

'I'm going to Saint David's.'

'But there's no service tonight, dear,' Sandra replied, 'there won't be anyone there.'

'The Lord is there and I want to pray to him.'

Sandra and her husband exchanged puzzled looks. The Leightons rarely went to church except at Christmas time, when they went because they enjoyed the cosy atmosphere and the carol singing. Nevertheless, they were sure there was no church service this particular Sunday evening. 'Couldn't you speak to the Lord from here?' asked Mike, hopefully.

'It's much better in the house of the Lord,' Doreen responded.

'How about I put on a hat and come with you, dear?' Sandra suggested. She was worried about Doreen's mental state and thought it wise to accompany her to the church and back.

'No thank you, Sandra. I prefer to go on my own.'

'There's no need for you to feel you have to talk to me, Doreen. If I accompany you, I promise I'll keep quiet. It's just nice to have someone along for the company. I won't come into the church if you prefer I didn't.'

Doreen didn't bother to reply. She looked in the hall mirror, adjusted her hat slightly, and walked boldly towards the front door. Mike went to the door to see her on her way. 'We usually eat around half past six, Doreen. We're just going to have mushrooms on toast tonight. If you're not back in time we'll keep yours for you and reheat it when you return.'

Doreen gave him a limp smile and let herself out.

The weather was delightful. The recent hot weather had abated somewhat and been replaced by slightly cooler damper westerlies. Constable-like cumulus clouds floated overhead while a gentle breeze rustled the leaves of the poplars beside the path that Doreen followed. She had walked this path many times with her dear Rolf to attend matins, but seldom had the pathway seemed so gloriously inviting as it was this evening.

Rolf and Doreen had been faithful parishioners of St David's Anglican Church since arriving in Upper Bybridge fifteen years ago. Doreen's faith had been wavering until she met Rolf, who worshipped the Lord with a passion. He never missed matins on Sunday mornings and occasionally attended evensong as well. Doreen sometimes wondered whether her husband was trying to repent of something sinful in his past. Over the years she had gradually learnt to accept his reluctance to speak of his life in Germany and to recognise he wished to remain a private man. Rolf would have been seventeen towards the end of the first World War but had been excused military service. Sometimes, she asked herself whether he really had arrived in the UK prior to World War II as he claimed or whether Rolf had remained in Germany and perhaps become part of that ghastly Nazi juggernaut. Now she would never know.

The path to the church meandered through a small wooded glade full of ferns, blackberry bushes and leafy deciduous trees that afforded soft dappled shade. In a few weeks' time these trees would start to lose their leaves and a lovely thick carpet of red, yellow and brown would cover the ground. There was the sound of a blackbird's shrill song and somewhere nearby a hen proudly proclaimed a new arrival. Doreen loved this part of the walk; it seemed so perfect as she went to the house of the Lord.

As she wandered up the gentle hill she was startled by a sudden crashing sound behind her. Looking around she couldn't see anything and put it down to some creature moving about in the undergrowth or perhaps a branch falling. She had heard rumours a small herd of deer lived in the glade although she had yet to sight them. Unperturbed, she walked slowly on. At the top of the rise the path wandered on into Saint David's ancient cemetery, a place of peace and solitude. Some of the graves dated back to the sixteenth century and remained virtually undisturbed except for the occasional gravestone leaning over or a lichen encrustation. Soon, her dearest Rolf would join the souls buried here. Already Doreen sensed she was close to her Lord in this beautiful, holy place.

Doreen knew if she had been the one attacked, Rolf would make this same short journey to pray at this lovely old church. In the house of the Lord, it might be possible to make some sense of the awful happenings of yesterday afternoon. Through prayer she might find the strength to carry on, to start the long process of forgiving the perpetrator, to come to terms with the massive changes in her future life. Half an hour talking to God in this sacred place of worship would be more restorative than the well-intentioned wishes of her friends and the silly sleeping pills prescribed by the doctor.

None of her family, or Rolf's had ever been buried here. Doreen wandered slowly over to a section of the cemetery where the most recent graves had been dug, a peaceful spot under an ancient yew tree. Dear old Mrs Kirkenvin was the most recent addition, barely a month ago. Bunches of dead or dying flowers still lay across her special mound of dirt while her headstone was being prepared. It was right here that the mutilated body of her darling Rolf would be laid to rest in a few short days' time. She noted grimly that the ground retained some moisture which would make the digging easier for the grave-diggers. She knew the grave-diggers, the two Barton brothers.

Doreen knew little about what happened next.

A massive force crashed down between her shoulder blades causing her to collapse slowly to her knees. As she crumpled another massive blow smashed violently through one of her kidneys and then another… and another…

The pathologist examining Doreen's battered body later was convinced death would have been almost instantaneous.

☾

The Reverend James Arbuthnot, Vicar of Saint David's Anglican Church of Upper and Lower Bybridge, was partial to a glass of dry sherry in the evenings. Hazel, his wife of forty-two years, usually joined him although she preferred the sweeter sherry variety. He looked at the grandfather clock tick-tocking gently in the corner of the drawing room and noted with pleasure it was almost six o'clock… sherry time.

'Six o'clock, my dear…' he called out as he pushed his tired old bones into a standing upright position. At seventy-two he was at that stage in life when you started to question how much longer you can adequately serve the Lord as the vicar of a small country parish.

There was no reply. Hazel was in the kitchen but she must not have heard him. He shook his head; she's definitely getting hard of hearing. She needs to consider purchasing one of those new-fangled hearing-aids.

'Six o'clock, Hazel,' he called again, louder this time.

'Yes, I heard you the first time,' came the slightly irritated reply. Once again the Reverend James wondered if perhaps it was *he* that was getting hard of hearing.

He shuffled towards the kitchen to pour the sherries himself and stopped at the kitchen door to survey the domestic scene. The aproned Hazel Arbuthnot was surrounded by an impressive variety of pots and pans, clearly too busy to attend to his need for a dry cherry. What's more her hands were white with some kind of powder or flour. She looked up holding her white powdered hands out in front of her.

'Have you forgotten dear that the tiler has asked you to ring him first thing tomorrow morning with the number of tiles he needs to bring to replace the ones damaged in last week's storm? Best do it now dear or you might forget. Oh…and will you have time tonight, after dinner, to pop round to see poor Doreen Summers? She must be devastated about that awful business with Rolf.'

'Yes…yes, of course,' he replied.

The vicar had completely forgotten about the tiler, but had thought it best to wait another day before visiting Doreen Summers. In his long experience waiting a day or two before visiting the bereaved was usually wise. He believed they were more receptive by the second or third day. Doreen and Rolf had been devoted members of his flock and he fully intended to do what he could to comfort Doreen. But he did agree he should go to the cemetery at the back of Saint David's to count the number of missing or damaged tiles. Sadly, his dry sherry would just have to wait awhile.

The Reverend James Arbuthnot retraced his steps and went out to the hall to put on a pair of sturdy walking shoes. Fortunately, the Vicarage was right next door to Saint David's and he would not need more than ten minutes to count the damaged tiles. Glancing out of the window he saw it was a beautiful evening so a stroll through the graveyard would not be unpleasant. No need for a coat but his trilby would not go amiss. Rufus, their energetic red spaniel, had noticed his master going into the hall and this signalled he was going out and that meant the chance of a walk was in the offing. Rufus scrambled out of his wicker basket, charged down the hall and stood looking expectantly up at his master with large pleading eyes and barking. His master weakened and a moment later Rufus was out in the garden with its plethora of enticing smells.

The vicar's left knee was playing up as he headed for the church cemetery, the result of a lifetime of kneeling before the altar of the Lord. He flexed it gingerly a few times but that made no appreciable difference so he walked on with a bit of a hobble. Rufus was charging about like a mad thing delighted to be out in the fresh air. They never put him on the leash when visiting the church grounds. Rufus was never permitted inside Saint David's Church though, unless it was Harvest Sunday when pets were welcomed. The vicar pushed open the squeaky gate that led into the graveyard and cast his eyes up to the hundreds of grey tiles covering the roof of Saint David's. He started counting the number of tiles missing, broken or dis-lodged. Not many he was relieved to see.

He counted fifteen problem tiles and was just beginning a re-count to make sure he had the correct number when Rufus started barking and carrying on over by the old yew tree in the corner of the cemetery where the most recent burials had taken place. It was only four weeks ago he had committed dear old Mrs Kirkenvin's coffin into the ground there. Surely Rufus wasn't trying to get at her coffin? Concerned at the dog's delinquent behaviour, the vicar called out, 'Come here Rufus. Stop that… come here.' Rufus ignored him. Normally he was an obedient dog. The vicar repeated the command, more forcefully this time. Still no response from Rufus who continued to bark fanatically. Annoyed, the Reverend James Arbuthnot made his painful way over to Rufus to see what was provoking this unusual behaviour.

It was the bloodied body of Mrs Doreen Summers. Blowflies were already feasting on her wounds.

☾

Belinda and Hank had been home barely an hour when each received a call from Chief Inspector Nigel Sandham shortly after six o'clock. His news was not good. The body of a woman had been discovered in the graveyard behind Saint David's Church in Upper Bybridge. It was thought to be Doreen Summers. The woman had been stabbed to death. Ten minutes later Hank and Belinda were racing back to the sweet little village where not-so-sweet things were happening.

The detectives had spent the whole of Sunday in Upper Bybridge and now they were being sent back again. If they were tired, they didn't show it because the adrenalin fired up whenever something as serious as a double murder occurred. It was another warm, sunny evening and they knew they had a couple of hours of full daylight remaining, enough time to examine the scene of this second crime. They arrived to find the two local uniformed police, Sergeant Frank Smithton and Constable Brian Brooks already had matters well in hand. The graveyard was cordoned off and the two policemen were patrolling the perimeter to prevent any inquisitive villagers from coming too close.

The detectives immediately set about their gruesome task. It was definitely Mrs Summers' body. She had been attacked from behind with a sharp implement. There were several stab wounds. The crime was obviously connected to her husband's demise. There were no signs of a struggle, Mrs Summers probably never saw her killer and death must have come almost instantaneously. There was a large pool of drying blood. Two vicious murders within twenty-four hours! Belinda shuddered to think she had been talking intimately with Doreen Summers earlier in the day. This second murder seemed to bear out her theory that Mrs Summers knew more than she was prepared to reveal. The murderer must have known this and didn't want her talking to the police. Doreen's mutilated body was discretely covered and left in situ. The finger-print specialists were contacted and promised to carry out their intensive work first thing

Monday morning prior to arranging for the removal of the body. Hank made sure additional uniformed police would be brought in to guard the site overnight.

The press soon arrived. Like hungry vultures they had to be fed scraps of information to quieten them down. Their questions were predictable.

'Who's the victim?'

'Is it another stabbing?'

'Is this now considered to be the work of a serial killer?'

'Do you have any prime suspects yet?'

'When will the murderer attack again?'

'How can the residents of Upper Bybridge feel safe with a murderer running amok?'

Belinda was full of admiration for the calm way Hank handled the demanding media. He remained polite but authoritative assuring them he would consider giving another press statement in the morning after the police had had more time to carry out their investigations.

Belinda and Hank then conducted their own rudimentary but fruitless search of the graveyard. Next, they door knocked the houses closest to St David's and finally reported back to Chief Inspector Sandham. Disappointingly, nothing helpful had turned up. As the light began to fade, the exhausted pair made their way back to the car and returned to their respective homes.

7.   **The Duncans**

Monday morning began slowly and sleepily at the Duncan's abode. After a crazily busy weekend they needed the time to de-stress, re-focus and enjoy time together as a family. Mondays were relatively quiet days in the lives of most pubs and "The Squirrel and Porcupine" was no exception. Furthermore, young Jenny was on school holidays so there was no need to rush about getting her off in time to catch the school bus.

Jenny had recently sat her "O" levels and passed seven out of the eight subjects she had attempted. She had failed Latin, probably because she had never considered the learning of an ancient, virtually "dead" language, relevant. When the next school term started Jenny would be in fifth form ready to commence her "A" levels in the three subjects she enjoyed the most: Biology, Mathematics and Geography. This was an unusual combination of subjects reflecting the fact Jenny didn't yet know what she wanted to do for a career.

Betty was always the early riser in the Duncan household. She had tidied the house, filed last week's invoices and receipts and set the table for breakfast before Jack and Jenny made an appearance. There was an unwritten rule observed by the residents of Upper Bybridge that you never rang a neighbour before nine in the morning, so Jack was more than surprised when the phone rang at twenty minutes to nine just as he padded into the kitchen in his new red bed-socks and striped pyjamas. He walked over to the phone.

'Hello…' he said, somewhat groggily.

Whoever was ringing spoke for several minutes without stopping, while Jack interjected occasionally with exclamations of shock and grunts of disbelief. When the call was over, he sat down at the kitchen table, visibly shaken.

'You're not going to believe this but there's been another murder in the village, this time its Mrs Summers. Her body was found yesterday evening in the graveyard around the back of St David's. Her body wasn't discovered till after pub closing time which explains why we didn't hear about this last night.'

'What's this village coming to?' exclaimed Betty, angrily, 'this has always been such a peaceful place.'

'How was she killed?' asked Jenny.

'Stabbed, like her husband,' Jack replied.

'Who is this murderer? That's what I want to know. If I go down the street, how do I know I'm going to be safe?' asked a visibly concerned Jenny as she joined her father sitting at the table.

'We don't know! That's just it. Until further notice we must all drive everywhere. No walking, no running or bike riding about the village please,' urged Jack in his most authoritative voice.

'What about me then? I don't have my driver's licence yet,' inquired an anxious Jenny.

'One of us will drive you, dear,' Jenny's mum quickly responded.

'Can I still go to see Michael this morning, then?' Jenny asked.

'Of course, dear. I'll drive you over and come and pick you up before lunch.'

'Thanks, mum.'

Michael Benton was Jenny's latest flame. He was one year ahead of Jenny at the same high school studying "A" level Mathematics, Chemistry and Physics and was the eldest son of the Bentons who owned a mixed farm located halfway between Upper and Lower Bybridge called "Bramble Farm." Michael was regarded by his peers as a "brainbox," however, working hard physically on the family farm kept him fit and grounded. Michael and Jenny had started seeing each other about six months earlier and Jenny now had a serious crush on the young man. They'd had a quick kiss and a cuddle in the barn a couple of times but Mr and Mrs Benton kept them under constant surveillance such that the young couple never felt safe from their prying eyes.

Breakfast finished, Jenny showered and dressed in her horse-riding gear. Michael had promised to take her riding if the weather was fine and his dad gave his approval. She looked at herself in the full-length mirror and decided a light application of lipstick would enhance her appearance. Jenny needn't have worried since she was naturally good looking and had a lovely healthy complexion. She helped her mother dry the breakfast dishes before the two of them left in the family car and wound their way along the narrow country lane with its high hawthorn hedges that led to "Bramble Farm." It was another beautiful late summer's day, the long warm spell showing no signs of easing. A red fox loped on to the road a hundred yards ahead, stopped, looked at them quizzically with its ears pointed then hurried on.

As Jenny creaked open the ancient wooden gate to "Bramble Farm" she heard the sound of the Brenton's tractor ploughing their small front field and hoped it wasn't Michael who had been dragooned into this task. She needn't have worried because a moment later they had a friendly wave from Tom Benton, Michael's dad, sitting up behind the tractor's steering wheel. No recent rain meant the driveway was firm and reasonably dry so there was no danger of skidding or becoming bogged as Betty turned the car around. Jenny was busy gathering up her riding gear when Mrs Brenton, a buxom woman with wrestler's arms, hurried over to their car intent on talking to Jenny's mother. No guesses what she wanted to talk about.

'Hello, Rhonda.'

'Isn't this murder business simply awful, love!' Rhonda Benton exclaimed. She called everyone "love" whether they were male or female, young or old, family or strangers.

'It certainly is. Let's hope the police catch the brute quick time.'

'That's for sure, love. Do the police have any inkling as to who it is?'

'Not that I've heard.'

'Well, something strange happened here last night. I'm wondering if I should tell the police. It seems a bit petty though, but then you never know do you?'

'What happened, Rhonda?'

'I think someone may have been in our barn.'

'What makes you think that?'

'Do you know where our barn is, love?' Rhonda switched her gaze and looked pointedly at Jenny, who blushed a deep red remembering the brief intimate interlude she had shared there with Michael.

'I can't say I've ever seen your barn, Rhonda.'

'That's because it's hidden from view just down the other side of the hill. Anyway love, I was down there an hour ago and somebody's been stealing food from the fridge in there. When Tom's working at the far end of the farm or in the barn he often doesn't bother to come back to the house for lunch. So, we have a fridge in the barn that I stock up every few days with stuff that will last a week or two. There's bread, cheese, apples, a bottle of milk, a packet of biscuits, even some butter. Whenever Tom feels a bit peckish, he raids the supplies in the barn.'

'Sounds sensible, Rhonda.'

'Well love, when I went down to the barn this morning, I found almost everything had gone. The bottle of milk had been drunk and nearly all the food was missing. The only things left were some butter and a couple of broken biscuits. Tom has assured me he's only eaten a couple of apples and a hunk of bread with some cheese during the last week, so someone has been raiding his rations.'

'Oh dear, Rhonda, that doesn't sound good.'

'Do you think I should bother the police? They must be so busy with these two murders I'm sure they wouldn't want to be bothered with a spot of petty thieving.'

'Agreed mum.' Michael had suddenly appeared and now stood next to his mother with a private wink reserved for Jenny. 'I'm sure the police don't want to have to mess about with piddling matters like dad's emergency rations getting nicked.'

'I tend to agree with him, Rhonda,' added Betty, looking a trifle embarrassed to be siding with Michael.

'Okay I won't bother them then. But if it happens again this week, I'll definitely report it.' Rhonda crossed her substantial arms, pleased she had come to a resolution.

So, the matter was settled. Betty drove off home and Jenny walked with Michael and Rhonda to the stables to saddle up the horses. Rhonda claimed she was only going with them to check up on the horses, but Michael and Jenny knew otherwise. In their view Rhonda was going with them primarily to keep an eye on *them*!

8.   A Few More Clues...

West Sussex was a relatively affluent part of Britain and this affluence partly accounted for the low crime rates. Murders were rare, double murders almost unheard of. Chief Inspector Nigel Sandham was horrified to hear of Mrs Summers' demise and immediately assigned all the resources at his disposal to the case as well as persuading Scotland Yard to loan him the services of two additional detectives. Detective Inspector Ivan Digby and Detective Sergeant Ruby Schneider arrived at the cemetery at Saint David's on Monday morning where they were briefed by Hank Zagalski.

'Doreen Summers was the sixty-year-old wife of Rolf Summers who was brutally murdered Saturday afternoon at the entrance to his house. Both murders involved multiple stabbings, viciously delivered using some kind of knife or dagger. We have yet to find a murder weapon. Our number one suspect is a character spotted in the local pub on Saturday afternoon shortly before the first attack. This person smokes foreign cigarettes thought to be manufactured in Germany which he foolishly discarded in the pub and also at the scene of his first murder. We have a reasonable description of the man and all major air and sea embarkation points have been alerted to watch out for him attempting to leave the country. Presumably, this person of interest slept somewhere in or around Upper Bybridge last night awaiting an opportunity to kill Mrs Summers.'

'If the suspect wanted to murder both Mr and Mrs Summers, why on earth didn't he kill the two of them at the same time?' Schneider asked.

'Yes, that's been baffling us too,' replied Hank.

'I think I know what might have happened,' volunteered Belinda.

'Do you remember some of the people who lived near Hollyhock Cottage reported hearing a gun shot at the same time we estimate the first murder took place?'

'Yes, that's correct, but the guy who was ex-army swore it was only a car backfiring,' added Hank.

'Well, my theory is this. The murderer *was* intending to kill them both when he came to Hollyhock Cottage but the sudden sound of the car backfiring spooked him. He had just stabbed Rolf and was about to go in to finish off Mrs Summers when he heard the bang. Thinking it was someone with a gun he panicked and fled.'

'Makes sense,' conceded Ivan Digby, 'so, this guy waited around Saturday night in order to finish the job off late Sunday evening?'

'Correct.'

'Where did he stay Saturday night then?' asked Hank, 'perhaps he stayed with someone in the village?'

'Surely he wouldn't have had the nerve to stay at the pub, would he?' asked Belinda.

'There are a couple of Bed and Breakfast places in the village,' remarked Hank, 'that's where he probably went. Let's get to them straightaway. Do you remember where they are, Belinda?'

'One was "Ye Olde Bakery" in the main street. The other was a farm house on the edge of the village, but I can't remember its name.'

'That's good enough. Ivan and Ruby, can we leave you two to supervise the search here in the cemetery while we check out the pub and the two Bed and Breakfast places?'

❦

Michael Benton and Jenny Duncan eventually managed to escape the watchful eyes of Michael's mother. Once Rhonda had supervised the saddling up of their horses there really wasn't any other reason for her to stay, other than to go out riding with them which she didn't want to do. Michael was a reasonably confident horseman having entered heaps of gymkhanas when small, although Jenny was still a beginner.

Aware of his girlfriend's inexperience, Michael planned a short ride around the perimeter of their farm. They would take it slowly. If everything went according to plan, he calculated they would still have enough time to stable the horses and retreat to the barn for a "snog." Michael never liked that word "snog." It sounded cheap and common. "A kiss and a cuddle" were much better.

Jenny did surprisingly well and enjoyed her ride. He gave her a few tips along the way and they returned in good time, safely stabled and settled their horses and holding hands headed for the barn. Jenny's mother wanted to pick her up at mid-day so they had thirty minutes to spend together.

The previous two occasions they had been together privately they had remained standing when they kissed. Today they had more time and Jenny wondered whether Michael would ask her to lie down with him. Like all decent barns there was a pile of clean, dry hay up one end and this would be the natural and inviting place to go. She had already mentally prepared herself to lie down with Michael if he invited her so to do. What Jenny hadn't thought about was how far she should go. She liked Michael tremendously and didn't want to lose his friendship. A couple of her girlfriends had boasted they had allowed their boyfriends to touch their breasts. And then there was crazy Lizzy Barnstaple who bragged she had been the whole way more than once. Nobody knew whether to believe Lizzy or who the boy was.

Michael squeezed Jenny's hand as they entered the barn to be greeted by the rich sweet smell of dry hay. She could feel her heart beating faster as she anticipated the kiss to come. Another of her girlfriends had told her about something called a "French" kiss when you put your tongue into the other person's mouth. She and Michael hadn't ever done that. Michael, she suspected, was as naïve as she was and may not have even kissed a girl before he'd kissed her. Their first kiss had certainly been a clumsy affair. She resolved to ask him if she was the first. Jenny somehow liked the thought that she might be the first girl Michael had ever kissed. He was certainly her first.

It was pleasantly cool in the barn and they were surrounded by a strange collection of farm implements some covered in dust and no longer in use. A green Massey Fergusson tractor took pride of place. Along one wall were several large hessian bags containing nutritional supplements for the chickens that free ranged around the yard. In one corner stood the old refrigerator she reasoned must be the one from which Tom Benton's food had been stolen. Jenny didn't have time to notice anything else because Michael was clearly intent on a bit of intimacy.

He pulled her gently towards him and told her she was beautiful. She smiled shyly. Not knowing quite what to say in reply she just whispered, 'Thank you.' Then he put his arms around her and they kissed. It was better this time and they lingered longer, enjoying the closeness. Jenny put her hands up to his face and felt the roughness of his skin where he shaved. She wondered if she should be forward and try to do a "French" kiss, but then thought better of it. After all, it was generally accepted among her girlfriends that it was up to the boy to make the moves. No "French" kiss eventuated so she presumed Michael didn't know about them. He was becoming more confident and passionate now so she thought it best to break away for a moment.

'Michael, can I ask you something personal?'

'Depends what it is…'

'Am I the first girl you've ever kissed?'

'Why? Don't you think I'm any good at it?'

'Oh no, I didn't mean that. If I am your first that's a bit special, don't you think?'

He shrugged his shoulders, 'I suppose…' and he bent down to kiss her again.

Suddenly, Michael straightened up and moved away, 'Hi dad, are you taking the tractor out?'

Tom Benton surely must have seen them kissing although it's always dark when you first enter a barn in comparison to the brightness outside. The teenagers were embarrassed and felt like naughty school children getting up to mischief and being caught red handed by the teacher. Rather sheepishly they left the barn together and slowly returned to the farm house to await the arrival of Jenny's mother at mid-day. However, Mrs Rhonda Brenton was anxious to talk and wanted their opinion about something.

'Oh, hello you two. Have a good ride? Did Trixie behave for you Jenny?'

'Yes, she was fine, thanks Mrs Benton.'

'That's good. I'm glad you two are back a bit early. I've been worrying all morning about this stealing business and now I'm thinking I really should ring the police. What do you two reckon?'

Michael pulled a non-committal face, 'If you want to, mum. No harm in it but I think you'll find they'll be too busy to do anything about it for a few days.'

'Yes, of course. What do you think, dear?' she turned to Jenny.

'What did Mr Benton say?' asked Jenny, tactfully.

'Oh, he's happy to go along with whatever I decide. He's far more worried about getting his turnips in the ground,' and she laughed.

There was a toot from outside. It was Jenny's mum. Jenny gave Michael a quick peck on the cheek as she left, thanked Mrs Benton for her hospitality and ten minutes later mother and daughter were back in the pub serving drinks.

☾

Belinda and Hank drew a complete blank at the pub and the two Bed and Breakfast places. "Ye Olde Bakery" was closed for restoration work and "The Rookery," the name of the farm house, had had a young family staying there for the last few days. Saturday had not been a cold night so it was quite possible the suspect had slept rough somewhere. There was a plethora of likely places; in the woods, a garden shed somewhere, under the bridge or in one of the numerous barns on surrounding farms.

Returning to their police car, the detectives checked in again with Chief Inspector Nigel Sandham. He had one additional piece of valuable information. The foreign looking cigarette butts found at the scene of the first murder and in "The Squirrel and Porcupine" had been identified. They were "Mercedes" brand, one of the Batschari cigarettes and cigars manufactured at the Batscharifabrik (factory) in Baden Baden, West Germany. If the stranger in the pub was the murderer, leaving his German cigarettes lying about could prove important evidence down the track. The cigarettes were difficult to procure outside Germany and virtually unheard of in the UK. The suspect must have brought them with him.

The detectives next move was to return to Mike and Sandra Leighton's cottage, in a bid to discover more about the background of Rolf and Doreen. Quite possibly, apart from the murderer, the Leightons were the last people to have seen Doreen alive. Mike let them in at the door and appeared relieved to see the police again. Sandra Leighton was deeply upset by the shocking murder of another friend. She put the kettle on. Five minutes later the four of them were sitting around the kitchen table making polite small talk. Soon Hank raised the serious matter for discussion.

'How long have you two known Doreen and Rolf?'

'Ever since they moved in next door some fifteen years ago,' replied Mike, as he plopped three white sugar lumps into his tea and stirred.

'We've always got along very well. I don't think there's ever been a cross word between us,' added Sandra, as she passed a plate of home-made biscuits across to the detectives.

The Leightons were recently retired. Mike had been a sub-editor with the local paper and Sandra a primary school librarian. Mike presented as a genial sort of fellow, a bit too wide around the girth to be healthy which probably helped explain why the garden was so over-grown. Sandra, on the other hand, was trim quite smartly dressed although rather "school-marmish." She had her hair up in a formidable bun.

Belinda spoke next. 'What mystifies us is *why* your neighbours have been murdered. There must be a powerful reason. It seems they were specifically targeted. But why? We are hoping that as their closest neighbours you may be able to shed some light on their background and provide some clues to help us determine what motivated someone to do this.'

Mike and Sandra looked at each other. Mike shrugged his shoulders and grabbed another biscuit.

'Well, I got to know Doreen quite well,' volunteered Sandra, 'us women talk about things more than the men do, I think.'

'Please go on…' urged Belinda.

'Since I retired in December last year, Doreen and I went out together quite regularly for shopping or afternoon tea. On other occasions we would just have a cuppa together at her home or mine.'

'It was chin-wagging all right!' interrupted Mike, 'I usually made myself scarce and left them to it.'

'Anyway, we used to chat about the news, village gossip, that sort of thing,' continued Sandra slightly annoyed at her husband's unnecessary and disparaging comment.

The detectives sipped their tea and waited patiently for Sandra to tell them more.

'Sometimes Doreen seemed a bit down in the dumps. You know, depressed. I used to jolly her along and usually she would brighten up after a short while and things would be back to normal again. Anyway, one day she seemed to be worse than usual so I took her hand and asked her what was worrying her. I thought there might be something wrong in her relationship with Rolf.'

'And was there?' asked Hank.

'No, she assured me she and Rolf were fine and perfectly happy together.'

'They always seemed to get along well,' Mike chimed in and copped another dirty look from his wife.

'Who's telling this story, Mike?' challenged Sandra. Mike looked sheepish and consoled himself by taking another biscuit.

'So…' prompted Belinda, 'what *was* worrying her?'

'She never told me exactly but it must have been something awful in Rolf's past, back in Germany. Apparently, Rolf had partially confessed to her one day. He said it had become too much of a burden for him to bear on his own so he had opened up. He swore her to secrecy, though. Told her she must never tell anyone, ever.'

'But she told you?' said Hank.

'Not really. That's all she would admit to. Rolf had done something bad back in Germany but she never told me what it was. It must have been early in the war. Shortly after it happened, he escaped to England to get away from the situation. When he arrived in England Rolf was captured by the British authorities and placed in an internment camp on the Isle of Man because he was German. Doreen said she first met Rolf after the war when he had been released and was working in Reading.'

'Interesting,' mused Hank, 'it's beginning to sound as though it might be a revenge crime. Whatever it was Rolf did in Germany it was devastating enough to have someone hunt him down here in the UK many years later. Whoever murdered Rolf murdered Doreen as well. I think the murderer assumed Doreen knew all about Rolf's crimes and consequently could help the British police to track the murderer down.'

'That makes sense,' agreed Belinda.

'I'm sorry I can't tell you any more,' apologised Sandra as she finished off the last of her tea. 'More tea anyone?'

There were no takers. The detectives thanked the Leightons for their help and departed.

Belinda and Hank decided to grab a pub lunch at "The Squirrel and Porcupine" but dropped in to see their two detective colleagues first. During the morning Digby and Schneider had completed another door-to-door round of interviews with the locals but without success. Nobody has seen a suspicious stranger or heard anything. The murderer, the detectives concluded, must be blessed with abundant luck. No trace of the murder weapon had been found either.

As they drove down to the pub for their lunch, a call came in from the police station at Lower Bybridge. The police there had just received a call from a Mrs Rhonda Benton at "Bramble Farm." She had been most apologetic about ringing but thought she should report they had had food stolen from their barn on Saturday night. Hank and Belinda checked the address and headed off directly to visit "Bramble Farm." Lunch would have to wait.

Ten minutes later the detectives pulled into the farmyard to be met by the formidable Rhonda Benton clad in a colourful apron with her sleeves rolled up and hands on hips. Because the detectives were in an unmarked police vehicle, Rhonda had no idea who her visitors were.

'Can I help you?' she challenged, in a less than friendly voice.

Hank showed Mrs Benton his ID and her tone abruptly changed. 'Oh, I'm *so* sorry I thought you were sales people. We get them here, you know.'

Hank came straight to the point, polite, firm and professional. Once again Belinda was impressed.

'Thank you for letting us know about the food stolen from your barn, Mrs Benton. You did the right thing. May we inspect the area, please?'

'Yes, of course,' Rhonda replied, quite surprised a small theft of food stuffs had required two young detectives to land on her doorstep within half an hour of her informing the police. 'Please follow me.' On the way she ran through what had been taken and assured the detectives it must have happened on Saturday night. Her husband could vouch for it, she added.

'Mrs Benton, we would like to spend half an hour carefully examining your barn please. Would you mind leaving us to get on with it?'

Rhonda Benton got the message and left them to it.

Two intriguing things came to light during their search. They found another "Mercedes" fag end and the pile of clean dry hay appeared to have been recently slept on. One more piece of the puzzle had been solved. The suspected murderer had slept for at least one night in the Benton's barn, possibly for two nights. When Belinda and Hank returned to the farmhouse, they left strict instructions with Tom and Rhonda to allow a car-load of uniformed police to go over the interior of their barn even more thoroughly.

This was the most exciting thing to have happened at "Bramble Farm" for many a year and the Brentons knew they would now be the centre of attention in the village for several days to come.

9.   The Murder Weapon

The two detectives eventually arrived at "The Squirrel and Porcupine" in time for a very late lunch. Hank ordered "Toad in the Hole" with chips and Belinda "Roast Beef of Olde England" with English mustard. Since they were on duty, they requested orange squashes made from freshly squeezed fruit. After chatting again briefly with young Jenny they retired to a table near the window to await the arrival of their meals.

'I get the feeling we're going nowhere fast,' Hank grumbled.

'That's not really the case,' replied a more positive Belinda, 'circumstantial evidence is building that the murderer is this German guy. He appears to have had powerful revenge motives for eliminating Rolf Summers and by association his wife. We have a good description of his appearance and we know he smokes these unusual "Mercedes" cigarettes.'

'I guess you're right. Let's hope he gets picked up at an airport trying to leave the country or at one of the many sea ports. I'll get Nigel Sandham to send out a second alert notice to every embarkation point. We know this guy's English is limited and he speaks with a heavy German accent. That should also help the authorities.'

'There's something else Hank that we haven't followed up on yet. It's not much but when you're clutching at straws, it might be worth looking into.'

'Oh yes, what's that?'

'When I first interviewed Doreen Summers shortly after the murder, she told me when her husband lay on the ground dying he gasped out a single word.'

'Good thinking Belinda, remind me what was that word?'

'Doreen said she thought the word was "rose."'

'Rose? How the hell does that help us?'

'I have no idea, but it struck me as being a strange word to utter with your last breath.'

'Umm…the Summers' garden was full of roses if I remember correctly. After lunch we might go back and have another look, although I have no idea what the heck we'll be looking for.'

Their conversation was interrupted by the pretty Jenny Duncan bringing them their lunch.

Until the meal arrived they had not appreciated just how hungry they were and they polished their meals off in quick time. Belinda paid the bill, making sure she collected the receipt so they could put in a claim later. Then they set off to examine the garden at Hollyhock Cottage more closely.

Neither Belinda nor Hank claimed any expertise in the vast world of roses. Between them they reckoned they could correctly recognise the flowers of a rose plant, be it a rambling rose, a carpet rose, a rose bush or a climbing rose. They were also aware roses came with nasty thorns and there were a great number of varieties, some with perfume, some without and they all needed to be pruned during the winter months.

As they approached Hollyhock Cottage, Hank reflected on what a smart woman Belinda was to have picked up on Rolf's final utterance. The word "rose" might not lead them anywhere, but it was another line of inquiry when they were desperately looking for more clues. He parked the car.

'I have an idea,' he blurted out, 'perhaps the names of the roses can be found on those little labels they put on them. Maybe there's a German rose here somewhere which might tell us something? Belinda, how about you write down the names of all the roses we can definitely identify?'

'Good idea,' agreed Belinda, 'the Summers were keen gardeners so the names of their roses might still be there.'

'Wow,' exclaimed Hank, as he surveyed the front garden, 'there must be a couple of dozen roses here in the front garden alone and maybe more at the back. I'll start on the right-hand-side.'

They set to work. About three-quarters of the front garden's roses did still have their names attached. The back garden, they discovered, had only fruit trees and a small pond. It took them the best part of half an hour to examine each rose plant carefully, hunt for its label and compile a list. In the end they had confirmed the names of seventeen of the twenty-four roses. Six other rose bushes that had lost their labels could still be identified because their flowers and leaves looked exactly the same as one of the roses they had already successfully listed. In the end the name of only one rose still remained a mystery.

'We did well,' said Hank, sucking at a couple of nasty scratches, 'come and sit with me on the garden bench and read the names of the roses out loud to see if they make any sense.'

Belinda had avoided any thorns because she had mostly been busy recording the names of the rose varieties. She sat on the bench, as requested, but careful to maintain a respectful distance. She would have loved to have sat closer to Hank but decorum dictated she stay professionally aloof. She read out the common names of the roses on her list slowly and deliberately.

'Snowdrift, Madame Hardy, Iceberg, Macy's Pride, White Meidiland, French Lace, Climbing Snowbird, Prairie Star, Secret's Out, Sally Holmes, Sombreuil, Climbing Iceberg and Cinderella.'

They sat quietly, non-plussed for a couple of minutes, trying to find something helpful from this list, some kind of a clue, anything…

'Read through the list again please.'

'There are some roses that possibly come from overseas,' suggested Belinda, brightly, 'Prairie Star is probably American and there are some French ones such as French Lace and Madame Hardy, but none with an obvious German sounding name.'

'Agreed,' replied Hank, pensively. 'I noticed some of the names have to do with cold weather conditions. There's Snowdrift, Iceberg,

Snowbird and Climbing Iceberg. Does that tell us anything?'

'Not much,' Belinda responded.

'I think this is a waste of time,' concluded Hank, still sucking on one of his cuts that refused to stop bleeding.

'I've just realised something,' announced Belinda excitedly, 'all twenty-four roses are white. There isn't another coloured rose in the whole place. It's a front garden made up entirely of white roses. Every other rose garden I've ever seen has a mixture of different coloured roses, but not this one.'

'So what? The giving of white roses is supposed to signify love, loyalty and devotion. They probably planted all these white roses when they first came here and had just been married. They'd still be all lovey-dovey then, wouldn't they?'

Belinda didn't answer immediately because she thought Hank's explanation might well be correct. Nobody had ever given *her* a bunch of white roses she lamented, but then nobody had wanted to express their undying love and devotion to her. For a brief moment she wondered whether it would ever happen.

Then another idea came to her. When she had been looking for the labels on the rose bushes she had noticed there were some new, smaller bushes amongst them. So, she reasoned, if the Summers ever lost a rose, they always replaced it with another white one. Perhaps they only loved white roses and it was as straightforward an explanation as that, but somehow, she sensed there may be something more to it. She looked at Hank but decided he would probably dismiss her attempt at lateral thinking as nothing more than "women's intuition." She said nothing.

℃

When they returned to the police car they received a call from Detective Inspector Ivan Digby. He was thrilled to inform them the murder weapon had been found discarded in the glade of trees behind the graveyard at Saint David's. He had been trying for the last fifteen minutes to get in touch. Hank and Belinda drove back to the church, hurried through the graveyard and on down the short track that led to the small wood. Here they were met by beaming uniformed police delighted at their success. It had taken them the best part of two days to find the murder weapon and they were now looking forward to resuming their normal duties. It was almost a festive atmosphere.

Digby and Sergeant Ruby Schneider came forward to meet them displaying the precious find on a board as if presenting medals at an Olympic ceremony. Properly gloved, the four detectives each carefully inspected the object. Covered in dried blood and dirty from where it had lain on the ground, they were unable to decipher the name of the manufacturer. The knife would now be rushed to the fingerprint experts for a full examination. It looked like a normal kitchen knife easily obtainable from hardware stores such as Woolworths or Marks and Spencers. Hopefully, any finger prints found on the knife would match the finger prints discovered on the door of the Summers' house, the fridge at "Bramble Farm" and the "Mercedes" cigarettes.

After uniform were sent back to Petworth to deliver the knife to the laboratory, the four detectives remained at the site for another hour discussing the case. They were convinced the murderer had fled the scene at the graveyard in great haste and had raced down this path. No serious attempt had been made to hide the knife. In his rush to get away the murderer had simply hurled the weapon into the trees. Once again, this was not the action of a professional killer who would take care to ensure the murder weapon was very difficult to locate. The more they learnt about this man, the more it pointed to an amateur killer. Unwisely appearing in the pub and then leaving his cigarettes lying about certainly supported this theory. Perhaps the most powerful evidence was the amateurish, frenzied stabbing of Doreen Summers. An expert killer would have slit her throat in one deft movement. This killer stabbed her randomly, four times.

That evening as Belinda and Hank drove back to Petworth, they felt quite elated. Finding the murder weapon was a huge boost to their morale and they now had high hopes the fingerprint experts would deliver the results they were looking for in the coming days. If only somebody had seen the German when he made his escape from Upper Bybridge or they could hear from Immigration that he had been detained at one of the departure points. The detectives agreed it was vital they urgently ascertain the name of their mysterious suspect.

☾

Their shared elation and positivity were affecting Hank in another way, too. The pent-up feelings he had been developing for this beautiful woman who had been working so closely with him for the last three days had reached breaking point. No longer could he contain himself. Bugger professionalism! There was a strong powerful attraction. What could be more normal than that? He was sure Belinda, likewise, was strongly attracted to him but was quite rightly also holding back. If their relationship was to ever grow and flourish it was up to him to make the first move. He still had not had the time, or perhaps it was the courage, to tell Suzie that he wanted to end their relationship. So, in this heady mood, Hank cleared his throat and started what he hoped would be a very special conversation with Belinda.

'Belinda…do you mind if we forget the murders for a bit? I'd like to talk to you about something else.'

Belinda didn't know what to expect. Perhaps Hank was displeased with something she had done during the last three busy days with regard to her police work. After all he was her superior officer and it was quite within his rights to express any concerns. Next, she thought he might want to talk about rugby. She knew he was crazy about the sport and desperate for the season proper to get underway. And then there were a number of other topics they had touched upon briefly over the last three days: politics, parents, religion, Jamaican independence, the success of the Beatles. These were also possibilities.

'No, that's fine with me,' she answered, wearily, sitting up straighter in preparation for what was coming.

There was a moment's silence while Hank fumbled with competing words buzzing around in his head, trying to put them together meaningfully, the way he wanted.

'I…I'm wondering… are you going out with anyone?'

Belinda was pleasantly surprised by the question. At first, she felt like saying bluntly, 'none of your business,' but she held back long enough to re-consider. This kind of question, she sensed, could be the fore-runner of something more exciting. Belinda knew if Hank was about to ask her out, she was mad not to accept. Nevertheless, she answered guardedly.

'Don't forget Hank I only received my promotion to Petworth three weeks ago. As it happens, my move here meant breaking up with my boyfriend. So, I guess the answer to your question is no, I'm not currently going out with anyone.'

'Then I'd like to change that for you. Please come out with me tonight?'

This sudden invitation was unexpected and Belinda was ill-prepared. She really admired this man and several times had wondered whether she would ever get to know him better. And now, here was her chance! However, she was aware he already had a girlfriend whom he had been dating for some time. Was Hank one of these "two-timers" nonchalantly taking two or more girls out at the same time? If so, she wasn't interested.

'Hank, aren't you already dating someone?'

'Yes, I have been but I'm breaking it off.'

'So, you *are* still going out together? Thank you for asking me but if you two haven't both agreed to split up, then forget about asking me out.'

Belinda's blunt response hit Hank like a scrum collapsing on top of him. She was quite right. He should never have asked her out until sorting things with Suzie first and that he had not done. He felt ashamed but full of admiration for Belinda's principled stance.

'I'm sorry Belinda, you're quite right. I've been meaning to break things off with Suzie for some time but the right time hasn't presented itself.'

'Well then…if the right time ever *does* present itself perhaps you could ask me out again?'

Appropriately put back in his place, Hank was somewhat subdued as they drove back into Petworth and he dropped Belinda off at her flat.

Later that evening, Hank plucked up courage and called round to see Suzie to tell her he wanted to end their relationship. In the end, it was not nearly as difficult as he had feared. Suzie had been thinking along the same lines.

10.   Tuesday, 27th August

Tuesday morning brought a change in the weather. The near heat-wave conditions of the last week had been chased away overnight, replaced by damp misty south westerlies and a significant drop in temperature. In the early hours of the morning blankets were pulled up in bedrooms and later out came the raincoats and umbrellas for those who had to leave home that morning. Belinda fished out her umbrella and braved the moist conditions to walk to Petworth's Police Station. Hank also made his own way, having decided after last night's rebuke it might be wise not to offer Belinda a lift. On arrival they both learnt Chief Inspector Nigel Sandham wanted a "catch-up" at eight-thirty.

When Hank and Belinda arrived at Sandham's door they found him stubbing out yet another cigarette with the usual haze of blue smoke hanging in the air. Their superior officer was a relentless chain-smoker and his silver ash-tray was testament to this with its mangled cigarette butts sticking up in all directions like a grotesque floor of stalagmites.

'Come in,' he rasped, 'cigarette?'

They politely declined his offer. This was only the third time Belinda had been in Sandham's office and she supposed smoking was typical of any policeman who had occupied the same office for twenty years. One wall was covered in black and white photographs, framed and arranged chronologically. There were photos of Sandham graduating from the Police Academy, the exteriors of various police stations he had been posted to, receiving his sergeant's stripes, graduating as a detective, becoming an inspector and then chief inspector. In pride of place was a photograph of Sandham being presented to Her Majesty the Queen, although precisely why this happy event had occurred was unclear.

The chief inspector's desk was reasonably tidy as befitted a man of his rank. A sad cactus plant struggled for survival in one corner of his desk and his "IN" and "OUT" trays occupied the other corner. A large blotting-paper pad sat directly in front of Sandham decorated with a plethora of weird doodles. The grim ash-tray was strategically positioned just to Sandham's right where he spent much of his day expertly flicking ash. Opposite Sandham's desk the standard issue large imitation Victoria Station clock was attached to the wall and above this a youthful Queen Elizaberh II smiled down regally on the proceedings. A number of current police files lay about on the floor. Government issue filing cabinets ran along another wall. Belinda and Hank sat down and looked at Sandham, expectantly.

'Good and bad news,' wheezed the chief inspector who had another bout of chesty coughing before being able to continue, 'which do you want to hear first?'

'The bad...' responded Hank.

'There's no sign of this German bastard. Immigration is looking out for him as well as every police station...' He stopped for another chesty rattle, 'every police station in the UK has been informed this guy is a wanted man and dangerous. It's a waiting game, I'm afraid. Hopefully, he'll show up somewhere very soon. Are you quite sure (another cough) he has actually left Upper Bybridge?'

'It's a small close-knit community. Anything out of the ordinary is likely to be quickly spotted by the locals. My feeling is he would have scarpered out of there faster than the speed of light and is now hell bent on getting home to Germany,' said Belinda. Hank nodded his agreement.

'Okay, now to the good news. The fingerprint boys have been busy and have confirmed the same set of fingerprints were found on everything. How amazing is that! The German's fingerprints were found on the murder weapon, the fridge where he pinched some food, in the pub and on the front door of the Summers' home. That's truly damning evidence. We just have to find the blighter now to get a conviction.'

'The thing that strikes me about this guy is what a rank amateur he is. Wearing gloves when you murder somebody must surely be rule number one in the Murderer's Manual. Rule number two would be learning how to kill your victim cleanly and efficiently. Stabbing someone four or five times and in the wrong places is not very efficient,' said Hank.

Belinda laughed, 'And rule number three would surely be don't expose yourself in the local pub for an hour or two before you murder someone.'

Sandham was going through his methodical routine of lighting up yet another cigarette. 'What do you propose to do now?' he asked.

'There's not much more we can do in Upper Bybridge, sir. I think I'll spend the day working on one of my other cases, interviews, reports… that sort of thing.'

'I also need to finish writing up the full reports for the Summers' murders,' added Belinda.

And so, with the blue smoke of Sandham's latest cigarette smoke enveloping them, Hank and Belinda thankfully left his office.

❦

Shortly after two o'clock, Sandham called Hank and Belinda back to his office. A matter of urgency, he claimed. Once again, they entered the boss's smoky den and found their seats. What Sandham had to tell them was encouraging.

'We think we may have caught our man!' Sandham declared triumphantly, 'the silly bugger got hit by a car and is in hospital.' He watched as Belinda and Hank congratulated each other.

'Where is he? Is he badly hurt?' asked Hank.

'Apparently, he was hit trying to cross the road as he came out of the Gatwick Airport underground railway station. Probably forgot we don't drive on the same side of the road as the Germans.' The Chief Inspector had to stop for another round of coughing to subside. 'His injuries are not serious it seems, but he was knocked unconscious and taken to hospital. They admitted him. The London Police, not realising this injured man was a suspected murderer, followed up in the usual routine way they adopt for all traffic accidents. They sent a young constable up to the hospital to get a statement from the injured man. The police simply wanted to advise his next of kin that he had been injured and check that his account of what caused the accident matched that of the driver who'd crashed into him.'

'And…what happened?' asked Belinda.

'Lots,' replied Sandham as another cough took hold, 'when he was admitted he was still unconscious and nobody knew who the heck he was. So, the hospital staff opened up his backpack and, lo and behold, inside they found his passport and an airline ticket. The bloke was three hours away from catching a flight to Bonn in West Germany. Immigration would possibly have recognised him and detained the man when he checked in. Anyway, we have him now. How about that for a bit of luck?'

'Great news,' agreed Hank, 'and who is he?'

Sandham looked down at his writing pad. 'According to his passport, his full name is Doctor Heinrich Gustav Ziegler. Born in a village called Stieldorf near Bonn in the German state of North Rhine-Westphalia on November 7th 1930. His occupation is listed as a senior lecturer at the University of Bonn.'

'Good heavens,' exclaimed Belinda, 'a doctor?'

'That's right,' echoed Sandham, 'but he may not be a medical doctor. He probably has a PhD in whatever his academic field is.'

'Murdering people is hardly what you would expect from a university academic,' commented Hank.

'Oh, I don't know,' replied Sandham, 'murderers come from all walks of life. In my forty years in the force, I've seen nurses, teachers, housewives, a retired judge, even an Anglican priest join the ranks of killers. Nobody's immune.'

'What about police officers?' Belinda asked.

'Worst of the lot,' laughed Sandham.

'Why the hell would an academic from Bonn University come over to England and stab the Summers couple to death? It doesn't make much sense,' said Hank.

'That's your job to find out,' replied Sandham, as he fished out an unopened packet of Players from his desk drawer.

'When did you say he was born?' asked Belinda.

'November, 1930.'

'So, he's nearly thirty-two. That means he was about nine when the second World War broke out, fourteen when it ended,' mused Belinda.

'What are you thinking?' asked Hank.

'The war must have been a terrifying experience for a young kid growing up in Germany.'

'True, but no worse than it was for our kids,' added Sandham.

'Maybe something happened to him as a kid during the war that really upset him?' surmised Belinda, thinking out loud.

'What's your German like?' asked Sandham.

'Non-existent,' they replied in unison.

'Well, I want you to visit the doctor in the hospital, urgently, and arrest him on suspicion of the murders of Mr and Mrs Summers. When I received the news that our suspect had been admitted to hospital, I asked the Metropolitan Police to mount a guard outside his ward twenty-four hours a day. As the investigating officers it is now your responsibility to make the arrest and see him officially detained for further questioning. Go home now pack your bags and get down there as soon as you can.'

'Which hospital is he at, sir?' asked Hank.

After yet another bout of coughing, Sandham finally read out what he had scribbled down on his writing pad. 'He's in the Lady

Armitage Ward, bed six at Crawley Hospital, West Green Drive, Crawley. It's the National Health Service's hospital closest to where he had his accident. Now get cracking. Ring me at home as soon as you have him officially charged and under lock and key. There's a police station at Crawley so if the doctor is well enough to leave hospital he can be held there overnight. I'll contact Crawley to appraise them of the situation. Any questions?'

'Do you want the doctor brought back here to face court?'

'Definitely.'

Belinda and Hank left together. It was agreed Hank would pick Belinda up at three-thirty at her flat. All they needed was overnight bags. If the traffic was not too heavy they should be at Crawley Hospital by six o'clock.

☾

Once again "The Squirrel and Porcupine" was buzzing late Tuesday evening. Somehow, news had leaked out that the murderer had been caught trying to catch a flight out of Gatwick Airport. The silly man had managed to get himself run over and was now languishing in a hospital somewhere in London under heavy police guard. Nobody could recall so many exciting topics of conversation happening in the little village of Upper Bybridge before!

The usual crew were there downing beers at a furious rate. Jack and Betty Duncan were hard pressed to keep up with demand and once again had been obliged to ask Jenny to help out for a few hours. 'Murders are excellent for business,' Jack remarked to his wife, 'do you think we could organise a few more over the winter months when business is quiet?'

'Don't be so crass! That's an awful thing to say, Jack,' admonished Betty.

'It's true though,' added Jenny, as she passed a non-alcoholic cider over the counter to Michael. Jenny was hoping she and Michael might have a little private time together sometime during the evening.

Tonight, the usual regulars had been joined by a number of other villagers hungry to hear and digest the latest gossip. Mike and Sandra Leighton, the Summers' next-door neighbours were there as well as Rhonda and Tom Benton, Michael's parents from "Bramble Farm." Even the Reverend James Arbuthnot was putting in an appearance, something he very rarely did. Apart from gossiping these folk had been touched by the events of the last few days and needed companionship and support. The Anglican minister was sharing a table with the Leightons and Bentons and the discussion turned to the topic of motivation. Why had this young man from Germany suddenly turned up in Upper Bybridge and murdered the Summers couple? What was his motivation for such horrific attacks?

Tom Benton was holding forth. 'Rolf Summers was German and they reckon the guy who's the murderer is German too. In my reckoning it all goes back to something that happened in Germany during the war.'

'I'm not sure I'd agree with you Tom,' reacted Sandra Leighton. 'As their next-door neighbours we got to know Rolf and Doreen well. After all, they lived next door for fifteen years! Rolf was adamant he spent the whole of the war in an internment camp on the Isle of Man.'

'So perhaps Rolf met his murderer there then,' suggested Rhonda Benton as she grabbed another mouthful of salted peanuts.

'That sounds feasible,' agreed the man of the cloth, sipping his red wine, 'but how did they become such bitter enemies? What happened for this man to come after Rolf Summers fifteen years later and then kill his wife as well?'

Mike Leighton chimed in, 'hopefully the police will do their research work thoroughly and find out what went on in that internment camp. There must be some officials who worked in the internment camp who would still remember.'

'Some would be dead by now, the war ended seventeen years ago,' added Tom.

'I'm sure records were kept. If there was serious trouble between inmates it was probably noted down in the daily reports. These should be archived somewhere.'

'Yes, I'm sure you're right,' agreed Rhonda. 'There's another gap in our knowledge though. Rolf and Doreen didn't come to live in the village until 1947, that's two years after the end of the war. What was Rolf doing between the time he was released from internment camp and getting married?'

'Courting Doreen, of course!' laughed Mike and they all joined in.

Jenny arrived at their table, looking as coquettish as ever. 'Would you like another round of drinks folks?' It was agreed another drink might help with the "motivation" issue they were endeavouring to solve. Jenny picked up the empties and placed them on her tray before checking what they wanted for the next round. Then, with a swing of her hips she left them to it.

'There was one strange thing that happened as poor Rolf lay dying on the floor of his house,' piped up Sandra. 'Doreen told Mike and me and the two detectives that Rolf uttered the word, "rose."'

'That's weird,' said Tom, 'maybe he once had a girlfriend called Rose?'

'Or it had something to do with those white roses he fussed over in his front garden?' suggested the Reverend Arbuthnot who had sometimes visited the Summers. The couple were, he remembered sadly, well respected parishioners.

Nobody could suggest any other explanation as to why the word "rose" was of relevance and the conversation quickly moved on to other topics.

It was late when the group finally broke up. Meeting for a good old chin-wag at "The Squirrel and Porcupine" was the little bit of therapy they needed, but sadly they were no closer to fathoming out the murderer's motives.

Belinda and Hank had a frustratingly slow journey to Crawley Hospital. Steady rain reduced visibility, there were several minor car accidents and roadworks were seemingly everywhere. When they finally arrived at the hospital's reception office, they were tired, hungry and irritable. The formal charging of Doctor Ziegler could only happen if Ziegler was fully conscious and the doctors considered he was well enough to see them. If Ziegler had been placed in an induced coma, or was having emergency surgery, they would be obliged to wait around for a day or two before proceeding with the formalities.

As usual, Hank took the lead at the window marked "Reception."

'Good evening. We are here to see Doctor Heinrich Ziegler.'

'Is he staff or a patient?'

'He's a patient. He was admitted today.'

'I see. Was he booked in for treatment or was it an emergency?'

'An emergency.'

'If he came in as an emergency patient you should go round to Accident and Emergency and inquire there. Go back the way you came in, turn left and follow the signs. It's not far, a five-minute walk.'

'Okay, thank you.'

A few minutes later they fronted up at the reception desk in Accident and Emergency. The lady on duty thumbed through the lists of patients admitted, patients discharged and patients still waiting to be seen.

'Ah yes, here we are. Doctor Heinrich Gustav Ziegler was brought in by ambulance at eleven fifty-six this morning. It was a trauma case. The triage nurse assessed him at twelve-eighteen and sent him to bed six in the Lady Armitage Ward for further observation and tests if necessary. At the time of his admission, he was unconscious, but we found his passport in his bag. That's how we got his name.' She looked up and smiled, pleased she had the details readily to hand.

'We would like to go and see him please.'

'Are you family?'

'No.'

'Then I'm sorry, but I can't allow you to see him.'

Hank wasted no time and flicked out his police ID. 'This is an urgent police matter. We wish to apprehend him. Unless a doctor can give us a very strong reason why we can't see him immediately, I am instructing you to let us through. Do you understand?'

'Yes, yes, of course,' replied the frazzled receptionist, 'please wait a second while I call the senior registrar.' A moment later she returned with an apologetic look on her face, 'I'm awfully sorry but Doctor Ziegler appears to have discharged himself. He hasn't been seen for an hour or two.'

'That can't be right,' Hank responded, curtly. 'The Crawley Police Station sent a uniformed police officer here to guard him.'

'I'm sorry, I can't comment on that. I only came on duty ten minutes ago so I don't know whether a policeman arrived or not.'

Belinda stepped in, 'I think it best if we speak to the Senior Registrar about this matter, please.'

'Yes, of course, I'll call him straightaway and let him know you're coming.'

A few minutes later, Hank and Belinda were taken in to see the Senior Registrar who was bending over the body of a young boy lying on a bed whimpering miserably. Seeing them, the Senior Registrar straightened up, stretched his back and extended a hand.

'Good evening, Stephen Cameron. How can I help?'

Hank explained they had come to the hospital to charge one of Stephen Cameron's recent patients with suspected murder and were not pleased the patient had been allowed to discharge himself.

Doctor Cameron was an impressive looking fellow as tall as Hank and a couple of years older. A shock of unruly red hair gave him a fierce appearance not unlike a Viking of yesteryear. Somehow Hank sensed a kindred spirit and within a couple of minutes had established that Stephen played full back for the London Scottish, a team with an enviable rugby reputation. Once this was established, the rest of the discussion came easily. Belinda marvelled at the efficacy of the "old boy" network clearly still alive and well.

'Doctor Ziegler came in by ambulance late this morning after being hit by a car. I checked him over and found no broken bones but he'd taken a nasty blow to the thigh on his right leg. It seems the impact threw him to the ground where he hit his head and knocked himself unconscious. Head injuries are always a worry so I admitted him for further observation. I wanted to do some scans to check for any brain damage and possible concussion.'

'So, what happened? We arranged with the Crawley Police Station for uniformed police to stay with him until we arrived with an arrest warrant.'

'This is a busy place, Hank. At any one time I'm dealing with up to fifteen demanding patients, trying to diagnose their problems and instigate the most appropriate medical procedures. In Doctor Ziegler's case he needed no life-threatening urgent attention. Apart from having a nurse to clean up and bandage a couple of his abrasions it was quite okay to leave him while I dealt with life and death cases.'

'Okay Stephen I understand. What's happened to his passport?'

'When Doctor Ziegler first came in, we needed to know who he was. He had a backpack so the office staff rummaged around in it and surprisingly they found his passport. We used it to record the usual patient details full name, date and place of birth, all that stuff. Then the passport was put back in his backpack and it travelled with Doctor Zeigler on the end of his bed when he was sent off for x-rays.'

'Then what happened?' asked Belinda.

'He must have come round and found himself lying on a bed in a hospital. I guess he panicked, especially if he knew you guys were after him. Obviously, he was strong enough to get himself up, grab his bag and scarper.'

'Why didn't someone stop him?'

'People are coming and going here all the time, Hank. It can be as busy as Paddington Station. It doesn't happen often but if a patient decides they don't want treatment they are perfectly free to get up and go. Any doctors or nurses who saw Ziegler leaving probably thought he'd been officially discharged and was fine to leave.'

'Did a policeman turn up?'

'Yup but he was too late. Your man had already discharged himself.'

'It must have been a small window of opportunity,' bemoaned Belinda.

'One thing may help you as you look for this guy. He'll be seriously limping for a few days. The right leg was hit quite hard. He also has plasters on his hand, left, I think. Wait on, I'll check on his medical record.'

It turned out it was his right hand and arm that had been dressed. His shirt had been torn too. There was also a plaster on his forehead, left hand side.

There was no more information to be gleaned from Doctor Cameron. Hank thanked him and the two men hoped they would meet again on a rugby pitch somewhere, sometime.

11. A Night in London

Belinda and Hank were starving. Before they left Crawley Hospital they asked the receptionist, the same one they had spoken to earlier, to recommend somewhere to eat. They didn't really mind where as long as it wasn't a Lyons Corner Café. Her suggestion was to go to Gatwick Airport only three miles away where there was a wide selection of eating places. Accepting this advice, Hank left the car in a parking place reserved for police and placed his police ID card on the dash-board. They found an Italian restaurant and ordered. Once they'd consumed some wholesome food and polished off a carafe of vino, they felt almost human again.

There was little doubt the chemistry between Belinda and Hank was becoming increasingly powerful. For four days they had tempered their feelings for each other and endeavoured to remain professionally aloof. Admiration was flowing in both directions and their sexual desires were intensifying. Furthermore, tonight they were obliged through no fault of their own, to find accommodation in a hotel somewhere close to the airport. The temptation was there particularly after a relaxing meal and the wine had lessened their inhibitions.

They did, however, talk business while waiting for the meal to arrive. Hank had already rung Sandham to break the news that Doctor Ziegler had given them the slip. The suspect had missed his flight and was probably lying low somewhere in London planning another way out of the country. Sandham was understandably furious. The angrier he became, the more his dreadful cough overpowered him. Hank told Belinda that by the end of the call he felt he was talking to a cough! Sandham's orders were simple and predictable. 'Find him!'

Theoretically, the task of finding Doctor Ziegler should not be difficult. Lame and wounded he should be readily spotted if walking around the streets. Sandham went quickly to work. Extra police "on the beat" were moved into Crawley and the surrounding suburbs. Gatwick Airport's immigration staff were placed on highest alert anticipating Ziegler would try to procure another flight. The international airport at Bonn was warned of Doctor Ziegler's possible arrival over the next few days. Interpol was appraised of the situation and asked to make contact with the University of Bonn to confirm Doctor Zeigler was employed there. Even the local Crawley travel agents were warned to look out for the doctor. The net was surely closing on the suspected double murderer.

The evening, however, was too special an occasion to be talking shop all night. For the time being there was nothing more they could do about Doctor Zeigler. Hank brought the conversation round to more personal matters.

'Suzie and I have officially broken up, you know.'

'Was it awfully difficult?'

'Yes and no. We'd been dating for around six months but in the end we both knew it wasn't going anywhere. We'd had lots of fun together and will always remain good friends.'

Emboldened by the wine Belinda asked, 'Did you sleep with her?'

'No.'

'Am I supposed to believe you?' probed Belinda.

'You may find this hard to believe but I'm actually a virgin.' There was a moment of silence as Belinda absorbed this unexpected revelation.

'Really! How old are you, Hank?' Belinda reached for his hand.

'Twenty-nine.'

'Are you seriously telling me that after many years celebrating umpteen rugby match victories no girls have ever tempted you into their beds?'

'True. Perhaps it explains why I'm still single and trying to find a woman like you to be my special partner for life.'

'Wow…Hank…I need a moment to take in what you've just said.'

'And… what about you, Belinda? Are *you* a virgin?'

Tears came to her eyes as she nodded enthusiastically. 'Quite a few have tried their darndest to seduce me I can assure you but I've hung on to the precious belief that my body, my heart and spirit are unique and special and not things to share until I'm absolutely sure the right man has arrived and I finally marry him.'

'Belinda, I'm so full of admiration. If it's possible you are now even more special to me.'

They squeezed hands.

'Hank, are you religious? Is it a Christian belief that has convinced you to remain chaste?'

'Not really. My parents are church-goers and I was always expected to go to church when I was a kid along with my little brother and sister.'

'So religious teachings about not having sex before marriage didn't influence you?'

'Well, I guess they did to some extent but only indirectly. No, I came to this decision myself. I genuinely believe we humans are on a higher plane than other creatures on this planet. We have powerful brains to think about our actions, unlike animals. For animals the sexual act is simply a basic instinct. There is no genuine love or adoration attached. They don't even understand the consequences of intercourse. Animals are driven by nature to mate and reproduce. Humans are better than that…on a higher plane… Now, it's your turn, Belinda. Please tell me why you have remained pure.'

'That's a hard act to follow, Hank. I suppose my thinking is similar to yours. My family were not church-goers so I don't have much knowledge of what's in the Bible. Like you though, I have marriage up there on a pedestal. It's the coming together of a man and a woman to share their lives and bring into this world children to love, protect and nurture. Deep love between a man and a woman should only be fully expressed when both have made serious vows to share their lives together and care for any offspring. For me, this is what "union" means, in every sense of the word.'

Between them they had said it all. They squeezed hands again and Hank left to settle the bill. There was no more to be said for the time being. Later they checked in at the Gatwick International Hotel and collected the keys for rooms 407 and 408. Before retiring they had a loving embrace. That night for the first time, Belinda and Hank dared to dream of a future together.

12. Wednesday, 28th August

Betty Duncan announced at the breakfast table she was driving to Lower Bybridge to spend a little time with Eva Spindle, an elderly parishioner not well enough to attend services at Saint David's on a regular basis. Eva was a sweet little widow living on her own in a cottage that was slowly falling into decay. She didn't have the money to carry out the much-needed repairs and was obliged, because of chronic arthritis, to spend much of her day confined to an armchair. Betty planned to take Eva some home-made biscuits and lend her a few of her women's magazines.

'What time are you going, mum?' inquired Jenny, showing a surprising amount of interest.

'As soon as we wash up these breakfast dishes.'

'Can I thumb a ride with you, please? Then you can drop me off at Michael's place on the way.'

Betty liked Michael, he seemed a decent enough lad and was doing well at High School. She knew Jenny had a crush on the boy, her first serious boyfriend.

'No problem, dear. If you help me with these dishes we can leave in half an hour.'

Jenny barely had sufficient time to help her mum, ring Michael to let him know she was coming over and put on some make-up.

It was a typically gloomy English day. Grey clouds scudded across the sky creating a light drizzle that came and went. It was enough to make everything damp so Jenny put on wet-weather gear in case she and Michael went walking, although she suspected Michael shared her desire to get away from his parents and spend time in the barn with her. She liked Rhonda Benton but Michael's mother didn't trust them. Perhaps Rhonda was right to worry because Jenny was longing to go further than just kissing and cuddling with her boyfriend. This whole business of sex fascinated her and she knew there was a world of passion and thrills out there to be explored and enjoyed. Today, she was determined to really encourage Michael. It was time she became more adventurous and, hopefully, experienced.

Her mother dropped her off at Bramble Farm at ten o'clock with instructions to be ready for her to pick her up again at mid-day. 'Don't be late dear, we have to relieve your dad in the pub at one.'

Meanwhile, Michael had well and truly got the message Jenny was keen to go down to the barn again and was already clad in his wellies and rain gear when she arrived. Tom, his dad, had gone to the markets for the day and wasn't expected home till dusk. Michael told his mum he and Jenny would be going for a walk.

'But it's too wet to go walking, Michael. Why don't you watch some telly or play board games?'

'It's hardly raining, mum. Besides, I promised to take Jenny mushrooming. It's ideal weather for mushrooms but she needs help identifying which ones to pick and which ones are poisonous.'

His mother replied with a disapproving sniff and thrust her formidable arms deep into the soapy washing-up basin to rattle the cutlery about noisily. Rhonda had conveniently forgotten that twenty years ago she too had been intrigued with the teenage world of romance, love, crushes, sex and experimenting. Life as a farmer's wife had soon knocked that past life on its head. Now, it was the daily grind of moving the sheep, feeding the chickens, checking on the horses and keeping her family properly fed and cared for. Rhonda couldn't remain grumpy any longer though because there was a knock on the front door and Jenny appeared appropriately dressed for the inclement weather. Against her better judgement Rhonda wished them well for their walk and hoped it would result in a generous supply of wild mushrooms. She even gave them a large bowl to put them in.

Picking wild mushrooms was, of course, far from the minds of the young couple. They were headed for the hay bales in the barn. Once out of sight of Rhonda's kitchen window they held hands and giggled their way through the farmyard, past the stables, past the chicken yard and down the slippery track towards the barn. Michael already had a fierce erection which he couldn't arrange more comfortably since he was holding hands with the gorgeous Jenny and at the same time holding up an umbrella. As soon as they were safely in the dry, inviting barn they embraced and for the first time Jenny felt his hardness pushing up against her. Breaking away she ran to the hay bales with a squeal of excited anticipation and started scrambling up calling to Michael to follow. This he did. Reaching the top, they fell down clumsily in the hay together laughing and giggling.

Covered in flecks of straw they stared at each other, feeling embarrassed and not quite knowing what to do next.

'I think you're supposed to take off my clothes,' said Jenny.

'Do you really think we ought to do this? asked Michael.

'Are you scared?' Jenny baited him.

'A bit.'

'Here touch my breasts,' and she took hold of his hand and placed it there. Through three layers of clothing, the outer one a damp raincoat, this did little to further excite the young man. 'Come on put your hand in.' Michael did so and felt her blouse and what must be her bra underneath.

'Wait a jiff I'll get them off.' Jenny stood up, removed the damp raincoat and unbuttoned her blouse. Dropping the blouse to the ground she stood before him. 'Want to see more?' she teased.

Now Michael *was* aroused. Seeing Jenny partially naked with only a bra covering her generous breasts was stimulating and he knew he wanted more. His erection was bursting against his pants. But then Jenny suddenly changed her mind. 'It's time you showed me what you've got, Michael. Come on get your trousers off,' she dared.

Acutely embarrassed about his penis so large and uncomfortable, Michael hesitated. Nobody had ever seen his erection before. 'Come on Michael.' Still, he dithered. 'Come on Michael you can keep your underpants on if you're scared.'

He sat up and pulled at his wellies. There was no way his trousers would come down with his wellies still on. Throwing the muddy boots aside he fumbled with the buckle on his belt and then, half lying, half sitting, clumsily yanked at his trousers revealing the bursting bulge in his underpants.

'Wow…you must be big!' exclaimed Jenny, ogling his still hidden crown jewels with a mischievous smirk. 'Now it's my turn again,' and she began to remove her walking shoes and trousers. A moment later she was standing before him proudly clad only in her bra and panties blowing kisses at him. Helpless now Michael stood up and held her against him. Jenny, feeling aroused pushed him over and they sprawled in the hay knotted together face to face, kissing frantically. Michael knew this was it; he had to have everything now and Jenny was definitely wanting it.

'Get your gear off Jenny, all of it. Quickly! We've got to do it, I can't wait.' Jenny loved the authority in her boyfriend's voice and it thrilled her to know how easily she had seduced him.

This was it. There was absolutely no turning back now. The chance of a pregnancy flashed fleetingly through Jenny's mind but she'd get Michael to pull out at the last minute. She'd heard this is what couples did if they didn't want babies. As she undid her bra she suddenly froze. They both did. There was someone else in the barn, someone whistling. Michael recognised the whistling immediately. It was his dad! What the hell was he doing here? His dad was supposed to be at the markets for the whole day…

❲

Tom Benton had had a frustrating morning. He had driven the truck over to Heatherington for the monthly market with the intention of purchasing a few more lambs for fattening to replace the half dozen

99

he had lost in the unusually late cold spell in May. However, he was not impressed with the quality of the stock on offer. After a yarn with a few farming mates, he decided to head home. Rather than drop in unexpectedly for morning tea with his wife, he planned to grab something from the fridge in the barn and then finish off the fencing job around the Swampy Oak field.

Tom drove in through the farm's bottom gate and headed up to the barn, cursing the continuing damp weather that threatened to prevent him working on the fence. Parking the truck, he buttoned up his raincoat and trudged into the barn. Tom was an inveterate whistler, whenever he had to walk anywhere, he whistled. It was a habit he had picked up at boarding school where all the boys whistled. It was a habit that had really annoyed Rhonda when they were courting. They would be out in the country somewhere having a romantic walk and Tom would open up with his whistling. Much of the time he didn't even know he was doing it. Rhonda used to joke that Tom could never be able to rob a bank because they'd always hear him coming.

On this particular morning, Tom's whistling served as an early warning for Michael and Jenny seeking sexual pleasures in the hay. Tom walked straight to the fridge and rummaged around looking for the packet of biscuits and whistling the whole time. Next, he wandered over to the electric jug to make a cup of tea. Meanwhile, Michael peered nervously over the edge of the hay carefully observing his father's movements, whilst Jenny, furious that Tom's intrusion had totally ruined everything, lay low on the hay struggling to get dressed. As she pulled up her trousers, she felt something cold and sharp push up against her leg. To her surprise she found it was a metal badge with a pin. She popped it in her pocket. Michael would probably know what it was.

By now, the rain was pattering steadily on the roof and Tom remained in the barn enjoying his cup of tea and the four chocolate biscuits he had found. With difficulty Jenny and Michael finished dressing and stayed hidden and silent atop the haystack. Jenny was beginning to get worried though. She had promised to be back at the house for her mother to pick her up at mid-day and it was already half past eleven. What were they going to do if the rain continued and Michael's dad decided to stay longer in the barn? They were effectively trapped!

To their great relief the rain lifted and Tom, whistling another unrecognisable tune, picked up a couple of fencing tools and made his way out to his truck. As soon as they heard him drive off the teenagers scrambled down off the hay and bolted back to the farmhouse arriving there just as Jenny's mum pulled up. Jenny left it to Michael to concoct some sort of a story to explain why they hadn't returned with a bowl full of field mushrooms. Before she left, she handed Michael the metal badge she had found in the hay intending to ask him about it next time they were together.

Rather sheepishly, Michael went indoors and straight up to his bedroom. His mother was on the phone. After cleaning himself up and having a wash he ventured back down to the kitchen famished and ready for some lunch. Fortuitously, his mother was still distracted by her long phone call and had completely forgotten about the mushrooms. Michael didn't even have to make up any lies to explain what he and Jenny had been doing.

After lunch Michael remembered Jenny had handed him a metal badge just as she was leaving. He pulled the badge from his trouser pocket and examined it. It was the size of a shilling, round with a pin at the back for attaching to an item of clothing. It was unlike any badge he had ever seen before. Presumably the badge had been left, unintentionally, on top of the hay bales by the murder suspect when he slept up there. Michael studied the badge more carefully. It was a simple design. Three white rose blooms were arranged symmetrically on a jet-black background. He wondered what the badge represented and came to the conclusion the murder suspect must be either an enthusiastic gardener or a member of some club that propagated roses. He had heard of various horticultural organisations that existed in the

United Kingdom and it seemed perfectly logical their members would like to wear badges. Perhaps there were German equivalents? Clubs, or groups of enthusiastic gardeners, who liked to identify themselves with special badges like this one? He turned the badge over to see if there were any markings on the back, but found nothing.

Then another thought came to him. Last year he had sat "O" level History and passed. Not surprisingly, the examination had been designed to test his knowledge of British history. One of the topics in the history curriculum was "The Wars of the Roses" which lasted for some thirty-two years during the fifteenth century. Essentially, these wars were fought between the followers of the House of York and the House of Lancaster for the right to sit on the English throne. The symbol of the Lancastrians was a red rose. The Yorkists' symbol, a white rose. Could this strange badge in some way be connected to those events five hundred years ago? Highly improbable Michael concluded and he left the badge on the side of his desk.

Stretching out on his bed he picked up his latest acquisition, a novel called "Trust the Saint" by his favourite author, Leslie Charteris and began reading. Charteris had written heaps of books about a sleuth called Simon Templar, also known as "the Saint" and Michael couldn't get enough of his books. Absorbed in his novel, he completely forgot about the mysterious metal badge with the white roses.

Next morning, to Michael's surprise, his mother spoke to him about the badge. She had been prowling through the house looking for clothes that needed washing and had found the badge sitting where he had left it on the side of his desk.

'What's this badge, dear?' she asked, holding it up so her son could see it.

'No idea, mum.'

'Where did you get it?'

'Found it.'

'Where? Somebody would probably like it back.'

'Yeah, maybe.'

'Come on Michael don't be so evasive. Did you find it at school?'

'Nope.'

'Well, where then?'

Michael realised his mother was on the war path and wouldn't relent until she received a satisfactory answer. 'Jenny and I found it yesterday.'

'Where? On the farm?'

'Yep, it was in the barn.' No way was Michael going to admit to precisely *where* in the barn Jenny had found it.

'In the barn?' His mother was getting quite animated. 'Are you sure?'

'Yes, mum.'

'Do you know what I think? I think this probably belongs to the murderer who was sleeping in our barn.'

'He's only a suspected murderer,' Michael gently corrected his mother.

'Well, I'm going to ring the police. It might be important evidence.'

'They won't be able to get fingerprints because Jenny and I, and now you, have all held it in our hot little hands.'

'True but you can get into trouble Michael for withholding evidence. This could be important for the police. We don't know. I'll drive down to the police station at Lower Bybridge and hand the badge in.'

'Okay, mum.' Michael was hugely relieved his mother didn't probe further into exactly *how* and *where* the badge had been found.

Constable Brian Brooks was on duty at Lower Bybridge Police Station when Rhonda Benton bowled in and handed him the metal badge displaying the three mysterious while roses. He duly recorded the details in his ledger as "an item of lost property" and realising it could be of interest to the detectives investigating the two murders, rang them immediately.

Rhonda returned home to her washing-up duties, satisfied she had promptly fulfilled her civic duty.

13. Thursday, 29ᵗʰ August

Belinda and Hank met in the hotel foyer at seven and set off for a run without doing warm-up exercises. The sun was up but not yet visible hiding behind a plethora of tall buildings. They didn't know this patch of London and had no maps. To avoid getting lost they resolved to simply run along the main road for twenty minutes and then turn back. Breakfast was beckoning. The exertion of running meant they hardly spoke yet were more than conscious of each other's company. Without overtly showing it they both quietly admired the other's physique. Belinda, tall and slim with a graceful well-toned body. Hank, typical of a super-fit rugby player, strong and muscular.

Once back at the hotel they showered and breakfasted and were on their way back to Petworth shortly after nine. It was a great trip because they spent the whole time discovering more and more about each other. Their free-flowing exchange covered several important topics: families, schooling, hobbies, travel and hopes for the future. The more they learnt about each other the more they wanted to know. As they pulled into the car park outside the Petworth Police Station, they realised with a pang of guilt, they had not spent a single moment discussing their double murder case. This changed abruptly as soon as they walked in. Chief Inspector Nigel Sandham was waiting for another update.

If Sandham noticed the new-found closeness between his two sleuths he didn't comment. He listened patiently, coughing occasionally, to what they had to report of their visit to Crawley Hospital. He then told them no further sightings of Doctor Heinrich Zeigler had been forthcoming and they agreed Zeigler probably couldn't avoid detection much longer. If his injuries were still painful, he might seek further medical attention at a chemist or a doctor's surgery. Money could well be a problem for him too. While the warm summer weather lasted Zeigler could find shelter and sleep rough but he still needed to eat. Eventually, any money he had with him would run out and he would be forced to visit a bank or beg, borrow, or steal. Surely Zeigler would make a wrong move soon and they would get him. It was only a matter of being patient.

Sandham forcefully stubbed his cigarette out in his half-full ashtray. He was annoyed they were not making fast enough progress. His mantra was that the longer it took to detain a criminal, the harder it became. It was already four days since Mrs Summers' demise. Sandham might have a shocking cough but there was nothing wrong with his brain.

'If I remember correctly, Zeigler is known to have spent a night or two sleeping in that barn at Bramble Farm half way between Upper and Lower Bybridge?'

'Correct, sir.'

'Our boys checked that location thoroughly and didn't find anything except some food had been stolen and there were signs Zeigler had slept on top of the hay.'

'They also found finger-prints there on the fridge, linking him to the murder weapon, sir.'

'Yes, of course, vitally important. But it seems our boys missed this...'

The chief inspector slowly unravelled a piece of yellow cloth, allowing a small metal object to fall onto his desk. 'It's a badge. Constable Brooks brought it in half an hour ago. It was found yesterday by the young lad who lives at Bramble Farm. What do you make of it?'

'Never seen a badge like it before,' responded Hank, turning it over and over in his hand before examining the back. He passed the badge over to Belinda who did likewise.

'The Benton family say they have never seen a badge like this one before either. So, I'm thinking it belonged to Zeigler and he dropped it there unintentionally.'

'That seems a reasonable assumption sir,' Belinda remarked, 'I think we should try and find out more about it. A badge like that must mean something to somebody.'

'Exactly. It's not much, but it may lead us to find out something more about Zeigler.' Sandham was overcome by another bout of coughing and had to wait a couple of minutes before proceeding. 'I want you two to find out what this badge signifies, who wears them and why.'

'Might be a rose club?' posited Hank, brightly.

'Maybe it's just ornamental, like a piece of jewellery and doesn't really mean anything?' Belinda suggested.

'Well, you two, it's your job to find out. Let me know if you find out anything of interest.'

The meeting over, Belinda and Hank filed out while their boss went through his routine of lighting up another cigarette. The pair headed for the staff room to have a cup of tea and discuss how they might solve the mystery of the badge with the three white roses. It was agreed Belinda would contact gardening clubs, nurseries and horticultural organisations. Hank would spend part of the day with the police archivist who had an enviable reputation for coming up with successful research findings. Before they parted company, Belinda reminded Hank that the Summers couple had been keen gardeners and the whole of their front garden was full of roses...every one of them, a white rose!

❦

The police archivist was rather disparagingly referred to as "Fossil" by most of his colleagues. He was one of those rare men who seemed ageless and had pottered around in his private downstairs quarters since pre-Cambrian times. Nobody knew exactly how old Fossil was, but he was ancient. There was a whiteness about him, a thick unruly snowy mop of hair and a white beard that covered most of his face. Even his skin was pale, probably the result of being closeted underground for so many years and rarely seeing the sun. A pair of half-glasses perched precariously on his nose needing cleaning every five minutes. Nobody knew much about Fossil's past, although it was rumoured, he had been in the Intelligence Corps during the first World War. If so, this would mean Fossil was in his late seventies or even his eighties. It was a mystery to some why he was still taking home a weekly pay packet but others knew it was because he had an uncanny ability to research topics successfully after everyone else had given up. His real name was Bert Pallister.

Hank descended the stairs to Bert's private kingdom two at a time. He knocked on the thick glass window that proclaimed "ARCHIVES" and waited to be invited in. Hank found "Fossil" sitting comfortably in an easy chair eating a banana and reading "The Times." Hank had only once before spent time with Fossil during which he had found him highly intelligent, well read and relentless in his pursuit of the truth.

'Good morning, Mr Pallister.' Hank felt it wise to treat "Fossil" with respect if he was to get his full cooperation.

'Ah, my boy…let me think for a moment. Yes, I believe its Hank… Hank Zagalski? Never forget a name like that,' and he chortled quietly to himself pleased his memory was still trustworthy.

'You're quite right, sir.'

'And to what do I owe this honour, Hank?' Bert took the last mouthful of his banana and laid the empty skin down carefully on his side-table.

'You may have heard, I'm investigating the Summers' murders from last weekend?'

'Indeed, I have heard. A nasty business. I've kept up with what's been reported in the papers but that's all.'

'Well, I'm hoping to tap into your research expertise to assist with an interesting object that's been found. We are keen to ascertain exactly what it is and whether it might be helpful.'

Hank dived into his pocket, produced the badge and went on to outline the details about where and when it was discovered. He stressed the need to get some answers as soon as possible because they were hoping to detain the murderer soon.

Fossil picked up the badge and examined it carefully. Then hoisted himself up from his arm-chair a little unsteadily and took the badge over to a table where he examined it again under a bright light with a magnifying glass. Next, he tried to scratch the back with the point of a knife. 'Definitely metal but there are no identifying marks naming the manufacturer or a date,' he concluded. 'I've never seen the like before. Leave it with me and I'll do some digging.'

They exchanged a few more niceties and Bert promised to contact Hank promptly should he turn up anything useful.

ℭ

Thursday evenings at "The Squirrel and Porcupine" were Darts Nights. Jack expected a good crowd since the annual grudge match between Upper Bybridge and Lower Bybridge was due to start at eight o'clock. Betty had a meeting at Saint David's so Jack had dragooned Jenny to once again work the evening shift. Earlier in the day Jenny had chatted at length with Michael over the phone and he had assured her he was coming tonight with his parents. His dad was playing for Upper Bybridge, always a controversial selection because Bramble Farm was equidistant from the two villages. It was more complicated than that though, because the gate to Bramble Farm was fifty yards closer to Lower Bybridge than Upper Bybridge. However, Bramble Farm's farmhouse was thirty yards closer to Upper Bybridge and eventually it was this fact that clinched the argument. Tom was an excellent darts player and Lower Bybridge had never quite forgiven him.

The current holder of the "Bybridge Trophy" was the team from Lower Bybridge who had won it back in a closely fought encounter in August 1961 after being in the wilderness for the four previous years. A keen contest was expected tonight with the bets slightly favouring Upper Bybridge. Last year's losing team was always invited to nominate which kind of darts game would be contested. Upper Bybridge had chosen "Round the Clock."

Whereas some of the pub's chatter was about who was expected to win tonight's darts match, there was still considerable interest in the two unsolved murders. Wild stories continued to circulate about whether or not the murderer had been caught and, if so, who he was. There had been extensive coverage in the local newspapers but then you couldn't believe everything you read in the papers. Some folks wanted to talk to a member of the Benton family to find out more about the strange badge that had been discovered at Bramble Farm. Like any piece of information that passes through several people's lips, the "truth" had gradually metamorphosed. Some had heard it was a white badge with three black roses; others insisted the badge included a German inscription at the base. Some thought the name of the manufacturer was engraved on the back showing it was of German origin. Few had it correct. Rhonda, in particular, lapped up being the centre of attention as she spun her story of the mysterious badge to those who were interested and a few unfortunate individuals who were not.

Michael was also the centre of attention amongst his small group of mates. When he unwisely disclosed it was actually Jenny who had discovered the badge and that they were sheltering in the barn at the time, his friends jumped to the obvious conclusion, Michael and Jenny had been enjoying a bit of rolly-polly in the hay. He did his best to deny this at first, but the more he protested, the more they knew he was lying. Observing the highly attractive Jenny working busily behind the bar, Michael's mates were more than a tad envious of their friend's romantic adventures.

The darts match was a close, tense affair. Upper Bybridge eventually threw the deciding bull's eye and Tom Benton was proclaimed the hero of the evening. The Bentons were in celebratory mood as they drove the short distance home that evening, although Rhonda had one niggling problem she wanted solving and decided she could wait no longer.

'Michael, exactly where in the barn did you find that badge?'

Michael and Jenny had hoped like hell nobody was ever going to ask that question, but here it was suddenly out of the blue and there was no way Michael could avoid answering. 'It was in the hay,' he mumbled colouring red, which he hoped didn't show in the dark.

'Okay, be honest with us Michael. What were the two of you up to in the barn that morning?'

'We were having a kiss, that's all.'

'And is that *all* you were up to, son?'

'Yeah.'

To his great relief, Michael's father entered the conversation, 'Steady on Rhonda. There was a time, not too many years ago, when you and I were not averse to a bit of a kiss and cuddle in that very same hay barn.'

Rhonda knew he was right and she pulled her horns in and was more circumspect, 'Well Michael, make sure you're completely honest with us in future please.'

They had arrived at the farm gate and Michael, whose job it was to be the gate-opener, couldn't get out of the car fast enough. The subject, thankfully, was dropped.

As they went to bed that evening Rhonda followed through with her husband. 'It's time you had a proper talk to our son, dear. He seems very keen on this young Jenny and we don't want an unwanted pregnancy on our hands. You will talk to him, won't you Tom?'

'Yes, dear.' Tom had been meaning to have a chat with his son for many months but never seemed to quite get round to it. He switched the light off.

14.   Friday, 30th August

Bert Pallister, police archivist, loved a challenge. Friday was a pleasant morning weatherwise with only a slight breeze and he enjoyed riding his ancient "bone-shaker" to work. The traffic was not too heavy and the roads dry. The forecast was good for the remainder of the day so his trip home should be a comfortable one too. He was looking forward to doing more work on the origins of the mysterious badge young Inspector Hank Zagalski had brought to him yesterday. Since this badge could be an important clue in the hunt for the suspected murderer of the married couple in Upper Bybridge, Bert had placed it as the top priority on his "to do" list.

Fossil parked his bicycle in its usual place and gently eased his back-pack off. Hesta, his wife, always gave him three carefully cut cheese and tomato sandwiches and an apple on Fridays and these were safely wrapped up in grease-proof paper snug in their picnic box. He removed his bicycle clips and clicked them onto his bike ready for the evening's ride home. He never locked his bike, although recently he had heard alarming stories of bicycles being stolen. He wondered what the world was coming to. Fancy having to lock up your bicycle!

Soon he was walking down the sixteen poorly-lit steps that led to his underground domain. It was strange, he mused, that all the archivists he knew were housed in out of the way places, tucked away where nobody was likely to find them, in cellars, backrooms, rooms at the far end of never-ending corridors. It was as though archivists were regarded as second-class citizens, people from another world. And yet, it was often the archivists who made the break-throughs that lead to the solving of major crimes. Despite the efforts of his police colleagues to push him down into what amounted to an underground cave, he loved his work and never wanted to retire.

When you have worked in the same building for thirty years you inevitably become a creature of habit. As always, Bert made himself a pot of tea and enjoyed one of his favourite Bath Oliver biscuits. Whilst enjoying this little repast he flicked through the pages of the local newspaper. He always made a point of arriving at the police station fifteen minutes early so nobody could ever accuse him of not starting work on time. Repast over, Fossil began his search for information about the mysterious badge in an almanac entitled, "Badges of the World," and thumbed through to the chapter headed "Secret Badges." Nothing helpful there. Next, he went to his beloved 1960 edition of the Encyclopedia Brittanica. Nothing there either. Stumped, he decided to tap into the extensive network of archivists who were members of the Royal Society of Archivists (RSA) for the United Kingdom and Ireland. Again, he was unsuccessful.

It was then Fossil realised he was probably looking in the wrong places. The man who was murdered had spent much of his life in Germany and it was known the murder suspect was also German. Possibly he could trace the badge's origin by consulting the German archives. With the help of the RSA he learnt the German Federal Archives were based in Koblenz. Next, he sought permission to make an overseas trunk call to the National German Archives to speak to a member of their English-speaking staff. The German staff were most obliging. Professional archivists the world over appreciated the value of fully cooperating with their international colleagues. Bert meticulously described the dimensions, weight and appearance of the mysterious badge and then left the detective work to the German archivists who promised to get back promptly if they found anything helpful.

❦

On the coast of East Sussex there is a village called Rottingdean. "Dean" is an old English word that means a dry valley, an unusual geological feature commonly found along this part of the English coastline. Rottingdean is flanked by other "dean" villages: Ovingdean, Saltdean and Woodingdean. The picturesque village of Rottingdean is popular with retired genteel society who crave the peace and quiet of the English countryside. Although people have lived in this vicinity for over five thousand years, these days Rottingdean is famous for having been the retirement home of the famous colonial author and poet, Rudyard Kipling, who for years resided at "The Elms." In the past, Rottingdean was also the haunt of a notorious Anglican clergyman known to have been at the centre of a lively and lucrative smuggling business.

One of the genteel Rottingdean retirees was dear old Mrs Godfrey, who retired to this quaint village some ten years ago with her husband, now sadly deceased. Mrs Godfrey loved the friendly village life and had made many friends so was quite content to stay in her small flint stone cottage, just off the High Street. She felt perfectly safe. There was seldom any crime in historic Rottingdean. The village shops were close by and Mrs Godfrey didn't need a car to bring back her groceries.

On this particular Friday afternoon, Mrs Godfrey walked down the street to do some light shopping for the weekend. She purchased cooked beetroot and Coxes Pippin apples at the greengrocer, collected her prescriptions from the obliging chemist and indulged in three juicy lamb chops from the family butcher. Shopping done, Mrs Godfrey slowly made her way back home carrying two manageable shopping bags. Unless it was raining, she always stopped to talk to one or more friends along the way. Today was no exception. She bumped into Mrs Sheldrake with her two French poodles both as black as coal and then Mr Sidebottom, the verger at Saint Margaret's. It was while inquiring about Mrs Sidebottom's shingles that she noticed a stranger watching them from across the road. Tourists were increasingly coming to Rottingdean for weekends nowadays so she assumed the man was a tourist who must have arrived early.

Satisfied that Mrs Sidebottom's shingles was on the improve,

Mrs Godfrey walked on past the bright red letter-box that had just received a shiny new coat of paint and turned right into Squires Lane, a one-way street that led down to her cottage. She stopped for a moment to change hands with her shopping bags because the beetroots were becoming rather heavy and her shoulder was aching. It was then she sensed someone behind her and turned to see who it was; she knew most of the folk who lived along Squires Lane. Strange to say, there was nobody there.

Arriving at her cottage she unlatched the low gate, carefully closed it behind her, then walked the few yards to her front door. Here she put down her two bags, took out her purse and fumbled around inside looking for the front door key. Mrs Godfrey unlocked the door, picked up her shopping and entered. When she tried to close her front door, she had the shock of her life. A strange man was standing there blocking the door and preventing it from closing. Next moment, the man pushed his way inside and slammed the front door closed behind him. Mrs Godfrey stood there, terrified. Her immediate thought was, this man is a rapist!

'No talk!' the man snarled wagging a quivering forefinger at her, 'telephone, where telephone?'

For several seconds Mrs Godfrey remained rooted to the spot frozen with fear, unable to move. The man angrily repeated his demand. Then her body responded and she walked unsteadily to the corner of the room where the telephone sat on a small side-table next to her armchair. The man followed her then savagely ripped the telephone connection from the wall. Whatever he was planning, Mrs Godfrey now had no way of contacting anyone to raise the alarm.

'Food, get food,' he gesticulated to his mouth several times, 'much food, now, much food!'

For the first time Mrs Godfrey had a chance to study her intruder. He looked like a desperate fugitive on the run from the law, youngish, perhaps mid-thirties. It occurred to her that if she ever got out of this scrape alive the police would want an accurate description so she tried to concentrate on his appearance. She thought him intelligent looking, reasonably handsome but unshaven. He seemed large but when she thought about it, she realised he was actually only average height. He carried a dirty back-pack which he now threw on the floor. His clothing was filthy and she suspected he hadn't washed for days.

'Hurry, get food! Get food, now!'

Mrs Godfrey jumped into action. Realising this man's English was limited she led him to the kitchen to show him what she had. No point listing the items. She waved at a fruit bowl on the kitchen table displaying a tempting array of apples, pears and plums then threw open the fridge door for him to see what was there. The man looked inside and pointed to the bottle of milk. She reached in and passed it to him. In a flash he removed the silver top and drank straight from the bottle, downing most of it before wiping his mouth vigorously with the back of his hand.

'Goot, more food, more!' he raged.

Apparently, the intruder wasn't interested in the meat and vegetables stored in the fridge so she took him to the kitchen cupboards. He hastily scanned the shelves and picked out a few tins to look at the pictures on the labels then shook his head disapprovingly and returned them. Next, he found the bread bin which he grabbed and conveyed to the kitchen table. Plonking the bread bin down loudly he indicated with signs he wanted something with which to cut the bread and something to spread on the slices. Mrs Godfrey hurried to get him the bread-knife and from the fridge collected New Zealand butter, home-made strawberry jam and a small jar of Marmite. He seized the knife and roughly cut the bread into chunks at least an inch thick. Next, he ordered a knife for spreading. The butter was too hard having been in the fridge all day. He pushed the Marmite jar aside with a grunt of disgust and settled on the strawberry jam which he proceeded to spread generously across several hunks of bread. Clearly, the man was starving.

Mrs Godfrey allowed herself to relax a little as the man was desperately hungry and not intent on rape. Quietly, she put the kettle on and dropped three spoonfuls of tea leaves in the teapot, one for her, one for the stranger and one for the teapot. While the kettle boiled, she observed the stranger devouring his thick wedges of bread, licking his fingers and hacking another hunk of bread off her loaf. It looked as though the man was going to consume as much bread as she ate in a whole week. Once the kettle boiled, she filled the teapot and turned it three times, anti-clockwise. Then she poured the stranger a cup of tea and placed what was left of the milk and a sugar bowl next to him. He stopped shovelling in bread for a moment and looked up at her. The slightest of smiles played across his lips.

That hint of a smile took her back to the Field Hospital where she had nursed during the first World War. So many men had passed through her hands physically, psychologically and emotionally damaged. Young men who called out for their mothers in their sleep, men lost in the brutality of war and above all seeking love and kindness, reassurance that the whole world hadn't gone completely mad. She had done what she could in her own gentle way for almost three years until the terrible war ended. A year later, she walked up the aisle with a young subaltern she had nursed, still lame from his shrapnel wounds. These far away thoughts were soon rudely interrupted.

'Money, want money, money now. Get money, I go.'

Mrs Godfrey had not anticipated this and it caught her by surprise. Her natural instinct was to deny she had any money. She shook her head strenuously, 'No money, sorry, no money.'

The man jumped to his feet and grabbed hold of the bread knife, 'Money, get money,' he demanded, brandishing the knife at her threateningly.

Of course she did have some money in the house. There was her purse, which she estimated had around five pounds and ten shillings as well as one hundred pounds she kept safely locked away for emergencies. Mrs Godfrey moved to collect her purse. Taking it to the table she tipped out the contents, making sure the coins didn't roll everywhere. She reckoned there was somewhere between six and seven pounds all up. The stranger shovelled the coins up and dropped them in his pocket.

'More money, more!' he growled, threateningly.

Mrs Godfrey stood her ground. Shaking her head from side to side she denied having any more money in the house. It was a bare-faced lie but a hundred pounds was a lot of money and she hoped she could get away with it. The intruder had other ideas. He moved round the kitchen table and advanced menacingly towards the old lady holding the bread knife high in the air and thrusting it downwards as if stabbing her. He came right up close to her and seized her arm roughly still threatening to stab her and shouting, 'Money, more money!'

Terrified, she nodded vigorously and called out, 'Yes, yes, I have more.'

'Now, money now!'

Mrs Godfrey pointed to her writing desk standing against the wall in her sitting room, 'Yes, yes, I have money, come with me.' She led him to her desk and using sign language indicated she had to find the key. The man stood behind her still brandishing the knife. For a horrifying moment Mrs Godfrey couldn't recall where she kept the key to her desk drawer and stood there with her hand to her mouth looking confused. She seldom opened the drawer these days and her memory was beginning to let her down. Perhaps the key was with the other keys in the hallway? She beckoned for him to follow her into the hall. But the key was not there! Where was it? Where had she put it? She was still trying to recall where the key was when the intruder returned to her desk and with a mighty heave smashed it to the floor. The force of the impact resulted in two of the three locked drawers flying open and spewing their contents over the floor.

'Where money? Where money?' screamed the man becoming more and more agitated.

'The money's here,' blubbered Mrs Godfrey. She fell on her knees and rummaged desperately through the papers in the drawer that had remained locked, but was now exposed by the shelf above it falling out. She looked up clutching a brown envelope with "Emergency Savings" written in large letters. 'Here take it. Now please, please go.' The intruder tore the envelope open and counted five crisp twenty-pound notes. Throwing the bread knife on the table he stuffed two apples in his pockets and picked up his back pack as if leaving. Then he changed his mind and turned to face Mrs Godfrey again.

'Here,' he shouted, pointing to a kitchen chair, 'here, sit.'

Meekly, she scrambled up from the floor and obediently sat on the chair, white and shaking. The man knelt down in front of her and his hands flew up her thighs and he yanked off her stockings. 'No, no, please no.' Mrs Godfrey tried feebly to push him away but he was far too strong. Then she remembered reading somewhere it was better to submit to a rapist than fight so she sat stone still her bony white legs sticking out in front of her without shoes or stockings, like chicken bones. One stocking he used to tie her hands to the back of the chair, the other to tie her ankles together. Next, he looked around the kitchen and grabbed a tea-towel. This he used to crudely gag her.

A moment later he was gone, closing the front door quietly behind him.

15.   Saturday, 31ˢᵗ August

Seventy-one-year-old Mrs Godfrey remained gagged and bound to her chair for twenty hours. Frequently wrenching her hands and feet against the stockings in feeble attempts to free herself, only served to tighten the bindings and rub her skin raw. At some stage in the middle of the night she wrestled too hard and the chair tipped over leaving her lying on her side on the cold slate kitchen floor. A couple of times she drifted off into a horribly uncomfortable sleep between bouts of excruciating cramps. She was too weak to drag herself to the front door or reach the bread-knife tantalisingly close lying on the kitchen table. Around ten o'clock that evening she could hang on no longer and soiled herself.

Every second Saturday at ten o'clock Mrs Godfrey had a regular meeting with her closest friend, Diana Dyson, who hailed from the nearby village of Saltdean. They met at the Rottingdean Windmill, then walked for half an hour along the sea shore before retiring for "elevenses" at the "Rikki Tikki Tavi," a cute café named after the famous mongoose in one of Rudyard Kipling's books. There they would chat for an hour or so before going home. Mrs Godfrey prayed countless times during the night that Diana, puzzled by her non-appearance, would come to her house to check on her well-being and finally her awful plight would be discovered. And this, more or less, was what happened.

Diana Dyson realised something was wrong when her friend didn't arrive at the windmill by ten-thirty because Mrs Godfrey always rang if unable to come to the Rottingdean Windmill. Fearing she was ill, or perhaps hospitalised, Diana drove to the cottage in Squires Lane and knocked on the front-door. No response. She tried again. Still no response. Fearing the worst Diana tried once more, then put her ear to the door and listened intently. She thought she detected a faint banging sound. It happened several times. Perhaps her friend had a tradesman in there and had forgotten to ring her to let her know she was unable to come. She knocked one more time and listened again. Yes, she was sure there was some sort of muffled banging sound coming from inside the house.

A narrow concrete path ran along the side of the cottage leading to Mrs Godfrey's back garden. Now curious, as much as concerned, Diana followed the path to the rear of the cottage and squinted through the sitting-room window. What she saw horrified her. Mrs Godfrey's antique writing desk had been overturned and papers and stationery were strewn across the floor. Something awful had happened. Diana quickly moved along to the kitchen window. Here she saw a bread-knife on the kitchen table, a mutilated loaf of bread together with an open butter container, an open jar of jam and an unopened jar of Marmite. One of the two kitchen chairs was missing. Mrs Godfrey was a meticulous house-keeper insisting her house always be tidy in case visitors called unexpectedly.

But where was Mrs Godfrey? Diana dragged a garden bench up to the kitchen window and climbed up to get a better look inside. And there she was over by the hallway, lying on her side tied to the missing kitchen chair. Something ghastly had happened here. Diana tapped on the window loudly and the chair moved. At least her friend was alive. Once, when she had called in to see Mrs Godfrey, she had shown her where she kept her "emergency" front-door key. Hurriedly returning to the front of the cottage, Diana went to the low wall and began looking into the gaps between the stones. She couldn't remember exactly where the key was hidden but within a few minutes found it covered in cobwebs. As quickly as possible Diana entered the cottage and released her good friend.

Mrs Godfrey was conveyed by ambulance to the small Rottingdean hospital where she was thoroughly examined and admitted overnight for observation. Her physical injuries were minor, chafing on the wrists and ankles where she had struggled to get free. However, emotionally, she was in a rotten state. The shock of being confronted by the intruder, the hours of pain followed by feelings of abandonment during the long uncomfortable night, had combined to make her a nervous wreck. She was loathe to leave the security of the hospital until Diana agreed to stay with her in the cottage for the next few nights. The Brighton Police were quick to interview Mrs Godfrey while she was recovering in hospital and soon realised who her intruder had been. Numerous sets of fingerprints were examined at Mrs Godfrey's home confirming her intruder was, indeed, the suspected double murderer, Doctor Heinrich Zeigler.

☾

Chief Inspector Nigel Sandham was relaxing at home watching the BBC coverage of the fourth test at the Oval when the Brighton Police rang. Cursing this unwelcome interruption to his viewing of an intriguing encounter, he telephoned Belinda and Hank and ordered them to immediately drive to Rottingdean to take charge of the search for Zeigler. Understandably, the two young detectives were less than impressed with the boss's orders to drive to Rottingdean on a Saturday afternoon. Nevertheless, they left Petworth together around five o'clock and arrived at the police headquarters in Brighton shortly after six-thirty. They were fully briefed before driving on to the Rottingdean Hospital to interview Mrs Godfrey. Road blocks had been set up and local police stations notified that Doctor Zeigler had been sighted in the immediate vicinity. He was now officially described as "highly dangerous."

The dear lady had recovered somewhat by the time the detectives arrived and was sitting up in bed having supper. They questioned her gently but learnt nothing new. Hank and Belinda came away convinced Mrs Godfrey's intruder was indeed Doctor Heinrich Zeigler. By now the chances of finding the doctor hiding out around

Rottingdean were poor. All they could do was add break and enter, assault and theft to the growing list of Zeigler's offences. They bought fish and chips served up in soggy newspaper and drove back to Petworth. The quick trip had been unproductive, but Belinda and Hank relished the opportunity to spend more quality time together.

16. Monday, 2nd September

Bert Pallister, the elderly police archivist, was not known for making appearances in the police station proper, preferring instead to conduct his research quietly in the nether regions where he was surrounded by his shelves of familiar resource books, folders, police records and scientific equipment. Down there Fossil was in complete control of his private domain, a place where he could ponder and probe, think and explore and more often than not come up with something positive to assist "his clientele" upstairs. Normally, he would get on the blower to talk to police officers who had requested his help but this morning something especially interesting had come to light and he was so excited he decided to break convention and go in person to talk to the two young detectives working on the Zeigler case.

Fossil had come to work as usual a quarter of an hour early, safely parked his bicycle and enjoyed his first cup of tea with one Bath Oliver biscuit. He was settling down to investigate some details about a spate of robberies that had been taking place in and around Horsham which had the police mystified when a trunk call came in from the archivists in Koblenz, Germany. Generously, the Germans didn't request him to reverse charges. Even better, they were prepared to spend time on the trunk call. It was the content of this phone call that drove Bert excitedly upstairs to talk with Sergeant Belinda Purcell and Inspector Hank Zagalski in person.

Bert's appearance upstairs was so unusual he garnered several comments from his colleagues, not all of them respectful. Ignoring the taunts, he made his way straight to Hank's office where Belinda was already seated. The two detectives were more than keen to hear what Fossil had unearthed.

'Good morning, Bert. Thanks for coming. I take it you've had some good fortune?'

'Indeed. The German National Archives rang a little while ago with some intriguing news.'

'We're all ears,' smiled Belinda, encouragingly.

'When I realised the murdered man was a German and the alleged murderer was also a German, I reasoned the white rose badge might well be of German origin. Hence my call to Koblenz where the German National Archives are based. I forwarded details of the badge to them on Friday morning. Amazingly, they already think they know what the badge is.'

'That's great news, so what do we know?'

'It's an extraordinary story and will take me a bit of time to fill you in but I believe it may well have a bearing on your murder case.'

Belinda and Hank looked meaningfully at each other wishing Fossil would get on with it. The elderly archivist was not to be hurried, however, and took his time choosing his words deliberately and making sure he was covering everything.

'As I'm sure you know, Hitler and the Nazi movement began in earnest in 1933 when Hitler was appointed Chancellor of the Third Reich.' The young detectives nodded, surprised Fossil had elected to go back almost thirty years. In fact, as they soon found out, he was intent on going back even further into Germany's history.

'The origins of the Nazi Party actually emerged after the end of World War I with Hitler becoming Nazi leader in 1921. By 1927 he had published his two volumes of "Mein Kampf" in which he expounded his Nazi ideology. Essentially, Nazism was stridently anti-semitic, expansionist and claimed Aryans were a super-race destined to rule the world for a thousand years. This ideology immediately appealed to the war battered, impoverished working-class Germans who had lost the first world war and were embittered by the continuing occupation of Germany by the allied forces. Germans saw Hitler as their saviour, a man who could restore German pride.

Fossil stopped to clear his throat. Removing his glasses, he breathed heavily on the lenses and pulled out a large white handkerchief to remove any dirt. Belinda and Hank wondered how much longer he was going to talk about the Nazis and how all this could possibly be relevant to the white rose badge. Fossil was certainly not finished and appeared to be enjoying himself. He went on…

'By July 1934 the Nazis were firmly in power in Germany and declared they were the *only* legitimate political party in the country. Shortly afterwards Hitler was proclaimed Fuhrer (leader), Chancellor and Commander-in-Chief of the army. Between 1934 and 1939 the Nazis steadily established total control of all social, political and cultural activities throughout the country. It was total domination of German society. Membership of the Nazi party became mandatory for everyone in public office and everybody was required to take Hitler's "Oath of Allegiance." The nation had become a totalitarian regime intent on the complete extermination of Jews, Roma and homo-sexuals. The dreaded Gestapo were everywhere.'

'It must have been horrific,' echoed Belinda.

'It was,' agreed Fossil, 'but amazingly, despite the dangers, there were still a few courageous German souls who remained determinedly opposed to Nazism and worked quietly and secretively to challenge the evil ideology. Nobody was game to speak up openly in public against the Nazis. Anybody suspected of even wavering in their Nazi beliefs was reported to the authorities. Those suspected of being a dissenter disappeared mysteriously overnight!'

Hank was shaking his head, 'Thank God we defeated the bastards.'

'Now,' said Fossil, reassuringly, 'I'm getting to the part about the white rose badge. My German archivist friends have been most generous with their time and they believe your badge is a secret badge used by members of the "White Rose" group that started in Germany in June, 1942.'

'Never heard of them,' commented Hank.

'Few people have,' Bert responded, 'it's an inspiring but tragic story.'

Once again Bert found it necessary to polish his glasses before continuing. 'Three medical students at the Ludwig Maximilian University of Munich founded the White Rose movement. Their names were Hans Scholl, Willi Graf and Alexander Schmorrell. The three men had witnessed the atrocious treatment of Jewish people while they were doing their compulsory three-month military service on the Eastern front. The three men were horrified at what they saw and decided they must do something about it. Secretly, they started writing and distributing anti-Nazi leaflets urging passive resistance to the regime. Soon they were joined by other students, a professor of philosophy and a few people from outside the university. They produced six leaflets and were working on a seventh before they were caught. The small group mimeographed thousands of copies of their leaflets and smuggled them out to other universities in Stuttgart, Cologne, Bonn, Ulm, Vienna, Hamburg and Berlin. Some leaflets were even mailed to prominent members of the establishment. Many were left in phone booths for the public to see. They also began a graffiti campaign. In the dead of night members of White Rose crept out and painted slogans such as "FREEDOM" and "DOWN WITH HITLER" on prominent public buildings across Munich.'

'That would have taken a lot of guts,' remarked Belinda, 'what happened to them?'

'The Gestapo became increasingly alarmed. They couldn't work out who was behind these acts of treason. However, on February 18th 1943, eight months after the release of the first leaflet, three students were finally caught distributing them. They were arrested and put on trial for treason at a public "show trial" at the Volksgerichtshof, the peoples' court. Sentenced to death, they were guillotined four days later. Shortly afterwards a number of other students and the professor were also caught and subsequently executed or imprisoned.'

'Did their courageous defiance make much of a difference?' asked Hank.

'It's hard to know. Perhaps not immediately but their actions may well have helped start or inspire other resistance groups. We know their efforts were not entirely in vain because the New York Times reported on the "White Rose" saga in their papers. In Britain, the Nobel prize winner for literature, Thomas Mann, spoke about the White Rose in one of his anti-Nazi BBC radio broadcasts. Mann was actually German and his broadcasts were relayed, in German, to the German people every week. The sixth leaflet was successfully smuggled out to Britain and in July 1943 Allied aircraft dropped over 43,000 copies of this leaflet across parts of Germany.'

'Whew…it's quite a story,' exclaimed Belinda, 'but I don't see how this white rose story is connected to our suspected murderer.'

'I'm not sure, either,' admitted Bert, 'but it could be important. A white rose badge believed to have belonged to your suspect has been recovered. The other thing I noticed was that one of the universities where students managed to distribute the subversive leaflets was Bonn University. If I remember correctly, the suspect's passport showed Doctor Zeigler was born in, or near, Bonn. Perhaps that's the connection?'

'It's possible, I suppose,' replied Hank, somewhat doubtfully, 'Zeigler was certainly born near Bonn.'

'But why would Zeigler be carrying the badge of the White Rose Group around with him?' asked Belinda, 'does the group still exist today?'

'I very much doubt it,' answered Fossil, 'there's no need for anti-Nazi organisations these days.'

'Exactly,' echoed Hank, 'so why is a double murderer running around with a White Rose badge? The White Rose people, it seems, advocated non-violent passive resistance. That's not what Zeigler has shown us. In fact, his actions are the exact opposite!'

Belinda gave a little snigger.

'What are you laughing about?' queried Hank.

'I just had a funny thought,' replied Belinda, 'do you remember the Summers' front garden?'

Hank looked blank.

'It was full of one thing. Rows and rows of beautiful white roses. Don't you remember, Hank?'

'Yeah, I do remember. There was a whole lot of different varieties of white roses and nothing else.'

'That's right. Perhaps that white rose garden meant something too,' suggested Belinda. 'Maybe the Summers couple had something to do with the White Rose Group?'

Hank shrugged his shoulders, 'Could be, I suppose. Alternatively, it could be just a coincidence.'

'Well,' concluded Fossil, 'I hope I've at least given you something to think about.' And with that, Bert got up to leave and return to his nether regions. As he did so he placed the White Rose badge on Hank's desk.

☾

Belinda and Hank walked to the cafeteria for a hot chocolate and a chance to discuss Fossil's revelations. There had been no more sightings of the elusive Zeigler who must still be hiding out somewhere or possibly managed to leave the country. Since nothing else had materialised, Fossil's tenuous line of thinking was all they had to work on. Any time now Sandham would call them back to his office for another update and they would have precious little to tell him because their cupboard was bare.

They collected their hot chocolates and a Mars Bar each and sat in the corner where it was quiet. Belinda was the more positive of the pair.

'A white rose garden, a white rose badge, students at Bonn University who were members of the White Rose Group and Zeigler, born near Bonn who possessed a white rose badge. It's all got to be connected, surely?'

'I'm beginning to think you're right, Belinda. We've nothing else to work on so let's follow this white rose trail.'

Belinda flashed him a beautiful smile. She liked that sometimes she could influence Hank and even persuade him to accept her way of seeing things. It was another plus in her estimation of the handsome man sitting opposite her.

'I guess we start by finding out everything we can about Doctor Zeigler. How long did he live in Bonn? Did he study there? And the trickiest question of all, how was he caught up with the White Rose movement? It must have meant something significant to him if he owned and carried around a White Rose badge.'

'Yup, I agree with that,' replied Hank, as he tore the paper off his Mars Bar and took his first bite. The stickiness of the inside of the chocolate bar prevented him speaking for a moment, 'I guess we start by contacting the University in Bonn to find out if Zeigler gained his qualifications there.'

'One thing is worrying me,' added Belinda, 'the descriptions we have of Zeigler place him in his mid-thirties, no more. That means twenty years ago, in 1942, when White Rose became active, he would have only been a teenager fourteen or fifteen years old. Surely, he wasn't old enough to be involved with the White Rose movement? He was far more likely to have been a member of Hitler's Youth.'

'True,' agreed Hank, 'but don't count him out just because he was so young. Perhaps he had a brother who was at Bonn University and was a member of the White Rose? Or a sister? An uncle or an aunt? And, using a teenager to run messages or help distribute leaflets could have been a clever way to do things. The Gestapo would be less likely to suspect a young lad of treachery.'

Belinda nodded, 'Anyway, I think we have to talk with Sandham to get his approval for us to start probing Bonn University and the local authorities there.'

They didn't have to wait long. Chief Inspector Sandham summoned them half an hour later and agreed to their request to start digging in and around Bonn to find out more about Zeigler's past.

❦

After lunch Hank had a call from the police station at Shoreham-on-Sea, a small town not far from Rottingdean, the town where Zeigler had terrified Mrs Godfrey over the weekend. A boat owner in Shoreham had reported being threatened by a foreigner who had demanded he take him across the English Channel to France. It was only when the boat owner was able to convince the foreigner the engine in his boat was not functioning that he ran off, probably to try someone else. Sixty or seventy sea-worthy private boats were anchored at Shoreham, yachts, rowing boats and motor boats safely tied-up in the small sheltered harbour. Hank checked that the Shoreham police had despatched every available policeman to the harbourside to search for Zeigler and promised he'd be there in a couple of hours. Belinda declined to go with Hank this time because she was following up the Bonn situation.

The weather was changeable as Hank drove south. It was early September, the start of Autumn, so unstable conditions were to be expected. Fast moving westerlies brought a succession of brief showers scurrying across quickly followed by patches of blue sky. He felt more positive this time that his trip might culminate in the arrest of Doctor Zeigler who was clearly desperate to get over to Europe. It would be most interesting to hear what more this boat owner could tell him.

After first reporting at the Shoreham Police Station Hank drove to the home of Dan Phillips, the aggrieved boat owner who lived along the Shoreham Esplanade. The house was typical of so many sea-shore homes erected along the Sussex coast; double storey white, late 1920s with red brick chimneys, heaps of windows and a brightly painted front door. No problem parking. As he got out Hank pulled his coat closer around his body, the wind had a nasty bite to it.

The door was opened by an attractive young woman who made eyes at him and confirmed her dad was expecting him. She took him along the hallway decorated with a row of colourful flying china ducks and into a sitting room at the rear of the house overlooking the back garden.

'Inspector Hank Zagalski,' he announced. The pretty girl took another longing look at him and made herself comfortable on a high chair near her father's arm-chair, intent on being involved in the ensuing conversation. Dan Phillips introduced himself and his daughter, Jane, and offered Hank a strong weather-beaten hand. They shook. Dan looked the part of a fisherman, his face prematurely lined and creased by the elements and a sturdy build with a thick crop of sandy hair.

'Sit yerself down. Care for a wee drop of rum?'

'Sorry mate, not when I'm on duty. It's against the rules,' smiled Hank, apologetically.

'So, you're the detective lookin' into this case afore me?'

'That's right. Just a few questions, if you don't mind?'

'Fire away, detective.'

'Could you start by running through everything that happened this morning.'

'Well, Monday's me day off so I likes go down to see Betsy, that's the name of me boat. The engine's buggered and I'm waiting for me mate to come and 'ave a look at it. Once he's fixed it, we'll be sea-worthy again…'

Their conversation was interrupted by a buxom woman sailing in, unannounced, bearing a trayful of scones with a jar of strawberry jam and a bowl of what looked like real clotted cream. 'Ere you are love, get them into ya.' The good lady plonked the tray down in front of Hank and was gone as quickly as she'd arrived.'

'That's the missus,' offered Dan, with a casual wave of his arm, 'best bloody cook in Shoreham.'

The freshly baked scones were delicious and hungrily sampled by Jane too. Licking his fingers, Hank asked Dan to continue.

'Well, I were down below decks when I 'eard this voice from up there on the wharf, see. I wasn't sure at first if I'd 'eard right. Blow me down if this bloke wasn't offering me a hundred quid! "One hundred pounds, mister," he was saying and waving these bank notes about in the air. I thought at first, he wanted to buy me boat and was about to tell 'im to piss off 'cause Betsy's worth a lot more than a hundred smackers. Then this geyser says, "Go France, go France, go now." Now he was talking! A hundred pounds to take him o'er the channel sounded a good deal and I'd make a quid or two out of it and all, until I remembered me engine was bloody stuffed.'

'Did it occur to you that this man might be a criminal?'

'Nah not at the time. Anyhow, I tried to tell this geyser the engine's stuffed and apologised to 'im. Then he got all angry like and pulls a bloody great knife out of 'is jacket and starts waving it about like a banshee. He was threatening me! I thought he was going to jump on board and slash me up like a bloody pirate.'

'So, what did you do, dad?' asked the pretty daughter.

'I didn't do nothin' love, 'cause, just at that moment two other guys happened to come walkin' along the wharf towards us and this scared the crap out of 'im. He stuck the knife and money back in 'is jacket and scarpered like a bloody scared rabbit. Could 'ave been nasty though, bloody nasty!'

'Did you get a good look at him?' Hank asked.

'Too bloody right. He looked scrawny, probably a week's worth of beard, 'is clothes dirty and he had a desperate look about 'im, and all. A nasty bit of work, I reckon.'

'Can you describe his stature? Tall, thin?'

Dan grabbed another scone, which he generously layered with jam and cream, as he gave this question some serious thought. 'Without 'is knife, I'd beat 'im up quick smart. Average height I reckon, average weight. He was a good deal younger than me. I turned fifty last month. This geyser would be in 'is thirties. Now, here's the thing… this bloke was a bloody German! I fought the buggers so I reckon I can pick a German accent when I 'ear one.'

'Dan, you've been a terrific help. Thanks for your cooperation. I'm pretty sure the guy you tangled with is Doctor Zeigler, a suspected double murderer.'

'You bloody kiddin' me, officer?'

'I'm almost one hundred percent certain… One last question Dan, where do you think he was headed after he left you?'

'Probably going to try it on with some other poor bugger.'

'Do you remember who else was down at the wharf with their boat at the time Zeigler approached you?'

'Cor blimey, now yer asking a difficult one. I was down inside me boat see, mindin' me own bloody business.'

'Think hard please Dan. It's possible Zeigler's already escaped and is over in France by now. He's a wanted man!'

You could almost hear Dan's synapses stretching out desperately as he tried to recall if anyone else was down on the wharf at the same time. At last, a light came on.

'Oh yes, I remember now. There was another geezer further along the wharf probably about anchorage fifteen. It was old Dougie. He's about bloody eighty years old but still owns a small motor boat. He's as deaf as a post and half blind into the bargain,' he laughed. 'You wouldn't want to rely on old Dougie to get you across to France, he'd probably go round and round in bloody circles.' The thought of taking such a crazy trip with Dougie brought on a series of chuckles from Dan.

'Do you know the name of Dougie's boat, Dan?'

'No problem there, officer, everyone knows 'is boat's name. Apparently, Dougie never married so he called 'is boat, "The Sea Virgin."'

'Dan, do you mind if we go down to the wharf together to check you're right? I need to know what's happened to Dougie, his boat and the suspect.'

'No problem, Governor. I'll get me coat.'

Ten minutes later Dan and Hank walked briskly along the wharf towards anchorage fifteen. There was no sign of old Dougie, Zeigler or "The Sea Virgin."

17. Tuesday, 3rd September

As soon as Hank returned to his car, he made several calls to alert police and the English Coast Guard that Zeigler was making a dash for France in a small motor boat called "The Sea Virgin." He also arranged for the French authorities to be notified. It was impossible to predict where the boat was likely to land since this depended on weather conditions and the tides as well as the sea worthiness of the small vessel. Leaving from Southend meant the boat faced a journey of some forty miles across the busiest shipping route in the world. A tiny boat like "The Sea Virgin" wouldn't stand a chance if it sailed in the way of a large ship. Furthermore, it was not known whether the boat had sufficient fuel to make the trip. If "The Sea Virgin" ran out of petrol or the engine broke down, the boat could wash ashore anywhere along the French coast between Calais and Le Havre.

Concerned for the safety of the two men bobbing about in the middle of the English Channel, or La Manche as the French called it, Hank decided to stay in Southend. He dropped Dan off at his home and drove on to the Shoreham Police Station to await news. No sightings were reported throughout the remainder of the day so he booked a room at a small hotel for the night. Next morning, there was still no news. Hank comforted himself by thinking that no news was good news. Somehow "The Sea Virgin" must have made it across to France and the men were safe. No doubt Zeigler was already hitch-hiking his way back to Germany by now. Goodness knows what shape the elderly Dougie was in after such an unplanned and frightening ordeal.

Around lunchtime reports started coming in from the French authorities. "The Sea Virgin" had safely come ashore on a small isolated beach twenty miles north of Dieppe sometime during the night. There had been enough moonlight for Zeigler to climb the low sand hills and race off into the dark. Dougie, totally exhausted by his terrifying journey, was too weak to leave his precious boat and stayed there for the rest of the night. Shortly after dawn, a young French couple doing their usual fitness run along the beach spotted Dougie and "The Sea Virgin" and came to investigate. The old man stubbornly refused to leave his boat until much later in the morning when two English-speaking police arrived. The police promised to look after his boat and to make arrangements for it to be transported back to Shoreham. Only then did Dougie agree to be driven to a hospital in Dieppe for a medical check-up and a good feed.

There was nothing more Hank could do in Shoreham, although he rang Dan to give him the good news that Dougie was safe. After a quick bite to eat he drove back to Petworth. It was intensely annoying that Zeigler had managed to escape the country. It would be far more difficult to apprehend him now that he was back in the vastness of Europe. Perhaps, Hank thought, he had better start learning some basic German.

❨

While Hank was away in Shoreham, Belinda had started investigating the Zeigler family, thought to be residing in or around Bonn and it wasn't long before she discovered a promising group of Zeiglers living in a small town called Stieldorf, situated some seven miles east of Bonn. The German telephone directory for North Rhine in Westphalia listed three Zeigler telephone numbers. Not being competent in the German language, Belinda was not prepared to ring these numbers herself. Instead, she contacted Scotland Yard who had a number of police on call who were conversant with one or more European languages. This was a service provided by Scotland Yard Belinda had not used before and she was impressed when she was put straight through to a German speaking detective by the name of Marjorie Williams.

'Good morning, Inspector Marjorie Williams speaking.'

'Oh…good morning, this is Sergeant Belinda Purcell CID ringing you from Petworth in Sussex.'

'Lucky you, I know the place well, a lovely little town.'

'I guess so, although I've only been based here for three weeks.'

'How can I help you Belinda?'

'I'm working on the double murder case of the Summers couple who lived in the nearby village of Upper Bybridge.'

'Yes, I remember reading reports about the case. It happened a bit over a week ago if I recall correctly?'

'You're right. The main suspect is a Doctor Heinrich Zeigler, who yesterday made it across the channel to France in a boat he had forcibly purloined. We're pretty sure Zeigler comes from near Bonn in Germany. We think he may have graduated with a degree in Economics from Bonn University and then, after gaining higher academic qualifications, was appointed a senior lecturer in the Faculty of Law and Economics at the same university. We know he was born on November 7th, 1930, which makes him only thirty-one. The murders were particularly vicious. What we cannot fathom out is why he committed these murders. What motivated him? If we can learn more about his family and his family's background it could be helpful.'

'I've also been to Bonn. A nice city, until we bombed it to pieces.'

'I have three phone numbers for Zeiglers living in a small town called Stieldorf, near Bonn. My German, sadly, is non-existent so it would be useless for me to try to contact them. Could you do this for me please, Marjorie?'

'That's what I'm paid to do Belinda as well as a hundred and one other things. I take it this is urgent?'

'Yes, it is.'

'Right, then you must hot-foot it up here to Scotland Yard and we'll do this together. I need to know every detail you can give me about this case before I ring anyone. When can you get here?'

'A couple of hours, depending on the traffic.'

'You had better stay overnight then,'

'Okay, can you recommend somewhere?'

'If you're prepared to come out with me tonight, eat tons of sauerkraut, drink German beer and gobble up some delicious Black Forest cake, you can stay at my place for the night.'

'That's very generous of you.'

They arranged to meet at three o'clock in Inspector Marjorie Williams' office on floor three.

❧

Bert Pallister had done such a magnificent job of researching the likely origins of the white rose badge, Belinda and Hank had no hesitation in giving him another research project. This time they wanted to know more about the background of Rolf Summers. Rolf had let it be known he had spent the whole of the war incarcerated in an internment camp for enemy aliens on the Isle of Man. At war's end he, along with other aliens, had been released and Rolf moved to Reading where he met and married Doreen. Rolf had been adamant he had come to the United Kingdom before the outbreak of hostilities and was none too pleased when war was declared and he was arrested and interned. Nobody, including his wife, had any reason to doubt his version of events. Detectives however, are trained to be curious and not accept everything they are told without checking and, if necessary, re-checking the facts. A more comprehensive understanding of Rolf's past might shed light on Zeigler's motivation for murder.

Assigned his new project, Fossil wasted no time contacting a police colleague working on the Isle of Man with access to the lists of interns held on the island throughout the duration of World

War II. A couple of hours later his mate rang him back with the intriguing news that there was no record of a "Rolf Summers" ever being held on the Isle of Man at any stage during the war. Perhaps, Bert's colleague suggested, Rolf Summers was a newly acquired name legally adopted after the war. A new name for a fresh start as it were. Fossil immediately contacted the office in London responsible for keeping the official records of those who had applied for legal name changes between the years 1940 to 1950. Did the office have any record of someone applying to become known as Rolf Summers? The answer came back an hour or so later in the negative. Rolf Summers had lied.

Fossil decided he had better check out other internment camps in the United Kingdom and overseas, just in case Rolf had been sent elsewhere and his file had gone with him. Nearly 80,000 people living in the United Kingdom at the start of World War II were of German or Austrian nationality and deemed "enemy aliens." It was feared these people's loyalties lay with Hitler and the Nazis. Some could even be spies, others were likely to assist Hitler if, and when, Hitler invaded. Within a few weeks all enemy aliens were arrested, imprisoned and made to appear before specially convened tribunals. Here they were categorised as being level "A," "B" or "C". Category "A" aliens were considered highly dangerous and immediately interned. Category "B" aliens were suspects and had to report to the local authorities once a week. Category "C" aliens were assessed as being "friendly" and could resume their normal lives.

Fossil was familiar with this recent history because he had investigated other "enemy aliens." Many caught up in this process felt mis-treated and had ended up turning anti-British. Resentment was strongest amongst the German Jewish who had escaped to Britain fearing Nazi persecution and had consequently been rounded up and sent to internment camps as "suspicious" Germans. There were so many interns the British Government decided to ship some of them off to Canada and Australia.

In June 1940 the first ship load of 1600 category "A" interns were put aboard the Arandora Star headed for Canada. Tragically, the ship was sunk mid-ocean by a German U-boat with only approximately half the passengers and crew being rescued. The survivors were promptly re-assigned to "The Dunera", a ship bound for Sydney, Australia. On arrival these well-travelled interns were despatched to a new camp established in Hay (New South Wales) with a few going to Orange (NSW) and the remainder to Tatura Camp (Victoria). Fossil provided the name "Rolf Summers" to the authorities in the Home Office who advised him they would get back to him the next day.

18.   Wednesday, 4th September

Belinda had a thoroughly enjoyable evening with Marjorie Williams. Marjorie had recently been through long and unpleasant divorce proceedings so was glad to have someone new on whom to off-load. In return, Belinda regaled Marjorie with every possible detail about Zeigler and the Summers murders. When they surfaced on Wednesday morning, slightly the worse for wear from a beery evening, they felt they had known each other for years. The pair arrived at Scotland Yard shortly after nine o'clock keen to explore the three Zeigler telephone numbers in Stieldorf that Fossil had unearthed. Marjorie had studied German at University and a framed certificate displayed in her office proclaimed she had been awarded first class honours in Germanic Studies from the University of London.

Marjorie set-up her desk the way she wanted it. She would use ear-phones. Any conversations would be recorded and she had pen and paper ready. Belinda was instructed to sit next to her and remain silent unless spoken to. Marjorie explained she may need to stop the telephone conversations sometimes to ask her for further clarification. Before trying the first number Marjorie warned her new friend that, on average, only one in three phone calls were answered first time. In other words, be patient, very patient… they could be there all day!

According to Marjorie, Zeigler was not a common family name in Germany like Smith, Jones, Cook or Brown in England. This could be helpful she claimed. The fact there were three Zeigler phone numbers in Stieldorf, a town of less than seven thousand inhabitants, augured well. Chances were these three Zeiglers were in some way related. Fortified by a strong cup of Earl Grey tea and a cigarette, Marjorie called up European long-distance trunk calls and assured the operator Scotland Yard would pay for the three calls to Germany. Belinda did her best to stay out of the cigarette smoke that curled relentlessly around her like some kind of misty apparition and resolved to stay silent and patient. They were, as it happened, in luck. At the first attempt Marjorie's phone call was answered by an elderly woman. The old lady and Marjorie quickly bonded and enjoyed a twenty-minute amicable conversation, not one word of which Belinda could understand. Marjorie frantically scribbled down a string of strange German words on her writing pad while she conversed.

The call over, Marjorie stubbed her cigarette out several times with her nicotine-stained thumb as if the butt needed a few goes to squash the last bit of life out of it. 'Excellent,' she exclaimed, 'that was a great start. They're all related and I can just about draw up the Zeigler family tree for you.'

'Is Doctor Heinrich Zeigler part of the family tree?'

'He sure is. Let me get a clean page and I'll have a go at drawing the tree for you.'

This Marjorie did but then paused for a couple of minutes while she went through the routine of lighting up another cigarette. Then, feeling more composed, she placed the fresh cigarette on the lip of the already full ashtray and wrote "Zeigler's Family Tree" at the top of the clean page.

'Okay, here we go,' exclaimed Marjorie, full of enthusiasm, 'that lady I was talking to was die grobmutter.'

'Die what?'

'Die grobmutter...oh sorry, the grandmother. She's Doctor Heinrich Zeigler's grandmother.'

'That's fantastic! What did she tell you?'

Marjorie flicked back through her note-book to where she had first started scribbling. She inhaled deeply then launched into a summary of their conversation.

'Die grobmutter Zeigler is now a widow, lonely I suspect, because she really welcomed having someone to talk to for twenty minutes. She and der grobvater Zeigler, that's grandpa Zeigler, had two children. She was more than happy to talk about them. Die dochter's name is Hilda and she's still alive and living with her husband in Stieldorf. The younger child was Fritz Zeigler. He married at the start of the war a lady by the name of Fraulein Von Mark who came from Bonn. These two were academics working during the war at the University of Bonn. Fritz was a senior lecturer in philosophy and der chefrau…'

'Hang on,' interrupted Belinda, 'der…what?'

'Oops, sorry, I can't help dropping back into German sometimes. Der chefrau means the wife. As I said before Fritz was a philosopher and der chefrau an historian. Die grobmutter reckoned they were both really brainy.'

'How come Fritz wasn't serving in the German forces?'

'I asked die grobmutter about that. Apparently, Fritz had always been a sickly child, he suffered from severe asthma. As an adult it was still so bad the poor man could only walk a few steps at a time before he started to get breathless. Anyway, the army didn't want him.'

'Lucky for him, he would probably have been killed in the war anyway,' commented Belinda.

'Well, he *was* killed and his wife Hildegard was also killed.'

'Really! How? Were they bombed?'

'No, not according to die grobmutter. She became all cagey about how they had actually died and I didn't feel comfortable pushing it too hard because Fritz was her only son and she had sadly lost her daughter-in-law as well.'

'It seems strange, doesn't it? They both died in the war but not from being on active service or from the bombings. So, what the devil happened to them? Oh God! Don't tell me they were Jewish?'

'That was one question I felt I could legitimately ask her. Die grobmutter insisted there were no Jews in her family and never had been.'

'So, their deaths remain a mystery. What else did she tell you?' urged Belinda.

'Here's the most exciting bit! Fritz and Hildegard had a child. His name was Heinrich Gustav Zeigler. Surely, it's got to be the person you're looking for?'

'Wow, that's just amazing! Now we've been able to track down Heinrich's family and get some background. Did you ask the grandmother anything about Heinrich?'

'Sure did,' Marjorie replied, as she inhaled deeply allowing the chemicals to do maximum damage. 'She was very proud of der enklesohn. Heinrich was only fourteen when his parents died and for a long time was really angry and bitter about it. At one stage he was suicidal and the family who rallied around to care for him were desperately concerned. However, Heinrich met Greta, a beautiful girl when he was sixteen and it was Greta who brought him out of his despair. She was an absolute tonic, it seems. They fell in love and Heinrich recovered and began to live a normal life again. He resumed his school studies, qualified for university and four years later graduated with first class honours and even won a university prize. Apparently, he had inherited his parents' brains. From then on there was no looking back. Heinrich excelled in his advanced studies and became a lecturer at Bonn University, the same place his parents had worked at. Like his parents he now has a PhD; not in Philosophy or History but in Economics.'

'Did you ask the grandmother if she knows where Heinrich is staying?'

'I did. She said Heinrich had been given overseas study leave but she didn't know where. A little time back she received a post card from him from somewhere in England. That's all she could tell me.'

'Did she say when Heinrich was coming back to Stieldorf?'

Marjorie shook her head and at the same time thumbed back through her notes to check whether she had missed anything.

'Ah…a couple of important things I missed…the other two Zeigler phone numbers in Stieldorf. One actually belongs to Heinrich and his wife, Greta. The other number is der onkel and die tante.'

'Okay, let me get this straight,' bubbled an excited Belinda, 'you mean the uncle and aunt?'

'That's right, Hilda and her husband, Carl. Hilda, you remember was Fritz's older sister.'

'Got it. Now we have to ring the other two numbers in Stieldorf, Heinrich's own number and his aunt and uncle's place. Let's do it straightaway.'

'Hang on a second,' advised Marjorie, 'let's think strategically for a moment or two before we blow our cover.'

'How do you mean?'

'Die grobmutter was very friendly and amenable over the phone but now she must be wondering why on earth she had a long-distance phone call from England. She's probably in her eighties and a bit slow on the uptake. Very likely she doesn't have a clue what Scotland Yard is. If she'd known we were the police she might have behaved far more guardedly and become worried about her grandson. At present I don't think she suspects there's anything amiss with regard to her grandson, Heinrich. She certainly doesn't know he's wanted for questioning on murder charges.'

'That makes sense,' replied Belinda.

'When we try ringing the other two numbers, how do we best handle it? As soon as these younger members of the family receive a call from Scotland Yard they're going to be mighty concerned. Why are the British police ringing us? Something must have happened to Heinrich? Is he sick or injured? Is he lost? Bankrupt? British police wouldn't be ringing unless there's a problem.'

'I see what you mean, Marjorie. Softly, softly is the approach we need to take.'

'Exactly.'

'Whatever we say we mustn't let slip we are investigating a double murder.'

'Right again. I suggest I fabricate a story about Heinrich being admitted to a hospital in England, a car accident perhaps and use this as a pretext to gather more information. I've had to do things like this before. I know, strictly speaking, it's not being quite honest but I think it's necessary. Are you happy for me to work along those lines, Belinda?'

Belinda nodded, 'Yes, that sounds the right way to proceed. It's not really a lie because Heinrich did have a car accident and was taken to hospital. He discharged himself before we could get to him. Okay, which number shall we try next?'

'Definitely, die tante and der onkel,' replied Melissa, 'but not until I have another fag on the go.' She rummaged around in her handbag and happily procured another packet of Players.

They rang the second Stieldorf telephone number but there was no answer. Half an hour later they tried again. Still nothing. They tried several more times during the day without success. Very likely they concluded, the uncle and aunt were working full time and wouldn't be home until late in the evening. Melissa invited Belinda to stay a second night and they decided to stay home for dinner and telephone later in the evening. Once more the call was unsuccessful.

☾

During the morning Hank received news that the elderly Dougie of "Sea Virgin" fame was being flown back to Gatwick and would be arriving at fourteen twenty-two hours aboard British European Airways flight 46 from Paris. The message stressed Dougie was in a "confused state" and requested police and a medical person be at the airport to meet him. There was no news yet about the return of his boat "The Sea Virgin."

Hank was keen to meet up with Dougie. The pirate-like theft of his small motor boat and the forced enslavement of the old man to crew Zeigler across to France were additional crimes to add to the ever-growing list of misdemeanours committed by the infamous Doctor Heinrich Zeigler. Like all crimes this had to be professionally investigated, the facts recorded and reports written. At this rate Zeigler was keeping both him and Belinda fully employed. Hank left for Gatwick in good time, parked in one of the spaces reserved for police and sauntered into the "Arrivals" part of the airport. He had twenty minutes to spare so he grabbed a coffee and sat down to wait at the designated gate. A flight coming in from Paris was likely to be full with as many as 350 passengers disembarking. He would need to keep his eyes skinned for elderly men, one of whom would be the unfortunate Dougie.

While enjoying his coffee he was approached by a Saint John's Ambulance employee who had also been sent to meet up with Dougie. They sat and chatted for a few minutes until the flight arrivals sign flashed. BEA 46 had safely landed. The Saint John's Ambulance fellow reckoned Dougie would be last off the plane because they would bring him off in a wheel chair. He was right. Fifteen minutes later a wheel-chair finally emerged from the corridor bearing a tired looking old man and being pushed by one of the air crew. After handshakes all round Hank stood back to allow the Saint John's fellow to do his medical checks unimpeded.

'He's okay,' the ambulance man announced, 'poor bugger's exhausted and still in a bit of shock. I can't find anything physically wrong and his heart and blood pressure are not too bad. How's he going to get back to Shoreham from here?'

'I'll drive him down. It will give me plenty of time to question him about what he's been through,' Hank replied. With that, he took hold of Dougie's wheelchair and headed for his car.

☾

It took the best part of two hours to get back to Shoreham-by-the-Sea with a stop along the way for refreshments. After a coffee and a feed of hot chips Dougie sparked up noticeably and opened up about his frightening experiences with Zeigler.

It turned out Dougie had recently become an octogenarian but his age and general infirmness were not enough to stop him going down to the docks to check on "The Sea Virgin" at least twice a week. He did so, he admitted, against his wife's wishes. He seldom took the boat out to sea, preferring instead to potter about within the sheltered harbour walls. Visiting his boat was, he told Hank with a mischievous wink, a chance to get away from the "missus" for a couple of hours of peace and quiet.

Dougie explained he was just about to leave the harbour when this joker came rushing along the wharf brandishing a knife with a wild look in his eyes. Dougie said he recognised a desperate man when he saw one and quickly agreed to take him across to the French coast. It wasn't until he was leaving the safety of the harbour that he began to worry about fuel. He needed a full tank to get across the ditch and his gauge was only showing about 90%. He knew it was going to be touch and go. As for his unwelcome passenger, he just sat in the tiny cabin smoking like a chimney.

Dougie went on to say they were fortunate the conditions were perfect; no wind or nasty currents and they managed to dodge the monstrous vessels moving through the channel. Before dark they beached on a sandy spot, seemingly deserted. Zeigler helped Dougie haul the boat out of the water then surprised him by giving him a twenty-pound note. This done, the stranger abruptly left. The last Dougie saw of him he was disappearing over the sand-hills carrying his back-pack. The petrol tank was virtually on zero and Dougie said he was simply too tired and weak to leave his boat. He spent a cold hungry night trying to sleep in horribly cramped conditions. Early next morning a young French couple came running along the beach and found him.

Hank tried to find out more about Zeigler. What was he like? His appearance? Any obvious peculiarities?

Dougie was not particularly forthcoming. 'I didn't spend much time looking at him,' he confessed. 'He scared the shit out of me. I was frightened that if I upset him, he'd turf me overboard.'

'Fair enough,' Hank conceded.

'The fellow looked like he'd been sleeping rough and I don't reckon he'd had a bath for weeks. There was a nasty smell about him like a pile of dead fish. You wouldn't expect that from a married bloke now, would you?'

'How did you know he was married?'

'He had a ring on.'

'Dougie when we catch this bugger, he'll be tried for umpteen crimes. Would you be prepared to be a witness?'

'Aw…I'm getting a bit long in the tooth for that sort of caper. I just want my boat back safe and sound with a full tank of petrol.'

'Well, if I guarantee to get your boat back safe and sound with a full tank of fuel and, in addition, we treat you like royalty at the trial, would you be in it?'

'Guess so if I'm still alive and kicking.'

Satisfied he had extracted all he could from the elderly seafarer, Hank dropped Dougie back with "the missus" and headed back to Petworth and more report writing.

19. Thursday, 5ᵗʰ September

Belinda and Marjorie spent another pleasant evening together, staying indoors this time and savouring Marjorie's home cooking. They left ridiculously early next morning to make calls to Germany before breakfast in the hope of contacting the Zeigler families before they left for work. The ploy worked and they had instant success. The first call lasted about ten minutes. The person at the other end was Frau Greta Ziegler, Heinrich's wife who fortunately spoke excellent English.

Marjorie introduced herself as a policewoman and then calmed Greta down because, quite naturally, she immediately thought something terrible must have befallen her husband.

'I do apologise for ringing you so early Frau Zeigler but I'm anxious to catch you before you go out for the day.'

'That's all right I'm an early riser anyway.'

'You speak remarkably good English, Frau Zeigler.'

'I'm glad you think so. I spent my early teenage years in a private school in the south of England.'

'That's interesting. May I ask where?'

'Roedean Anglican school for girls.'

'Really, that's a famous school.'

'I know. When the war broke out, my father was worried about what might happen in Germany so he enrolled me there. I was at Roedean until I did my "O" levels. Then my father brought me back home to Bonn.'

'Did you meet Heinrich then?'

'Of course. We were both sixteen and at the same school. Now, before I go on, I think you owe me a bit more of an explanation. Scotland Yard doesn't go ringing people out of the blue unless there's a very good reason. Why are you ringing? Is it about my husband, Heinrich?'

'Yes, it is. Apparently, there was an anomaly on his passport and we have been asked to double-check the passport details,' lied Marjorie, pleased to have concocted a reasonably plausible excuse for calling.'

'I find that hard to believe. He has never before had any problems with his passport and he often goes to other countries in connection with his work as an academic. Surely you could have asked Heinrich, couldn't you?'

'True but we can never be too careful Frau Zeigler,' replied Marjorie, 'could you confirm for me where Heinrich was going in the United Kingdom, please?'

'Oh, I don't know… I think he said he had three conferences to go to and was planning to spend a couple of days doing research.'

'Can you be more specific than that?'

'No, I can't, sorry.'

'Do you have a date for Heinrich's return?'

'This weekend sometime. I can't remember exactly when his flight gets in. We're close to the airport here and he just jumps in a taxi which saves me having to go to pick him up.'

'Would you mind checking his arrival date and time please so we know precisely when he is due to arrive?'

'All right. Wait a moment while I check on the calendar.'

Marjorie and Belinda exchanged positive, confident looks.

'Hello, are you there?' Greta's voice.

'Yes, I'm here.'

'Heinrich was supposed to get back a few days ago but then he rang to say he'd been delayed a few days.'

'Did he give you a new time for his return?'

'No he didn't. He said he still had to make his flight bookings. It's not like him to be so vague. I suppose he could breeze in any day now.'

"Do you know where he's flying from?'

'Gatwick, I presume.'

'Frau Ziegler, there is something else the police are interested in. Do you know, by any chance, know what happened to Heinrich's parents?'

'Funny you should ask that because Heinrich never mentions them. All I know is they were killed during the war. Heinrich was about fourteen when it happened. Is this the real reason why you're ringing me?'

'Partly, yes. One final question please. Have you ever seen a small badge belonging to Heinrich that is shiny black with three white roses on the surface?'

'Yes, I've seen it in his desk drawer. Why?'

'Do you know what it represents?'

'Heinrich has never talked to me about it. I've asked him a couple of times but he wouldn't tell me. My guess is the badge is some kind of a nostalgic memory associated with his parents.'

'Is the badge still in his desk drawer?'

'Wait a second and I'll have a look for you.'

A moment later Greta returned. 'He must have taken the badge with him. It's not in his drawer.'

'Frau Ziegler you have been a great help, thank you so much. Have a good day...'

With the call ended the two detectives knew exactly what had to be done next. Within the hour Scotland Yard's senior staff had contacted the German police in Bonn to inform them Doctor Heinrich Zeigler was expected to return home very soon and should be regarded as highly dangerous. He was to be arrested immediately for the suspected murder of two British citizens. The German police were concerned the precise travel details were not forthcoming, since it was not even known whether Zeigler planned to fly into Bonn or choose another mode of transport. Perhaps the best strategy, the German police were advised, would be to watch Zeigler's house day and night and make the arrest there.

❦

Hank was sitting in his office typing up a report with two fingers and feeling the pain in his right leg. Last night at rugby training he had somehow turned an ankle. The ankle was swollen and he wondered whether he may have chipped a bone or torn a tendon. Worse still, Belinda was not around to give him any sympathy. There really did seem to be some truth in the old saying that absence makes the heart grow fonder. He was definitely missing Belinda who had now been up in London for two nights. He had been speaking to her over the phone a few minutes before and was delighted to hear how successful she and her colleague had been in contacting the Zeigler family in Stieldorf. Hopefully, even more would come from these contacts. Here in Petworth, Hank was feeling frustrated because he had not heard anything more about the whereabouts of Doctor Heinrich Zeigler who seemed able to go to ground so easily. Hank was annoyed he was not contributing much to his capture.

Hank was re-reading the final two paragraphs of the police report he had been working on when he heard a familiar smoker's cough outside his office and a moment later the substantial figure of his boss appeared at the door. Chief Inspector Nigel Sandham wheezed his way into Hank's office and with a sigh of relief plonked himself down on the vacant chair There he sat for a couple of moments getting his breath back and his thoughts in order. Then he reached into his top pocket to pull out a packet of Players, but realising he was in someone else's office, thought better of it and reluctantly shoved the packet back where it had come from.

'I have two pieces of information for you, one important, the other not.'

'Fire away, sir.'

'The unimportant one first…I'm being retired on medical grounds. I've been officially declared, "unfit for duty."'

Hank and everyone else at Petworth Police Station had anticipated this might happen for many months but it still came as a shock to actually hear the news.

'I'm sorry to hear that, sir.'

'Apparently, I'm in a bad way. Bloody emphysema. It's choking up my lungs. Doctors reckon I might only have a year or two.'

'It's serious then?'

'Too bloody right. I saw the Police Commissioner yesterday and he gave me my marching orders. My last day at work will be Friday next week. Would you believe it? Bloody Friday the thirteenth!'

Hank allowed himself a slight smile. Personally, he didn't go along with the silly superstitious nonsense some folk espoused. Walking under ladders brought bad luck, black cats running across your path ensured good luck, putting an umbrella up indoors encouraged wet weather. It was all a load of codswallop as far as Hank was concerned. Since Sandham was his boss, however, he was prepared to humour him.

'We'll have to have a bit of a farewell shindig for you, sir.'

'I've made it to sixty-two, but won't get to retirement age. Nevertheless, I'll get some kind of an invalid pension. That'll please the missus. Now, let me tell you the important news.'

Hank lent back in his chair and drummed his fingers impatiently on the side of his desk while he waited for another coughing episode to subside.

'The Bonn police have just been in touch. They had a message from Scotland Yard this morning warning them that Zeigler was expected home very soon. Well, it seems he's already back there. The police have moved fast and they reckon they're closing in on him. According to the German chief inspector who spoke to me, Zeigler returned to Bonn University earlier today where he's been working as a senior lecturer for a few years.'

'Why didn't they arrest him there?'

'He gave them the slip.'

'Bugger! Did his academic colleagues know he was wanted by the police?'

'Apparently not. The police are now working on the belief Zeigler has abducted a female student. When the police questioned the academics with whom Ziegler works, they claimed he was madly in love with a second-year Economics student, who was equally infatuated with him. The pair were last seen driving away from the university campus together in a white Volkswagen.'

'But Zeigler's married!'

'What's new? This is not the first time a bloke has abducted a young woman and it won't be the last.' The strain of talking so much brought on another round of barely controlled coughing.

'Do the police know where they've gone?'

'It seems not...'

'They're bloody useless! I thought the German police were supposed to be ultra-efficient. Somehow, they've let a double murderer slip through their fingers.'

Sandham shrugged his massive shoulders, 'Calm down Hank I'm sure they'll locate a white VW easily enough. Give them time. As the officer in charge of the investigation, you had better get yourself ready to fly to Bonn at a moment's notice. Contact Belinda, fill her in and tell her to get back here pronto so she can fly out with you.'

'Happy to do that, sir.'

The Chief Inspector struggled to his feet, pulled out his packet of cigarettes and lumbered back down the corridor to his own retreat.

☾

At the same time as Chief Inspector Sandham was visiting Hank, up in Scotland Yard Inspector Marjorie Williams and Belinda finally managed to get through to the third Zeigler on their list. The person who answered did not speak English so Marjorie conducted the interview entirely in German, while Belinda sat next to her feeling less than useless. The conversation was a lengthy one and at times tense. When Marjorie eventually replaced the receiver, she was clearly excited about what had transpired.

'Whew, that was a really interesting call. I was speaking to Doctor Zeigler's uncle and he was very open with me. He had no idea his neffe, sorry, nephew is wanted for murder or he would have clammed up.'

'Tell me more…' urged Belinda.

'This uncle's name is Carl. He's proud of his nephew Heinrich who he described as highly intelligent, gifted, hardworking and a good husband. Carl would have been absolutely devastated if he had known the real reason why we were ringing him.'

'Go on…'

'According to Carl, his brother Fritz and his sister-in-law, Hildegard, Heinrich's parents, were both murdered by the Nazis in 1943.'

'Murdered! Why?'

'They were leaders in a resistance movement working against the Nazis. Even today few people know about this but there were small groups of people who were totally opposed to Nazism and dared to do something about it. The resistance movement started in German universities…'

'Interesting. I think I've heard about this resistance movement once before.'

'Well, Heinrich Zeigler's parents were part of this resistance movement but they were caught. Four days later they were executed for treason. Guillotined, would you believe! According to Carl, young Heinrich who was fourteen when his parents were executed, was traumatised. At the time, he completely fell apart and even attempted suicide. They were a tight-knit family. Carl and his wife Hilda stepped in and looked after Heinrich. They took him in and tried their best to be substitute parents. After a year or so Heinrich suddenly turned a corner, returned to school and began working obsessively at his studies. Carl and his wife were thrilled. Heinrich, it seemed, had finally found a way of dealing with the hatred and anger that had been boiling up inside him like molten lava for eighteen months since his parents died. He did well in his studies, went on to university and never looked back. Carl doesn't know for sure how Heinrich managed to get over his anger and depression but thinks it was after meeting the lovely Greta at school when he was about sixteen.

'Fascinating, but how does this relate to the double-murder?' asked Belinda.

'I have no idea.'

'Perhaps the Summers couple was involved somehow with Heinrich's parents? Perhaps they had something to do with their capture and subsequent trial? We still need to find out more about them,' Belinda added.

'That sounds like a good line of inquiry. Now, there's one other thing that Carl told me that will interest you. The resistance movement had a secret name. It was called, "The White Rose."'

'Really! That might explain a couple of things. Ziegler's badge had three white roses on it, the Summers' garden was full of white roses. There's still a big part of this puzzle missing though. How was the Summers couple caught up in this story? I wish we knew…'

'Sorry Belinda, I can't help you with that.'

20. Friday, 6th September

nspector Hank Zagalski rolled out of bed at seven. His ankle was still sore so a morning run was clearly not a possibility. This lack of physical exercise annoyed him intensely since he was the kind of person who needed to get rid of excess energy on a daily basis. A work-out in the gym, a five-mile run or a half hour of swimming laps in the pool were all acceptable ways of exercising and re-charging his batteries. This was the second day his ankle injury had been too painful for normal activities. For a moment he pondered whether there was something more than just a sprain and whether he should perhaps arrange to see a doctor. Not one to whinge about aches and pains Hank decided against seeing a medical person, time was nearly always the great healer. After every rugby match, he came away with bruises and sore muscles but these ailments nearly always resolved themselves before the next Saturday's game.

The thought that Belinda would be back in the office this morning cheered him up. Belinda had completed a first-aid course recently so he would let her have a look at his ankle. He valued her opinion and a little bit of her feminine touch and charms would not go amiss. He showered, dressed and went to the kitchen where he chopped up a tomato and an onion and threw them into the frying pan along with a tin of Heinz's curried baked beans. Stirring it up he served the tasty mix on top of two pieces of buttered toast and washed it down with a large glass of pure orange juice. Still peckish, he added another slice of toast with a generous spread of chunky marmalade.

Belinda had rung yesterday excited about the success of her phone calls to the Zeiglers in Germany. She had decided to stay one more night in London to make a final call to Bonn in the early morning and take in a show in the Westend with her Scotland Yard colleague, Marjorie Williams. They were going to see Agatha Christie's newest play, "The Mouse-Trap." Hank wished he was there with Belinda.

As Hank limped into the police station he was joined by their elderly police archivist, Bert Pallister. He refrained from calling him "Fossil" which Hank felt was both unkind and disrespectful. Bert had devoted his life to fighting crime and had already come up with some valuable information for Belinda and himself. Bert had a twinkle in his eye this morning and assured Hank he was "on to something" in relation to the Summers couple. If his police contacts in Germany turned up trumps, he hoped to give Hank and Belinda more details about Rolf and Doreen Summers later in the morning.

ℭ

Belinda drove into the Petworth Police Station's car park mid-morning. The first thing she did was head to Hank's office where she greeted him with one of her stunning film-star smiles. A few minutes later he had his painful foot in her lap while she gently rolled down his sock. Belinda was quick to remind him she had no formal medical qualifications and he shouldn't rely on her inexpert opinion. No doubt they both savoured this little bit of intimacy because Belinda seemed to take a long time to make up her mind that the ankle was only bruised. Gently, she pulled the sock back up Hank's leg caressing his tight calf muscles as she did so. Hank watched her intently, admiring the shape of her neck and catching a tantalising glimpse of the top of her breasts. Job done, Belinda rose to her feet and asked if he would like a couple of aspirin. He declined her offer and they spent the next half hour discussing in detail the content of the three phone calls to Stieldorf she had accomplished with the help of Marjorie's German language skills.

Later that morning they had a phone call from "Fossil." True to his word, he had dug up some more valuable factual information about Mr and Mrs Summers. Remembering Hank's painful ankle Bert offered to come upstairs to Hank's office. His offer was quickly accepted. Five minutes later the three of them were comfortably settled around Hank's desk eating chocolate fingers that someone had produced. Bert was excited about his discoveries and keen to unload.

'So, Bert you've been busy?' opened Hank.

'Not me so much but my excellent German contacts have been,' replied Bert as he consumed his third chocolate finger.

'Do you speak German?' inquired Belinda.

'Only about "O" level standard,' smiled Bert, 'I'm mostly reliant on the German police. Now first of all, let me tell you about Mrs Doreen Summers. She was as English as they come and had never even been to Germany. The couple met in Reading at a dance in 1946 and genuinely fell in love. As far as I can tell, Doreen never knew Rolf had been lying to her about being an intern on the Isle of Man during the war. We now know that Rolf was making all that stuff up.'

'So, that is now definitely confirmed?' probed Hank, 'he was lying when he told everybody he came to England before the war?'

'Seems so. What the German police discovered about Rolf's activities during the war is really interesting stuff. As a kid he was diagnosed with a weak heart and consequently was never accepted for military service at the start of the second world war. At the outbreak of war Rolf was a qualified carpenter and joiner working for a small family business in the centre of Bonn. Everything points to Rolf being an enthusiastic Nazi. He attended rallies, went to Nazi meetings and was committed to the extreme Nazi ideology. At the end of 1942 the small family business he worked for was totally wiped out in a British bombing raid. The family members were killed, the workshop destroyed. Rolf was out on a job when it happened so he escaped unscathed. However, now that his job as a carpenter was gone, he signed up as a security officer at the University of Bonn.'

'Wow! This is getting really interesting. So, Rolf Summers and Doctor Heinrich Zeigler's parents were all working at the same institution in 1942?'

'Exactly!'

'This is an incredible breakthrough,' enthused Hank, 'something shocking must have happened between them that has now been avenged twenty years later.'

'Wait till I tell you the rest of the story,' urged an excited Bert. 'First, you have to understand the Nazis controlled absolutely everything in Germany. The Nazis decided what events you could attend, where you went, who could travel and even who landed the jobs. A security officer at a university was considered by the Nazis to be a vitally important position because it was at the universities where there could be dangerous free-thinking students who might dare question Nazism and what it stood for. Rolf Summers as a security officer would have been rigorously trained by the Nazis to spy on students and staff and report anything he saw that was in any way suspicious. Before knocking off at the end of every shift Rolf would have had to report any concerns to his superior.'

'What a God-awful system the Nazis created!' exclaimed Belinda, licking her fingers clean of chocolate.

'The spying even extended to listening to student conversations in the toilets. Rolf might have been a bit of a pervert because his reports sometimes disclosed discussions he'd over-heard in the women's toilets,' continued Fossil.

'What? Was he going into the Ladies' toilets?' demanded Hank.

'Oh no, things were much more sophisticated than that. The toilets were set up with listening posts and a security officer could listen in, unbeknown to the occupants. Anyway, one evening Rolf reported hearing two or three young female students talking in the toilets about white rose leaflets that had been smuggled into the university ready to be distributed. Rolf would have been briefed about the white rose underground resistance movement that sought to bring down the Nazi regime and he immediately knew he was onto something big.'

Belinda passed the chocolate fingers around, while Hank carefully shifted his sore ankle.

'The crux of what Rolf over-heard was alarming. The girls were going to meet up with the other white roses at six o'clock that evening in the university's gymnasium to collect their batches of leaflets from the two lecturers who were the instigators and leaders of the white rose movement at Bonn University. Rolf was a cunning bastard. He didn't challenge the girls. He waited nearby to see who they were when they exited the toilet then he reported the whole conversation to the Nazi authorities, who thereupon set up an ambush. The white roses had planned to meet in the gymnasium dressed in their sporting gear and carrying bags with their clothes to change into afterwards. The leaflets were to be hidden in their carry bags ready for circulation that evening under the cover of darkness. The Nazi squad pretended to also be university students working out in the gym at six o'clock. Well... you can guess what happened,' said Bert.

'This is not going to have a happy ending,' murmured Hank, 'go on Bert, put us out of our misery.'

'Apparently, there were nine white roses who turned up clad in their sporting gear and ready with half-empty carry-bags. And guess what, the two lecturers who had the leaflets ready to hand to the students were Doctor Heinrich Zeigler's parents! The whole group was caught red-handed. The Zeiglers were carrying 2,000 leaflets, a thousand each. Rolf Summers who had dobbed them in, couldn't help himself and it is recorded he physically attacked the Zeiglers and had to be restrained. All this is written up in great detail in the trial papers. One thing about the Nazis was their super-efficient meticulous recording and documentation of events such as arrests and trials.'

'So, what happened to the white roses?' asked Belinda.

'Within a few days they were tried and all nine found guilty. The students were sent to prison for five years and the ring-leaders, the Zeiglers, sentenced to death. Heinrich's parents were executed four days later. They had their heads chopped off!'

'Good God!' exclaimed Hank.

There was silence for a minute or two as the three police tried to absorb the horror of what had happened nineteen years ago in that gymnasium at Bonn University. Thanks to Bert's marvellous research work, Belinda and Hank now knew Heinrich Zeigler had a strong motive to murder Rolf Summers. Nineteen years after his parents died, Zeigler must have finally discovered where Rolf was hiding out and consequently came to England where he brutally avenged the shocking murder of his parents. The execution of Zeigler's parents had been a bloody affair. Perhaps this explained why Doctor Zeigler had chosen an equally bloody method to dispose of his victims.

21.   Monday, 9th September

Chief Inspector Sandham summoned Hank and Belinda to his office early Monday morning. This Monday was the start of his final week at work and he felt he was not keeping fully abreast of what was happening in the Zeigler case. There had been a couple of small farewell parties for him over the weekend and everyone who attended had wanted to hear the latest news about the Summers' murders. As a senior police officer, Sandham needed to be circumspect about what he divulged but he was also aware there had been some further developments on Friday that he needed to get his head around. It really had been most inconsiderate of this Doctor Zeigler fellow to have committed two grisly murders on his patch just before his retirement. The week or two prior to a person's retirement should be enjoyed in a leisurely manner with a few quiet drinks with colleagues. Instead, his officers were racing about dealing with the worst crime event in West Sussex for twenty years.

Sandham noticed the cleaner had emptied his ash tray and wiped his desk free of some spilt ash. He pulled out a cigarette and lit up. Inhaling deeply, he reflected on the calming effect a decent fag had on his temper. He was well aware of the disparaging views his two young detectives had about his smoking habits. What was it they called his cigarettes? Ah yes… they called them "coffin nails." Rude buggers but in his heart of hearts he knew they were right. It was chain smoking for many years that was killing him. Too late now to try and stop, the damage was done.

There was a knock on the door and he invited his two young detectives to join him. They probably thought he was too old to notice but he had observed the chemistry between the two. Making eyes at each other, a gentleness between them. These were two beautiful young people and so well matched. They were most discrete. However, it was clear to everyone at the station that they were falling deeply in love. As the officer-in-charge of the station he probably should be recommending that one of them be transferred to another police station. Too much romancing in the one place was not considered wise by the powers that be. However, with only a week to go, he wasn't going to be a killjoy. He would leave it to his successor to act if they thought it necessary.

Hank was still hobbling on his sore ankle. A fine young man, the sort the police force wanted to encourage, blessed with a fine set of values and a strong moral compass. Already an inspector at twenty-nine, Hank should go far. Over the weekend Sandham had written up his final assessment of young Hank and it had been a glowing report. It sat on his desk in front of him now ready to be dispatched to head office.

And then there was the stunning Belinda. What a treat she was! Quite apart from her good looks she had already impressed him in the four weeks since she had been posted to Petworth. Reliable, considerate, respectful, hardworking and intelligent. It was particularly gratifying to find a young woman progressing up the ranks. If there were more women of her calibre then equality of the sexes was indeed achievable.

'Good morning, Hank, good morning, Belinda. Thank you for coming to my office first thing on a Monday. I hope you both enjoyed a good weekend?'

Through the blue cigarette smoke he saw a knowing look flash between the pair. No doubt they had been enjoying each other's company.

'Now, I want a complete update on what transpired on Friday. Who's going first?'

The next ten minutes were dominated by Hank and then Belinda with Sandham interjecting occasionally to get further clarification about some point or other. Chief Inspector Sandham also spent some of the time scribbling down notes.

'Thank you for that,' he declared when they had finished. 'What now?'

Hank took the lead. 'I guess we must rely on the German police to do their job. Hopefully, they'll find and arrest Zeigler and we can then extradite him back to the UK to stand trial. I have a bag packed in case they want us over there in a hurry.'

'Same here,' echoed Belinda.

Sandham remained silent for a moment. 'What about Mrs Summers? I can understand Zeigler wanting revenge on Rolf for dobbing in the white roses and specifically his parents but why did Zeigler kill Mrs Summers?'

'Clearly, she was not involved in any way with the white roses,' replied Belinda. 'She hadn't even been to Germany as far as we can tell, so it seems a bit tough that Zeigler went after her as well.'

'I reckon Zeigler believed Rolf had confessed to her. If Zeigler had only killed Rolf he would eventually be caught because Doreen would spill the beans. Zeigler's plan, therefore, was to kill them both and escape without anyone knowing who did it. He might have got away with it if it hadn't been for that car back-firing at the precise moment he stabbed Rolf. Rolf, like some of the Upper Byford neighbours, thought he had heard a gun-shot so he fled. Then frustratingly, he had to hang around for another night in Upper Byford waiting for an opportunity to kill Doreen. Her lonely walk up to that church was his chance and he took it.'

'Makes sense,' conceded Sandham. 'I'm not one for wanting to go out in a blaze of glory but it would be wonderful if we had this Zeigler bloke safely locked up in custody by Friday the thirteenth, my last hurrah!'

Belinda and Hank laughed and promised to do their best.

☾

Hank and Belinda lunched together in the police canteen. Canteen grub was limited in choice and basic in quality. The only reason many police ate there was because it was convenient and offered a chance to catch up with colleagues. Fossil rarely dined in the canteen but came wandering in on this particular Monday and asked if he might sit with Belinda and Hank. They welcomed him and congratulated him once again for the highly successful research he had conducted to date. Not surprisingly their conversation revolved around Heinrich Zeigler and the imminent retirement of their boss on Friday the thirteenth.

Hank had hungrily gobbled down his steak and kidney pie with chips smothered liberally in tomato sauce but was still hungry. The desserts didn't look particularly appetising yet there remained a hole in his stomach that needed filling so he decided to risk the last cold apple pie sitting out on display. Surely, nobody could spoil the taste of such a humble item as a simple apple pie? He was wrong. One mouthful revealed the presence of cloves; a flavour Hank could not abide. In disgust he pushed the plate away and mumbled something about ruining the taste of healthy flavoursome apples with unnecessary exotic flavours. Belinda smiled at him and reached across for the abandoned dessert. It was whilst she was finishing off the much-maligned dessert that Hank was called to answer a phone call that had been put through to his office.

Ten minutes later Hank returned just as Belinda and Bert were about to leave. He bade them resume their seats because they would be interested to hear what the phone call was about. Belinda tried to read the expression on her boyfriend's face but it was non-committal. Instead, she allowed herself to admire his good looks for a moment while he pulled out his chair and settled.

'That, my friends, was the Bonn Police. Inspector Adolf Fuchs, the one who speaks English fluently. He wanted to update me on their search for our friend Heinrich Zeigler. Not good news, I'm afraid. The last they heard he had driven off the Bonn University Campus in the company of a second-year student he was reputedly having an affair with. At that time, he was driving a white Volkswagen. By the time the police had despatched a chase car, Zeigler had already dropped his girlfriend off, hijacked another car and disappeared. The Germans learnt this from the distressed female student who thought she was eloping with her lecturer. Zeigler must have had second thoughts and decided taking her with him would be more of a liability than a pleasure. The jilted lass turned up at a police station an hour later in the suburbs somewhere to tell her story. In that one hour Zeigler could have travelled a long way.'

'He may have been thinking of using the girl as a hostage,' suggested Fossil.

'Whatever the reason, she must have been traumatised by the whole experience,' added Belinda.

'The police took statements from her and returned her home. She described Zeigler as being "very agitated and short tempered." In the end, the police reckoned she had come to her senses and was greatly relieved to have been dumped on the side of the road next to a shopping centre car park. She didn't know where Zeigler was headed and couldn't even provide any useful details about the car he stole except it was shiny black and had four doors.'

'Every other car in Germany is probably shiny black with four doors,' laughed Fossil.

'Anyway, this is where the trail goes cold. As we know all too well, Zeigler has a canny knack of disappearing.'

'Have there been any more recent sightings?' Belinda inquired.

'Nope! The police found out the Zeiglers part-own a chalet up in the mountains where they sometimes go in the ski season and figured he could be headed up there to hide out. They've checked the joint but there was no sign of him there.'

'That means he's on the loose again and nobody knows where he's headed,' said Belinda, gloomily.

'The police have also been speaking at length with Heinrich's wife, Greta. I think you spoke to her, Belinda?'

'I certainly did. Seemed a very pleasant lady.'

'Obviously, Greta's incredibly worried about her husband. The police didn't tell her why they were hunting for him but they sure put the wind up her. They stressed that harbouring Heinrich or obstructing them in their police work were criminal offences punishable with a prison sentence. They also searched the house just to be sure he was not hiding there.'

'Poor woman,' said Belinda, 'she's in an awful predicament. Suppose Heinrich tries to sneak back home then she has to decide whether to hide him or dob him in. I know if I was in a similar situation, I would be very reluctant to betray my husband.' She glanced up at Hank who was watching her carefully and immediately regretted it.

'One interesting thing Greta told the police was that Heinrich's behaviour changed suddenly a few weeks ago. She said he was really excited about something he had discovered but wouldn't tell her what it was. He was usually open and transparent about his research work or anything that was troubling him but not this time. Several times she tried to ascertain what it was that he'd come across. Whatever it was, it made him nervous too. Greta described him as being strangely driven. It was at this time that he became pre-occupied with planning his next overseas trip during August and September. Greta went on to say that he became strangely withdrawn. When she asked him where he was going in August and September, he became very guarded.'

'This all makes perfect sense to me,' said Hank, excitedly. 'Ever since Heinrich was fourteen and witnessed the shocking execution of his parents, he has been determined to avenge their killing. The person he blamed most was Rolf Summers who had dobbed the white roses in and then appeared as the chief witness at their trial. Zeigler must have been looking for Rolf Summers for years. Finally, he discovered Summers living quietly in the small village of Upper Bybridge. At last, he had an opportunity to carry out his awful payback. He had waited bloody nineteen years! No wonder he was excited but also nervous and secretive. Don't you agree, Belinda?'

'I do. I think you've nailed it!'

22. An Important Introduction

Belinda awoke in a nervous sweat. She had not slept well and the reason was abundantly clear. Tonight, she planned to have dinner with her parents and she had invited Hank to join them, the first time Hank had met them. Hank Zagalski was actually the third young man she had introduced to her parents. Both the earlier suitors had fallen by the wayside. The first young man, a pharmacist, was so in to his medications, vitamins and cure-alls he'd already become a virtual hypochondriac. Belinda had been very fond of him and they had dated on and off for years having attended the same high school. However, the thought of how this young man, already unhealthily pre-occupied with his wellness in his early twenties would be like by middle age was truly concerning. Today, they remained good friends but that was where the relationship stayed.

The second young man had been an up-and-coming novelist. A graduate of Oxford University where he had studied English Literature, he was a true romantic. Handsome, clever, funny and charming, and dare she say it, sexy. She had instantly fallen madly in love with this incredibly attractive young man. The relationship lasted less than two weeks, however, because she refused to go to bed with him. Her gorgeous Casanova dropped her like a lead balloon when his moves to seduce her were not reciprocated. In the very short time, they had dated she had managed to introduce him to her parents who were greatly impressed with him and genuinely disappointed when nothing eventuated. Belinda often thought about her short-lived novelist boyfriend and still wondered whether sticking so rigidly to her strict moral principles had been wise.

And now she was about to introduce her third serious boyfriend,

Hank, to her parents which was why she was so nervous. Belinda turned twenty-six soon and most women of her age were already married or at least engaged. Nobody had said anything to her yet about being in danger of being "left on the shelf" although she was conscious of some growing concerns in her family. She had heard a couple of snide comments such as, "all the best young men have already been snapped up" from a married niece who was three years her junior. Being a policewoman didn't help either, it terrified some men. Belinda found it interesting to see the reactions of eligible males when they asked her what she did for a living. Without exception they would express surprise and in a number of cases took no more interest in her as a potential partner. At least Hank understood policing which was a promising start.

Belinda's parents had been married thirty years and were in their mid-fifties. Like most married couples, they had their ups and downs but had stayed together to provide a stable, loving environment for their three children. Now that they were empty-nesters they were forging a new path as they contemplated retirement in ten years' time. Alice Purcell, Belinda's mother, had returned to work as a nurse after years staying home to care for the kids. She had completed a six-month, full time, compulsory nursing update course to get back into the profession and was enjoying her work in the paediatric ward at her nearest hospital.

Belinda's father, Major Allan Purcell, had signed up for the army at the outbreak of war when he was thirty-two and was immediately selected for officer training. Six months later he was seeing active service in France. Shortly after the end of the war he was discharged with a distinguished military service record and the rank of Major, something he was intensely proud about. Like most of his colleagues, he came back as "damaged goods." Although not physically wounded, he had suffered psychologically and had become "difficult." Settling back into civil life had not come easily because he had wanted to impose army discipline on his wife and children. Somehow, they had survived this harsh military environment and fortunately the Major mellowed somewhat over the years. Belinda thought her dad would like Hank as they would have much in common; rugby, physical fitness and both having served in well-disciplined organisations.

Belinda's parents lived in Clifton, just outside of Bristol and were on a travelling holiday. This evening, they were booked into the Petworth Arms, a small hotel in the centre of town. It was there they were to meet for pre-dinner drinks at six o'clock. Belinda picked Hank up in good time and they walked into the saloon bar together a few minutes before six. They were a fine-looking couple, both tall and fit and in the peak of health. Hank was still nursing his sore ankle but managed not to limp noticeably. Belinda wore a long light green evening dress that tastefully accentuated her feminine form.

The evening was a great success. Belinda's parents were in sparkling form and she had forgotten how amusing her dad could be with a couple of drinks under his belt. They both immediately liked Hank and fell into easy conversation with him. The evening was a relaxed, fun affair. The food was excellent, served piping hot just as mum liked it with properly pre-heated plates. Service was brisk and polite. Belinda noticed her dad left a generous tip under his plate at the end of their repast. They retired to the guests' lounge for a port afterwards and Belinda and her mum grabbed the opportunity to disappear into the ladies to "powder their noses."

'What a gorgeous young man you've found dear and you only moved to Petworth four weeks ago.'

'I know and we get along famously.'

'How old is he?'

'Twenty-nine.'

'Three years older than you then, dear…'

'Correct.'

'Do you think this could be *the* one?'

'Oh come on mum, we've only known each other for four weeks!'

'Well, the last boyfriend of yours we met you had only known for *two* weeks and your father and I thought he was definitely the one. We really liked him. What on earth happened for that romance to end so abruptly?'

'It just did.'

'Come on Belinda dear, something must have happened? You seemed to be so in love, infatuated?'

'I was and I still am in some ways. But he's gone now, gone forever.'

'Who broke it off?'

'I did.'

'Why? What on earth happened?'

'I want to remain a virgin until I take my marriage vows but he wasn't prepared to wait. One night he really tried to persuade me to change my mind. He plied me with alcoholic drinks and started fondling me all over. I told him to stop, as nicely as I could, but he was really determined. He wouldn't take no for an answer. I ended up slapping him across the face. I'm pretty strong after doing all my police training and I hit him so hard it knocked him over and he fell off the couch onto the floor. That really angered him. I'm sure he'd had his way with other girls before me and always got what he wanted. Suddenly he realised I wasn't like the others.'

'Oh dear, that's sad. He seemed such a lovely fellow...'

'He was and I fell for him, big time!'

'I'm going to tell you something I've never told anyone else.'

Belinda looked at her mother and could see that what she wanted to say was going to be difficult for her. Her mother hesitated, uncertain whether to go on. Finally, she plucked up the courage.

'You are not going to like what I'm going to say, dear. I hope you'll forgive me. When I was courting your father, he was quite the dashing young man about town. All the girls swooned over him. In those days, and I'm talking about the early 1930s, we used to go to formal balls and pre-book who we were going to dance with. It was all very prim and proper. Like several other girls I fell for your dad who, like your Hank, was a fine rugby player. He was a real hunk of a man. Hard to believe now when you see him with his paunch and receding hair.' She gave a little laugh before going on. 'Anyway, to cut a long story short, I was desperate to win him. He had everything I yearned for. A good family, an excellent job, money, good looks and a fun personality. My parents were keen too…'

'I think I know what you might be going to tell me, mum.'

'Yes…I slept with him and what's more we found sex wonderful. I really believe I won him over this way. Of course, I was worried I'd get pregnant. However, if that happened, I reasoned he would have to marry me then, anyway. So, to hell with it. I forgot all my Christian teachings and enjoyed every minute. Are you terribly ashamed of me?'

'No mum. Sex before marriage is a very personal decision. You might be surprised to know that Hank thinks the same way as me… wait for the right person to come along, marry them and then enjoy each other in a unique and special way. Sex is something precious, almost sacred, that a married couple can explore together once they've tied the knot.'

'Heavens, look at the time…we've been talking in here for at least ten minutes. The men will think we've fallen down the plug hole.'

❧

Hank and Allan Purcell had been talking Rugby, big time. They had re-lived the 1962 Five Nations Championship with England beating Ireland 16-0 but then losing to France 0-13. Amazingly, England had recorded draws against Scotland and Wales and both men were convinced England had been robbed by poor refereeing. They were equally disappointed about the British and Irish Lions tour to South Africa where they had lost three matches to one and were just getting started on the Australia versus New Zealand matches for 1962 when the ladies re-appeared. Belinda's mother spoke first.

'I only need one guess to know what you two men have been discussing…'

'Oh yes, and what would that be?' asked the Major looking up at his well-powdered wife.

'Rugger?'

The men smiled. 'Bullseye. And what about you two ladies? That was an awful lot of powder being wafted about out there?'

'That's private,' Alice replied, with a faint blush.

'Umm…what do you think they were discussing, Hank?'

'The latest fashions?'

'Oh, don't be silly Hank,' Belinda responded slapping him affectionately on the shoulder.

'Another port for everyone?' asked the Major, 'the night is still young.'

Hank and Belinda were on duty early the next day and politely declined. Shortly afterwards they excused themselves and drove the short distance back to their respective homes.

The evening had been a great success and Belinda was thrilled her parents had so easily related to Hank. They spent ten minutes kissing and cuddling in the car before Belinda reluctantly returned to her flat, alone.

Belinda had been surprised by what her mother had confessed to but it didn't change her own thinking. She still intended to remain a virgin until her very special marriage night.

23. November, 1962

It was the first heavy frost of winter as Belinda left her cosy unit to walk briskly to work. She loved these crisp clear mornings with soft blue skies and a timid sun struggling to rise above the tree-tops. Everything was covered in a layer of glistening white ice; the smoke from numerous chimneys rising straight up undisturbed by air currents. At the edge of the mill pond a group of noisy young boys were daring each other to be the first to test the strength of the ice. A pair of robins chattered at her from the top of a wooden fence but flitted off as she drew close.

Belinda wrapped her scarf more tightly around her neck and slightly adjusted her bright red beanie, part of her birthday gift from Hank. As she passed the corner store, she noticed a huddle of housewives chatting away outside the shop. There were red noses and puffs of breath coming from their mouths. They waved or nodded as she strode past. The locals rather liked a young policewoman living in their midst; it made them feel safe and secure.

It was now nearly two months since they had heard anything more about Doctor Heinrich Zeigler. It was as if he had completely disappeared from the face of the earth. The Bonn Police didn't bother to make their weekly calls anymore because the trail had gone stone cold. Zeigler's university girlfriend, who had been found abandoned but unharmed, now had a very different opinion of her handsome lecturer and was thankful he hadn't used her as some kind of hostage. Only Zeigler's wife had heard anything. An undated card arrived a couple of days after Heinrich disappeared with a German postage stamp and postmark. It was brutally brief. Translated, it read as follows…

Darling Greta,

I'm in a spot of trouble and must stay away for a time, probably a very long time. I love you dearly and very much hope you will come and join me sometime in the future when I have settled down elsewhere.

Heaps of love to the family,

Heinrich

Greta handed the card to the police as soon as it arrived but it was little help. The card had traces of Heinrich's fingerprints all over it so it was certainly from him. The picture was a foaming tankard of beer and the postmark the same small town where the girlfriend had been dropped off.

For a time, the Bonn police remained upbeat confident Zeigler would make a wrong move and give himself away. There were "sightings" which were speedily followed up but to no avail. Every "sighting" ended up as a false alarm except for one in Hamburg where the police arrived just too late to detain him after Zeigler had successfully removed a substantial sum of money from his bank. Thereafter, his bank account was frozen.

As the weeks rolled by, the police theorised Zeigler must have left the country, probably disguised and with a new name and identity. Where he had gone, however, was anyone's guess. During his academic career Heinrich had visited a number of countries to attend, or present papers, at international conferences so it seemed feasible he would try to hide in one of these countries because he would have some familiarity with them. Greta was able to supply the police with a list of conference locations Heinrich had visited. The list included eight European countries, the USA, the United Kingdom (twice), Canada, Australia and Brazil. The police authorities in these nations were encouraged to be extra vigilant.

Belinda timed her arrival at the police station perfectly. Hank was scrambling out of his car with his briefcase as she walked into the car park. They kissed briefly and hurried into the over-heated police station. Chief Inspector Nigel Sandham had retired, as planned, on Friday the thirteenth having enjoyed an appropriate farewell function at which he confessed he was disappointed the case of the Summers' murders remained unsolved. Last week, Sandham had been admitted to hospital suffering from severe respiratory problems. His replacement was expected in the new year. Hank, now the most senior officer at the Petworth Station, had assumed a wide range of additional managerial duties. With Hank tied up with extra administrative work, Belinda was busier than ever dealing with a spate of petty crimes that required the attention of a detective.

Romantically, Belinda and Hank's relationship was deepening as each day passed. There was little doubt that marriage was in the offing, although Hank had yet to "pop the question." Belinda had taken Hank to spend a weekend with her parents which had also been a great success. Each time Hank and Belinda went out together, she wondered if this was going to be the occasion he would propose. Hank, however, wanted his proposal to be something very special and the right time had not yet arrived.

PART TWO

24. Western Samoa, Late November 1962

Chief Inspector Rod Benson, his wife Susan and their son, Sammy, had been living at Aggie Grey's Hotel in Apia, Western Samoa for three weeks. Rod Benson was in Western Samoa at the invitation of the Western Samoan Police Force and was "on loan" for three months from Scotland Yard. His task was to advise the Western Samoan Police Force on the future establishment of an investigative arm as an addition to their normal day to day policing duties. In other words, Rod was to recommend how best to set up a small group of Western Samoan detectives to handle major crime.

On January 1st 1962 Western Samoa had finally celebrated its independence from New Zealand which had administered the small group of nine tropical islands since 1915. Prior to New Zealand's involvement, these islands had been governed by Germany. Shortly after the outbreak of the first World War Great Britain asked New Zealand to peacefully occupy the islands and "remove" the Germans. This they did without any armed resistance.

Germany had become the sole colonial power in Western Samoa in 1899. For many years prior to 1899 the United States, Great Britain and Germany had hotly contested ownership of the Samoan islands. Eventually, as a result of The Tripartite Convention of 1899, it was agreed the United States would take over the eastern islands which became known as American Samoa. The islands to the west became German controlled, Western Samoa, while Britain ceded all her rights to the Samoan islands in exchange for additional territorial rights in Tonga and elsewhere.

The Germans soon realised the potential for large scale

plantations and quickly established farms of cocoa beans and rubber. Chinese and Melanesians were brought in to do the hard work, some of whom stayed when the Germans were forced out in 1915. A small number of Germans, who had married local women, or fallen in love with the lush islands, also managed to stay after the great majority of their countrymen were given their marching orders in 1915.

Aggie Grey's Hotel had, by 1962, become famous as the only reasonable quality hotel in the whole of Western Samoa. The colourful matriarch, Aggie Grey, now sixty-five, had opened these premises back in 1933 and was a clever operator. Half English, half Samoan, she had a foot in both worlds which helped her create an establishment that appealed to most tastes. Many dignitaries and famous actors had stayed at Aggie Grey's over the years and American serviceman based in Samoa during the second world war had adopted the hotel as their favourite drinking hole.

Acclimatising to the humid tropics was proving a challenge for the Bensons although little Sammy seemed to manage well. The three of them lived in a cramped apartment at the back of Aggie Grey's that thankfully possessed an ancient air-conditioner. It was a noisy beast of a thing that grunted and groaned but managed to cool the air enough to let them sleep at nights. Most of their meals were taken in Aggie Grey's restaurant courtesy of the British Foreign Office that was paying the bills since Western Samoa was now a member of the British Empire.

Chief Inspector Rod Benson was short and stocky. He had originally been refused entry to the British police force on account of his low stature but a sympathetic MP had taken up his case and persuaded the recruiting officer to think again. Apparently, what had sealed the change of heart was the fact Rod played scrum-half for the Harlequins and would be a great asset for the Metropolitan Police Rugby team. What Rod lacked in height he made up for with brawn and speed. With bright red hair and a well-muscled body, he was a terror on the rugby pitch. Fortunately, his sporting prowess was accompanied by a highly active mind and he had risen up the ranks to be a Chief Inspector in near record time. Rod had just turned thirty-five.

Rod's petite wife, Susan, was a ball of fun, full of energy although temporarily somewhat constrained by the debilitating heat and humidity of Apia. A bright charismatic character with a winning smile and an infectious laugh, she was the sort of person everyone gravitated to at parties and other social events. She was not strikingly attractive to look at but made up for her rather ordinary looks with her effervescent personality. A qualified primary teacher, Susan was keen to do something voluntary to help the youngest nation on earth during her three months stay. The Western Samoan Education Department was unsure what to do with Susan Benson when she unexpectedly sailed into their head office one morning. Concerned Susan might not be well received in the remote village primary schools; the department asked her to review their primary school curriculum and come up with some suggestions for improvements. She was happy to help in this way and trundled off to the education office every day after taking Sammy to the small international school nearby.

Each evening after work, the Bensons went for a walk along the sea front to enjoy the cool sea breezes. It was a way to unwind at the end of the day; quality family time. The blazing sun dropped quickly below the horizon around six o'clock which helped lower the temperature a little but not the humidity. Many locals had the same idea and were often to be seen strolling along the pavement chatting and laughing, playing touch rugby or eating pineapples, coconuts, bananas or breadfruit, whatever had been for sale that day at the local fruit stalls. It was a pleasant friendly atmosphere. After taking the sea-air, the Bensons retired to the restaurant at Aggie Grey's for dinner. Three weeks staying at Aggie Grey's meant they were now well known to the staff and as regulars were made to feel welcome. After the evening meal, Sammy was showered and put to bed and Susan or Rod would read him bedtime stories.

In some ways this was an idyllic life-style for the Bensons. The pace was more relaxed, nobody was in a hurry to get things done, tomorrow would do…. The gentle Samoans were friendly and polite although few spoke English, so language was at times a serious barrier. The half a dozen policemen Rod was working with were keen to learn about detective work in the United Kingdom and amazed to hear about the amount of crime there. The Samoans were keen to point out that there was little or no crime amongst the Western Samoans and the need for detectives in the small nation was to better handle the crimes of the foreign visitors to their country. Tourists were arriving in increasing numbers as well as traders, consultants and public servants on short term assignments.

Rod soon learnt about "fa'a Samoa." This was the traditional Samoan way of handling matters. Samoans were gifted sailors, fishermen and boat builders, as well as subsistence farmers. The great majority lived in small villages dotted around the coast of the two largest islands, Upolu and Savai'i. Every village was governed by its senior villagers known as the "Matais". The Matais met regularly and arrived at decisions for the common good of their villagers. Typical matters that came up for discussion were marriages, the upkeep of the church, the appointment of the minister as well as the maintenance of the primary school, the fales (homes) and the gardens. Land disputes were settled by the Matais too, as was any anti-social behaviour.

The Matais were so effective in seeing there was little or no anti-social behaviour in their villages that for a very long time having a police force was deemed unnecessary. Any misdemeanours were handled by the Matais, who sagely considered each case on its merits and then meted out appropriate punishments, if required. However, with the gradual emergence of the first and only town in the country, Apia, it was realised the village Matais system did not function well in a larger urban community so an embryonic police force was created together with a supportive legal system. Most of the police work was dealing with foreigners who over-imbibed, cheated, molested local women or stole something. If a crime was committed in one of the many Samoan coastal villages the Samoan police left it to the local Matais to manage and didn't get involved unless invited to do so. This strategy worked brilliantly.

Foreigners were not welcome in the peaceful coastal villages and could only enter at the invitation of the village chiefs. Once invited, there were a number of traditional rituals to be observed; speeches, sharing of ava (Samoan type of kava) and then more speeches. These welcoming ceremonies took place in the large village fales with the invitees and the Matais sitting together in a circle cross legged on tapa mats.

After three weeks living in Apia, the Bensons were beginning to recover from the cultural shocks commonly experienced by those who travel to distant lands for the first time where things are done very differently. They had tried a few local dishes, sampled the soporific ava, experienced their first hundred mosquito bites and marvelled at their lush tropical surroundings. No longer were they surprised when the heavens opened up and soaked everything and everybody mid-afternoon. They had even learnt a smattering of the local language. On Sundays Samoans went to church without exception. The ladies decked out completely in white puletasis, the men wearing white shirts and dark formal lavalavas (rather like kilts without pleats). The Bensons were irregular church goers back in England but here in this deeply Christian society they felt it disrespectful not to attend. Besides, the singing was fantastic! The long, bombastic sermons always in Samoan were harder to endure. Little Sammy was always able to escape to Sunday school.

Towards the end of the Benson's fourth week on assignment, Rod announced that next weekend the three of them had been invited to visit a village called Salamumu on the southern side of Upolu. The road over the mountains to Salamumu was dirt, bumpy with heaps of potholes, but had views of beautiful scenery and waterfalls. The invitation had come from Andrew Ra'a, a Salamumu Matai, who was the most senior policeman in the group that Rod was working with. Rod had tentatively accepted the invitation on behalf of his family. Young Sammy was immediately excited by the possibilities.

'Dad, will we see animals in the jungle? There could be lions, elephants, bison and even crocodiles. We've got to go, dad. Better take a gun in case we are attacked by wild animals.'

'Darling, those animals don't live here in Western Samoa, they are in places like Africa,' explained his amused mother.

Sammy looked sad, 'Aren't there any wild animals?' he asked, pleadingly.

'Snakes maybe… perhaps some wild goats or pigs,' conceded his sympathetic father.

'Then I don't want to go,' moped Sammy.

'Well, I suppose I could ask Aggie Grey to look after you when Dad and I go away for the weekend,' suggested his mother.

Sammy was terrified of Aggie Grey! There was actually no need to be but to a very small child she seemed old and domineering. The thought of having to stay with Aggie Grey was enough for Sammy to do a rapid re-think.

'Okay, I'll come then.'

'If we're all happy to go, I'll tell Andrew we'll join him on Saturday morning. He has an old truck, an ancient Ford that he drives. He'll be very pleased to hear we're all coming.'

The plate of crispy chips that suddenly appeared in front of Sammy quickly cheered him up.

❡

Not many people in Samoa owned a truck of any size or description. The truck Ra'a was driving when he turned up outside Aggie Grey's on Saturday morning was jointly owned by Ra'a, his dad and Ra'a's two younger brothers. It was a four-way split, although Ra'a's dad had paid rather more than each of his three sons. The 1955 model Ford parked on the side of the street had originally been bright red, but it was hard to discern much of that colour now. It was more of a rusty, dusty nondescript blend of tones. Ra'a had reserved the two vacant front seats for the Bensons with five or six Samoan friends sitting about in the back of the vehicle. Nobody ever travelled without passengers in Samoa since transport was at a premium. One of the passengers in the back of the truck was hanging onto a couple of less-than-happy chickens intent on letting everyone know of their displeasure. Between their squawks, a pig could be heard grunting and snuffling also unhappy about his predicament. The pig's owner kept telling it to "shut up" but the pig didn't seem to understand. The pig's owner then demonstrated with his hand that the poor animal was due to have its throat cut. Fortunately, Sammy either didn't see the gruesome gesture or failed to comprehend.

There were only two main roads on the island of Upolu. One was the coast road that hugged the coves and beaches the whole way round the island and the other one was the road that Ra'a and the Bensons were taking now which climbed inland over the central range and down to the southern side of the island. It wasn't long before they left the bitumen and began the twisty climb through dense tropical foliage. A few enterprising farmers were attempting to run cattle up in these hills where it was slightly cooler. They had been obliged to erect fences along the sides of the road to keep the animals from straying. To do this, the farmers had cut down tree saplings and stuck them in the ground for posts. Intriguingly, in the rich volcanic soils these saplings quickly took root and the fences rapidly turned into hedges. Sammy, fortunately, had lowered his expectations with regard to meeting fierce untamed beasts of the jungle and in the end was quite satisfied to spot an occasional parrot, a couple of feral cats and to wave to the people they saw walking along the road carrying baskets of fruit and vegetables for sale at local markets.

Ra'a was in excellent spirits, pleased to be pointing out familiar features as the old Ford chugged faithfully uphill through a series of sharp bends and over innumerable pot-holes. He stopped at one place to show them an excellent view looking north over the sleepy capital of Apia and the sea beyond. There was a sign at this lookout but it was barely visible since a large leafed plant had grown almost over it. Ra'a yanked the plant off the sign and laughed, 'This plant is called Mile-a-Minute,' he joked, 'if we leave our vegetable garden for a few days when we come back it will be covered with Mile-a-Minute plants.' Sammy thought this very funny and for the rest of the trip yelled out, 'Mile-a-Minute,' every time he saw the plant starting to creep across the road or over a building.

As they dropped down the southern side of the mountain range, they could feel the heat and humidity intensifying. When they met the coastal road, they turned right and headed west through a series of small villages each with a splendid white church, colourful gardens and a small roadside store. Ra'a stopped a couple of times to drop off his grateful passengers including the man with the pig. Just before mid-day, Ra'a turned off the coastal road and drove slowly into his own village of Salamumu. It was just as well he travelled slowly because from nowhere a couple of dozen kids of all ages surrounded them, yelling and laughing. 'They like having visitors,' grinned Ra'a, as he waved back. The kids followed the truck as they drove on for a few hundred yards and finally pulled up at the large village fale.

Samoan fales are intriguing. Built upon large slabs of concrete, they have no walls and consist only of a few sturdy wooden posts holding up a corrugated iron or thatched roof. It's a sensible design as it allows any sea breezes to blow through and keep things cooler. When it rains protective awnings can be dropped down the sides of the fale where the rain is coming from. No walls, of course, means no privacy. The children play, adults chat, smoke and argue in full view of their neighbours. It is said the first missionaries from the London

Missionary Society found living in a fale highly stressful because they couldn't enjoy private times of prayer and contemplation.

Ra'a and the Bensons had arrived at the large village fale in the centre of Salamumu where meetings and ceremonies were held. All around this central building, in a rough circle, were the much smaller family fales. Every fale had a corrugated iron roof painted bright red giving the village a powerful feeling of "togetherness." Great pride was taken in maintaining the colourful village gardens. Still surrounded by the excited village children, the Bensons climbed stiffly down from Ra'a's truck and followed their host into the village fale. Ra'a pointed to where the Bensons should sit on a beautifully decorated tapa cloth in readiness for the welcoming ceremony. Ra'a walked to the other side of the village fale and found his correct place in the circle of Matais. There were close to twenty Matais present. All, except two, were men. Sitting on a hard floor cross-legged was not something Rod and Susan Benson were used to but they knew they were expected to sit this way for at least half an hour. Sammy had been excused this ordeal and had already teamed up with a few of the Salamumu youngsters for some fun and games.

The welcoming ceremony was more or less what the Bensons expected. Ra'a had briefed them well. A lengthy speech from the village chief, the sharing of the traditional dirty brown ava drink consumed from a half coconut shell and then a number of shorter speeches from certain Matais who felt moved to add something more to the occasion. The proceedings were conducted entirely in Samoan so the Bensons sat quietly smiling when there seemed to be some jocularity and keeping a straight solemn face at other times. Finally, with much shaking of hands, the formalities were over and Ra'a led them over to his family's fale for lunch where they found Sammy waiting for them. He had been playing kilikiti, a Samoan form of cricket thought to have been enjoyed in the islands for hundreds of years, long before the MCC was founded in London.

When lunch was over and Rod and Susan had thanked their

hosts, Ra'a announced it was time to go down to the water-hole, a favourite place for the village's young at heart to cool off and have fun. Once again, they were accompanied by a large group of boisterous Salamumu youngsters anxious not to miss out. It was only a five-minute walk and they could hear the sound of the waterfall almost as soon as they left the village. It was an ideal spot. A group of teenagers were already diving and jumping into the deepest water close to the waterfall itself. Hot and steamy, it was at least shady around the waterhole and just the sight of the water had a cooling effect. The younger children were swimming naked and Sammy was desperate to join them. Susan didn't have the heart to say no. Quick as a flash he was down at the water's edge along with a couple of little mates he was already best friends with. Sammy was only starting to learn to swim while his new mates swam like otters!

Rod and Susan found a flat shady rock to sit on since they had not brought their swimming costumes and so could only relish the beauty of the place and watch the kids having fun. Sammy was easy to see since he was the only white skinned kid there. Ra'a's children were there too, also accomplished swimmers and perfectly confident in the water. Ra'a joined the Bensons on their rock.

'So Ra'a, this swimming hole belongs to Salamumu village?' asked Rod.

'Well, there are no maps saying that but we are the closest village so we look after it. A few of the other villages are lucky enough to also have waterholes nearby. Every village is close to the sea though so we can all swim and fish there too.'

'Are there any nasty things the children have to watch out for when they're swimming?' asked a slightly nervous Susan as she watched Sammy trying to pluck up the courage to jump off a rock his friends had just dived off.

Ra'a though for a moment. 'In the sea there are sea-snakes. If you see one you get away as quickly as you can. They can kill a small child but they stay out in the deeper water usually. Then you have poisonous jellyfish. Again, don't go near them. On land, the worst creature is the giant centipede. Its bite is toxic and one bite can kill a baby or a very elderly person.'

'Oh gosh!' exclaimed Susan, 'Are there any around this waterhole?'

'Probably,' replied Ra'a, 'you rarely see them here though. Too many people about.'

Rod was about to ask about venomous snakes and spiders when he noticed a small group of white skinned people approaching the waterhole from above the waterfall. A well-used track wound its way through the trees and ferns. A couple of minutes later two white men and a white woman emerged at the far side of the waterhole.

'Who are those people?' asked a curious Rod.

'Those are the Schmidts,' replied Ra'a, giving them a friendly wave, 'they have a large property further up the hill.'

'That's interesting. I didn't know foreigners were allowed to own land in Western Samoa.'

'Well, they aren't.'

'So, how come these folk have land here?' Susan asked, as she swatted a persistent mosquito.

'I don't know how much of our recent history you know?' Ra'a responded.

Susan and Rod admitted they had little or no idea about Western Samoa's past.

'Western Samoa was a German colony from 1899 to 1915. During that time adventurous Germans settled here. They grabbed land, cleared it and planted crops on a big scale. We Samoans had never realised you could have commercial crops of the things we have been growing for thousands of years around our villages on a small subsistence scale. We only grew what we needed.'

The three white-skinned Schmidts were now pulling off their gear to reveal they had swimming costumes underneath. As Rod and Susan watched, the three dived into the cool refreshing water. Being a policeman, trained to be observant, Rod naturally took careful note of their appearance. He thought they were probably in their thirties and looked fit. One of the men could be a little older, in his early forties perhaps. The woman, wearing a discreet modest swimming costume, had an attractive figure.

'So, what happened in 1915 to end the colonisation?' asked Susan.

'New Zealand sent troops here and ordered all Germans to leave the country. It was the first World War and the allies were worried about the Germans being here. It could easily have become a German base.'

'I can understand that,' agreed Rod, 'were the Samoans pleased to see the Germans get kicked out?'

'Definitely!' exclaimed Ra'a, 'we didn't like them taking our land. We had skirmishes with the Schmidt family when they first settled up there above the village. They cleared the land and planted rubber trees, cocoa beans and copra. The Schmidt family arrived here in 1900 and by 1905 they were starting to make big money.'

'How come the Schmidt family wasn't sent home like all the other Germans?'

'It was very hard for the Kiwis to round everyone up. Probably 95% were put on ships and sent back home but a few Germans found ingenious ways of staying. The Schmidt family certainly did.'

'How did they manage that?' questioned Susan.

'The Schmidt family was clever. They did a deal with our village chief at the time. They promised to give the chief 25% of their profits and to employ more of the young Salamumu men on their plantation. All they wanted in return was to be able to stay and not be betrayed to the New Zealand authorities. It worked. Samoa was administered by the New Zealanders until this year when we finally won our independence. The Schmidt family has farmed here commercially and successfully, for sixty-two years. They have made heaps of money but also helped Salamumu to become one of the wealthiest villages. We have the grandest church on the south coast, can pay a generous stipend to our minister and have a well equipped school. This is all possible because we still get 25% of the Schmidt's profits.'

The Schmidt family members were now hauling themselves out of the waterhole and drying down with towels. Towels were not really necessary as the hot sun did it for you in a few minutes. Then one of them spotted Rod and Susan sitting on the other side of the waterhole. Very few whites, apart from the Schmidt family, ever visited this waterhole so they were naturally interested to meet them. More or less dry and still drying their hair the three wandered over.

'Malo,' greeted the older Schmidt.

'Ua mai oe?' asked Ra'a.

'Manuia fa'afeta,' responded the older Schmidt.

Ra'a then apologised to his guests. 'Sorry, we were just saying "hello" and asking each other how we are. We'll speak English now. Let me introduce you to Carl Schmidt and his lovely wife, Sophia. Carl and Sophia this is Rod and Susan Benson. Rod is all the way from Scotland Yard, London. He's running a course I'm attending in Apia.'

The four shook hands and greeted each other.

'And we have a visitor from Germany. He's a cousin,' announced Carl, turning round to introduce the third member of his party. However, the young man had suddenly hurried away and was heading back to the path that led uphill along the side of the waterfall. 'Strange,' remarked Carl, 'I don't know what happened to him all of a sudden.'

25.   The Cousin

That Saturday evening the Bensons enjoyed a village feast with virtually everyone from the village present. A very special night. There was no alcohol because Salamumu was a "dry" village. Instead, they had a choice of fresh pineapple, noni or soursop. After the feasting was over there was an exhibition of fire dancing given by a couple of the young village lads. Sammy, although exhausted by the excitement of the day, managed to stay awake until ten o'clock when the church minister closed the evening's proceedings with a prayer and a blessing. The villagers melted away quietly and respectfully back to their fales. Tomorrow was the Sabbath and everyone needed their sleep before church at nine o'clock.

Ra'a had warned the Bensons to bring clothes appropriate for church so they were prepared. The singing of hymns was just as joyous and spirited as in Apia, while the minister was even more long-winded with his fire and brimstone sermon. Sammy was invited by his new-found friends to join them sitting together in pews at the back of the church. He sat surprisingly still and quiet throughout the service because there was a "controller" standing behind the children holding a very long bamboo stick. If a child started to fidget, or tried to whisper, the ever-attentive controller used his long pole to tap the miscreant on the head. A warning! Two taps and you were reported to your parents which usually meant being deprived of play for a whole day.

Susan and Rod were intrigued to observe a "naming and shaming" session at the end of the service. As with all other churches, a plate was passed around during the singing of one of the hymns and each family placed an envelope on the plate with their name written on it. Inside each envelope was the family's gift to the church for the week. After the minister had delivered his final blessing, one of the matais walked to the microphone at the front of the church and proceeded to read out how much each family had donated. You could hear a pin drop.

'Vaai, twenty talas,

Fapuleai, twenty-five talas,

Teuila, fifteen talas,

Faafafa, eighteen talas…' And so it went on until every family in the village was accounted for.

Everyone knew exactly how much each family was expected to give every Sunday. Most of the announcements were met with complete silence but occasionally there was a collective groan if a family had fallen short or a joyous murmur of approval if a family had exceeded its weekly tithe. This "naming and shaming" process lasted nearly ten minutes before the congregation started to slowly file out of the church. Rod had placed a twenty-tala banknote on the plate as it went by and was greatly relieved that the matai making the announcements didn't mention the amount his family had given.

After the service, the villagers drifted back to their fales to sit in the shade and enjoy a family lunch. Sundays were set aside to be a time of relaxation and quiet contemplation. No work was attempted and the children were expected to play quiet games only. Boisterous behaviour was immediately called out. It was faithfully observed as God's Day of Rest. Rod, however, was anxious to talk to Ra'a so he collected his lunch and sat down cross-legged next to him.

'Ra'a, can I ask you about the Schmidt family we met yesterday at the waterhole?'

'Of course,' replied the matai as he scooped up a piece of taro swimming in coconut milk, 'I'm sorry they didn't stay longer.'

'So am I. Actually, it was the Schmidt's visitor who interests me.'

'Oh, why is that?'

'Two things. I had the feeling I'd seen him somewhere before. Carl said he was his cousin but I never heard what his name was. And then the cousin behaved very strangely. As soon as he heard you say I was from Scotland Yard, he couldn't get away fast enough and bolted back up the path as if I had the plague.'

'Yes, I noticed that. I thought he might have been in a hurry to get to the toilet or something.'

'I'd really like to follow him up. Do you think we could possibly call in on the Schmidt's this afternoon before we leave for Apia?'

'I don't see why not. Their access road is on the other side of the village. It only takes ten minutes to drive up to their luxurious home.'

☾

Half an hour later Ra'a and Rod climbed back into the beaten-up old truck and headed up into the verdant, thickly forested hills overlooking Salamumu. Susan and Sammy were happy for them to go off together because they had been invited to the fale of an elderly female matai to look at her intricate tapa cloth work. Of course, no work was allowed today but there was nothing to stop a person admiring someone else's handiwork. And this lady had a reputation for exceptionally beautiful work.

The dirt access road snaked its way up to the Schmidt's property through no less than three hairpin bends and heavily forested surrounds before abruptly popping out into intensely bright sunshine. They had reached a plateau covered with rows and rows of rubber trees, each with a tin container attached to the trunk collecting the milky coloured latex. Before they could follow the road through the rubber trees, they had to open a gate to the property with a sign reading, "Schmidt and Sons Pty Ltd." Rod jumped out and deftly handled the gate duties.

The road was now as straight as a die with a considerably smoother more comfortable surface. Apart from the occasional bird, there were no signs of life. They must have driven for half a mile through the plantation with the rubber trees on either side lined up like ranks of soldiers standing at attention. The road then took a sharp turn to the right and there before them, a hundred yards farther on, stood a splendid bungalow surrounded by a variety of palms of varying heights. Rod thought the residence looked a bit like Robert Louis Stevenson's mansion, where the famous writer had lived for seven years just outside Apia, although the Schmidt's house was on a smaller scale.

On their way up the hill Ra'a had outlined the relationship that currently existed between his village and the Schmidt family. Things had been extremely tense when Fritz Schmidt had first arrived, escorted by a group of armed white men back in 1900. They had brandished guns at the villagers and demanded a villager to guide them up into the hills behind Salamumu. The Germans liked what they found up there and immediately built a rough shelter and started felling the native trees. They bought food from the Salamumu villagers and soon Fritz replaced the Germans with Chinese workers, who did the hard work clearing the forest, building the access road and planting out the seedlings for less than half the wages he would have had to pay his compatriots. This was a very difficult time for the villagers of Salamumu. A couple of times fierce fighting broke out when Chinese workers raped some of Salamumu's young women.

Things improved after the New Zealanders arrived and kicked the Germans out of Samoa in 1915. Fritz Schmidt, who had married a German woman by that time, was desperate to stay. Once the villagers started to share in the profits and could see the benefits of all this money coming in, village attitudes began to change. Today, we all get along quite well. The Schmidts hardly ever come to church, but they financed the bell tower and still pay for the church's maintenance. Thanks to the Schmidts, the church gets re-painted every few years.

'So, Carl and Sophia Schmidt, who we met yesterday, are direct descendants of Fritz Schmidt?'

'Correct. Carl is Fritz's grandson. Old Fritz died in 1955 at the age of eighty. He had several children, most of whom went back to Germany. Carl now runs the place with his wife Sophia and they're still doing very well exporting their produce.'

'Was the village using the land up in the hills before Fritz turned up and seized it?'

'Yes and no. Our vegetables, fruit and flower gardens have always been grown around the village; however, we did come up into the hills from time to time to hunt or pick berries and mushrooms. We can still do that today but we have to stay well away from the Schmidt's farm. It means we have to walk farther, that's all.'

Ra'a and Rob soon came to a second gate that enclosed the tropical gardens encircling the house. The name of the house was inscribed on a white board, "Mananaia." 'It's a Samoan word meaning "beautiful"' Ra'a commented, as Rod closed the gate behind them. It was indeed a beautiful place, some sixty years in the making. Rod already recognised a few of the tropical plants: red ginger, bamboo, the stinging nettle tree, hibiscus, breadfruit and kapok and Ra'a identified a few more for him: chilli peppers, mango and lemon grass. The aggressive mile-a-minute weed had been kept out of the garden allowing the colourful profusion of plants to thrive.

The Schmidts had heard the truck as it pulled up on the loose white gravel and Carl appeared at the front door to welcome them.

'Talofa Ra'a, Talofa Rod. This is a pleasant surprise. Come on in…'

Carl was wearing shorts, sandals and a colourful loose Samoan top. Years of living and working outside had left him with a permanent tan and he looked fit and healthy. A mop of blonde hair in need of a good cut gave him a slightly rough, surfie appearance, otherwise he was a strikingly good looking fellow.

They followed Carl through the house and out to a lovely shady area out the back beside a swimming pool. Sitting there on a deck-chair was Carl's wife, Sophia. Sophia had film-star good looks and a bright personality to match. Rod thought she looked even more beautiful than when she had been swimming in the waterhole the day before. Friendly greetings were exchanged and a young Samoan girl appeared at the door to ask what should be served. Sophia ordered cool drinks and a small fruit platter for four. The lass, who Ra'a knew because she was from Salamumu, smiled sweetly and hurried away.

They spent a little time talking about the international export market and the two full-time gardeners Carl employed to maintain his private house garden. Then Rod was able to move the conversation towards what he wanted to discuss.

'It must be very peaceful with just the three of you living here,' he opined.

'Yes, it is at the moment,' replied Sophia, unlocking her long legs, 'our two children are in Germany at their private schools.'

'And I think we met a visitor yesterday who is staying with you?' probed Rod.

'True,' replied Carl, 'for the last six weeks my distant cousin from Germany has been staying here. But he left in a hurry yesterday, just after coming down to the waterhole with us.'

'As you know, I'm with Scotland Yard and I'm naturally a curious man, which probably explains how I got to become a sleuth.'

'A sleuth? What is a sleuth, please?' inquired Sophia.

'It's another word for a detective,' apologised Rod, forgetting that Sophia's mother tongue was German.

'We're sorry my cousin left,' continued Carl, 'because we had been training him up to do a number of tasks around the property. He arrived suddenly and left suddenly, most peculiar! We got along well enough. He said he had come because he had had a nervous breakdown and his doctor recommended getting away overseas and doing physical work for a change. He was an academic, you know. It nearly killed him working in the heat every day but he was coming good and starting to enjoy life.'

'Perhaps he felt he was cured, darling,' suggested Sophia, 'or more likely, he was keen to get back to his wife?'

'Who knows? He was a secretive sort of bloke. We weren't paying him. He said he wanted to work to pay for his board and keep. I was beginning to think he wanted the arrangement to go on for months…'

'Yes, you're right,' interjected Sophia, flashing a lovely smile towards her husband, 'I was thinking the same thing. In fact, I was beginning to wonder whether he had left his wife.'

'You might be right, dear. He didn't say much about her and no letters ever arrived for him either.'

'The reason I'm so interested in your visitor comes back to my training as a policeman,' said Rod, 'right from the beginning of my training I was encouraged to observe and memorise. If something wasn't quite right, I noticed it. Yesterday, when it was mentioned I'm from Scotland Yard, your cousin couldn't get away quickly enough. In my humble opinion, he's horribly guilty about something.'

'I guess that's possible. It never occurred to me we could be harbouring a fugitive,' Carl added, 'after all he's my cousin, although twice removed, I think.'

'There's one other thing,' continued Rod, 'your cousin's face looked vaguely familiar. I have a feeling I may have seen his visage on a "wanted poster." This is a bit of a long shot, I know, but I do try to memorise most of the people on the recently issued wanted lists.'

'I guess we should be trying to do the same thing on our course,' added Ra'a, impressed by what Rod was saying.

'Did your cousin tell you where he was headed Carl?'

'No. Did he say anything to you, dear?'

Sophia shook her head, 'No nothing. He just grabbed everything and left. I asked Reuben to drive him as far as the turn-off. He'd be able to catch the bus from there over to Apia.'

There was a moment's silence as Rod reflected on what he'd just heard. He was wondering whether his suspicions were well enough founded for him to take the matter any further, or whether he was over-reacting. His gut instinct told him this man was guilty of some major crime but he didn't have an ounce of evidence to back it up. Without evidence police are powerless and even more so when they are a guest in a foreign country.

'What's your cousin's name?'

'Doctor Heinrich Zeigler.'

26. Follow-up

The Benson family was dropped off at Aggie Grey's Hotel at dusk. Tired, they strolled back to their unit listening to the chorus of birds settling down for the night and keeping a wary eye on the colony of fruit bats nearby already stirring in readiness for another night's feeding frenzy. It had been a big weekend for little Sammy. It was all he could manage to have a quick shower and stay awake long enough to eat his scrambled eggs, followed by pawpaw doused with lemon juice. By eight o'clock he was fast asleep. Rod spent the rest of the evening preparing the workshop he was running next morning while Susan read a novel.

Susan thought her husband was unusually quiet during the evening, a sure sign something was bugging him. When they went to bed, she tried to get Rod to talk about it.

'You've been very quiet this evening, dear. Is something worrying you?'

'I've been getting my work prepared for tomorrow.'

'Yes, I know but usually you talk to me a bit during the evening when you're working. You've hardly said boo to a goose tonight.'

'Umm, sorry. Yes, there is something worrying me. It's silly really but it won't go away.'

'Come on darling, spill the beans.'

'It's that guy we met.'

'Which guy? We met heaps of people in Salamumu.'

'The white guy at the waterhole on Saturday afternoon. The one who had disappeared by the time we went to visit Carl and Sophia Schmidt this afternoon.'

'Ah yes, the German cousin.'

'It might just be my suspicious mind, but I have a feeling he's a wanted man.'

'What, in Germany?'

'No, in England.'

'But he's German, isn't he?'

'Yes, I know, but I remember the name vaguely from a couple of months ago.'

'What was the name again?'

'Doctor Heinrich Zeigler.'

'It doesn't ring a bell with me,' answered Susan.

'Well, if my hunch is right, Zeigler's hiding out here in Samoa to escape the English police.'

'What sort of crime do you think he committed?'

'I can't remember. It could have been drugs, embezzlement, rape, murder…I don't know. Something serious anyway.'

'Is there anything you can do?'

'I have no authority to do anything here in Samoa, but I might send a telegram to my off-sider in Scotland Yard tomorrow morning and ask him to let me know if my hunch is right or not.'

'That sounds sensible, dear,' and Susan gave him a goodnight kiss.

True to his word, next morning Rod called in at the Apia post office during his lunch break and sent this telegram to his off-sider in London:

MET DR HEINRICH ZEIGLER HERE IN SAMOA STOP IS HE WANTED BY POLICE IN ENGLAND? STOP URGENT REPLY NEEDED STOP ROD

The telegram was transmitted at 12.26 Western Samoan time, the middle of the night in London.

☾

Rod received a return telegram next morning while having breakfast in Aggie Grey's dining room.

ZEIGLER WANTED ON DOUBLE MURDER CHARGES STOP

ARREST IF POSSIBLE STOP YARD TALKING TO SAMOA
GOVT TODAY STOP JOHN

Without a word, Rod passed the telegram across to Susan.

'Looks like you're going to have an extra busy day, darling,' was all she said handing the paper back.

'I'll see if I can catch-up with the Chief Commissioner sometime today.'

Rod and his family had already met the Chief Commissioner of the Western Samoan Police Force on their arrival at Faleolo International Airport four weeks earlier. Mike Arbuthnot was a New Zealander who had successfully handled the national celebrations on January 1st when Western Samoa had officially become the world's newest nation. Mike had felt it his duty to meet the Benson family and make them welcome. Establishing an investigative branch in the fledgling Western Samoan police force was a major initiative and he wanted to give it the best possible chance to get off the ground. Mike agreed to meet Rod in his office at the end of the day.

The police headquarters was a modest long timber single-storey structure badly in need of a paint job and some basic maintenance. Over the last two years every spare tala in the country's coffers had been saved to be splurged on the January 1st Proclamation Day events so virtually nothing was left in kitty to pay for such mundane jobs as the upkeep of the Police HQ. Mike Arbuthnot was pleased to meet Rod and keen to find out more about the fugitive. Things had moved surprisingly fast during the day while Rod had been busily conducting his workshops.

'Welcome Rod. The family well?' asked the Commissioner with his pronounced New Zealand drawl.

Yes, thank you sir, beginning to really like the place, I think.'

'That's good. I'm into my third year here. It's quiet but the Samoans are lovely people, most hospitable.'

'I'd agree with you there. We spent this last weekend over in Salamumu as a guest of Ra'a who is a matai there.'

'Fine fellow Ra'a. I have my eye on him as a possible future Police Commissioner one day after they push me out. And how's the detective course going?'

'Well, enough, thank you sir. They're all keen, although poor English is a problem for a couple of the fellows. Slows us down somewhat and I have to ask Ra'a to translate much of the time.'

'Yes, I'm not surprised. Now, let's get down to business. First of all, congratulations on spotting this escapee trying to hide on these shores and for moving so quickly.'

'Thank you, sir. Let's hope we can do something to detain him.'

'There's nothing we can do here in Western Samoa to arrest or detain a foreigner, unless...' the Chief Commissioner paused, '...unless, we have the explicit permission of the Samoan Home Secretary and the relevant diplomatic service. In this case it would be the UK's High Commissioner. I have already talked to the Home Secretary. That was a simple matter of sharing a bowl of ava with him at lunchtime and he's happy for us to find our man and extradite him back to the UK. Problem solved...'

'What about the High Commissioner, sir?'

'I'll ring Norman right now...'

Rod waited while the Chief Commissioner and the British High Commissioner chatted for several minutes. They seemed more interested in discussing the upcoming British Lions rugby tour of New Zealand than hunting down a brutal murderer. However, when the conversation was finally over the police chief replaced the receiver and spoke to Rod again.

'It's all systems go. You now have all the permission you need to hunt this Zeibler bloke down.'

'It's Zeigler, sir.'

'Ah yes, Zeigler. What do you propose to do first up?'

'My gut feeling is the guy has already left Western Samoa by air. We are probably too late. I'll check with security out at Faleolo Airport for lists of all passengers who have left the country in the last twenty-four hours. If he has left Samoa, we will at least know where he's flown to.'

'That shouldn't be difficult. Faleolo is the only international airport and there are only one or two commercial flights in and out of the country each day. Better check the private planes too,' the Chief Commissioner advised.

Rod thanked the Chief of Police for his help. Then he dropped into Aggie Grey's to advise Susan he would be late for dinner and drove the twenty-five miles out to the international airport. The road was one of the very few in the country to have bitumen and he arrived shortly after dark. Checking the passenger lists was easy. Only three commercial flights had left Faleolo since yesterday afternoon. Doctor Heinrich Zeigler's name did not appear on any of the passenger lists. Nor was Zeigler listed as being aboard a private plane. Unless he had escaped by boat, Zeigler must still be in the country.

27. Wednesday, November 21st

Another miserable day weatherwise. Inspector Hank Zagalski was at rugby training practising scrummaging under the watchful eye of the new coach. The cold drizzle penetrated all parts of his body and had not cleared all day. It must be at least three days since they had seen even a glimpse of weak autumn sunshine. The ground was boggy enough to make it hard for his football boots to get decent traction in the slippery mud. His mates weren't doing any better either and were letting the coach know this scrummaging business was a waste of bloody time. With an angry blast of his whistle, the coach abandoned the scrum practice and started setting up teams for a quick seven-aside game. It was at this moment Hank noticed Belinda parking her car in the carpark that overlooked the ground. Belinda had recently started coming to watch his rugby matches at weekends but coming to a mid-week training session was a first. He wondered why she was here this time.

Wisely, Belinda remained warm and snug in her car watching the men slipping and sliding about in the gathering gloom of a bleak English evening. The occasional late autumnal leaf blew across her windscreen to join the millions of others piled up along the base of the nearby fence. She had some exciting news to pass on to Hank. It was so urgent and so important Hank would appreciate discussing it with her immediately. It would be almost dark by five o'clock so she knew she had only another fifteen minutes to wait. Even fanatical rugby rats have to stop playing in the dark.

Training over, the boys headed off to the pub for a couple of beers but Hank used the arrival of his girlfriend as a perfectly legitimate reason for not joining them this particular evening. He collected his clothes from the changing room and endured the unavoidable ribbing from his mates. There was no malice in their comments, yet some were crude and he was glad Belinda's ears had been spared any embarrassment. He was horribly wet and covered in mud when he reached Belinda's clean car. She wound down her window and looked him up and down, disapprovingly.

'Guess what, Hank? You and I leave tomorrow evening for Western Samoa!'

'What?' a stunned Hank replied, 'where the heck is Western Samoa?'

'West of Eastern Samoa, I presume,' laughed Belinda, 'go home and get cleaned up, then come round for dinner and I'll tell you everything I know.'

Hank didn't need any further encouragement. 'I'll be at your place by sixish.'

☾

Belinda had a platter of cheese and biscuits and a half pint of Guiness ready when Hank arrived on the stroke of six. There was something cooking in the oven that smelt delicious and Belinda was looking particularly fetching in a dress he had not seen her wearing before. On the coffee table sat a globe of the world and after a few minutes searching they finally located Western Samoa sitting fifteen degrees south of the equator and just west of the International Date Line. Try as they might, they couldn't locate an Eastern Samoa. 'Perhaps it's called Western Samoa because it's west of the International Date Line?' suggested Hank. They could just make out the names of two Samoan towns marked on the globe: Apia and Pago Pago.

'Shortly after you left to go to rugby training, the boss was looking for you. He'd forgotten you leave early on Wednesdays for rugby training. Anyway, there's been a definite sighting of Zeigler in Western Samoa and the government there has asked Scotland Yard to come and get him. Scotland Yard knew we were the detectives working on the case, so they've passed it over to us. Isn't that exciting!'

'So, what's the climate like there?'

'Stinking hot and humid,' replied Belinda, 'pack your tropical clothes.'

'I don't have any!'

'Then just wear your swimmers,' she giggled.

'Okay, as long as you just wear a bikini.'

Belinda smiled seductively, 'I do have a bikini, as it happens, and I think you'll like it.'

'I'm sure I will!'

'Everything has been booked for us. We leave tomorrow from Gatwick at seventeen hundred hours on a BOAC plane. We even have a day stopover in Sydney before flying on to Apia, the capital of Western Samoa.'

'Wow, I still can't believe this is happening.'

'This dish smells as though it's ready,' and Belinda opened the oven door and checked. 'No, another five minutes.' She walked back to where Hank was sitting.

'We've been booked into a hotel in Apia on an open voucher, which means we can stay for an extended time if needed. All expenses paid. Oh, I nearly forgot…we have anti-malaria tablets to take every day, starting tonight. I've already got them from the chemist.'

'You said there's been a definite sighting of Zeigler, so that means he's still on the loose?'

'I guess so. By the way the boss said we don't have to go to work tomorrow. We'll need the time to pack, get organised and tell our families what's happening.'

'I'd like to see if the library has anything about Western Samoa so I can bone up on the place.'

'That's a good idea. We have to pick up our tickets at Gatwick. They'll be waiting for us at the BOAC information desk.'

Belinda had little else she could pass on to Hank, except it was a senior English detective working in Western Samoa who had contacted Scotland Yard with the information about Zeigler.

Hopefully this wasn't a false alarm. They would look a bit silly if they went half way round the world for nothing!

☾

Never having flown before, Hank and Belinda were ill-prepared for what was ahead. They arrived at Gatwick Airport an hour before their flight, showed their passports, collected their tickets from the BOAC information desk and checked in their luggage. The first shock was discovering the flight to Sydney involved thirty-eight hours of travel with eight stops! According to the travel documentation, their Boeing 707-138, the world's most up-to-date aeroplane, would stop to refuel and take on new crews in Rome, Cairo, Bahrain, Karachi, Calcutta, Bangkok, Singapore and Darwin before finally touching down in Sydney. Fortunately, all meals were provided en route.

They had been warned to wear business clothes for the flight and Hank looked smart in a tweed jacket and tie while Belinda had taken care to be dressed as if attending church. She decided against wearing a hat, however. As the passengers assembled in the waiting area they were offered refreshments prior to boarding. A beautifully dressed air hostess called Rosemary took them to their seats and fussed over them, making sure they were comfortable and had everything they needed. Next, Rosemary handed them each a menu that was four pages long and contained choices for every meal as well as morning and afternoon teas for the entire thirty-eight-hour journey. Grandly presented, Belinda and Hank couldn't believe the variety and sophistication of the meals they would be enjoying.

Rosemary was most attentive and had sole care of about ten passengers. They took off on time, with Hank holding Belinda's hand… first flights can be somewhat unnerving. Once the initial excitement of being air-borne had worn off they settled down for the long, tiring grind ahead. Alcoholic drinks were free and it soon became clear some passengers were determined to be the worse for wear before they arrived in Rome. A delicious three course evening meal appeared, one course at a time, just like in a classy restaurant. Clean, folded napkins were provided and Rosemary wore white gloves whenever serving. The evening meal was a leisurely affair taking over two hours. Hank and Belinda then lay back in their generous reclining seats and enjoyed a port with their after-dinner mints.

Despite the wonderful service, occupying thirty-eight hours of flying time was a challenge. Many passengers smoked cigarettes, cigars or pipes and very early in the 12,753 mile journey the cabin filled with smoke and a blue haze hung heavily in the still air. Supposedly, there was some air circulating but it was largely ineffective. Before long some passengers started coughing while others developed sore eyes and even head-aches. There was not a great deal to do. If you had a book, you could read and Rosemary handed out a few fashionable magazines and newspapers. At the rear of the plane was a cocktail bar with a fulltime barman where you could go to stretch your legs and try out some exotic concoctions whenever it was safe to do so. BOAC even supplied each passenger with six free postcards showing a BOAC aircraft and you could write on these to fill in a bit of time.

Landing and taking off at the eight fuel stops relieved the boredom somewhat, although even these breaks in routine became tedious when you felt tired and grumpy from sitting for so many hours. Some fuel stops were a little longer than others and passengers were allowed to leave the plane and walk around the airport if they wished. The two detectives found it was a relief to have a stretch and breathe some fresher air but there was not much to do in the airports except look at the shops. Unless you had the correct currency, you couldn't buy anything anyway.

After nearly two days flying around the world, their plane banked steeply on its approach into the airport at Darwin. The captain welcomed passengers to Australia and warned everyone to remain seated until the quarantine officer had been through the plane spraying insecticide as a precaution against nasty, unwelcome insects entering the country. The temperature the captain informed them, was thirty-three degrees with almost one hundred percent humidity. Heavy clouds could be seen building up over the sea and torrential rain was expected. After enduring two days of cigarette smoke, the smell of insect spray was but a minor irritant and Belinda and Hank took the opportunity to file out and walk across the blistering tarmac to the airport building. Once again, the heat hit them as they stepped out of the aircraft. They were grossly over-dressed for a tropical climate and had already made up their minds when they reached Sydney, they would spend their day there purchasing clothes more appropriate for tropical Western Samoa.

What little they saw of Darwin from the air didn't impress, although the beaches looked inviting. As they continued their journey south-east across Australia the terrain changed from lush green tropical to arid red desert until several hours later when the country slowly started to improve again. They circled once before landing smoothly at Mascot after dark. Coming in, the city lights were a fantastic sight. The famous harbour and the Sydney Harbour Bridge were easy to spot. They sailed through customs and caught a taxi to their motel where they at last enjoyed a good night's rest on beds that didn't shudder and shake and where they could breathe in clean air.

Saturday, November 24th was a pleasant sunny day in Sydney. Hank and Belinda spent the morning shopping for their tropical clothes. In the afternoon they caught the tram to Bondi Beach where they sun-baked in the barmy spring sunshine. They found the water rather too cold for comfort and later returned to their motel for a shower before dinner at the motel's restaurant.

Three days living in such close proximity had allowed the

couple to discover more and more about each other. Belinda now knew Hank was a snorer and Hank found Belinda twitched and mumbled in her sleep. They had made good use of their waking hours though, learning more about each other's childhoods, families, likes and dislikes, hopes and ambitions. Belinda had an adventurous streak but also wanted a settled married life with several children. A happy family life was what she craved above all else. Hank shared her longing for a family but was ambitious for his career too. He wanted to rise up through the ranks of the police force to become, at least, a Chief Superintendent and was even considering one day establishing his own private detective agency.

The physical attraction between the pair was as intense as ever. However, true to their strict principles, they limited their physical contact to embraces, kisses and hand-holding.

28. Western Samoa

Sydney to Apia, via Suva, was aboard a Qantas plane half the size of the Boeing 707-138 which had conveyed Hank and Belinda all the way from London. Nevertheless, they were well cared for and landed safely at Faleolo Airport at ten past ten at night. During the flight for the first time Belinda and Hank heard softly spoken Samoans speaking in their native tongue. It is often said that first impressions are the lasting ones and they liked what they saw and heard. Their fellow passengers were polite, respectful folk of similar stature to the British. But, joked Belinda, they were better looking.

Faleolo Airport was virtually deserted. They sailed through passport control and customs with the sleepy officials keen to finish work for the day and get home. There was no air conditioning, although a few ancient ceiling fans struggled valiantly to move the air. They were horribly hot and sweaty well before they reached the exit where they planned to hail a taxi to take them into Apia. Outside they found three decrepit cars lined up with taxi signs, the first two of which were already taken. Appreciating there may not be sufficient taxis available for everyone, Hank moved quickly towards the last one only to encounter a man in a peaked cap who suddenly appeared holding a sign that read, "SCOTLAND YARD VISITORS."

Hank introduced himself and was relieved to find the man in the peaked cap spoke some English and had been expressly sent to collect them. The man said his name was Elijah and then gave a long unpronounceable family name with a heap of vowels in it. Elijah went on to explain he was the chauffeur for the Chief Commissioner and had been sent to convey them to Aggie Grey's Hotel. Thankful, the two detectives piled in with Elijah handling their luggage. They saw no speed signs along the twenty-five-mile journey east into the capital and travelled at a sedate pace befitting a chauffeur driven vehicle. With the windows wide open there was some relief from the sapping heat and humidity.

Being dark it was difficult to see much. The road passed through a number of poorly lit villages where villagers could be seen inside houses with no walls that Elijah told them were called "fales". Sophisticated gardens and healthy crops of strange vegetables surrounded the villages. Every village boasted an impressive church and what looked like a large village fale, presumably for meetings. Not much else was visible until they drove into Apia where the main roads had basic street lighting.

Elijah pulled up outside a charming old grey timber building of late Victorian Colonial style. It was past eleven and they walked in to find there was nobody about. Once again Elijah came to their rescue. He disappeared out the back somewhere and emerged five minutes later with a security fellow in tow. There were a few "talofas" (hellos) all round and much shaking of hands. Accustomed to tipping, Hank pulled out a one-pound note and handed it to Elijah with his thanks. Elijah looked at the note for a moment or two as if it was toxic or cursed. Tipping was not customary in Western Samoa. Then, realising it was meant as a thank you gesture, Elijah grinned and thrust the one-pound note into a trouser pocket. With a cheerful wave, he was on his way.

The security man dispensed with the bother of filling out guest forms and led them out the back along a concrete path that wound about between a row of accommodation units. It was quiet, most people already asleep. The security man stopped outside unit 26 and unlocked the door. He then grabbed their luggage and started taking it into the unit. At this point Belinda and Hank tried to explain they were not married and wanted two separate units. The security man did not understand at first, but eventually got the message. Not looking too pleased, he trudged back to reception to collect another key. Belinda ended up taking unit 26 and Hank a bit further down the path at unit 30.

The pair met for breakfast next morning in the large, airy dining room. The Victorian décor had been carefully preserved so that the room, like the rest of Aggie Grey's Hotel, oozed with "atmosphere." Both felt refreshed after a reasonable night's sleep and enjoyed a leisurely "European" style breakfast. They discussed what they should do and decided to report to the police station situated only a couple of hundred yards away from their hotel. However, before their meal was finished an envelope was brought to the table addressed to Inspector H. Zagalski. Inside was a brief letter.

Dear Inspector Zagalski,

I trust you and your colleague had a good trip and a restful night?
Please report to my office at 9.30am for a full briefing.

We are most grateful to Scotland Yard for your assistance with this matter.

Michael Arbuthnot, OBE
Chief Commissioner of Police, Western Samoa.

After their pleasant breakfast they checked in at reception, showed their passports, completed their accommodation forms and returned to their units to freshen up before their briefing with the Chief Commissioner. They arrived five minutes early and were asked to wait in a small waiting room complete with a fan that kept the air moving and the perspiration just bearable. They didn't have to wait long before being invited into the Chief Commissioner's office.

Belinda thought it was uncanny. There seemed to be some sort of telepathy between rugby union players. Almost immediately Hank Zagalski and Mike Arbuthnot instinctively knew they were both smitten by the sport and were talking "rugby." Perhaps, mused Belinda, rugby was indeed the game they played in heaven. The Chief Commissioner had been close to winning selection for the All Blacks in his prime so the first ten minutes was devoted solely to the two men extolling their athletic virtues and discussing the upcoming clash between the All Blacks and the British Lions. Belinda felt surplus to needs and sat there in bored silence. Finally, both men realised they were being somewhat disrespectful to her and apologised. Mike Arbuthnot started his briefing.

'A few days ago, Rod Benson, one of your men, made a positive sighting of Doctor Heinrich Zeigler. He spotted him on the other side of the island near a village called Salamumu. Rod is a great operator, here for three months to establish an Investigative Unit for our embryonic police force. I don't think he makes mistakes...'

'Why would Zeigler have come here do you think, sir?' asked Belinda, delighted at last to participate in the proceedings.

'Ah, good question,' responded the Chief Commissioner, 'few people know the Germans ruled this country for a short time before the first world war. We Kiwis kicked them out in 1915. A few Germans managed to stay, however, and have since become successful plantation owners. It seems that the bloke you're looking for has a distant German relative still living here. When Zeigler wanted to evade your close attentions, he must have thought he could escape to the far away islands of Western Samoa and start a new life here, in cognito. Clever, but not clever enough it seems.'

'The long arm of the law will catch-up with you eventually,' laughed Hank, 'so, you want us to extradite Zeigler back to England?'

'Indeed. There's only one problem; he's still on the loose.'

'I'm not surprised. He's a slippery bastard. Excuse my French,' said Hank, 'we've nearly caught him several times.'

'So, do we have any idea where he is now?' asked Belinda.

'Not really,' admitted the Chief Commissioner, 'he was last spotted on the side of the road with his suitcase waiting for a bus to take him across Upolu from Salamumu to Apia. That was on Sunday afternoon.'

'Then it's quite possible he's left the country by now,' suggested Belinda.

The Chief Commissioner shook his head, 'We've been checking

the passenger flight lists for commercial and private aircraft every day and have police stationed at Faleolo, the only international airport.'

'But what's to stop him jumping on a boat and escaping? There must be heaps of small islands and trading going on between them,' queried Hank, 'he's escaped once on a boat, already.'

'I agree that's a possibility but not a likely one. Most of the boats around these islands are fishing boats for hunting tuna. They go out overnight and return next day. You also have to appreciate the population of Western Samoa is only about 200,000 and news travels surprisingly fast village to village. We sent a couple of police wagons out to visit all the coastal villages to warn them to look out for this Zeigler guy. He'll stand out here like a horribly sore thumb.'

'What about tourists? asked Belinda, 'would there be private yachts coming here?'

'Again, a very slim possibility. Unless Zeigler's going to try and work his passage as a crew member, or pay a hefty sum of money to be a passenger, he's most unlikely to escape that way.'

'But he could stow away!' exclaimed Hank, 'it might be possible aboard those large sea-going schooners.'

The Chief Commissioner had had enough, 'Hank and Belinda, you are both detectives. Get on with your detective work and find your man and get the bastard out of the country. I don't want a double murderer floating around these beautiful peaceful islands. There's rarely any serious crime here because the matais run a tight ship in every village.'

'Matais?' echoed Belinda and Hank in unison.

'Village chiefs. The only reason we have to have a police force here is because of the bloody tourists!'

'That's interesting,' exclaimed Belinda.

'We badly need the foreign currency from the tourists but we don't want to have to deal with the problems they bring.'

'What sort of problems, sir? inquired Hank.

'Mostly drunken disorderly behaviour, although we are increasingly dealing with trespass, theft and even rape.'

While Hank and Belinda were digesting this information, Mike Arbuthnot made a generous offer.

'You two will be like fish out of water here. Not only will it be a major cultural shock for you but you won't have a bloody clue how things tick. So, I'm assigning you a police vehicle and an experienced local police officer who will be your driver, guide and interpreter. You can trust him with your life. We don't carry arms in Western Samoa but as we are dealing with a particularly nasty character likely to resist arrest, you will each be issued with a firearm.'

They thanked the Chief for his generous offer.

Mike Arbuthnot called his secretary, 'Gloria, has Sergeant Samo arrived yet?'

'Yes, he has sir.'

'Bring him in please.'

A moment later there was a knock on the door and the secretary, Gloria, appeared followed by a genial looking fellow dressed in a tidy police uniform with three stripes proudly displayed on both arms. Sergeant Samo marched in, came smartly to attention and saluted his superior officer.

'At ease, sergeant...'

The sergeant stood like a soldier "at ease" still looking straight ahead at the Chief Commissioner, who made the necessary introductions. 'I have briefed Sergeant Samo with regard to his duties. His English is excellent and he has been in the police force for how long...?'

'Twenty-seven years, sir.'

'Sergeant Samo has a first-class police record and must be one of our longest serving policemen.'

'Only two have been in the force longer, sir.'

'What's more... he's played rugby for Samoa!'

Belinda rolled her eyes. Was she going to be subjected to more long and tedious discussions between these two men about drop-kicks, scrums, centre halves, tight-head locks and a host of other rugby phenomena over the next few days?

'So…there hasn't been another sighting of Zeigler since Sunday afternoon? Today is Friday. So where has he been hiding all this time?' inquired Hank.

'What do you think, sergeant?' asked the Chief Commissioner.

'Sounds to me he has headed up into the hills where nobody lives, sir.'

Sergeant Samo turned to the two British detectives to explain his comment in more detail. 'Apia is the only reasonable sized town in Western Samoa. Almost everyone else lives along the coast where the land is flat and the fishing good. A few have tried to run some cattle or goats up in the hills with mixed success. Some of these hill farmers have built small huts up there where they stay for a night or two when checking on their stock or building fences. It's just possible this gentleman has found an empty hut and is living up there.'

'He's no "gentleman" sergeant,' exclaimed Hank, 'he'd cut your throat as quick as a flash if he felt the need to do so. He's a dangerous man!'

Sergeant Samo nodded.

'Fortunately, sergeant, we have seldom had a vicious killer like this Zeigler fellow in Western Samoa before,' added the Chief Commissioner.

'What would he be doing for food?' asked Belinda.

'If you know enough about our flora you can harvest edible roots, fruits and nuts. It rains daily so fresh water wouldn't be a problem. But having recently arrived here, he wouldn't know much about our native vegetation. My guess is he sneaks down and steals food from the villages under the cover of darkness.'

'Sounds feasible,' agreed Hank. 'Sergeant, would you recommend we start by visiting the closest villages to where Zeigler was last seen to find out if any food has been disappearing?'

'Sounds sensible, sir.'

'Good, that's settled then,' interrupted Mike Arbuthnot, impatient to get on with other matters. 'I want a report on progress around five o'clock every evening. Any more questions?'

The three police filed out having thanked Mike Arbuthnot for his support.

29.   The Hunt Begins...

It was a quarter past ten when Hank, Belinda and Sergeant Samo left the Chief Commissioner's office in time for a morning tea break.

'Sergeant Samo, what is your Christian name please? If the three of us are going to be working closely together over the next few days we might as well use our Christian names. I'm Hank and this lovely lady is Belinda.'

Shyly the sergeant nodded, 'My Christian name is Jacob.'

'Jacob?' echoed Belinda, 'that's an unusual name.'

'Not in Samoa,' smiled Jacob, 'many people have been given names from the Bible.'

'Good, that's settled then. I'm dying for a drink. Any cafes nearby, Jacob?'

'Cafes? Er…no…we don't have cafes like you do. If you would like a cup of tea, I can take you to the police mess.'

Hank looked at Belinda who gave a non-committal shrug. Then, remembering her manners, 'Yes thank you Jacob, we are happy to join you.'

They followed Jacob to a rather dilapidated building behind the main office where a few old wooden tables and metal chairs were scattered about haphazardly. 'The urn is always on,' declared Jacob and they each selected a mug from the odd collection of drinking receptacles available near the urn.

There was no milk so the two English detectives drank black tea. A long line of hungry sugar ants was raiding the sugar bowl so they did without that too. What a contrast this set up was to back home where everything was clean, in plentiful supply and there were numerous choices. For the first time it really hit home that in the

223

UK they lived in great comfort and luxury in contrast to the basic conditions endured by the Samoan people.

With their mugs full they pulled over three metal chairs and sat at a table that wobbled on the uneven floor. As usual, Hank took the initiative.

'Jacob, please tell us where these villages are, what we need to take and when you suggest we leave.'

Jacob took a sip of his tea, then pulled out a pocket-sized notebook and a pencil. 'Let me draw you a map. It will be easier for you to understand then. Assuming Zeigler hasn't escaped to the island of Savaii, where we have police guarding the sea crossing, then he's still hiding out on this island somewhere. The island of Upolu is around 47 miles long and 20 across at its widest point. Our islands are geologically very young, the result of recent volcanic activity so the hills are steep and, in some places, almost impenetrable. There's a coastal road that goes completely around the island connecting all the small villages. There's another road that goes from Apia straight over the mountains to the southern side of the island. As he talked, Jacob began drawing a map showing various prominent geographical features and then started adding a list of the south coast villages.

'Safa'atoa…Salamumu, that's where he was first spotted. Sataoa… Vaiee, which is my village. Then there's Tafiloala where my wife comes from, next is Manmoa then Sa'agafou and Saleilua. That should be enough to keep us going. Together these villages stretch across about twenty miles of the south coast.' Jacob looked up, pleased with his artistic efforts.

'Crikey, I hope you won't expect us to pronounce these villages correctly?' commented Belinda.

Jacob laughed, 'You can point to the villages on this map if you're worried. Better still, I'll get a copy of the official map of Upolu before we leave.'

'What's this place you've marked on the road, Jacob?' asked Hank, pointing to a long name.

'Oh, that's Papapapaitai Falls our largest waterfall. You get an excellent view of it when you cross the island. After heavy rain it's quite a scary sight. It even creates a mist that hangs over the falls like heavy smoke or a strange cloud.'

'Can you hike down to it?' inquired Belinda.

'It's easier to hike up to it,' replied Jacob, 'and you have to choose the right time. It can appear to be a beautiful, well-behaved waterfall one minute and then, ten minutes later, it's a raging torrent. A few people have died getting too close; swept away by a sudden flash flood.'

'Okay,' said Hank, a sense of urgency in his voice, 'what gear do we need to take?'

Jacob thought for a minute before reeling off a list of items. 'We'll need sleeping bags, mosquito nets, mattresses, eating utensils, drinking water, maps, a compass, rifles, ammo, camera, first aid kit and gifts for the villages. We have all those items in storage ready for us to take. It's only a matter of signing everything out and then loading up the vehicle.'

'No food?' queried Hank, always a hungry man.

'We'll be staying in the villages and they'll feed us handsomely. There'll be so much food you'll be groaning,' laughed Jacob. 'I'm a matai and that brings a level of respect with it, as well as my wearing of the police uniform of a sergeant. And having you two along as visitors from overseas will encourage the villagers to create some sumptuous feasts. Mark my words, we are assured of a warm welcome wherever we go.'

'When do we leave?' asked Belinda, keen to get started.

Jacob looked at his watch. 'It's half past ten now. If you would like to collect your gear we'll aim to get away by mid-day.'

☾

Belinda and Hank walked slowly back to Aggie Grey's Hotel. They had already learnt to slow down in this hot, humid tropical climate.

As they strolled, they discussed Sergeant Jacob Samo, their driver, guide and interpreter. Both felt he was an impressive man, ideal for the job ahead. Apart from a bit of an accent, Jacob spoke perfect English which led them to believe he must have been raised and educated in an English-speaking part of the world.

They packed up their personal belongings and checked out. It was impossible to predict when their assignment would be over; they could be away for a day or two, or perhaps as long as a week or more. The receptionist understood and advised them bookings were light for the next few weeks so they shouldn't have any problem getting rooms again on their return. Leaving their suitcases in the foyer, they walked the two hundred yards back to the police station to help Jacob. He was almost loaded up by the time they arrived. They were surprised to find they were going to be travelling in a humble Ford Transit, the only police vehicle currently available. Shortly after mid-day the threesome left the police station and started to drive across the beautiful island of Upolu.

Along the way they found out more about Jacob's background. Born in the village of Vaiee, his mother had died young from malaria. Jacob's father re-married a young English woman who had come to Vaiee as a volunteer primary school teacher in the 1920s. His father was ambitious for his two children and gladly accepted his new wife's generous offer to send Jacob and his younger brother, Joseph, all the way to England for their education. There was no shortage of money in his new wife's family and the two boys were educated at Haileybury and Imperial Service College from the ages of nine to seventeen. Haileybury had an enviable reputation. Jacob found boarding school tough but it taught him resilience. He learnt to speak English with "a plum in his mouth" and relished the opportunity to play rugby, or "rugger" as it was better known in those days.

'Were you tempted to stay in England? asked Belinda.

Jacob shook his head, 'No, I was always homesick. I could only come home to Vaiee once a year when we had our six-week school holidays in July and August.'

'Are your parents still alive, Jacob?'

'My father is. He's just turned eighty. My English step-mother contracted leukemia and returned to England for treatment, but sadly died a few years ago. Cancer's a dreadful disease. When we go to my village, you'll be able to meet my dad. He was the village headman for several years but has now handed that job over to a younger man.'

'And you are a matai, I believe?' queried Hank, 'how do you become a matai?'

Jacob laughed in a slightly embarrassed manner. 'You are selected by your family and the members of the village. Each village has a dozen or more matais. My father is now a matai sili, meaning he is a senior matai.'

'So, is it a hereditary title?'

'Certainly not. I didn't become a matai because of my father. I had to earn the status.'

Belinda found the whole village chiefly system intriguing and asked a few more questions. 'What must you do to be selected, Jacob?'

'Your family and the villagers must believe you are well suited to serve their needs. Selection is based on consensus and merit. There is a fono o matai, that's like a village council, at which only the matais may speak. What's more, only matais are permitted to stand for parliament!'

'Wow, so it's a prestigious honour then,' added Hank.

'Definitely.'

'Are there any female matais?' Belinda inquired.

'At the last count around twenty percent were female,' Jacob replied. 'The fono o matai makes the executive and judicial decisions for the whole village. It's not a particularly democratic practice, though. What the fono o matai decides, is final.'

'Very interesting.'

Belinda would have liked to explore the matai organisation further but Jacob was pulling over to the right-hand side of the road to park at a look out. It was a little cooler here, near the top of the range, and the blazing sun had obligingly disappeared behind a bank of cumulonimbus clouds that were starting to build up ready to deliver the afternoon's downpour. The three walked over to a dilapidated fence that held a rusty sign that warned of steep cliffs and rock falls. Peering over the edge they were treated to a splendid view of a long elegant waterfall cascading over a precipice.

'This is the Papapapaitai Waterfall,' said Jacob. 'I think it's the most impressive one in Samoa. Not much water in it today because it hardly rained yesterday, but if these clouds keep building it will be a raging torrent in a couple of hours.'

'I wish we could see it in all its majesty,' Belinda remarked, 'I love waterfalls.'

'We could leave you up here on your own if you like,' joked Hank, 'and pick you up at the end of the week.'

Belinda stuck her tongue out cheekily at Hank and climbed back into the Ford Transit.

It was half past twelve and Jacob invited the two English detectives to have lunch with him in his own village, Vaiee. 'We'll be there in half an hour and there's always heaps of food about. We might also drop off our luggage in my family's fale where we'll be sleeping tonight. You can meet my dad too. At the same time, we'll check whether anyone in the village has had any food stolen.'

Belinda and Hank were both hungry and delighted to accept Jacob's kind invitation.

❧

During the ensuing half hour of their journey as they descended the narrow winding road to the south coast of Upolu, Hank and Belinda took it in turns to tell Jacob about Doctor Heinrich Zeigler and the crimes he stood accused of. It was a sorry tale of vindictive murders followed by frustrating attempts to capture the man. Above all, the two detectives stressed the danger Zeigler posed for anyone who tried to apprehend him or even cross him.

Jacob admitted that in his twenty-seven years serving as a member of the Western Samoan police force, he had only once been involved in a murder case. Crime was minimal in his country and usually of a petty nature, best handled locally by the fono o matai. Murder amongst the Samoan people was virtually unknown. In all Jacob's time as a policeman, he could only recall five murders. Four were over the hand of a woman and the fifth was a land deal that went terribly wrong. 'We are a peace-loving nation, except on the rugby field,' he joked.

Once they were down the mountain they turned right and passed through the village of Tafiloala with its beautifully maintained gardens and subsistence crops of taro, coconuts, pawpaw, ginger, mangoes and others they didn't recognise. Before they reached Jacob's own village, he pulled over to the side of the road to tell them something he deemed most important.

'It is not acceptable to enter a village without the permission of the high chief. However, because Vaiee is *my* village and I have the standing of a matai, the chief has agreed to let the three of us come into the village to have lunch and leave our luggage. When we return later this evening there will be a formal ava ceremony to welcome you both as honoured guests. When I drive into Vaiee in a few minutes time, please remain quiet and respectful. We will go straight to my family's fale for lunch and leave as soon as it is polite to do so. I will give you a nod when it is time to leave. No photographs please. Taking photos will probably be acceptable after you have been living here for a few nights and the people know you.'

Jacob's advice made Belinda and Hank realise just how valuable his local knowledge was. Without Jacob's understanding of local custom, they would have ignorantly blundered into villages and then wondered why they always received a cold, hostile reception. Hank reflected on his own police training several years ago when it had been emphasised it was wise to work *with* the local people. That advice was valid in the United Kingdom, but even more so here in Western Samoa.

A few minutes later a road sign announced they had arrived at Vaiee. Jacob steered the police vehicle slowly along a road made of crushed coral towards a ring of some twenty fales. A bunch of lively children appeared from nowhere and surrounded them waving and laughing showing their dazzling white teeth. Belinda instantly warmed to these divine looking kids. Their vehicle skirted round what appeared to be a large village green, well grassed and muddy in parts. Jacob told them the area was used for ceremonies or important meetings when the whole village would be present. Sometimes dances and feasts were held here with neighbouring villages. 'And, of course, we play rugby and our own kind of cricket here,' added Jacob.

Jacob's father was introduced as Matai Sili Samo; a distinguished looking man with thinning salt and pepper coloured hair. He shook hands with a firm grip and a welcoming smile. Although eighty, he looked fit with a straight back and wiry build. Wearing a loose-necked blue T-shirt, a lavalava and no footwear, he seemed relaxed and pleased to be entertaining the two English detectives. They parked their suitcases in one corner of the fale under a tapa cloth and sat cross-legged on the ground. Only a light lunch was served by two elderly ladies from the village since there was to be a celebratory feast in their honour after dark. Jacob acted as interpreter because his father had forgotten some of his English. Interestingly, the old man spoke reasonable German still, having been a young man throughout the German occupation.

When Jacob sensed it was appropriate to leave, he signalled to Belinda and Hank who were relieved to stand up after sitting cross-legged for so long. They thanked their hosts, made use of the pit-toilets and climbed back into the Ford Transit.

Jacob suggested the first village to visit should be Salamumu, the village where Zeigler had first been spotted at the waterhole and where he had stayed with Carl and Sophia Schmidt in the verdant hills above Salamumu. Jacob thought it unlikely Zeigler would return to this village for food because he would be recognised by the villagers who were well aware he was a wanted man. Nevertheless, they felt they needed to check. It was possible Zeigler had befriended someone in the village, who might feel sorry for him and give him food. Of course, there was nothing to stop Zeigler sneaking about after dark to pick ripe bananas or pawpaw off the trees.

The threesome spent nearly two hours in Salamumu. Again, Jacob's status as a local matai smoothed their progress enormously. The head chief was anxious to help and waived aside the need for a welcome ceremony. He told them he was very worried Zeigler was still on the loose. They learnt that Zeigler had shown a particular interest in one of the attractive young women in the village and there was concern he might try to come back for her. There had been no further sightings, however, and nobody in the village had reported food disappearing. As an extra precaution they drove up the hill to the Schmidt's property. Zeigler had made no attempt to contact them after his sudden departure five days ago.

As they drove away from the Schmidt's lavish home, Hank gave vent to his naturally suspicious mind. 'Do you think we can trust the Schmidts? After all, they're family for Zeigler. Do you think the familial ties are strong enough for Carl and Sophia to close ranks and protect him? Perhaps the Schmidts feel it is too dangerous to have him in the house and are still feeding him and allowing him to stay in one of their sheds or outhouses?'

The same thoughts had already passed through Belinda's mind too; however, she had put the matter to rest. She felt she was an excellent judge of character. In her opinion, Sophia and Carl were convincing. She believed they'd been telling the truth and were totally honest when they declared they had had no further contact with their cousin. 'What do you think, Jacob?'

Jacob had been listening intently to the opposing views of his two colleagues, one suspicious, the other believing.

'All I can add to what you have said already is that I have known Carl and Sophia all my life. They work closely with the villages along this coast. We don't always agree on everything, but we have never had any reason not to trust their word. We matais have found them to be honest and trustworthy at all times.'

'Okay, that's good enough for me,' replied Hank.

☾

Torrential rain started as they drove back along the coast road to Vaiee. Puddles appeared almost instantaneously and steam rose like smoke from the baked tarmac. Trees swayed and the few people walking along the road crouched under trees or held fronds of palm trees over their heads. One or two hoisted colourful umbrellas but these were no match for the snarling wind that roared and blew their umbrellas inside out. A handful of chickens ran across the road screeching and squawking for cover. They heard a clap of thunder crashing above the noise of rain pounding everything around them. The windscreen wipers could not cope and Jacob was forced to pull over to the side of the road until the intensity of the downpour passed. As so often happened in Samoa, the rain storm passed as quickly as it had arrived, and they were able to resume their journey with bright sunshine and only a slight drop in temperature.

Jacob advised his two colleagues to be ready at the meeting fale for the formal welcome around dusk. He would be there, of course, sitting on the other side of the circle of matais who assemble for such occasions. 'Keep an eye on me,' he stressed, 'I'll be able to give you signals if you don't know what's going on.' The two detectives admitted to feeling apprehensive as they washed and dressed in their smartest gear.

The formal welcome was not as daunting as they had feared. As Jacob had indicated, the matais were seated in a large circle according to rank and Hank and Belinda were politely shown where they must sit as honoured guests close to the most senior members of the village.

Officiating was the village high chief. Sitting next to him was the village orator and next to him, Jacob's father, the senior matai. Next came Hank and Belinda. The other fifteen matais sat in order of seniority on either side of the official group of VIPs. Jacob, still one of the junior matais, was seated almost exactly opposite Hank and Belinda.

There were three speeches conducted almost entirely in Samoan. Each speaker frequently turned towards Hank and Belinda so they knew they were the subject of their remarks. It was a serious affair with no jokes, no laughter. First to speak was the village high chief, followed by the village orator who clearly relished the art of speech making and spoke the longest. When the high chief asked if any other matais wished to speak, Jacob took the opportunity and explained to the gathering why he was working closely with the two guests. His words were met with stern nods.

Then came the ava ceremony. Three fine looking young men displaying splendid tattoos, approached the high chief carrying a large carved wooden tanoa (bowl). Respectfully they sat down in front of him and proceeded to use the fau (strainer) a couple of times. Jacob had informed Belinda and Hank earlier that the tedious process of making ava would have been going on for an hour or two before the young men entered the community fale. A few more words and some clapping before one of the young men plunged a highly polished half coconut shell into the ava and then, with both hands, gracefully presented it to the high chief, who bowed solemnly and holding the container with both hands drank the ava without stopping. The empty coconut shell was then returned to the waiting young man who repeated the process before handing the re-filled shell of ava to the next most senior, the orator. After the orator came Jacob's father and then it was Hank's turn. He drank the muddy-looking liquid without flinching and Belinda determined she must do the same. She certainly didn't like the taste, or the numbing sensation, and prayed silently the ava shell wouldn't come back around the circle a second time. Thankfully, her prayers were answered. When everyone had participated once, the three young men bowed and departed. The high chief said something that might have been a prayer, or a blessing, and the ava ceremony was over.

Hank desperately wanted to hold hands with Belinda or give her a cuddle as they stood up, but he had already observed that physical displays of affection were taboo. Quite simply, it was not done. It was acceptable for a man and a woman to walk and talk together but touching in public was never permitted. Belinda had noticed this too and wondered how married couples ever managed to be intimate in the open fales with absolutely no walls.

The welcoming feast that followed was a far more relaxed affair. Tables and benches had been laid out at the far end of the communal fale and Belinda and Hank sat with Jacob, who acted again as both interpreter and guide to the various dishes on offer. They were introduced to a refreshing drink called soursop made from the fruit with the same name. Later they enjoyed KokoSamoa, a kind of sweet coffee made from roasted Samoan cocoa beans.

Several dishes appeared that they had never heard of. There was Palusami made from taro leaves, onions and coconut milk; Oka I'a, raw tuna salad marinated in lemon juice and coconut cream, also served with onions and finally Kale moa, a chicken curry with ginger, garlic, onions, carrots and potatoes. Belinda, not liking coconut, struggled with the first two but found the curry delicious. Dessert was also an eye-opener. There was Panipopo, Samoa's national dish, consisting of buns baked in sweet sticky coconut cream. Belinda managed to discretely pass her Panipopo to Hank when nobody was looking, but did manage some Pisua. Pisua was a tapioca dish drenched in a creamy sauce made of coconut milk and served with caramelised sugar.

All the excitement of the day meant by ten o'clock Hank and Belinda were ready to retire. Jacob escorted them back to his fale and checked they had everything they needed for a good night's sleep including mosquito nets. Hank slept at one end of the family's fale, Belinda at the other.

30. Stolen Food?

Belinda and Hank spent three days and three nights as guests of Vaiee village. It was not long before they started to form friendships, despite the language barrier. They were introduced to a large number of villagers related to Jacob and soon realised Vaiee consisted mostly of six or seven huge families and Jacob's clan was one of these. It seemed as though half the village claimed to be Jacob's children or grandchildren or were cousins, nieces or nephews. And then there were other "one talks," the aunts and the uncles, the in-laws and the great aunts and the great uncles. There was no way Belinda and Hank could remember everyone's name or their precise relationship to Jacob. The most pleasing thing about being in Vaiee was that everyone in the village appeared to be living in harmony and getting along well.

They were there on a Sunday and attended Matins with almost everyone else in the village. The village church was packed and the service dragged on for nearly two hours. However, they were sitting beneath a fan which made the experience more bearable and the singing was fabulous. After the service, Jacob told them the minister had prayed that all criminals be brought to justice.

Sunday afternoon was taken up with a game of kilikiti, or kirikiti, on the village green. There were bamboo stumps and a ball made from the leaves of the pandanus palm. Bats were three-sided clubs like those used in earlier times to batter your enemies to death. Striking the ball with a three-sided club ensured the flight of the ball was highly unpredictable. There were no boundaries, you just kept running. The game was essentially a social event open to all ages and genders. People came and play ed when they felt like it and left when they had had enough. There was more than ample food and drinks on hand laid out under the shady trees throughout the duration of the game. The hosting team must forfeit the match if the food runs out. Much to the amusement of the villagers, Belinda and Hank batted, bowled and fielded for around an hour.

It was back to work on Monday and the three police continued their visits to the various villages dotted along the south coast hoping to hear of a sighting of Zeigler or some sign of his recent presence. In all but one village, they were welcomed without having to sit through a formal greeting ceremony and this saved them considerable time. As before, these special concessions were entirely due to Jacob's status as a well-known matai enjoying considerable local prestige. The villages had soft-sounding, enchanting names: Safa'atoa, Tafiloala, Sataoa, Saleilua, Manmoa and Sa'agafou. They were all similar in lay-out: a village green surrounded by family fales, a fine church, a primary school and a sizable village fale. One feature that intrigued Hank and Belinda were the large above ground cement graves situated close to each family's fale. Apparently, Samoans found it comforting to keep the remains of their dearly departed physically close. Children freely played on these graves and the washing was often laid out to dry there. On some graves, coffee beans were left for weeks to dry in the hot sun.

It was Tuesday evening before they had completed a visit to every village on Jacob's map but with no sign of Zeigler. It was as if he had once again disappeared without trace. Hank called a meeting after they had enjoyed yet another evening meal as the guests of Vaiee. He was worried about continuing to accept the hospitality of the village without some kind of recompense. As instructed, each evening he had faithfully used the only telephone in the village to report to the Chief Commissioner on their progress. This evening, he planned to ask Mike Arbuthnot to make a payment to the village for three days and nights of food and accommodation.

Hank was also concerned about what to do next and he wanted Belinda and Jacob's views. They sat in the village fale around a hurricane lamp while hundreds of insects of all descriptions buzzed about them incessantly. Occasionally the pesky little creatures would pluck up the courage to land on their hair or bare arms and they had become expert in flicking them away. Mosquitoes, however, were never given a chance to escape. Their fates were instant slaps and their blood-ridden bodies then had to be scraped off the skin.

'We have now visited no less than eight villages along the South coast in and around Salamumu where Zeigler was last sighted,' announced Hank. 'Our man appears to have vanished without trace. I believe our strategy to date has been the right one, although sadly with no results. We now need to decide what to do next. I have a few ideas but first I want to hear your suggestions. Jacob?'

Jacob cleared his throat and swatted another mosquito before answering. 'I keep asking myself, what would *I* do if I was Zeigler? Obviously, I would want to escape police detection and at the same time survive. I must find food and water and to do this I would have to buy or steal from villages. I can get water from the free-flowing creeks but food is far more difficult. My guess is that Zeigler has moved further along the southern coast to some other villages we have not visited yet. There are many more villages along this coastline.'

'How easy is it for Zeigler to travel across country through the hilly hinterland, Jacob?'

'There are rarely any paths to follow so he would have to push his way through thick jungle-like vegetation and across steep gorges where the rivers run. It's possible, but tough going. You would need to be fairly desperate to try it.'

'Well, he's desperate all right. What do you think, Belinda?'

'My thinking is rather different to yours, Jacob. I'd be intent on escaping Samoa where I'm a wanted man and easily recognisable. I would assume the airport is being carefully watched so would look to get away by boat. Every village has a few fishing boats. Perhaps I could bribe someone to take me across to Tonga or Fiji, where I wouldn't be known.'

'He would need a hefty amount of money to persuade a boat owner to take him to another Pacific country,' added Hank.

'Agreed,' seconded Jacob, 'several thousand talas. I doubt he has that kind of money. Remember, he was only getting free food and accommodation at the Schmidt's place.'

'Unless he has stolen money,' suggested Belinda.

'Very unlikely,' responded Jacob, 'people don't hold much cash. He could try one of the small stores along the coast road though. They'd be holding the daily or weekly takings before depositing the money in the bank.'

'What about banks, then? asked Belinda, 'could he rob one, perhaps?'

Jacob shook his head. 'There are only four banks in Apia and one out at the airport. The only other bank is on Savai'i, the other big island. There are no banks on this side of Upolu. Perhaps Zeigler has managed to get to Apia where it would be easier for him to hide. There are a couple of hundred ex-pats living there and he wouldn't stand out like a sore thumb.'

'Okay,' said Hank, irritably, 'we have to come to a decision. As of tomorrow morning we need a definite plan. Listening to you two, the most sensible idea is to extend our checking of the coastal villages either to the west or the east. Which will it be?'

The consensus was the villages further to the east. There was no particularly valid reason for this; they just felt it was important to continue working as a cohesive team. Each member of the threesome was feeling disappointed they had had absolutely no leads to date.

This, however, was about to change!

31.   A Breakthrough?

Wednesday started much the same as the first three days in Vaiee, a large satisfying breakfast in Jacob's fale while the children dressed proudly for the village school in their bright red and white uniforms. Samoans never have much money, but they always make sure they send their kids off to school clean and tidy with their hair neatly done. The kids happily ran off to school bare-footed. On their backs were small satchels containing picnic lunches, pencil cases and exercise books. Sometimes, there was also a library book to be returned. The children loved school and were more than happy to race across the village green to the cluster of buildings that provided the most basic of classrooms. Only the top two classes had chairs and desks with a blackboard. The smaller children sat on benches or on the ground and used slates and chalks. There was no glass in the classroom windows and doors were left open to allow air to circulate better. Classes were regimented but the kids didn't seem to mind and enjoyed the chanting and sing song choruses. Jacob confided in Belinda and Hank that most of the teachers had only reached year three at high school.

The three police were clambering into their Ford Transit ready to set out for the day, when an elderly man approached. Jacob recognised the man as somebody from his village.

'Talofa, Isiah,' he sang out, 'good to see you.'

'Talofa, Jacob,' croaked the old man, 'I was hoping I would catch you.'

'What's up, Isiah?'

'I've been robbed.'

'Really?' The language being used was Samoan, but Jacob was quite the expert in interpreting everything for his two English colleagues. 'What's gone missing, Isiah?'

'Food and blankets,' the old man replied.

'Where from?'

'My mountain hut.'

'I'm sorry to hear that, Isiah. Are you quite sure these items have been stolen?'

'Of course, I'm bloody sure,' snapped the old-timer.

'I've never been to your mountain hut. Whereabouts, is it?'

'About a mile off the main road up above Papapapaitai Falls where there's excellent grazing. I'm worried my cattle might be stolen next. I spent all day yesterday making my way down the mountain because I'd heard you were here in Vaiee.'

'Well, you've done well, Isiah. What's more, we have two top police from England here to help us,' said Jacob, as he waved towards the two detectives. 'This is Inspector Zagalski and this is Sergeant Purcell.'

'Talofa, Talofa,' mumbled Isiah, clearly overwhelmed to discover the two "whiteys" were police from a distant land.

'How about you jump in Isiah and we'll drive up to your hut and take a look?'

'It isn't much of a place,' replied Isiah, suddenly becoming apologetic.

'It might be more important than you realise, my friend,' Jacob assured the elderly man, 'jump in.'

Isiah was well past the age when he could "jump in." Not only was he rather creaky in his dotage, but he was also nervous about accepting such an unexpected invitation. This was only the second time in his life he had ever been in a motor vehicle and he was still frightened by the noisy beasts and how fast they went. He stood his ground, hesitating.

'Come on, Isiah, you can sit in the front if you like.'

Reluctantly, the old fellow clambered aboard and sat in the front seat looking around nervously as if expecting something was about to jump out and bite him. Clearly, he had not had a wash for some time and his clothing was dirty and crumpled. Isiah gave off an unpleasant body odour.

As they set off, Jacob filled in his colleagues about the lonely cattlemen who spent much of their time in the highlands minding the cattle. He explained that very occasionally there was some poaching but their main problem was trying to keep the cattle from wandering, or joining another herd belonging to somebody else.

Isiah became distinctly nervous as they started to climb the twisty road to the top of the range and hung on to the hand-holds tightly. Fortunately, car sickness was not one of his challenges. After half an hour, Isiah indicated the place to stop. He had spotted the track that led off from the road towards his hut and the mob of cattle he was minding. Locking the Ford Transit, the party of four set off along the seldom trodden path. Isiah picked up his machete which he had hidden under a thick thorn bush and wielded it enthusiastically wherever a plant had dared encroach onto the track. For a man well into his seventies Isiah made surprisingly fast progress and scarcely a bead of sweat appeared on his brow. In contrast, Hank and Belinda were wet with sweat and had to keep wiping the perspiration away to stop it running into their eyes. After ten minutes a small hut came into view, Isiah's humble abode for much of the year.

The hut was basic. Constructed from slats of wood, it managed to keep out most of the rain and helped block the cool breezes that could sometimes blow at this higher elevation. Up here, Samoans thought it was cold. With difficulty the four of them crammed into the single room structure with what looked like a mast in the centre. There was no electricity, no running water and no toilet. An ancient metal tank captured water from the daily rainstorms and the surrounding bush and open grassland provided a more than adequate toilet. Food was a never-ending problem for Isiah. He made do with whatever he could buy from the few traders who travelled to Apia each day with goods for market.

The hut was almost totally devoid of furniture. There was a folding bed (now without blankets), a rickety wooden chair and an upturned fruit crate that served as the table. An oil lamp sat on the crate next to a tin plate, a knife, a fork and an enamel mug. Cooking was out of the question unless Isiah lit a fire outside. Surprisingly, a faded photograph of a young Queen Elizabeth smiled down on the proceedings from a rusty nail. Her Majesty was the only attempt at adornment. The only other item in the lonely hut was a tuck-box in the corner. Isiah explained he had to keep his food in the box as there were hungry mice, rats, geckos and cockroaches.

There was shade on one side of the hut so they sat there on the ground to ask Isiah more questions. It seemed clear Isiah's two army blankets were missing along with a half-eaten loaf of bread, two bananas and a pawpaw that had been safely stowed in his unlocked tuck-box. Jacob asked the questions and interpreted for his two English colleagues.

'Isiah, have you seen anyone around your hut recently?'

The old man shook his head, 'No, I haven't seen anybody, but yesterday when I came back after checking the cattle and discovered my things had been stolen, I found footprints. Not mine because I don't wear shoes. These were shoe prints.'

'Are they still visible?'

'No, got washed away in last night's rain.'

'Could you tell where the footprints were leading to?'

'Along the track that goes down to the village.'

'Which village?'

'Tafiloala.'

'Can you describe the footprints for us, Isiah?'

'They were shoes, I told you.'

'Yes, I know, but what size were they?'

Isiah seemed flummoxed. To him, a shoe was a shoe, something he never wore. Jacob used his hands to try to get Isiah to be more specific about the size of the shoes but it was a waste of time.

'Was there a pattern in the footprint, Isiah?'

Again, Isiah found the question confusing, 'A pattern?'

'The underneath of a shoe has a pattern which shows up when a person walks on wet ground. It might be circles or zigzag lines, all sorts of things…Here, look at the bottom of my boots.'

Isiah shrugged his shoulders, 'I just know it wasn't a foot. It was a shoe, probably a sandal.'

Jacob changed tack. 'This path down to Tafiloala, do you ever use it?'

'Sometimes, if it hasn't been too wet.'

'Does the track get flooded?'

'Yes, badly. There's a rope bridge that crosses over the water at the bottom of the Papapapaitai Falls.'

'Ah yes, I remember now,' responded Jacob, 'I went there once to see the flood waters raging out of the falls. Very scary place!'

The old man nodded, 'If the Papapapaitai is in flood, I have to walk the long way round, down the main road. If I start at sunrise I can make Vaiee by sunset but I'm getting too old for that now.'

'Okay, Isiah, if you would like to walk back to the vehicle with us, I can give you a blanket and a bunch of bananas. Sorry I can't offer you more.'

The old man was most grateful.

☾

As soon as they had safely despatched old Isiah back to his hut with his gifts, the three police discussed their next move. Although there was still no positive sighting of Zeigler, they felt sure the footprints and thieving pointed to the German. If they were in England, they could easily confirm Zeigler's recent presence in the hut with finger-print technology. However, such techniques were yet to be introduced to Western Samoa. Hank summed up the situation.

'Assuming this is Zeigler it would seem he's currently camping out somewhere between Isiah's hut and the village of Tafiloala. Being close to the Papapapaitai Falls he has no problems with fresh water, but finding food is his constant challenge. Jacob, you know the local terrain reasonably well, what can you tell us about the track he's probably on?'

'It's steep in parts and you're walking on rocky, black basaltic rock. The jungle on either side of the track will be thick and almost impenetrable. Without a machete, or a bull-dozer, he's not likely to be able to set up camp very far off the track. Of course, he could be lucky and find a lava tube…'

'What the heck is a lava tube?' asked Belinda.

'There are several along this coastline,' replied Jacob, 'they are quite rare geological features and are only found where lava has flowed down from a volcano. As you know the Samoan islands are totally volcanic, there are still a couple of active volcanoes over on Savai'i. As the massive rivers of lava come spewing down the sides of volcanoes they start cooling. A solid skin forms where the lava is exposed to the cool air but underneath the skin the white-hot lava keeps flowing like a river. Sometimes, this white-hot lava flows out completely leaving a hollow shell of basalt behind and, hey presto, you have a lava tunnel. It's a great place to hide or shelter if it rains. It's like a cave that goes a long long way back into the hill.'

'Wow, I'd love to see one,' Belinda remarked, 'are there any along the track do you think?'

'I can't remember,' Jacob admitted. 'If there is one, the track most likely goes past the entrance because people are curious to see what these lava tubes look like. One day they might even become tourist attractions.'

'If Zeigler is looking for food, realistically he has only two options…raid the cattlemen's huts or steal from Tafiloala or other villages,' stated Belinda.

'Correct. He might also stumble upon some fruits growing wild in the jungle, if he's lucky.'

'How many other huts are there that might have food stored in them, Jacob?'

'Not sure. At a guess, there could be half a dozen on this western side of the highway. If Zeigler crosses the highway to the eastern side he will find more there.'

'Right, we need reinforcements urgently. A couple of police on foot to patrol the mountain huts and warn the cattlemen about Zeigler, a vehicle patrolling the main road in case he tries to cross over to the eastern side, or make a dash for Apia and half a dozen more men to search the track entering from both ends. Any other ideas?'

Jacob and Belinda agreed. 'How quickly can we get the extra police?' asked Belinda.

'The nearest telephone is at Manmoa. If we ring on our way back to Vaiee in half an hour's time, the reinforcements should be here first thing in the morning, say eight o'clock,' volunteered Jacob, optimistically.

'Excellent. We can meet the reinforcements here at the top of the range, at eight. I'll get you to brief them, Jacob. We can delegate two men to check and patrol the huts and another three to start searching the track from this end. What sort of a vehicle will they come in, Jacob?'

'It'll be another Ford Transit. The British Government donated ten to Western Samoa last year as an Independence Day gift.'

'Good. Two men can patrol up and down this main road and we'll take the final three men down to Vaiee so they can set off up the track from that end.'

At last, the three police felt they were closing in on their quarry. The Chief Commissioner promptly agreed to Hank's request and promised to have ten men at the top of the range by eight next morning. Mike Arbuthnot warned Hank, however, that there was a complication. The Meteorological Office was predicting a cyclone, which was currently forming rapidly off the south coast and expected to head towards them. It was, after all, cyclone season and he urged them to listen carefully to any further warnings on the radio.

32. Cyclone Juliana

The Samoan Islands, on average, suffer one cyclone per year. Of course, the cyclones vary in intensity from category ones through to the worst kinds, category fives. Sometimes the cyclones simply brush the side of the islands leaving little damage, at other times these beautiful tropical islands can cop the full force of a massive cyclone head-on leaving a trail of catastrophic damage and serious loss of life. Most destructive are the cyclones packing force nine or force ten gales that batter the islands and enrage the seas. With most of the population living along the narrow coastal plains, the resultant tidal surges can also bring devastation and carnage.

The science of Meteorology in 1962 was primitive. Remote clusters of islands, such as Samoa, were poorly served. The locals, however, recognised the signs of an approaching cyclone. Fishermen reported sudden declines in their fish stocks and the old timers noticed different kinds of birds flying across the islands. There were even long-term signs when a bad cyclonic season was coming. For example, farmers who grew mangoes claimed the size of their crop was determined by future weather patterns and a small crop was a sure indication rough weather was on the way.

Jacob had experienced a number of cyclones during his many years living in Samoa, but Belinda and Hank had very little idea what to expect. Of course, there were winter storms in the United Kingdom, but they usually passed over within an hour or two and the force of the wind did not compare with the winds circling around the eye of a cyclone. Zeigler, hiding somewhere up in the hills of Upolu, would be dangerously naïve about what might be heading his way.

The path of a cyclone is difficult to predict. Sometimes they remain almost stationary with the result that damaging winds can persist for days on end before the system moves off, or they might weaken into a tropical storm. One extraordinary tropical cyclone that hit Western Samoa in March 1889 had a major influence on the history of the small country. Jacob enjoyed explaining what happened in 1889 as they drove back to Vaiee.

'The first Samoan Civil War took place between 1886 and 1894. The war was about power and influence and which Samoan chief would rule the Samoan Islands as the Paramount Chief. There were three contenders. This civil war was further complicated by the presence of three colonial powers who also wanted to control the islands: Germany, America and Britain. There was much plotting and intrigue going on as the three colonial powers sided with one or the other of the chiefs and started supplying military training, troops and weapons. Things came to a head in March 1889 when three American warships, three German warships and one British warship, HMS Calliope, were anchored in Apia's harbour. A major clash between the three colonial powers looked inevitable.'

'I've never heard this history before,' said Hank, listening intently.

'Nor me,' added Belinda. 'So, what happened?'

'On March 15th things looked like they were about to blow up when, guess what, a massive cyclone rolled into Apia Harbour. It became known as the "Apia Cyclone" and was probably a category four or five. It created absolute chaos. The three German warships were either sunk, or smashed to pieces, the three American ships likewise. The only ship to escape was the British warship that wisely had headed out to sea to ride out the cyclone.'

'That must have been one hell of a storm,' remarked Hank.

'It certainly was. Partly because of this cyclone, the three colonial powers signed the Tripartite Convention a couple of years later. This was the agreement that divided the Samoan Islands into two: American Samoa and German Samoa.'

'Crikey, I hope the cyclone that might be heading our way is not as ferocious as Cyclone Apia,' added Belinda.

Jacob switched on the car radio and they picked up a crackly voice coming from Radio Samoa. It was a Samoan announcer and the two detectives had to wait a few minutes before Jacob interpreted for them. His message was brief.

'The cyclone is intensifying and is already a category two. It is expected to worsen further and to hit Samoa somewhere along this southern coastline in about three or four hours. It's been named Cyclone Juliana.'

☾

News of Cyclone Juliana's proximity had certainly reached Vaiee when they drove in a few minutes later. The village was a hive of activity. There was no sense of panic though, since the adults knew exactly what they had to do. Anything that could possibly be blown about had been brought in to be safely stored inside the family fales. This included the washing, toys, gardening tools, sporting gear and cooking facilities. The elderly in each fale were responsible for selecting and packing enough food and clean water to last the family for up to three days. This would be taken to the village church where everyone would wait out the cyclone. The church was by far the most substantial building in the village and in its lifetime had already endured dozens of cyclonic storms.

The Vaiee fishermen were faced with a major decision and there was no easy answer. Should they simply tie up their boats more securely than usual in the hope they would safely ride out the storm, or immediately go out to sea until well clear of the reefs and battle the cyclone out in the deep? Most ended up taking the first option.

Even the children had tasks to do. A few of the older children ran down to the school to help the teachers make sure everything was stowed away and made secure. Others rounded up the family dogs, chickens and pigs and found safe places for them to stay well away from the full force of the coming cyclone. And, of course, the school children had to find their school books and pencils to put into their satchels so they had homework to do if forced to stay in the church for a couple of days.

Two hours later, Radio Samoa was in full cyclone warning mode. Cyclone Juliana, the announcers were saying, was going to be a large destructive storm and everyone must take shelter and prepare for up to three days locked away with enough food and water to last the distance.

Around five o'clock, a steady stream of villagers started heading for the church. The pews had been re-arranged to create more room and families were calmly setting up their own spaces with blankets, pillows and sleeping gear surrounded by their goods and shekels. There was no fuss, no panic, everyone seemed resigned to sitting out yet another storm. It was, after all, what happened every year or so. The fales had been battened down on all four sides and there was an eerie stillness; the calm before the storm. There was no wind and the sea looked placid and harmless. The only sign of the approaching cyclone was a strange colouring in the sky and sea birds flying in to seek cover.

Jacob had invited Belinda and Hank to stay with his family and share whatever they had by way of food and water. The Ford Transit was parked as close as possible to the back wall of the church under a large green tarpaulin that had been well anchored to the ground. Hopefully, the vehicle would avoid the most powerful winds and be protected from flying objects. Before they retired to the safety of the church Hank made a final call to the Chief Commissioner. Understandably, the arrival of the ten police reinforcements had been postponed until the cyclone had passed. Hank agreed to get in touch again as soon as possible.

For the first time Belinda felt a shred of pity for Doctor Heinrich Zeigler. Presumably, he was still hiding out somewhere along the track, blissfully unaware of the impending cyclone soon to crash remorselessly into the island. Did Zeigler have any shelter? Had he, perhaps, found one of those mysterious lava tubes that might save his life? After weeks hunting for Zeigler in England, Germany and now Western Samoa was it going to be Cyclone Juliana that would finally end it all?

33.   The Aftermath...

Shortly after dark the cyclone rapidly intensified. The wind shrieked and rain pounded the solid basalt walls of the village church. The noise was deafening. To have a meaningful conversation meant you had to shout at the top of your voice and then be virtually sitting on top of the person to hear their reply. Most people were resigned to the violent noises and sat in silence, read, slept, or took it in turns to nurse a small child. Some women used the time usefully to do craft work, not an easy task in the poor light within the church. Small groups of men congregated in corners of the church to play cards or chess. They respected the fact they were inside the Lord's house so no money changed hands. The church minister walked about his flock offering comfort, or prayers, if requested.

Belinda and Hank sat together slightly away from the rest of Jacob's family. It was abundantly clear to any of Jacob's family, who were in any way observant, that the two detectives from England were very much in love. The Samoans respected that and left them alone. The light inside the church was not really good enough for reading, but Belinda had brought along paper and pens and the pair spent time playing children's paper games with some of Jacob's young family: Noughts and Crosses, Battleships, then Heads, Bodies and Tails and finally Boxes. As the storm raged on and the hours ticked slowly by, first the children and then the adults gradually fell into an uneasy sleep lying about on the floor of the church or along one of the pews.

Shortly before dawn the wind and rain started slowly to ease. The villagers began to stir and before long started to put together whatever they had brought along for breakfast. There was a powerful feeling of relief amongst the villagers as they dared to hope the cyclone had already passed them by and it had not been as bad as they had expected. Soon the word spread from the two or three matai who were fortunate to possess battery powered radios, that Radio Samoa was still actively broadcasting. The announcer was urging everyone to stay under cover for at least another hour or two and wait for a message from the Meteorological Office that it was safe to emerge. Apparently, Cyclone Juliana had unexpectedly veered off its anticipated course and the eye of the storm had stayed at sea and passed between Western Samoa and American Samoa. This near miss meant the amount of damage, while extensive, was less severe than expected. The announcer went on to request the matais in each village to double check everyone was accounted for.

Jacob, as one of the more junior of Vaiee's matais, was assigned this task. Conscientiously, he spoke to every family group, taking notes as he went. When he returned, he had a comprehensive fix on almost everybody in the village of Vaiee. Everyone was present in the church except for three men known to be overseas in New Zealand and one in Australia. Two women were in hospital in Apia and five people were away visiting other villages. The only three villagers not yet accounted for were Thomas and his brother Saul, who had taken their fishing boat out to sea to ride out the storm in deeper waters, and Isiah up in his cattleman's hut.

Doctor Heinrich Zeigler was not counted as one of the villagers. Had he survived?

❧

The "all clear" came shortly before nine o'clock and the villagers streamed out to assess the extent of the damage. As cyclones go, Cyclone Juliana had been reasonably considerate. Damage was, on the whole, minor. Every fale remained basically intact, although there had been some shredding of bamboo protectors and a number of holes had appeared in roof thatch where projectiles had impacted. Trees and branches were down all over the place and one large branch had smashed the corrugated iron roof of one of the school's classrooms. Mostly, it was a case of everyone getting out around the village for a few hours to clean up the debris, let the dogs off their leashes, release other animals and start work on any necessary repairs. School remained closed for the day, while the damaged classrooms were cleaned up. Children were warned to stay away from the two nearby creeks that were now in flood. There had been a minor storm surge, estimated to be around four feet. However, the beach, the road and the three-foot-high wall in front of Vaiee had been sufficient to hold the water out.

Jacob was anxious to do his bit to help his village to clean up and Belinda and Hank joined him. The only village telephone line was down and there was no indication how long it would be before someone might be available to repair it. There was no way Hank could contact the Chief Commissioner unless they drove back over the range to Apia and spoke to him face to face. This seemed a reasonable idea but there was no way of knowing if the main road was open for traffic. The three police decided to wait and hope the telephone line would be repaired but If nothing had happened by four o'clock, they would try to get through via the main road.

They needn't have worried. Just as they were preparing to leave at four o'clock, a second Ford Transit appeared carrying the ten extra police. Thet said the main road was open, although they had to drive slowly and move debris along the way. The reinforcements had thoughtfully brought enough food with them for three days so they could remain independent of the village where food might be in short supply after the cyclone. That evening Jacob thoroughly briefed the ten men and instructed them to be ready to leave by eight next morning. The extra police had also brought their own sleeping-bags and mosquito nets and were easily accommodated in the village's fale for the night.

Next morning all was in readiness by eight o'clock. First aid kits had been checked and food rations distributed. Several torches were handed out in case they needed to be out after dark. The walkie-talkie was tested and operational. Hank, Belinda, Jacob and Sergeant "Stinger," the leader of the reinforcements, were issued with police revolvers.

The most likely scenario was that Zeigler would be hanging out somewhere along the lower part of the track, not too far from Vaiee. The plan was that Hank and Belinda would start out from Vaiee and walk up the track searching for the fugitive together with three of the reinforcements. Jacob and the other seven would head off back to the top of the range in their Ford Transit. Two men would spend the day patrolling the main road in case Zeigler tried to escape to the east of the main road. Two others would trek westwards across the range visiting the mountain huts and alerting herdsmen they came across to the possible presence of Zeigler and the fact he was dangerous. Jacob and the remaining three men would start to walk down the track towards Vaiee. Somewhere along the track the two groups expected to meet up, provided the rivers were not still in flood.

Hank issued strict instructions. He wanted Zeigler brought in alive. There was to be no shooting, except in self-defence.

☾

Hank and Belinda introduced themselves to their three new Samoan colleagues: Gideon, Samuel and Peter. Once again, the magic rugby connection came to the fore. It turned out the three young men still played rugby for their villages and were enthusiastic supporters of the Samoan National Rugby team. Of the three, only Peter spoke some English so he became the unofficial spokesman for the others and interpreter when required. The three men came from the larger island of Savai'i which they claimed was even more beautiful than Upolu and far less populated. It was good to have three cheerful fit young men to accompany them.

As they left Vaiee they were cheered on their way by the usual mob of laughing school kids, home from school for a second day thanks to Cyclone Juliana. Juliana had damaged more than one classroom, so the decision had been made to keep the school closed another day. A number of the bigger lads desperately wanted to escort the police along the track and had to be sternly told not to follow. It was difficult to know how much these children had heard. The kids must have been wondering why so many police had suddenly descended on their village. Initially, two detectives from England had arrived with Jacob and then a second Ford Transit had turned up with ten more police on board! What on earth was going on? The children were accustomed to the matais dispensing justice. It must be a really serious business if this many Samoan police had to be called in.

Cyclone Juliana had brought some welcome cooler air for a few brief hours but already this morning the temperature and humidity were climbing again and it felt oppressive as they threaded their way slowly along the narrow forest track. Wisely, Hank and Belinda had hidden their guns whilst in the village, not wanting to cause alarm. Now they stopped and retrieved their weapons from their back packs. It was easy to forget in this spectacularly beautiful environment they were hunting a desperate and dangerous man.

Hank insisted on silence as they walked further away from the village. There was surprisingly little damage to the thick jungle. Some of the higher branches had snapped off and there was a lot of leaf litter lying about. The main problem was the wetness of the ground. Everything had been drenched and much of the time they sloshed through mud and puddles. Leeches were about in abundance, something Belinda found particularly nasty to deal with. Every time she brushed past a branch or stopped for a moment to look at something the horrid little creatures found a way of attaching themselves to her exposed skin. They were hard to remove. Seeing her struggling, Peter came over with some crushed dock leaves which he advised her to rub on her skin. It seemed to help.

Hank and Peter were responsible for spotting anything to the left of the track that could be interesting. Belinda, Gideon and Samuel surveyed to the right. Several times they stopped to further investigate a bit of a clearing or a track leading off into the jungle. It was difficult to know exactly what they were looking for. A cave perhaps? Some sort of temporary man-made structure? Maybe an entrance into one of those rarely seen lava tubes? Before long they were thoroughly wet, a combination of dripping trees, sodden feet and perspiration.

It was curiously quiet and still in the jungle. There were few birds about, although sometimes one would take off suddenly, screeching and squawking madly at the sound of them approaching. There was the usual low-level hum of busy insects, mostly bees and mosquitos and sometimes the piercing call of cicadas. Occasionally, a lizard or gecko would scuttle out of their way. Once a feral cat raced across the track with some sort of a rodent in its mouth. There was no sign, however, of Zeigler.

After twenty minutes they heard the roar of water cascading down rocks and came across the first creek, now more a river. The villagers had once built a bridge here but it had been washed away in the next flood. The remains of the stone structure still stood defiantly on this side of the creek. They were forced to stop and discuss what best to do. Was it too dangerous to attempt a crossing? One thing they could be sure about was that this creek now formed a natural barrier preventing Zeigler coming down this part of the track.

Hank was a strong swimmer and he knew Belinda was too, but he had no idea how proficient Peter, Samuel and Gideon were. They were strong lads, rugby players, but could they swim? Peter became the go-between and questioned his two colleagues. They were unsure of their ability to manage such strong waters. A moment later Gideon pulled out a sharp knife and wandered across to some vines hanging from a nearby tree. He gave them an almighty yank then cut several vines off to make the equivalent of several short ropes. These the Samoans joined up so they had a length of vine that must have stretched at least twenty-five yards.

One end of the vine they attached to the base of a tree on the bank and tested to check it was secure. Hank then gave his pack, hat and revolver to Belinda and waded out into the fast-moving water taking the other end of the vine with him. His feet scrapped across rocks and he was thankful he had good quality boots. Half way across Hank was out of his depth and had to start swimming towards the other bank, fortunately only a few yards away. The current was too strong and he was swept down river still hanging on to the vine. Some twenty yards further downstream he was washed up onto the opposite bank. Looking like a drowned rat he scrambled out and doubled back along the bank to tie his end of the vine securely around another tree. There was now a rope-vine connecting both sides of the river. As long as each person hung onto the vine and proceeded carefully, hand over hand, they would be able to cross safely. The only problem now was keeping the two revolvers and the ammunition dry. Belinda wrapped them up in several layers of whatever she could find that was still dry in their back packs and then gave the heavy backpack to Peter, who hurled it across the river to Hank. It was like watching the throwing of the hammer at the Olympic Games but It arrived safely at Hank's feet.

Without the rope vine, the rest of the group would never have made it. It was a terrifying experience slowly crossing the raging river one hand at a time. A couple of times large branches or lumps of wood crashed into their bodies as they edged their way to safety. Belinda, who went last, was aghast to see a huge snake tumbling past her. It must have been some kind of python. She was relieved to see it disappearing downstream still managing to keep its head above water. On reaching the other bank they needed time to recover and squeeze the muddy water out of their clothes. Samuel had gashed his knee while making the crossing and they had to administer first aid. The bandages were sopping wet but they whacked on a heap of strong purple disinfectant called gentian violet.

Hank waited until he was sure Belinda and Samuel were fully recovered before he led off up the track again. They were starting to climb gradually now as they moved further away from the river. The group was unsure whether the river crossing they had just negotiated was the outflow from the Papapapaitai Falls or some other smaller river. If they were yet to reach the Papapapaitai River, it would be impassable for another couple of days. Again, they walked in silence while keeping up their careful surveying left and right of the track. At one point they came across what looked like the entrance to a cave but a closer inspection showed no signs of recent occupation. They squelched on with wet clothing starting to rub uncomfortably on various parts of their bodies.

Half an hour later they again heard the unmistakeable roar of water rushing down another river system up ahead and realised this one was considerably larger than the first one they had crossed. They had arrived at the mighty Papapapaitai River in full flood! As they emerged from the jungle and stood on the bank, they could see several magnificent waterfalls towering high up above them. There was no way they could cross this torrid mass of water. The sun was shining brightly and a brilliant rainbow arched across the water course. Hank decided this was the ideal place for them to rest again for a drink and to eat anything that remained of their food after the first river crossing. Further progress up the bush track was clearly impossible. They were now sure Zeigler was *not* hiding along their part of the track.

34. An Important Find

The roar of the water made conversing difficult so they sat in the hot sun for as long as they could to dry themselves out. Five minutes was more than enough for Hank and Belinda and they retreated to the welcoming shade of the trees. Their three colleagues had no problem staying out longer under the glaring tropical sun. It didn't matter that their food was no longer edible since thirst was their main concern. Fortunately, they were carrying ample supplies of water.

It was a wonderful place there by the river, wild and untamed. Hank and Belinda had heard there were stepping stones crossing the Papapapaitai River which were normally excellent for making it over to the other side without getting one's feet wet. It might be a few days, however, before these flood waters subsided sufficiently for the stepping stones to be exposed again. Large colourful butterflies gambolled around them floating on the slight breezes set up by the rushing water. Birds flitted and swooped hunting air-borne insects while an interesting assortment of small reptiles darted shyly between the rocks. Belinda looked longingly at Hank and wished she could be here alone with her man without the worry of having to find a suspected double murderer nearby. Perhaps one day the two of them would return to this beautiful country for a holiday? Dare she dream it would be a honeymoon?

Getting to his feet, Hank stretched and yelled above the sound of the cascading water, 'Okay guys, it's time to start heading back down the track.' He waited for Peter to interpret and continued. 'I'm almost one hundred percent certain Zeigler is not hiding along this part of the track. Nevertheless, I want us to repeat the same searching technique we used on the way up here. Peter and I will look to the left, you other three look to the right. Fresh pairs of eyes are always valuable. Anything interesting, let me know. Any questions?'

There were no questions so they collected their few belongings and hoisted backpacks. They were about to leave when there was an excited shout from Gideon. Most of what he said was in Samoan although Hank did understand the first two words, 'Hey boss.' Gideon was quite agitated and pointing in the water. Nobody could see at first what it was that had caught his attention. Frustrated, he was the only person who could see the object, Gideon ran along the bank to get closer shouting and pointing. The others followed him and then they all saw it at the same time. Jammed between two rocks, with only a corner visible, was a suitcase!

Very few Samoans owned suitcases. In fact, it is rare to find even one in a Samoan village. Gideon was clever to have spotted this brown suitcase wedged so tightly amongst the rocks on the edge of the muddy coloured flood waters. Gideon had probably seen suitcases before when on duty at the airport where international travellers seldom embarked on journeys without them. Belinda and Hank were thrilled this suitcase had been found because a few days ago Carl and Sophia Schmidt had told them when Zeigler suddenly announced he wanted to leave he had taken his brown suitcase with him. Chances were, this was the it!

The police rushed to where the suitcase was stuck. It proved a tricky business to extricate it from the surrounding rocks. It was far too dangerous to jump in the water so they had to start pushing and pulling at the rocks around the suitcase to dislodge it. They took it in turns to lie on their stomachs to prise the suitcase free while two others sat firmly on their legs to prevent them being dragged in. They were worried if the suitcase came loose suddenly, the force of the water would carry it away and they would never see it again. It was an uncomfortable and difficult exercise. After ten minutes, the suitcase finally dislodged and Samuel, who was hanging onto it at the time, was pulled back up the bank. Once again, they were thoroughly wet, but at least they had been successful. The slightly misshapen suitcase now lay sodden, but safe, under a shady tree ready for examination.

Hank and Belinda looked at the battered exterior. Amazingly, it had survived more or less unscathed apart from dents and scratches where it had been tumbled over rocks. There was nothing to indicate who the owner might be, no names or labels. They did, however, find a valuable clue on a small brass plate attached to the back of the suitcase. The brass plate simply read, "Horne Brothers, Made in England." Belinda and Hank felt confident they had rescued a suitcase Zeigler must have purchased whilst living in England recently and then brought out to Samoa.

There were two strong metal locks both firmly locked. They didn't like to further damage the suitcase yet it was vital they open it. Water most likely had leaked in. The case felt quite heavy and they were sure it was not empty. They tried hard to force open the two locks but they were good quality and resisted their efforts. Impatient to access the contents, Hank pulled out his revolver and told everyone to stand back so he could blast the locks open. No luck. His revolver was wet. Belinda passed her revolver to him and he tried again. This time the revolver obliged and the two locks were successfully blown open.

They crowded around. The suitcase contained a sodden pile of items, mostly men's clothing. Examining the labels on some of the clothes, they were found to be of German origin. There was a pocket on the inside lid of the suitcase firmly closed with a substantial zipper. Doing his best to contain his excitement, Hank whipped the zipper back and delved in. The contents of the pocket had remained relatively dry and immediately he pulled out a German passport for Doctor Heinrich Gustav Zeigler. Quickly flicking the passport open, Hank found the date stamp for when Zeigler had arrived in Western Samoa. But then he noticed there was something else in the suitcase pocket. Diving his hand in a second time, Hank pulled out a sturdy green hard-back notebook. Thumbing through the pages Hank found the names, addresses and telephone numbers of Zeigler's contacts. At the back of the notebook was a letter written entirely in German. 'Bugger,' he exclaimed, 'anyone here read German?'

Nobody did. 'Right,' announced Hank, 'we hotfoot it back to Vaiee and drive to Salamumu to visit the Schmidt couple again. They'll have no problems translating the letter for us. It could be really important since it has today's date at the top.'

'The letter doesn't seem to be addressed to a single person. It's more like one of those, "To Whom It May Concern" kind of letters,' suggested Belinda. 'It'll be interesting to see what it's actually about. Perhaps it's a confession? Or maybe a denial? Perhaps Zeigler has had enough and wants to surrender?'

'Maybe it's a suicide note!' chimed in Hank, 'that would save us a lot of trouble.'

The walk back to Vaiee was uneventful, apart from encountering a nasty looking snake that fortunately slithered off through the dense undergrowth. They had a walkie-talkie system but it was limited in its range and they couldn't make contact with Jacob and his team. They would have to wait until they could access the more powerful police radio in the Ford Transit. Before setting out, Jacob and Hank had agreed to be back in their respective Ford Transits, ready to exchange messages, at two o'clock.

They made it back into Vaiee shortly after one o'clock and managed to scrounge some lunch and have a short rest before climbing back into the Ford Transit in time for the two o'clock link up with Jacob. The Samoan policeman had some startling news. Jacob and his men had found a hide-out in a small cave not more than half a mile from the top of the Papapapaitai Falls. The cave was barely deep enough to keep someone dry when the tropical downpours occurred. Jacob was certain it was being used by Zeigler since they had found two army-style blankets and banana skins, the items recently nicked from Isiah's cattleman's hut. They had seen nothing of Zeigler, however.

Hank ordered Jacob to collect up his men and return to Vaiee as soon as possible. Once he knew what Zeigler's German letter said, he would be better able to advise the men what they would be doing over the next few days.

☾

Belinda was pleased just the two of them would be driving over to Salamumu. A little quality time together, without the others about, was something she had been missing. As they pulled out of Vaiee, the heavens suddenly opened again and they had to pull over to the side of the road for ten minutes until the rain cell had passed. The heavy rain pelting the roof was so loud they were forced to shout to be heard, hardly a romantic start to their short trip. The rain stopped as quickly as it had started and they were on their way again. Belinda and Hank had only been in the country for only a few days, yet they already accepted that an afternoon downpour was almost inevitable.

The roads were instantly slippery. It took but a few minutes for the heat and humidity to return. They hung their arms out of their respective windows to enjoy the cooling breezes. Hank kept his hand close to the horn so as to alert the wandering people and animals. Motor vehicles were few and far between along the coast road, so everyone and everything treated the road as their walking track. Squawking chickens were everywhere and mongrel dogs roamed freely. Hank was most concerned about the naked and semi naked little kids that had absolutely no road sense and often darted across the road chasing a ball or just wandering, absent mindedly. Occasionally, they saw a man or an older boy riding a pony bareback. Most of the women carried bulky piles of firewood, baskets of fruit or vegetables, even long sticks of sugar cane or bamboo and often with a baby wrapped to their bodies as well.

Belinda and Hank turned off the main road at Salamumu

and started up the quieter, winding lane that led to the Schmidt's property. Vehicles were even less common along this stretch of road and any children they came across stopped and waved excitedly. For these children it was still a thrill to see a motor vehicle.

Twenty minutes later Hank pulled up at the front entrance to Carl and Sophia Schmidt's elegant home. The house and gardens were bathed in sunshine, a piece of tropical paradise. The door was opened by a homely-looking middle-aged Samoan woman with generous bosoms and a smile to match. She studied her two visitors for a long moment, making up her mind whether to speak German, English or her native tongue. She made the right choice, 'May I help you? I'm Ruth, the house-keeper.'

The two detectives introduced themselves. 'Please, please come in,' she said, 'Mister Schmidt is out on the plantation somewhere, but the lady of the house is in. She's in her studio. Please follow me.'

Ruth led them along a wide airy hallway with paintings on both walls and doorways leading off to various other rooms. The hall led straight into a spacious art studio where the tall striking-looking Sophia stood before an easel with a paint brush poised in one hand and a cloth in the other.

'Excuse me, madam. There are two detectives here to see you.'

Sophia turned and looked admiringly at the two young detectives standing at the entrance to her studio. She didn't miss a beat and calmly re-directed her gaze towards her house-keeper, 'Thank you, Ruth. Would you please organise sherry and refreshments on the patio.'

Ruth left and Sophia smiled at her unexpected guests. 'This is a surprise,' she said, 'you will excuse me for not shaking hands, but I've been busily dabbling in my hobby and am rather grubby.'

'We're sorry to encroach on your time again, and without warning,' said Hank, 'however, we need someone with your expertise to assist us in a police matter, please.'

'Shall we move out onto the patio? Ruth won't be long,' suggested Sophia, putting aside her paint brush.

They moved outside into the shady garden and Sophia turned on an outside fan to create a welcome breeze. 'Coming from England you are probably dying of heat exhaustion,' she laughed. Sophia gestured for them to be seated and then sat down herself and crossed her legs in a way that was rather too revealing, at least Belinda thought so. 'Now, what sort of expertise are you assuming I have?' inquired Sophia, with a mischievous look on her face.

'We have found a note-book belonging to your cousin, Doctor Zeigler. We are still looking for him. He has totally disappeared and must be in hiding somewhere.'

Sophia immediately became defensive. 'I can assure you officer he is not hiding here. We are cousins by marriage, yes, but Carl and I are not in the business of hiding potential criminals. We have not seen Heinrich, or heard from him, since he left in such a hurry.'

'We are glad to hear that,' Belinda assured her. 'The expertise we are seeking is your ability to translate some German into English for us.'

At this point the conversation was interrupted by Ruth, who reappeared bearing a large silver tray on which were two bottles of sherry, side plates, serviettes, glasses and some nibbles. Politely, Ruth asked the guests and then her mistress whether they would prefer a dry or sweet sherry. Once the three drinks had been dispensed and the nibbles shared around, she quietly retreated.

'You have come to the right person,' smiled Sophia. 'Believe it or not, I am a trained German-English translator. I'm delighted to help you provided it's not a long piece you want to have translated?'

'It's a letter nearly two pages long,' answered Hank. 'I should warn you we found the letter in a suitcase that had been washed down the Papapapaitai Falls.'

'Sounds ominous,' admitted Sophia, uncrossing her legs. 'As a professional translator, I must insist this translation work is done properly. Quite likely, my translation may be required in a court of law one day. So, I will provide you with a properly considered *written* translation. In a case like this, a mere verbal translation is not acceptable. Can you give me half an hour or so?'

'Yes, of course, if you think a written version is necessary,' Belinda replied.

'It is absolutely necessary. There are so many nuances in any language that can drastically affect the meaning of the written word. If you want my professional services, that is my proviso.'

Sophia was determined and what she said made a lot of sense. They willingly agreed and Hank handed over the green notebook open at the right page.

'Do help yourself to nibbles and more sherry.' Sophia quietly left the patio carrying the notebook and her glass of sherry.

☾

It was closer to three quarters of an hour before Sophia returned and it was obvious from the moment she re-entered the patio she had shed a tear or two. She arrived armed with a clean white handkerchief.

'It's very bad news, I'm afraid. Heinrich claims in this letter to be about to throw himself over the Papapapaitai Falls which would mean certain death.' Sophia stopped to gather herself and dab her eyes. 'We had no idea Heinrich was wanted for murder when he came to stay. I hope we are not also in trouble now for harbouring a criminal? This letter is a suicide note!'

Belinda and Hank had suspected suicide might be the essence of the letter and so were not overly surprised. However, as always, their naturally suspicious minds took over. Was the letter a cruel hoax? Zeigler was clever. Was this no more than a ploy to try and convince everyone he had committed suicide when, in fact, he was still very much alive and doing his best to escape the country? They didn't mention this as a possibility to Sophia, who appeared keen to start reading her English translation to them. Tearfully, she sat back in her chair and began reading slowly from a sheet of blue paper.

To Whom It May Concern…

My name is Doctor Heinrich Gustav Zeigler, Senior Lecturer in the Economics Faculty, Bonn University.

For many weeks I have been on the run from the law in England, France, Germany and now, Western Samoa. I had high hopes I might forge a new life here in this beautiful country with my distant cousins, Carl and Sophia, but the long arm of the law has found me even here after only six weeks.

I have suffered terribly. I live in constant fear of being caught and have had to sacrifice my freedoms. I cannot visit my beautiful wife; I cannot return to work or live at home in Germany. I remain in hiding like a despised rat. Finding food or accessing medical attention is almost impossible. Perhaps the worst aspect of being a fugitive like this is the ghastly, never-ending, aching loneliness. I spend my -time avoiding people for fear I will be caught and imprisoned for life.

I hereby confess to the murders of Rolf and Doreen Summers but please let me explain my reasons.

In 1943, when I was a vulnerable fourteen-year-old, my parents were viciously executed by the Nazis. Their so called "crime" was being members of White Rose, a passive resistance movement. I loved my parents dearly and have always admired them for their courageous stand for what they believed was right. Whilst the great majority of Germans lost touch with their human values and went along with the evil Nazi ideology, my parents had the moral strength of character to resist. They didn't deserve to die for being right!

At the tender age of fourteen, I made a solemn promise. My promise was to avenge the deaths of my parents. This was the only way I could overcome the deep depression I had fallen into at the time. The thought that one day I could put things right for my parents became my total motivation for living. My life turned around. I went back to school, I studied hard, I followed my parents' example and became an academic. I even went to work at the same university my mother and father had worked at until they were taken away and brutally murdered by the Nazis. I married a beautiful woman and bought a comfortable house in Stieldorf. I was doing well.

However, despite these successes, I never forgot my real mission in life was to avenge the wrongful deaths of my heroic, loving parents.

I became totally obsessed but kept my obsession secret. How could I best satisfy my need for revenge? Who could I find who had been involved in the capture and execution of my parents? I got lucky! By closely examining the legal records associated with the show trial of my parents, I was able to list four people who were heavily involved. Three were already dead but there was ONE still alive. His name was Rolf Gottliebson. This was the man who had first reported my parents' activities to the Nazi authorities when he was a security officer at Bonn University and later appeared as the key witness at their trial three days later. This man, in my view, was as responsible for my parents' shocking deaths as anyone. So, I decided, I must kill him.

I spent years and years looking for Rolf Gottliebson. He was a cunning bastard. He left Germany, changed his name to "Summers," became a skilled tradesman and married a woman in England. Eventually, I managed to track him down. He was living in a cute little village called Upper Bybridge in the South of England.

I planned things meticulously for weeks beforehand. Rolf and Doreen Summers had been living in Upper Bybridge for many years. I reasoned I had to kill them both because Rolf would have told his wife about his time in the war and what he had done. Remember, there are no secrets between married couples.

Things didn't quite go to plan though. I arrived in Upper Bybridge in a taxi. Needing a bit of "Dutch courage" I called in to the local pub for a couple of beers. I think it was called "The Squirrel and Porcupine." Then I walked along the main street to where the Summers couple lived. It was a pretty little cottage. I was surprised to find their front garden full of splendid white roses. Was this a feeble attempt on Rolf's part to atone for his feelings of guilt after having sent my parents to their deaths? I knocked on the door. A man answered. I asked if he was Rolf Summers. He said "yes," so I stabbed him several times with the kitchen knife I'd purchased specifically for this purpose. I was about to go in to kill his wife when there was a loud gunshot nearby. I panicked and fled, leaving Mrs Summers unharmed. I still had to kill her though because I was sure she knew too much. I murdered her the same way, behind the village church, the next day.

With the job done, I fled Upper Bybridge. My plan was to return home to my lovely wife in Bonn and go back to work as if nothing had ever happened. Sadly, it didn't work out that way. Somehow, the police got on my trail and I became a fugitive, constantly on the run trying desperately to stay one step ahead of the police.

Eventually, I managed to make it to Western Samoa where I knew I had a second cousin, Carl Schmidt. We had never met but we had always exchanged Christmas cards. Carl Schmidt was a "mysterious" cousin living in luxury in a tropical paradise tucked away in the middle of the Pacific Ocean. He presented my best chance of "disappearing" and enjoying a new life worth living.

A little over six weeks ago I arrived, unannounced, at my cousin's lovely property. I spun them a story about recovering from a nervous breakdown and begged them to take me in. They were very kind and did so. We agreed I should work for them for free for an indefinite time and in return they would give me full board and lodging. Carl could see some advantages in this arrangement because, with my background in economics, I could help him increase his exports to Europe.

It was all working out brilliantly until one horrifying afternoon two British detectives suddenly turned up at the swimming hole we frequented. I have no idea how they knew I was in Western Samoa. Anyhow, I had to escape yet again. So, taking my brown suitcase, I said goodbye to my cousins and headed up into the hills to hide.

I have been "existing" near this waterfall for a week now and I cannot take anymore. I don't think there is anywhere else I can go for safety. A life in prison is unthinkable so I have decided to end it all. I have just survived a terrifying cyclone by hiding in a small cave, but I'm starving, have putrid tropical ulcers on my legs and arms, am constantly attacked by mosquitos and leeches and I'm growing thinner and weaker every day.

I now deeply regret having made that promise when I was a naïve teenager. Furthermore, I wish to sincerely apologise to those I have hurt or let down; my wife and family, Carl and Sophia, my university colleagues and the good citizens of Upper Bybridge.

The river is raging. It's possible this tiny cave I have been hiding in may never be found. I'm putting this letter in the pocket of my suitcase. In a few minutes I will jump over this waterfall together with my suitcase. I sincerely hope the suitcase is found one day and this letter will be some small solace to my wife and family.

I love you darling...

Heinrich Gustav Zeigler (Doctor of Philosophy)

1929-1962

35.   Case Closed?

There was total silence when Sophia finished reading her translation to the two detectives. Sophia was the first to speak. 'What a terrible, awful waste of human lives.' Sophia had been deeply moved by Heinrich's letter as she dabbed her eyes with a handkerchief.

'May we please keep your written translation, Sophia?' asked the practically minded Hank.

'Yes, of course.'

Belinda wondered if they should offer to pay for Sophia's translation but then thought better of it. Instead, she decided they must be transparent and up front with Sophia.

'Sophia, I'm so sorry your cousin decided to take this action. The case will never be satisfactorily closed, however, until we find Heinrich's body. I'm sure you understand? We need evidence that proves Doctor Zeigler has not survived.'

Sophia nodded glumly.

'If we can find his body, would you, or your husband be willing to identify him?'

'Yes, I suppose so. I'll ask Carl to do it. He spent far more time with Heinrich working out on the plantation. I only saw him in the evenings.'

There was nothing more to be done. Hank and Belinda took their leave as quietly and calmly as they could and set off back to Vaiee. In their safe keeping was the original letter penned by Heinrich and Sophia's professional translation.

☪

Finally, it looked as though Hank and Belinda might achieve closure on this troublesome double murder case. Of course, they still needed to find Heinrich's body to confirm he had committed suicide. Then there would need to be an official post mortem. This would entail returning the body to England because the facilities to conduct post mortems in Western Samoa were non-existent. Last of all, certain legalities would have to be attended to. Belinda and Hank would need to appear in a court-of-law so that Doctor Zeigler's suicidal demise and the murders of Doreen and Rolf Summers would be formally recorded for posterity.

'How sure are you that Zeigler's suicide letter is genuine, Hank?'

'It sounds pretty convincing.'

'I thought so too. There must come a time when even the most determined fugitives have had enough. It would take a lot of courage though, to throw yourself over a mighty waterfall. His body, if we ever find it, will be smashed to pieces.'

'True. I just hope his body hasn't been washed out to sea. The torrent of water coming down that river may well be strong enough to do that.'

'When you contact Mike Arbuthnot this evening, be sure to ask him to extend the time the ten extra police can stay with us. Thirteen sets of eyes are much better than three!'

'Sure will. I think it would be wise to say nothing in Vaiee tonight about finding the suitcase and the contents of Heinrich's letter. I will confide in Jacob of course. We can quite truthfully say we failed to find Zeigler today and will be searching again tomorrow. I certainly don't want the villagers running around looking for his body! If they think he's still out there they'll be too frightened to stick their noses in.'

'Agreed,' said Belinda and leant over and gave Hank a loving kiss on the cheek.

The Police Commissioner was pleased to hear of the developments and authorised the continued deployment of Jacob and the ten police until Friday evening when they must be allowed to return home to their families in Apia for the weekend. This meant Hank and Belinda would have Jacob and the ten extra police to assist them for only two more days.

☾

Early Thursday morning the thirteen police assembled in the village's fale for a short briefing. Belinda, Hank and Jacob had spent last evening planning. It was Jacob who disclosed the plan to the men speaking in his native tongue.

Assuming the river was still too high to cross safely they would need two teams, one for each bank of the river. Jacob and five men would take one of the Ford Transits up the main road and walk down the track to the river from the main road. When they reached the river, they were to split up. One group would walk up-river until they arrived at the base of the waterfall. The second group would search the bank all the way down to the mouth of the river. It was estimated the total length of the river from Papapapaitai Falls to the sea was close to eleven miles so it was certainly doable.

The second team, led by Hank and Belinda, would walk up the track and also divide at the river with one group going up to the falls and the other group walking down the river bank to the mouth of the river. It was only at this point in the briefing that Jacob revealed why they were searching the river banks so thoroughly. The men were instructed to keep the likelihood of a suicide confidential. If they didn't find Zeigler's body today, they would be out looking tomorrow as well. Jacob also assured the men they would be returning to Apia late on Friday evening which brought smiles to their faces.

Alerted to the extreme danger of conducting a search along flooded river banks, the two teams set off, carrying their lunches and bottles of water. Massive cumuli-nimbus clouds were developing above. It looked as though they were in for a drenching earlier than the usual late afternoon downpour. The worst thing that could happen now was the weather conditions deteriorating so badly that everywhere became dangerously slippery with the river rising again and flooding even more extensively. This would mean their chances of finding Zeigler's body would be seriously diminished and they would have to cancel their search for the day.

Walking through the dense tropical forests with the heavy threatening clouds building above them, made it surprisingly dark. The Samoan police, used to these conditions, were not particularly perturbed and padded on confidently in their bare feet. For Belinda and Hank, wearing heavy bush walking boots, the going was more challenging. Tree roots, mosses and lichens were slippery enough when the light was good and you could see, but in these gloomy conditions it was easy to slip and slide on unseen snags. The bush was unusually quiet in anticipation of the looming storm. Half way along Hank called for a short break, more for himself and Belinda than the fit Samoans.

They were lucky. The storm passed them by with hardly a drop of rain and visibility steadily improved. Two hours after they set out, they reached the western bank of the Papapapaitai River. Here they dutifully divided into two groups. Hank went upstream with three men while Belinda headed for the coast accompanied by two police.

The plan was to thoroughly search the rocks and crevices along the river banks until each group reached its planned destination. Here each group would have lunch before returning. The groups were to be back where they had started by 3.00pm.

As planned, the four search parties re-convened between two-thirty and shortly after 3.00pm. The last group to check in was the one led by Jacob and it was his group that found Zeigler's smashed body. The body was sprawled across dark basaltic rocks near the foot of the Papapapaitai Falls.

It was a sombre group of men who returned to Vaiee that evening bringing the stark news of Doctor Zeigler's horrific death. The minister held special prayers that evening in the village's fale to which a surprising number of villagers felt moved to attend.

Bringing out a body along a difficult route is no easy task. Hank ordered all thirteen police officers to assist on Friday morning. Using a stretcher provided by the village's medical centre, they took it turns to carry out the body. Zeigler's body was then respectfully placed in one of the Ford Transits and driven back to Apia where it was placed in the morgue. The Schmidts were contacted and Carl drove to Apia on Saturday morning to confirm the body was that of his cousin, Doctor Heinrich Zeigler.

Hank and Belinda stayed at Aggie Grey's again that weekend. They were pleased to at last have closure. On Monday, they boarded the first of three flights that would eventually return them to London. They were still on duty during the three flights because they were officially escorting Zeigler's coffin. After the body had passed through a routine post mortem in London, it was eventually flown on to Bonn for a family burial.

36. "The Squirrel and Porcupine"

It was more than a week before Belinda and Hank were back at work in Petworth and life began to return to some sort of normality. They found there was a surprising amount of media interest in their exploits. The BBC had already featured much of their story on radio and television news and were hungry for more. The newspapers, likewise, had taken up the story with enthusiasm. They ended up having to give interviews for the BBC, the recently launched ITV station, the Daily Telegraph and The Times. Giving interviews was not something they had been trained to do and they were distinctly nervous speaking at the first one. By the time the last interview was conducted they felt far more confident.

A surprising amount of fan-mail greeted them too: postcards, letters, even a couple of small parcels containing gifts. They were positive messages coming from all over the United Kingdom. Belinda received far more fan-mail than Hank. Interestingly, the majority of her admirers were males which they laughed about. Clearly, many of the males were moved as much by Belinda's stunning good looks as her prowess in hunting down a dangerous murderer. Hank, on the other hand, received most of his mail from the fairer sex.

The rugby season was in full swing and Hank was anxious to earn his place back in his team. During the time he had been in Western Samoa he had lost match fitness and his first rugby training session nearly killed him. His coach told him to train for another week before he would risk playing him in a proper match. Belinda, similarly, had lost a degree of fitness and found getting back to her usual running standard took nearly two weeks.

Hank had been invited by Belinda's parents to have Christmas with them. He readily accepted. Hank planned to make this

Christmas a very special one because he intended to observe proper protocol and ask Belinda's father if he could marry his daughter. Hank had said nothing about this to Belinda, just in case he didn't get her parents' approval. He had spoken to Belinda, however, about appropriate Christmas presents to take for Major Allan Purcell and his wife, Alice. They had gone Christmas shopping together and ended up buying an attractive pair of ear-rings for Alice and two tickets to the January Rugby Test, England versus France, at Twickenham, for the Major.

❨

In amongst their fan-mail was a surprise invitation from the staff and clientele of "The Squirrel and Porcupine." The invitation read as follows:

December 2ⁿᵈ, 1962.

Dear Inspector Zagalski and Sergeant Purcell,

The residents of Upper Bybridge are most grateful for your professional policing in solving the tragic murders of Rolf and Doreen Summers, two respected members of our small community. As you can imagine, there has been considerable anxiety around the village about this horrid business but now there is a huge sense of relief that matters have finally been satisfactorily concluded.

The staff and patrons of "The Squirrel and Porcupine" would like to show our appreciation to you both. Accordingly, we invite you to a special celebratory evening to be held in your honour on Wednesday, December 12ᵗʰ at 6.00pm. As our honoured guests all expenses will be covered.

RSVP by Friday, December 7ᵗʰ

Kind regards,

Jack Duncan (Proprietor)

Belinda and Hank discussed the invitation at some length. They were concerned that accepting such an invitation might be seen by their superiors as being "unprofessional." Belinda sought a quiet word with the new Chief Inspector and was pleased to hear that he had no hesitation in giving his approval. The Chief Inspector admitted it was "unusual" but their acceptance would be in keeping with the new policing policy of being "closer" to the local community they served. So, with the Chief's blessing, they wrote back accepting.

Wednesday, December 12th dawned dark and gloomy. Heavy clouds rolled in from the North and it turned bitterly cold. It was only ten days until the winter solstice, the shortest day of the year. Normally, Hank didn't bother to check weather forecasts since he was happy to accept whatever nature served up, however, the intense cold and ominous clouds convinced him to turn on the weather forecast at eight, just before he left for work. The weatherman was throwing out warnings like confetti at a wedding. Heavy snow with snow drifts was already causing chaos across Scotland and this severe weather was steadily moving south. Southern England could expect the bad conditions to arrive sometime overnight. Road weather alerts were current for the entire country and the public was being advised to prepare for an extended spell of fiercely cold weather. Everyone was urged to stock up their food reserves and stay warm at home until the cold snap passed in a few days' time. Conditions were expected to get so bad that only essential services would still be operating.

Hank took the warnings seriously. He checked his food cupboard and finding it nearly empty decided to drop into the corner store on his way to work. A few tins of soup, baked beans, spaghetti and frankfurters would see him safely through for a week or so. Cold snaps seldom lasted longer than a few days before they petered out and life returned to normal. He checked where he had left his shovel and placed it where it would be easy to access should he be snowed in. Then, donning his ski gear, he left for work.

Belinda had also heard the weather warnings. She was really looking forward to their night out at "The Squirrel and Porcupine" and was determined to go unless they experienced unforgiving blizzard conditions. It was a fantastic gesture from the pub and community of Upper Bybridge. It would be so enjoyable to mix with the locals socially for a change and not as an authoritarian figure. Unlike Hank, Belinda already had a well-stocked pantry, although a few more fresh vegetables and fruit wouldn't go astray. She rugged up extra warmly and left for work.

Of course, demands on uniformed police increase in times of foul weather although those who had successfully transferred to the Criminal Investigation Department (CID) were spared being out on duty in these lousy conditions. Hank and Belinda recalled a number of occasions they had worked extra-long hours when "on the beat," controlling traffic if traffic lights failed, attending accidents and assisting at natural disasters. The weather was usually to blame; gales, torrential rain leading to floods, snow and ice. One of the worst situations they both remembered was a night of black ice. It had rained hard during the day and then, as night fell, it suddenly turned fiercely cold. The wet roads froze. It was dangerous because the roads appeared only to be wet and nighttime drivers failed to realise they were actually driving on treacherous ice. There were major pile-ups and every available member of the uniformed police force was out most of the night dealing with horrendous situations. A night of black ice only benefitted petty nighttime criminals who could work unimpeded with the police force otherwise engaged.

During the day Hank and Belinda kept half an ear open for further weather updates. The cold spell, it seemed, was still on its way, but the weather system had slowed somewhat and now wasn't expected to reach the South Downs until the early hours of Thursday morning. Good news! Hank had volunteered his car and they planned to leave at 5.30pm to travel the twenty miles to "The Squirrel and Porcupine" in Upper Bybridge.

❮

Excitement had been steadily building throughout the day inside "The Squirrel and Porcupine." The Duncan family had put up the pub's Christmas decorations a bit earlier than usual. It was to be a special night and they wanted everything to look especially inviting. The traditional Christmas tree was firmly embedded in its large red pot that came out but once a year and was looking splendid. It had been Jenny's enjoyable task to decorate the tree with an array of baubles and Christmasy items. Last year's paper chains had been slung across the ceiling and other paper chains livened up the bar. In the centre of the tables were candle-holders with shiny new red candles ready to light and surrounded by twigs of freshly picked holly. At Jenny's insistence, they had attached generous bunches of mistletoe to hang beneath the four roof lights.

Betty, the faithful Anglican, had set up a manger scene at one end of the bar, much to the annoyance of Jack, who claimed it took up too much bar space and would make it difficult to serve the clamouring hordes of patrons they were expecting. In the end a compromise was reached, when Betty promised to prepare a couple of gallons of her famous warm mead for the patrons, a drink that had been more than popular with the locals last year. Betty claimed to have a secret recipe handed down to her through the generations and refused to divulge the details to anyone. Whatever it contained, it had a kick like a mule!

As for the evening's entertainment, rotund Cecil had been roped in once more to be Santa and Caroline Sutter, the music teacher at Petworth High School, who conveniently resided in the village, had again promised to belt out some carols on the pub's ancient Steinway. The piano needed a bit of tuning but Jack Duncan reasoned nobody would worry about the odd flat note here and there when in a spirited festive mood. Everything was in readiness by 5.00pm and the doors were thrown open for the good folk of Upper Bybridge and even some from Lower Bybridge. Everyone was intent on honouring the two detectives due to arrive at 6.00pm.

Jack sported a silly Santa hat, Betty had new Christmas earrings (miniature Christmas trees) and young Jenny was dressed as the sexiest elf that Santa had ever had the pleasure to employ. Betty looked at her daughter with a deep sense of unease. She did not approve. Not only was Jenny showing far too much stockinged leg, but her bust looked as though it was about to burst out of her flimsy costume at any moment. What's more, Jenny knew all too well how to cavort about in a highly sexy, provocative manner. How, Betty wondered, had her daughter learnt to be so seductive? Where had it come from? Certainly not from her. Betty shook her head and went to serve a customer.

℃

A few minutes after half past five Hank pulled up outside Belinda's place. It was horribly cold and the occasional snow flake drifted down, a precursor of what might be coming in the next few hours. Belinda hurried out wearing a fur coat and some sort of booties with white fur inside. It was a relief to feel the warmth of Hank's car. They kissed and set off for Upper Bybridge. Along the way they recalled the many weeks they had spent on the Zeigler murder case; the frustrations, the people they had met and worked with, and how they had eventually pieced together the connection with the White Rose movement in Nazi Germany. It had begun months ago with Rolf Summers' last breathe when he uttered the word "rose." And then there was Rolf and Doreen's front garden full of splendid white roses. But why? This display of white roses must have been an attempt to atone for the actions Rolf had taken when a Nazi during the second world war. Rolf had been instrumental in bringing about the executions of several members of the White Rose movement including Heinrich Zeigler's much-loved parents. Linking everything together was the mysterious white rose badge discovered in the barn at Bramble Farm.

As they drove along the quiet roads towards Upper Bybridge the snow gradually became heavier and began to settle. The windscreen wipers were still coping so visibility was no problem, however, they needed to slow down because the roads were becoming slippery. Although they didn't say it, both knew travelling back to Petworth later in the evening could be a challenge if the snow continued. Soon they reached Lower Bybridge and turned left up the country lane that went past the entrance to Bramble Farm and on up to Upper Bybridge. Parking near "The Squirrel and Porcupine" was a problem. There were cars, trucks and even motor bikes and bicycles parked everywhere. Clearly, their special night was going to be well attended. They stopped outside the entrance to the pub where a man was gesticulating at them wildly. It was the young lad, Michael Benton, from Bramble Farm, who ran over to Hank to tell him they had reserved a special parking space for them at the back door. Very thoughtful of them.

Sure enough, they found a sign at the back door half covered in snow that said "Reserved for Police." They scrambled out and crunched the few yards to the back door where a shivering Michael Benton awaited them. He led them through the seldom seen and dimly lit back quarters of "The Squirrel and Porcupine." Then, opening another door they burst into a crazy bright world full of lights, people, smoke and noise.

"For they are jolly good fellows,
For they are jolly good fellows,
For they are jolly good fellows,
And so, say all of us…"

The patrons had lined up to form a ragged guard of honour through which, first Hank, and then Belinda, were obliged to walk laughing and clapping as they went and fully entering into the spirit of the occasion. The chorus was repeated and glasses raised as they came to the end of the tunnel of enthusiastic villagers and peeled off their winter coats. The ever-attentive Michael Benton took their coats and scarves away for safe keeping. Somebody thrust glasses of warmed mead into their hands while half a dozen other bubbly folk were busily saying things to them all at the same time. It was chaos but happy chaos, full of well-meaning and fun. A bell clanged, then clanged again and again until at last quiet descended on the revellers.

'Ladies and Gentlemen and anyone else…' there was a round of laughter. 'Ladies and Gentlemen, we are here tonight to honour two members of the police force.' It was the proprietor, Jack Duncan speaking. 'I call upon the Reverend James Arbuthnot to say a few words of welcome…'

'No bloody sermons, Reverend,' came a call from the back somewhere followed by much raucous laughter. The crowd parted to allow the elderly Anglican priest to emerge and take his place in front of the bar.

'We can't see him, give him a bloody stool to stand on,' came another voice.

A chair was hurriedly found and the Reverend Arbuthnot hoisted up by many willing hands.

'In the name of the Father and the Son and…' yelled another wag, followed by more laughter.

The Reverend James Arbuthnot had never before had to address such a rowdy, unruly congregation and at first seemed discombobulated. A few more wise cracks rang out from some of the fellows who had already put away a few too many beers before the minister found his tongue.

'Good evening everyone…I wish I could get a congregation half this size up at Saint David's.'

This opening comment elicited another round of responses, the gist of which was that the Reverend needed to put on free beer for his flock if he wanted to increase the numbers. Laughing, good humouredly, Arbuthnot continued.

'A couple of months ago, I walked over to the church to check how many roof tiles needed repairing and it was then I discovered the mutilated body of one of my dearest parishioners, Mrs Doreen Summers.' The pub clientele hushed to a respectful silence.

'It was the second dreadful murder in this village in the space of 24 hours. To say we were all shocked is putting it far too mildly. I remember praying with the congregation for several Sundays that the police would safely apprehend the person responsible. We lost a fine tradesman in Rolf Summers and Doreen was a much-loved school teacher. Two fine members of our community.

In charge of the case were Inspector Hank Zagalski and Sergeant Belinda Purcell who we are delighted to welcome here tonight. Hank and Belinda… from the bottom of our hearts, we wish to thank you for your tireless work in tracking down the murderer and bringing a sense of closure to us here in Upper and Lower Byfield. Now, at last, we can sleep easy at nights. The number of people who have braved the wintery weather tonight is testament to how grateful we all are. Please all join with me in giving Hank and Belinda three hearty cheers… hip, hip hooray, hip hip hooray, hip hip horray!'

Before the hoorays had ended big Tom Benton stood on another chair with a glass of wine in his hand.

'Folks…folks… I want to propose a toast to the best two detectives on the South Downs, Belinda and Hank. Thank you for your bloody hard work and cheers!' A chorus of "cheers" rang out around the saloon as a hundred glasses were raised in thanks and appreciation before chatter and laughter filled the room once again.

Belinda and Hank were pulled in different directions as people clamoured around them firing off questions and offering congratulatory comments. Plates of tempting finger food started appearing and were placed on the tables for everyone to enjoy. It was the usual pub food: hot pies, sausage rolls and hot dogs galore. These delights were soon followed by large plates holding a variety of cakes, biscuits and brandy snaps. As soon as Belinda and Hank were half way through one drink another was thrust into their hands. It was all a bit crazy but heaps of fun.

During the evening Belinda and Hank met up with almost everybody they had interacted with whilst conducting their detective work. From Lower Byfield they chatted with Senior Constable Frank Smithton and Constable Brian Brooks, the uniformed police who officially reported the murder of Rolf Summers one hot Saturday afternoon back in August. Then there was Mike and Sandra Leighton, next door neighbours and good friends of the Summers pair. They thanked the Reverend James Arbuthnot for his welcoming words and then bumped into Inspector Ivan Digby and Sergeant Ruby Schneider, the two detectives assigned to them when the second murder was reported and their work load had become too much to handle. In a corner of the saloon, they were regaled by Tom and the feisty Rhonda Benton, owners of Bramble Farm, where the mysterious white rose badge had been found.

Jenny Duncan, dressed as a sexy elf was everywhere, chatting up the men, collecting the empties and teasing her boyfriend mad by openly flirting. Michael Benton followed her around like a lost lamb, helpless and green with envy as Jenny lapped up admiring attention from all quarters. Occasionally, Jenny's mother would throw a disapproving glare in Jenny's direction but was far too busy serving drinks to intervene. Jack Duncan was the happiest man in the world when so much beer flowed and the pounds kept tumbling into his tills.

Jack's pleasure was short lived. On the stroke of eight o'clock, well before closing time, the relief policeman from Lower Bybridge unexpectedly entered "The Squirrel and Porcupine." The din was deafening but he had an urgent message. Realising that calling for quiet was a waste of time, he pulled out his police whistle and gave it an almighty blast. The result was instantaneous. He only had to blow it once. The relief policeman was a tall fellow head and shoulders above most of the patrons.

'I'm Sergeant Pike and I've an important announcement to make. It has been snowing heavily for two hours now and some roads are already impassable. The Meteorological Office has issued warnings of continuing severe weather for the next twenty-four hours with blizzard-like conditions, frozen pipes, icy conditions and heavy falls causing drifts. If you want to get home tonight, you must leave now, while most of the roads are still open. As the officer on duty, I'm ordering the proprietors to close this pub within ten minutes and the establishment to remain closed until further notice. Please leave immediately in an orderly fashion and take extreme care as you make your way home. Good night, everybody!'

Sergeant Pike's sudden announcement was *not* well received. A loud chorus of grumbles and complaints filled the room as the patrons downed their drinks with indecent haste. Sergeant Pike stood tall and firm by the pub's entrance, however, and simply ignored those who personlised their unsavoury comments. By the time the patrons had found their hats and coats, said their farewells and queued at the toilets, the ten minutes had stretched to twenty. Jack Duncan was particularly angry, but knew there was nothing he could do about it. Sometimes mother nature ruled supreme.

Belinda and Hank hurriedly thanked their hosts and left the building. The carpark was already a quagmire of slushy snow, six inches deep, making driving dangerous. Heavy snow falling dampens sound and it was eerily quiet as they swept the snow off the car's windows and clambered in. They made it home safely, but a half hour drive became an hour and a half of nightmarish slipping and sliding.

37.   Epilogue

The snowfall on the night of December 12th 1962, was the start of the famous "Big Freeze" of 1962-1963 that swept across the British Isles. Little did Hank and Belinda realise, as they headed home after their special night at "The Squirrel and the Porcupine," that the intense cold weather would prevail, virtually uninterrupted, until March the following year. Official English meteorological records stretching back over 300 years to 1659, showed only twice in all those years was there a worse winter. Strong Easterly winds set in bringing snow and icy conditions directly from the Russian tundra. Twenty-foot-deep snow drifts were reported; the sea froze as far as four miles out from the coast and there were days and nights of gale force winds. The shocking conditions created havoc on British roads causing many deaths. People chose to stay home and only ventured out to do essential work or shopping. Sports fixtures were hugely disrupted; some Football Association soccer matches had to be rescheduled as many as ten times!

Belinda and Hank's plans to spend Christmas with her family had to be cancelled. The roads were impassable. This was deeply frustrating for Hank who desperately wanted to ask Major Purcell for the hand of his daughter. He could have telephoned but Hank felt such a serious matter could not be appropriately discussed over a telephone line. It was late March when Belinda and Hank finally arrived at the Purcell's home and Hank had the opportunity to corner Major Purcell. Thankfully, the major had no objections and Belinda and Hank were duly married early in November 1963. Their honeymoon was three weeks spent in beautiful Western Samoa where they renewed their many contacts and re-visited Apia, Vaiee, Salamumu and the Papapapaitai Falls.

Belinda gave birth to their first child late in 1964. Later they were blessed with two more children in 1965 and 1967. The last born was a girl, who they named Rose. The national flower of England is the rose, but there were two other reasons for selecting this name. One was a deeply respectful nod to the White Rose resistance movement and the brave citizens who opposed Nazi ideology during the second world war. The third reason pleased Hank especially. A few years earlier the English Rugby Union team had adopted a red rose as their national symbol. To this day, the red rose is proudly emblazoned on the English players' white rugby jerseys.

Upper Bybridge and Lower Bybridge struggled for many years as their young folk drifted away to the big cities seeking work and adventure. With the rural population declining, the pubs, like other small village-based businesses, were in decline. Jack and Betty worked hard to keep "The Squirrel and Porcupine" financially afloat. They benefitted somewhat when the only pub in Lower Bybridge sold up and became a Bed and Breakfast facility. At least there was no more local competition. The Duncans finally retired in 1996 by which time roads had improved and there was a renewed hunger amongst the wealthy to seek a peaceful country lifestyle. The influx of many new cashed-up younger residents helped the pub to prosper and eventually they sold up profitably to a new manager.

Jenny Duncan soon lost interest in Michael Benton and left Upper Bybridge to train as a beautician. She later married a policeman, but divorced him four years later. For a number of years, as a single mum with two little ones, things were tough. Then, she met the love of her life and finally settled down in a happy stable relationship.

There is an extensive literature concerning the White Rose Resistance Group. Copies of their original leaflets may still be found in German museums and a number of books have been written about their activities and the lives (and deaths) of leading members of White Rose. The survivors of the group have also spoken freely of their experiences. The last surviving member of White Rose was

Traute Lafrenz, who died on March 8th 2023 aged one hundred and three. On her 100th birthday Lafrenz was awarded the Order of Merit of the Federal Republic of Germany.

Sadly, the White Rose movement was short-lived. By February 1943, eight months after its formation, White Rose was virtually non-existent. Almost every adherent had been executed, imprisoned or had escaped the country. At the time of its demise, White Rose was attempting to link up with two other Nazi resistance groups, the Kreisau Circle and the Red Orchestra.

It has never been established with any certainty how the name "White Rose" came about. The founders, we know, had admired a poem called "The White Rose" penned by the nineteenth century German poet Clemens Bretano. They had also read a novel by the mysterious, little-known author, B. Traven entitled "White Rose." Some historians think white roses came to be seen by the organisation as symbolic of purity and innocence in the face of evil. Perhaps, the name was a combination of the three? It is unlikely we will ever know.

Today, there is a monument in front of the Ludvig Maximilian University in Munich commemorating the White Rose Resistance Group which originated and operated there for eight short months. Brave people in many parts of the world continue to this day to use non-violent means to resist inequality and oppression in its many forms. Will we ever learn?

It is 1962, and on a hot summer day in the quiet English village of Upper Bybridge, a shocking murder takes place, closely followed by another. The police are baffled. Who could have done this and why? This is a story full of mystery, intrigue, colourful characters and romance.

The killer is identified but proves elusive. Long and frustrating police chases ensue and end up in a most unlikely part of the world. Do the police finally catch their suspect? Or is there one more unexpected twist to this tale?